FEATURED ALTE...
AND DOU...

Praise for Sa...
CARRY ME HOME

"Touching...surprisingly poignant...builds to an emotional crescendo...The book becomes so engrossing that it's tough to see it end."—*Washington Post*

"Heartfelt...Strong characters, a clear community portrait and a memorable protagonist whose poignant fumblings cloak an innocent wisdom demonstrate Kring's promise."
—*Publishers Weekly*

"Sandra Kring weaves an intricate and heartwarming tale of family, love, and forgiveness in her sensational debut novel....Kring's passionate voice is reminiscent of Faulkner, Hemingway, and Steinbeck....She will make you laugh, have you in tears, and take you back to the days of good friends, good times, millponds, and bonfires. This is a piece destined to become a classic and is a must-read for devotees of the historical fiction or the literary fiction genre."
—*Midwest Book Review* (Rating: five stars)

"Sandra Kring writes with such passion and immediacy, spinning us back in time, making us feel the characters' hope, desire, laughter, sorrow, and redemption. I read this novel straight through and never wanted it to end."
—Luanne Rice, *New York Times* bestselling author of *Dance With Me*

"Simpleminded Earwig Gunderman will capture your heart and challenge your conscience....*Carry Me Home* is a plainspoken, nostalgic account set in the 1940s, but the story of a brother's love, and the healing powers of family and community in the aftermath of tragedy, is timeless."
—Tawni O'Dell, *New York Times* bestselling author of *Back Roads* and *Coal Run*

THE BOOK OF
Bright
IDEAS

Sandra Kring

DELTA TRADE PAPERBACKS

THE BOOK OF BRIGHT IDEAS
A Delta Trade Paperback / June 2006

Published by
Bantam Dell
A Division of Random House, Inc.
New York, New York

Book design by Ellen Cipriano

Delta is a registered trademark of Random House, Inc., and the colophon is a
trademark of Random House, Inc.

Library of Congress Cataloging in Publication Data
Kring, Sandra.
The book of bright ideas / Sandra Kring
p.   cm.
ISBN-13: 978-0-385-33814-1
ISBN-10: 0-385-33814-7
1. Friendship—Fiction. 2. Sisters—Fiction. 3. Wisconsin—Fiction.
4. Domestic fiction.
PS3611.R545 B66 2006
813/.6 22   2005056008

Printed in the United States of America
Published simultaneously in Canada

www.bantamdell.com

BVG 10 9 8 7 6 5 4 3 2 1

For all those who longed to find a best friend
and found it in themselves.

THE BOOK OF BRIGHT IDEAS

1

I should have known that summer of 1961 was gonna be the biggest summer of our lives. I should have known it the minute I saw Freeda Malone step out of that pickup, her hair lit up in the sun like hot flames. I should have known it, because Uncle Rudy told me what happens when a wildfire comes along.

We were standing in his yard, Uncle Rudy and I, at the foot of a red pine that seemed to stretch to heaven, when a squirrel began knocking pinecones to the ground with soft thuds. Uncle Rudy bent over with a grunt and picked one of the green cones up, rolling it a bit in his callused palm before handing it to me. It was cool in my hands. Sap dripped down the side like tears.

"Here's somethin' I bet you don't know, Button," he said, using the nickname he himself gave me. "That cone there, it ain't like the cones of most other trees. Most cones, all they need is time, or a squirrel to crack 'em open so they can drop their seeds and start a new tree. But that cone there, it ain't gonna open up and drop its seeds unless a wildfire comes through here."

"A wildfire?"

"That's right," Uncle Rudy said, scraping the scalp under

his cap with his dirty fingernail. "See them little scales there, how they're closed up tight like window shutters? Underneath 'em are the seeds—flat little things, flimsy as a baby's fingernails—with a point at one end. If a fire comes along, the heat is gonna cause those scales to peel back and drop their seeds, while the ground is still scorching hot. Then that tiny seed is gonna burrow in and take root."

I was nine years old the summer Freeda and Winnalee Malone rushed across our lives like red-hot flames, peeling back the shutters that sat over our hearts and our minds, setting free our sweetest dreams and our worst nightmares. Too young to know at the onset that anything out of the ordinary was about to happen.

I was sitting on my knees behind the counter at The Corner Store playing with my new Barbie doll, her tiny outfits lined up on the scuffed linoleum. It was the first day of summer vacation, and Aunt Verdella was watching me because my ma was working for Dr. Wagner, the dentist, taking appointments and sending out bills and stuff like that. Aunt Verdella didn't work, like my ma, but she'd been filling in at the store for Ada Smithy (who was having a recuperation from an operation, because she'd had some ladies' troubles). It was Aunt Verdella's last day, then Ada was coming back, and we could stay at Aunt Verdella's while she looked after me.

Aunt Verdella was standing next to me, the hem of her dress like a blue umbrella above me. She was talking to Fanny Tilman about Ada, and Aunt Verdella's voice sounded almost like it was crying when she said, "Such a pity, such a pity," and Fanny Tilman asked her what the pity was for, anyway. "Ada's well past her prime, so seems to me that not getting the curse from here on out should be more of a blessing than a pity," she said, and Aunt Verdella said, "But still..."

While they talked, I was trying to get Barbie's tweed jacket on, which wasn't easy because her elbows didn't bend, and that tiny hand of hers kept snagging on the sleeve. While I was tugging, I was itching. I was looking at the little clothes spread out and trying hard to remember if she was supposed to wear the red jacket with the brown skirt or the green skirt. I cleared my throat a few times, like I always did when I didn't know what I was supposed to do next, and Aunt Verdella looked down at me. "Button, you're doin' that thing with your throat again. What's the matter, honey?" Aunt Verdella's voice was loud, so loud that sometimes it pained my ears when she wasn't even yelling, and her body always reminded me of a snowman made with two balls instead of three. The littlest ball was her head, sitting right on top of one big, fat ball.

I stood up. My knees felt gritty and I glanced down at them, hoping they weren't getting too dirty, because I knew Ma's lips were gonna pull so tight they'd turn white, like they always did when Aunt Verdella brought me home looking all grubby. "I can't get her jacket on," I said.

I handed Aunt Verdella my Barbie, the tweed jacket flapping at her back. Aunt Verdella laughed as she took it. Fanny Tilman peered at me, her puffy eyes puckering. "Is that Reece and Jewel's little one?" she said, like Aunt Verdella could hear her but I couldn't. I put my head down and stared at a gouge in the gray countertop.

"Yep, this is our Button," Aunt Verdella said. She wrapped her freckly arm—stick-skinny like her legs—around me and pulled me to her biggest ball. It was soft and warm, not snowman-cold at all.

"She looks like Jewel," Mrs. Tilman said, and she sounded a bit sorry about this. I saw her looking at my ears, which were too big for my head, and the face she made made me feel smaller than I already was. Aunt Verdella thought that long hair would hide my ears until I grew into them, but Ma said long hair was too much work to keep neat and she already had enough to do. Every couple of months, she'd snip it short, thin it with those scissors that have missing teeth, then curl it with a Tony perm. When she was done, my hair was bunched up in ten or eleven little pale brown knots. I wanted hair long enough to hang loose past my shoulders and cover my ears when I was around people, and to put up in a ponytail that swished my back when I wasn't. But, shoot, I knew I'd never have anything but those stubby knots.

Aunt Verdella finished dressing Barbie, then handed her to me. I stood there a minute, wanting to ask her which skirt matched, but I didn't want to talk with Fanny Tilman still looking at me, so I sat back down on the linoleum and stared at the two skirts some more.

Aunt Verdella had the door propped open with a big rock, because it was nice outside and the store was too hot with the sun beating through the windows. I was staring at the doll clothes when the sound of metal scraping on pavement filled the store.

"Uh-oh, somebody's losing their muffler," Aunt Verdella said. The racket from the scraping muffler got louder and sharper before it came to a stop. Aunt Verdella got up on her tiptoes, the tops of her white shoes making folds like Uncle Rudy's forehead did when she brought home a whole trunk-load of junk from the community sale.

"Good Lord, look what the cat's drug into town now," Fanny Tilman said. "Just what we need, a band of gypsies."

"Oh, Fanny!" Aunt Verdella said.

I heard a door creak open, then slam shut. A lady's voice started talking, but I couldn't make out what it was saying. I heard some banging and then, "Jesus H. Christ! Is anybody gonna come pump my gas or not?" Folks who got gas at The Corner Store pumped their own gas, except for a couple of old ladies and the outsiders. Aunt Verdella called out, "I'll be right there, dear!"

"Excuse me, Button," she said as she stepped over me and hurried around the counter. I put my fingertips on the counter and pulled myself up to take a peek. Mrs. Tilman was standing in the open doorway, her purse clutched in her arms like she thought the "gypsies" were going to try swiping it. She was busy gawking, so I stood all the way up and peeked out between the handmade signs Scotch-taped to the window.

The bed of the red pickup truck at the pumps, and the wagon towed behind it, were piled high with junky furniture I *knew* didn't match and boxes stuffed with bunched-up clothes and dishes that spilled out over the tops.

My eyes almost bugged out of my head when I saw the lady who was standing next to the truck while Aunt Verdella pumped her gas. She had the prettiest color hair I'd ever seen. Red, but like a red I'd never set eyes on before: shiny like a pot of melted copper pennies. Not dark, not light, but somewhere in between, and bright like fire. She stretched like a cat, the sleeveless blouse tied at her waist riding up a belly that was flat and the color of buttered toast. She was made like my Barbie doll, with two big bumps under her blouse, a skinny waist, and long legs under kelly-green pedal pushers. She was wearing a pair of sunglasses with a row of rhinestones at the corners that shot rays into my eyes when she turned toward the store. There was something about the lady too, that shined just as bright as her hair and those rhinestones. Not a warm kind of shining, but a sharp kind, like bright sun jabbing through the window and stinging your eyes.

Aunt Verdella cranked her head toward the store and yelled, "Button, bring Auntie the restroom key, will ya?"

I stepped up on the wooden stool and reached for the key, which was taped to a ruler so it couldn't get lost easy, and I hurried it outside. As much as I hated meeting new people, I wanted to see the pretty lady up close.

The Barbie lady took off her sunglasses and poked them into her fiery hair, which was piled high on her head in a messy sort of way. She had green eyes like a cat's, and her eyelids were sparkly with the same color, clear up to her eyebrows. She had real nice ears too. Tiny, and laying flat to her head like ears are supposed to. I handed Aunt Verdella the key, and she gave it to the pretty lady, who was glaring at the truck, a crabby look on her face. "The ladies' restroom is right around the west side of the building, honey," Aunt Verdella told her.

The pretty lady tapped the ruler against her thigh. "Winnalee Malone, I'm gonna blister your ass if you don't get out of that truck this instant and go pee. You hear me?" I'd never heard a lady swear before, so I know my eyes must have stretched as big as my ears.

The windshield of the truck was blue-black in the sun, so I couldn't see who she was talking to. Aunt Verdella put the gas handle back onto the hook alongside the pump, then headed over to the driver's door where the Barbie lady was standing, still tapping the ruler on her leg. "Oh my," Aunt Verdella said. "Ain't you the prettiest little thing! You've got a face like a cherub." Aunt Verdella said "cherub" more like "cherry-up." "Why don't you come out here and say hello? I got Popsicles inside. A free one for the first pretty little customer who uses the restroom today." Aunt Verdella looked at the lady and winked, then turned back to the truck. "Come on, now, honey. We don't bite."

The Barbie lady lifted her arms and slapped them against the sides of her thighs. "Ah, to hell with you, Winnalee. If you're gonna be stubborn, then sit there till your bladder bursts, for all I care. I'm too tired to argue with you."

"Winnalee? Now, ain't that the prettiest name. Where'd you get a pretty name like that?" Aunt Verdella asked.

"From my ma," said a voice from inside the truck. "It's a homemade name."

The lady cussed again, like ladies aren't supposed to do, then she said, "Winnalee, I'm not going to stand here and piss my pants waiting for you. You coming or not?"

Aunt Verdella cranked her head around. "You go on to the restroom, dear. I got a way with children," she said, then she winked again. The pretty lady made a growly sound in her throat, then she headed toward the building, her heels clacking against the pavement.

It took a while, but finally Aunt Verdella coaxed Winnalee out. When I saw her, I could hardly believe my eyes: She had long, loopy hair the color of that stringy part inside a cob of corn, but with some yellow mixed in too, and it hung clear down to her butt. It didn't have any rubber bands or barrettes in it, so it floated in the breeze like a mermaid's hair under water. Her face was round and pink, with little lips that looked like they had lipstick on them. She was wearing a lady's mesh slip, and it was rolled up at her round belly to keep it from falling down. She had on a white sleeveless blouse that belonged on a grown-up too. One side of it slipped down her arm and she crooked her elbow to keep it from falling all the way off. She didn't look at us but turned to reach for something on the seat. I scootched over by Aunt Verdella to see what the mermaid girl was getting.

"Well, my, what do you have there, Winnalee?" Aunt Verdella asked as the girl slid out of the truck holding a capped, shiny silver vase in her arms, cradling it like it was a baby doll.

"It's my ma," Winnalee said.

"Your ma?" Aunt Verdella asked, suddenly looking a bit shook up.

It was like Aunt Verdella didn't know what to say—which I was sure was because she was thinking the same thought as me. That there wasn't a lady anywhere small enough to fit into that vase. Either Winnalee was funning us, or else she was just plain nuts. Instead, Aunt Verdella asked her about the thick book she had tucked under her armpit. "Button likes to read big books too, don't you Button?" she said, putting an arm around me.

"It's her Book of Bright Ideas," said a voice behind us in the same tone that the snotty big kids who picked on us little kids at recess used. I turned and saw the pretty lady standing there, her hands on her hips, her legs parted. She was looking up and down the street.

It was like Aunt Verdella didn't know what to say again, so

she said nothing except that if Winnalee was a good little girl and went potty, she'd give her a Popsicle or an ice cream bar.

The lady grabbed a big black purse off of the seat of the truck and we all headed toward the store, Winnalee's loopy hair dancing, her mesh slip flapping in the breeze like fins.

Fanny Tilman backed out of the doorway and slipped behind a grocery shelf, where I knew she was gonna stay hid, like a mouse waiting for somebody to drop some crumbs.

"Where you people from?" Aunt Verdella asked as she scooted behind the counter. The pretty lady took a bottle of RC Cola and one of root beer from the cooler, then set them down on the counter alongside her purse. Winnalee was behind her.

"Gary," she says. "Gary, Indiana. We drove straight through."

"Yeah," Winnalee said. "We had to leave in the middle of the night. All because Freeda went dancing with some guy from the meat factory, when she was supposed to be Harley Hoffesteader's girl. Harley got so pissed he was coming after her with a shotgun. Probably would have killed both of us dead if we hadn't gotten out of there fast. It don't matter, though. Freeda would've moved us anyways. She always does." The lady cuffed her on the top of her head and Winnalee cried out, "Ouch!" Aunt Verdella flinched and told Winnalee that maybe she should go potty now, and would she like me or her to go with her. Winnalee's nose crinkled. "I'm not a baby," she said, then she grabbed the key from the counter and marched out the door.

"Oh my. Gary. That's quite a drive. That must be, what, a good three fifty, four hundred miles from here?"

"I don't know." Freeda shook her head so that wispy strands wobbled against her long neck. "Hell, I don't even know where we are."

"You're in Dauber, Wisconsin, dear. Population 3,263,"

Aunt Verdella said proudly. "You thinking of settling here, or are you just passing through?"

Freeda shrugged. "I guess one place is as good as another. There any places to rent around here?"

I swear I heard Fanny Tilman (who was peeking up over the bread rack) gasp.

Aunt Verdella squeaked her tongue against her teeth as she thought. Then her puffy lips made a circle like a doughnut. "Ohhhh, well, actually, there just might be! Well, if you don't mind living in a place that's being fixed up, that is. You see, my husband, Rudy, and his brother, Reece, their ma passed away a couple a years ago, and we've been talking about renting her place out once Reece gets it fixed up. I keep saying that a house that sits empty falls to ruin fast, but you know how men are. Reece—that's Button here's daddy—he ain't gotten around to the repairs yet, but if you don't mind him coming and going, I don't see why we can't rent it to you now."

Winnalee came back in and held the key out to me, but looked at Freeda. "Hey, you said we were going to Detroit! She lies," she said to me, her thumb jabbing toward Freeda. Then she leaned over and peered at the mesh slip she was wearing. "Can you see my undies through this thing?" I looked, saw a bit of white, and told her I could. She rolled her big, lake-on-a-sunny-day-colored eyes and sighed. "I tried to tell Freeda that I was in my underwear, but she went and packed up my clothes anyway."

Freeda grunted. "Like it matters. You're in dress-up clothes half the time, anyway, Winnalee."

Aunt Verdella talked about Grandma Mae's place, bragging about the nice closed-in porch with good screens (all but for the one a barn cat shredded) and about the flower garden that was already shooting up daffodils and hyacinths, while she went to the freezer so Winnalee could pick out a treat. She called me over to have something too.

"Oh dear, where *are* my manners," she said all of a sudden. "I didn't even introduce myself yet. I'm Verdella Peters, and this here is my niece, Evelyn Mae, but we all call her Button. She's nine years old. How old are you, Winnalee?"

"I'm gonna be ten on September first," she said.

Freeda smiled for the first time, and her smile was as pretty as her hair. "I'm Freeda Malone, and you already know the sassy one. She's my kid sister."

Things happened fast then. While Freeda Malone was paying for her gas and the pop, Aunt Verdella told her they could get something to eat at the Spot Café. "You girls come back after you're done eating," Aunt Verdella said. "I'm closin' up in an hour, and you can follow me then." While Aunt Verdella chattered, I watched Winnalee eat her grape Popsicle. She didn't seem to have one bit of worry about the purple dripping down her hand and streaking her arm. I had my wrapper cupped around my stick, like you're supposed to, so I didn't have to worry about getting all sticky and stained.

The minute the Malones left, Aunt Verdella got as light and floaty as bubbles. Fanny Tilman came out of her hiding place then, looking like a gray mouse in her wool coat, even though it was too warm for even a little jacket.

"Verdella! Jewel is gonna be fit to be tied, you offering Mae's house like that! And to some gypsy drifters, to boot!"

Aunt Verdella waved Fanny Tilman's comment away. "It's gonna be real nice having people in that house, Fanny. I get so lonely when I look across the road and see that big, empty place. Mae didn't take to me much, but still, it was just nice knowing someone was there." She looked down at me and grinned. "And Button here sure could use a little friend, couldn't you, Button?"

Mrs. Tilman's mouth pinched. "Good heavens, Verdella. It's not like bringing home a litter of abandoned kittens, you know. These are strangers, and most likely trouble, by the looks of them."

When the Malones came back, Winnalee had ketchup

splotched on her blouse, right over one of those points sticking out front like two witch's hats. Her eyes were a little red, and her cheeks had white streaks on them where a few tears had washed them. She didn't look unhappy at the moment, though, as she squatted to examine the tops of some canned goods where rainbowy shadows made by something shiny hanging in the window were flickering.

Aunt Verdella took her pay out of the till like she was told to—one dollar for every hour she worked this week—while I packed up my doll. She folded the envelope in threes and tucked it into her bra to take home and put in her jewelry box, where she kept all the money that was going toward the RCA color television set she wanted. A magazine ad of it was tacked to her fridge door, where it had hung since I was in the first grade. When she first came over with that ad, saying she was gonna save up and buy it even if it took her a lifetime, Ma had taken the *TV Guide* and showed Aunt Verdella how, at best, she'd only get three hours of color TV time a day. Mom repeated this story whenever she wanted to make Aunt Verdella look foolish. "I told her, look here, on Mondays, you'll only get forty-five minutes!" But Verdella just laughed and said, " 'Long as two of those hours are used up by *As the World Turns* and Arthur Godfrey, I'll be happy. Besides, by the time I save up $495, who knows, they might *all* be in living color!' " Aunt Verdella had no idea how much that TV set was gonna cost her once she finally saved up enough, but she still faithfully put away every spare dime she had to buy it.

Aunt Verdella locked up The Corner Store and we climbed into her turquoise and white Bel Air, which was cluttered with junk. A Raggedy Ann and Andy—bought from the community sale last summer, just because they were cute—were propped on the bag of romance magazines that somebody gave her weeks ago, and wadded-up candy and chip wrappers littered the floor. Aunt Verdella checked my door three times to make sure it was locked, so I wouldn't lean on it and fall out, then made me set down my Barbie case and climb over the seat to watch out the back window as she backed out, so she didn't run anybody over.

"It's okay," I said.

Once we got going, I climbed back into the front seat. I sat close to Aunt Verdella, her arm warm against my cheek. Aunt Verdella kept looking in the rearview mirror, making sure that the Malones were still following us.

The shortest way home was down Highway 8, but Aunt Verdella wouldn't drive on the highway, so we kicked up dust down one town road after another, driving for what seemed forever. By the time we got out of the city limits the insides of my arms were splotched with the red, pimply rash that sprouted up on them whenever I got rattled. I knew Ma wasn't gonna be happy. Not about my dirty knees, and not about the Malones. I slid my jaw over a bit so my teeth could grab at the bumpy clump of skin inside my cheek, even though Dr. Wagner told me that if I kept up the nasty habit, I was gonna bite a hole clear through my face. Aunt Verdella wasn't worried like me though. She sang lines from one of those country songs she always played on her record player and grinned like she was bringing home Christmas. The rash itchin' my arms, though, told me that maybe this was a package we weren't supposed to open.

2

Aunt Verdella chattered about having the Malones in
Grandma Mae's house, while she kept her eyes on the road
and drove with her hands choking the wheel. Now and then,
her head gave a little jerk as she looked in the rearview mirror.
I turned in my seat and took a peek back too. I couldn't see inside their windshield good, but I could see shadows moving,
like maybe Winnalee and Freeda weren't sittin' still.

We drove past a lot of farms where cows stood in the fields
doing nothing but chewing. Then we drove a long stretch seeing nothing but trees and brush crouched close to the road,
and a few old farmhouses. Finally, we came to Peters Road,
drove past Aunt Verdella's house, and crossed the highway.

Our house, which was sort of new, sat right on Highway 8,
our driveway across from Peters Road. Daddy had built it
when I was just a baby. It was one of those houses shaped like
a shoe box, with a garage next to it painted turquoise like our
house. Off to one side was a bigger garage, where Daddy and
Uncle Rudy worked on things, but that was just silver. Ma's
car was sitting in our garage, its butt facing out, so I knew she
was home.

Ma always did the same thing when she got home from
work. She got out of her nylons and suit and put on an old

housedress in case she spattered grease while cooking, then she'd start supper. I knew Ma would be in the kitchen when we pulled in the drive, and that wasn't gonna be good, because Ma always complained if company dropped in without calling first, especially if it was almost suppertime.

Aunt Verdella didn't care though. She pulled her Bel Air into the driveway and hit the brakes so hard that Raggedy Ann tumbled down to my feet. I scooped her up and put her back next to Raggedy Andy.

Aunt Verdella thumped on the horn. She got out of the car and hurried to the Malones' truck, which was parked behind us. "Button, go get your ma. Hurry up, now!" I got out of the car and stood there, not wanting to, while Aunt Verdella yelled out real loud, "Jewel! Come on out here! Jewel!" her words banging right through the screen door.

Ma came out on the steps. She had a stirring spoon in her hand and an apron slung around her middle. She didn't look real happy to see any of us.

"Jewel, come on over here. I got someone for you to meet." Ma looked at me like she was begging me to tell her what was going on.

"Evelyn, go get your father and your uncle out of the garage, please," Ma said to me through a smile that didn't spread up to her eyes.

As I was heading toward the garage, Aunt Verdella was tugging the Malones out of the truck. I was almost glad to be gone then, 'cause I didn't want to see Ma's face when she saw Winnalee Malone wearing dress-up clothes with her underwear showing through.

I stepped into the garage, which was so big that it took the clanking of tools and cranked them as loud as if they were sounding in a microphone. The whole place smelled like metal and oil. Daddy had the radio on, and the Beach Boys were singing so loud he couldn't hear me calling from the doorway. I went inside, right over to where Daddy and Uncle Rudy were working on Daddy's old 1934 Ford, doing what Daddy said was "restorin'" it. Uncle Rudy was leaned under the hood, and Daddy was scooted under the car, his legs sticking out of the side like somebody had drove over him, pinning him underneath.

Uncle Rudy smiled when he saw me. "Hey there, Button," he shouted. I tried to yell to tell him that Ma wanted him and Daddy to come out, but I knew by the way he was studying my mouth that he could only see it move, not hear what it was saying. He went over to the radio and turned it down, leaned over so he could hear me, then he told Daddy what I said.

Daddy rolled out from under the car on one of those little boards with wheels and sat up. His black eyebrows knelt down over his eyes. He didn't grin and pat my head when he saw me the way Uncle Rudy did. Instead, he looked through me like I was made of fog and asked Uncle Rudy what was going on. Uncle Rudy told him he'd go see.

When Uncle Rudy and I got to the driveway, Aunt Verdella waved and grinned. She didn't wait for Uncle Rudy to get to where they were standing on the lawn. Instead, she half-ran, half-walked to meet him and gave him a big hug and smooches on his cheek, as if nobody was even watching. She started talking a mile a minute, trying to explain things.

Uncle Rudy shook Freeda's hand and patted Winnalee on the head. She grinned up at him, her lips still purple from her Popsicle.

"So I told the girls to follow me right over here. That I was sure we could set something up."

"Rudy, I think Reece better come out here," Ma said. She crossed her arms tight, then said, "Evelyn Mae, go get your father. Now."

I didn't like talking directly to Daddy. It made me feel shy in my belly. But I went.

"Your dad looks like Elvis," Winnalee said when Daddy and me got back to the yard (not even bothering to whisper), but that wasn't so. He had black hair like Elvis, and eyes the color of a navy crayon, but not the same nose and mouth, just regular ones.

Aunt Verdella introduced everybody, and Daddy moved the tool he was holding from his right hand to his left, wiped his hand on his jeans, then held it out to Freeda. She grinned when she took it and got all squirmy. "Sorry to be barging in like this, interrupting your work, but your sister-in-law insisted on rescuing us." Daddy told her they weren't interrupting anything, even though they were. Winnalee went right up to Daddy, and she smiled up at him. "You look like Elvis," she said. Daddy laughed, then patted her on the head.

"Reece," Ma said, "I was just reminding Verdella how we agreed not to rent out Mae's house until you got those repairs done. Mae's things aren't even packed away yet." Ma's voice got quiet, like mine did when I had to tell her or Daddy something.

"Oh, Jewel," Aunt Verdella said. "These girls don't mind if it's not fixed up yet. And I'm done at The Corner Store now, so I can pack up Mae's things." Freeda's green eyes were staring at Daddy's arm, right below where the sleeve of his T-shirt was rolled up over a pack of Camels, showing his tattoo of a heart with a knife stuck through it, a drop of red blood falling from it.

I had never really looked at my ma when she was standing next to a real pretty lady before, but now that I was, I saw something that I never saw before—and what I saw made me feel sad for her, and for some reason, sad for me too. My ma wasn't pretty. Her eyes were too squinty and her lips were only skimpy gray lines. Her thin hair was the color of oatmeal and lay flat and dull against her head, except for a skirt of frizzies at the bottom and a lump of curled bangs sitting across the top of her long forehead like a pork link. She was tall like a man. And with no bumps that you could see poking against her pale green dress, she looked like a praying mantis bug.

Ma crossed her arms, which were pale like her face and

had blue streaks sitting close under her skin. I turned away from her and looked at pretty Winnalee, and I thought of how I must look just as ugly standing next to her as Ma looked standing next to Freeda Malone.

"And if you're looking for work, Freeda, Reece here was just saying that Marty, down at Marty's Place, is looking for another waitress. The new girl he hired a couple months ago just quit to get married." She turned to my daddy. "Weren't ya just saying that this morning, Reece?" She didn't wait for him to answer. She turned back to Freeda. "Reece here and his friend, Owen Palmer, they used to play guitars and sing over at Marty's Place every Friday night. The place wasn't much then, but he's remodeling with nice light paneling and a new dance floor. He'll be reopening in another week or so, isn't that what you said, Reece? They have the best fish fries in town, don't they, Rudy? Have you waitressed before, Freeda?"

Freeda laughed. "Hell, of course I've waitressed before. And served beer to old drunks, scrubbed other people's toilets, wound the eyes to fish poles, answered phones, hacked old ladies' hair—you name it, I've done it."

"Well, let's all go on inside and talk things over, over a pot of coffee," Aunt Verdella said, as she pushed everyone toward the house like they were her dolls and she was taking them on an adventure. "You two can stay outside and play," she said to me and Winnalee. "Aunt Verdella will bring you some nice lemonade and some of those peanut butter cookies I brought by this morning."

Soon as the screen door shut, Winnalee headed across the yard toward the tire swing that hung from our big maple, and I followed because I didn't know what else to do. She set her vase and book down on the grass, then she stuck herself through the tire, belly side down, and pushed herself with her bare feet. "You and your ma are gray people," she said as she waved her arms in the breeze like she was swimming.

My arms itched a bit when she said this, though I wasn't

sure why, since I didn't even know what she meant, much less if I was supposed to get mad 'cause she said it. Winnalee probably didn't know I was mad, though, because she wasn't looking at me. She was swinging and staring out at the woods that sat out past the yard. I wanted to ask her what she meant, but I couldn't make myself do nothing but stare and blink.

"Push me," Winnalee said, so I did. "No, wind me up!" she begged when I made both my arms use the same shove so she'd go nice and straight.

I took the tire and ran in circles till the rope was twisted up like a screw, then I let go. Winnalee squealed, "Wheeeeeee!"

When the swing was doing nothing but swaying side to side like a wobbly drunk, Winnalee pulled herself out of the tire and zigzagged across the grass, her arms stretched wide, then she fell down and giggled. I just stood there, staring at her. She sat up after a bit. "Hey, you wanna see my ma?"

She went over to where her vase and book were sitting. She sat down, her legs straddling the vase. She unscrewed the lid, tipped it toward me, then waited for me to bend over and take a peek. I wanted to look, yet I didn't. I knew there wasn't a lady inside there, so I knew she was just pulling my leg, but I didn't want to have to say so out loud. "Go on, look."

She waited, so I leaned over and looked, but I didn't see nothing but the shadow my head was making over the dark hole. "You see her?" she asked.

"It's too dark in there to see anything," I said.

She pulled the vase closer to her and took a peek. "Here," she said, "come around my side and you can see her."

I moved behind Winnalee and peered over her shoulder. I could see inside a bit then, but it just looked like somebody had emptied their ashtray in there, and I told Winnalee so.

"Those ashes *are* my ma," she said.

I forgot about being shy then. "Uh-uh!" I said.

She looked up at me, her eyes so pretty blue that I couldn't help staring. "It *is* my ma. She's dead and burned up to ashes."

I shook my head. "Uh-uh, dead people get buried in the ground." I said this knowing full well I was right, because Grandma Mae was dead, and so was Uncle Rudy's first wife, Aunt Betty. And on that day for the dead—that day that scared me—we'd all go to the cemetery and put plastic flowers next to the gravestones with their names on them.

"Well, not my ma," Winnalee said.

I wanted to call Winnalee a liar, but something in the way she said it, her eyes looking like they were turning into water, made me stop. "It ain't right, though," she said quietly. "Somebody being put into a jar and moving around town to town and never having a final restin' place. That's what Ma used to call graves. Final restin' places. So when I get big and get me some money, I'm gonna buy her a restin' place right under an apple tree. And I'm gonna buy her a nice, pretty white stone with a fairy on it and tell them to cut the words *Hannah Malone* right into the marble. That's what I'm gonna do."

Winnalee screwed the lid back on that thing she called an urn and set it back on the grass, gently, like she didn't want it to break. "Wanna see my Book of Bright Ideas?" she said. I nodded. She patted the grass beside her, but I didn't want to sit next to a dead, burned lady, so I sat on the other side of her. She picked up her book. "It's genuine leather bound," she said, her chubby hand brushing over the brown cover with gold letters sunken into it, so that I couldn't read the title because her fingers were in the way.

She was about to tell me more when Aunt Verdella burst out the front door, carrying a tray. "Aunt Verdella didn't forget about you two!" she yelled as she hurried toward us, her eyes watching the two pink, plastic cups on the tray so they wouldn't tip over. "Well, maybe for a minute I did," she said, then she ha-ha-ed all the way across the yard.

She bent over to set the lemonade and plate of four cookies on the grass. I could see a strip of silver sitting on both sides of her part, which told me that she wouldn't have her dark auburn hair long before she hauled me to the drugstore, where she'd hold boxes up to her head and ask me which colored, frozen wave would look the best on her. Winnalee picked up one of Aunt Verdella's peanut butter cookies and grinned at the crooked raisin-smile. I was gonna tell Winnalee that I helped Aunt Verdella poke the smiles into those cookies, but I didn't.

"How you girls getting along?"

"I like her," Winnalee said about me, and I could tell that she meant it by the way she said it. This made me happy, even though I wasn't sure I liked her, just yet.

"Well, good," Aunt Verdella said, "because it looks like you two are gonna be neighbors!"

As soon as Aunt Verdella went back inside, I peered back at Winnalee's book while she munched on a cookie. She was staring at it in between bites and humming while she chewed with her mouth open. "Says here the name of this book is *Great Expectations,* by Charles Dickens. Why you call it your Book of Bright Ideas, then?" I asked.

Winnalee shoved the last of her cookie into her mouth, even though it was too big of a piece, and it bulged the sides of her cheeks. She picked up her book and laid it across her legs and opened it toward the back. I blinked, because there wasn't any writing in that book at all, only white, blank pages.

When she talked, she was all mumbly, so I told her that maybe she should swallow first. She did, then she explained.

"I got this book at a rich lawyer's house, where Freeda cleaned for a time. He had a whole library of these leather-bound books, every one of them with nothin' inside. Freeda said they were just for looks. So I took this one. I tucked it right up my shirt and walked out with it. Freeda says I stole this book and that she had every right to blister my ass for doing it. She said she was gonna march me right back there in the morning so that lawyer could blister it some more, but she didn't do either. Not once I convinced her that it wasn't stealing at all. This here wasn't anything but an empty box, and nobody in their right mind would tell the folks who take the empty boxes out of the back room of the IGA that they were thieving. It's not like that lawyer was going to read it, anyway, so I took it and started a book of my own." She paged toward the middle of the book and, sure enough, there were words printed there in pencil.

"You're writing a story?"

"No, not a story. Just things I learn. I number them, see?"

"Why do you do that?"

"So I can find the things I want to read again, faster."

"No," I said. "Why do you write those things down?"

The wind tossed a strand of Winnalee's loopy hair between her lips and she took it out and flipped it. Her hair looked glossy and pretty in the sun, even with a few snarls and cookie crumbs stuck in it. "Because I'm writing clues. Itty-bitty clues that you have to put together. You know, clues to the secrets of life. So you learn how it works, and you don't keep makin' the same mistakes over and over again. That's what Freeda says people do. They keep making the same dumb mistakes over and over again. I don't want to do that."

Now Winnalee had me all mixed up, because she was saying this stuff like I was supposed to know what she was talking about, but I didn't.

She paged through the book, near the beginning, then stopped and rested her finger in one spot. "See? *Bright Idea #17,*" she read. *"If you don't give your ma a hug before you go to school because you're mad at her for not letting you wear your good dress, she might die while you're at recess. Then you ain't going to be able to give her that hug ever."*

Winnalee looked up and bit her lip. "You know what a great expectation is?" she asked. She didn't wait for me to answer. "Well, it's something you really, really hope for. It's my great expectation that when I get one hundred bright ideas written down, I'm gonna be able to fit them together like pieces of a puzzle and know all there is to know about how to live good. God knows, a kid ain't gonna learn these things by asking her sister, because she ain't gonna tell you shit, so I'm gonna figure it all out by myself. I figure by the time I get to one hundred, I'll know all there is to know. You can help me find the clues, then we can jot them down. I bet by the time school starts, we might even have this whole book filled up with one hundred bright ideas."

I didn't have any bright ideas, but I smiled because I was happy that Winnalee thought I might think of one. "How many you got written so far?" I asked.

"Eighty-three," she said. "I wrote the last one while we were driving out of Gary. See?" She held the book out and I read *Bright Idea #83: If you go dancing with a meat packer when you got a biker for a boyfriend, he might get his gun and shoot you and your sister dead, so you'd better get out of town fast.*

As Winnalee shut the book and reached for her second cookie, the door opened and the wind carried the grown-ups' voices over to where we were sitting, and I knew Winnalee had to leave then. I picked up the tray and Winnalee grabbed a glass from it and drank her lemonade as we headed toward the house. "If Freeda hadn't packed away all my pencils, I'd jot a bright idea right now," she said.

"What would you write?"

"I'd write *Bright Idea #84: When you go through a new town that don't look like much, stop anyway, because you just might find a best friend waiting there.*"

3

Soon as everyone left, Ma made Daddy and me come in for supper. The whole house was filled with the stink of liver and onions, so I didn't bother asking what we were having.

"I can't believe Verdella, bringing them here out of the blue like that," Ma said.

Daddy grabbed a slice of homemade bread, and as he buttered it, crumbs fell like snow onto his plate. "They need a place to stay, and she wants to help them out, that's all. Verdella is kindhearted that way." He didn't look at Ma when he talked, but then, he never did.

"Well, she could have checked with us first, before bringing them over and putting us on the spot like that."

I know Ma wanted to say more, but she didn't. As soon as Daddy left, Ma clanked the dishes into the sink and sprayed a yellow line of Joy over them. That's when the phone rang. "Oh, hello, Bernice." Bernice was the lady who worked with Ma. She had hair like mine, and a boy in my grade who punched girls in the arm. "Fanny? . . . Yes, you heard right. . . . Uh-huh . . . uh-huh, she certainly did bring them here."

While I sat looking at my plate, trying to get myself to finish my liver so I could leave the table, Ma started talking about the Malones and about Aunt Verdella. "Well, that's just what I was thinking, Bernice. Good Lord, she doesn't know the first thing about these people, but she's got eyes in her head, doesn't she? Uh-huh . . . yes . . . and you should have seen the way that child was dressed too. Why, I don't even know if I want Evelyn associating with her."

Ma said a string of "Uh-huhs," then she gasped, "Well, I'll tell you one thing for sure, Mae would not like this one bit! That Verdella, always sticking her nose where it doesn't belong. Course, I couldn't say much to Reece. You know how he is about Verdella."

I took my fork and jabbed at the slab of liver on my plate. The onions were cold now, coated with grease that looked like those thick gobs of spit men leave on the sidewalks. My stomach felt sick just from looking at them. And from hearing Ma talking about Aunt Verdella. I didn't care if Aunt Verdella talked too loud, or filled up her house with mismatched junk, or even if she had an old bathtub sunk halfway into the ground in her front yard, with Jesus' mother stuck in it, even though she wasn't Catholic. Whenever Ma talked mean about Aunt Verdella, it made those noises happen in my throat. And *that* made Ma turn and give me a crabby look.

Ma stood up her tallest. "She's picked up the line again, Bernice, so watch what you say till she hangs up." I knew this meant that the old lady down the road, Mildred Epson (one of four others on our party line), had picked up the phone to listen to Ma and Bernice yack. Ma tapped her foot and waited. After a bit she said, "There. I thought she'd never hang up. I swear, some people on this party line don't do a thing all day but wait around for someone to use the phone so they can listen in and get some gossip. The next time I see that woman, I'm going to tell her what I think of her eavesdropping." Ma said this all the time, but every time we ran into that bent-up old lady, she never did do anything but smile and shift from leg to leg, as Mrs. Epson went on and on about her hips, her elbow, her back, and every other part on her body that hurt.

Ma sighed. "There, now, where were we, Bernice? . . .

"No, no. Verdella and Rudy aren't on our line. They don't even have a phone. Verdella comes down here all the time to use ours—as if they can't afford one of their own—yet she's saving all that money to buy a color television set. That's Verdella, though. Not a brain in her head." I picked up a piece of cold liver and stuck it in my mouth. It felt like I was biting into the tongue of one of Uncle Rudy's old work boots.

"Oh, you know how Reece is though," Ma said, turning her back to me again. "He won't hear one negative thing about Verdella, even if it is the truth. He says she's the best thing that could have happened to Rudy after Betty died and that she's good to him. Well, maybe she is good to him in some ways, but still, from what Mae always said about Betty, you can't even compare Verdella to her. Betty kept a good house and had a good head on her shoulders. If Betty could see that place now, she'd roll over in her grave."

I watched Ma out of the corner of my eye. She was pacing as far as the phone cord would stretch. She didn't say no more about Aunt Verdella, though, because Daddy came back into the house to dig for something in the junk drawer. "Well, I'd best get back to my dishes now. I'll see you tomorrow, Bernice."

The next morning, Ma woke me up as she always did when the sun was first peeking through my window, and I hopped out of bed quickly, even though my eyes still wanted to stay shut. She had my things set out on the bed like paper-doll clothes, faded pink pants on the bottom and a pink flowered blouse stretched out above it. A pair of white anklets was wadded up in a ball, sitting beside my outfit. Even when wearing old clothes to go help her aunt clean an old house, a girl should match. This much I knew.

Once we got into the car, Ma tugged at her nylons, which wanted to bunch at her ankles. It was cold in the mornings

still—it being only four days since school let out—so even
wearing a sweater, my arms and legs bubbled up with goose
pimples.

"So, Evelyn," Ma said, then paused as we crossed
Highway 8 and headed down the road (named "Peters Road,"
since no other family ever lived on it except ours), the tires
spitting rocks up under Ma's car with little pings. "Did Aunt
Verdella tell you anything about these people?"

I knew I should probably tell Ma what Winnalee said
about some guy chasing them with a gun, but she always
harped at me if I was a tattletale. Yet I knew that if I said "no,"
then I'd be a liar, so I didn't say anything at all.

"It seems a little suspicious to me. If they arrived in town
in the afternoon—their belongings just tossed in the truck—
and came from Gary, that means that woman probably packed
that child up in the middle of the night. Who does a thing like
that, unless they had to leave in a hurry?" Ma was talking more
to herself now than to me.

Ma's knuckles got tight on the steering wheel as we pulled
into Aunt Verdella and Uncle Rudy's driveway. She leaned
over and reached across me to open my door. "Stay clean,"
she said, then leaned back against the seat, as though I were
already gone.

She pulled out of the driveway before Aunt Verdella could
even get to our car. "My, she sure was in a hurry this morning," Aunt Verdella said, then she gave me my morning hug.

Aunt Verdella was happy today because we were going to
start cleaning up Grandma Mae's house for the Malones. "I
told them we can have this place ready in a couple of days.
Three at the most. I don't want to see those girls paying those
high prices over at Daverson's Motel." She handed me a cardboard box stacked inside with smaller ones, then she grabbed
some more boxes, heavy with cleaning bottles, and we headed
across the yard.

Grandma Mae's house was big and covered with gray
squares that looked like sandpaper. It had red shutters that

needed paint sitting beside each window. Near the house was a big, red barn, and next to that was the field where Uncle Rudy's cows ate. Uncle Rudy milked fifteen of them every morning and every night.

Across the field, I could see Uncle Rudy pounding a fence post into the ground. From so far away, his maul looked like a pencil with a wad of gum stuck on the eraser part. Tommy Smithy, Ada Smithy's fourteen-year-old boy, was out there too, putting another post in place for hammering. I had sighed when I learned that he would be helping Uncle Rudy with chores around the place, just like he did last summer. Tommy had hair the color of speckled mold in the corners of old basements, and it was in tight, knotty curls that Aunt Verdella said didn't even come from a perm. He had pointy teeth like nails in front. He wasn't old enough to drive yet, but his daddy let him use their old truck to come to work. I didn't like Tommy, because he liked to scare me and tease me when he caught me alone.

Aunt Verdella was watching across the field where Uncle Rudy was working, while we walked across Grandma Mae's yard. She had a little smile on her face, like she always did when she looked at him.

When we got on the porch, Aunt Verdella took the key from her pocket and unlocked the door. She shoved the door open and it scraped across the wood floor. "Oh dear, I'll have to tell Reece to rehang this door. The house must be shifting."

Grandma Mae's house smelled like old dust, and it was quiet. Real quiet.

"Come on in, Button," Aunt Verdella said. "We'll start right here in the front room."

I didn't remember Grandma Mae real well. Only that she was skinny and stiff like a broom handle, and that she didn't smile or talk to me. She gave me a brush and comb set one Christmas, but Ma said it was too nice to use, so she made me put it on my vanity and leave it be. I didn't mind not using it though. Why would I need a brush as big as a bear's paw to brush a couple of little knots, anyway? Ma said it would be nice to have something to remember my grandma by once she was gone, but every time I looked at that comb and brush set sitting there on my vanity, all I remembered was that I had nubby knots for hair.

It took a bit to get myself to move from the doorway. I felt like I should take off my shoes and walk like a whisper, though I wasn't sure why. Aunt Verdella didn't feel that way though. She had on her old canvas shoes with garden and barn crud scuffed halfway up the sides, and as she thumped hard across the floor, tiny clumps of it sprinkled over the oval rag rug sitting in the middle of the living-room floor.

Aunt Verdella got a stack of yellowed newspapers from a basket sitting next to an old chair, and she dropped them down by the coffee table, next to the boxes. "We'll wrap up the knickknacks and pictures first and bring them up to the attic," she said. "I'd like to leave a little something out, you know, make it more homey for the girls, but I don't suppose your ma would like seeing any of Mae's things left out for strangers."

She showed me how to wrap the glass things by rolling them in a few sheets of newspaper, then she showed me how to tuck them in a cardboard box so we could fit lots in. I wrapped up a green candy dish, then a couple little ladies that Aunt Verdella said were from Germany, just like Grandma. I laid the wrapped ladies inside the candy dish carefully, while Aunt Verdella watched me. "You're doing a fine job there, Button," she said. I smiled, because I liked the way Aunt Verdella always told me that, even when I wasn't doing a fine job.

Aunt Verdella took the pictures off the mantel. She held up one of my ma and daddy. Ma was wearing a wedding dress and her lips were pulled shut in a smile. She looked shy, but happy. Her shoulders were dipped forward, like they were lots of times. My daddy looked real handsome, his dark hair combed neat off of his forehead. "Your ma sewed her own dress. She got a pattern, then altered it to just how she wanted it. It's beautiful, isn't it?" I nodded.

Then Aunt Verdella took down a picture of Uncle Rudy and that first lady that was his wife. She was wearing one of those wedding dresses too and a long veil that wrapped around her body, making her look all cloudy, like she was already a ghost, even though she wasn't then. Aunt Verdella talked a bit about Ma and Aunt Betty's wedding dresses, and what she liked on each one, then she told me that when I grew up and got ready to marry, Ma would make me the prettiest gown anyone ever saw. Prettier than a princess's gown, she said.

"Is there a picture of you in your wedding dress too, Aunt Verdella?"

She shook her head, and there was only a hint of a smile on her face. "Oh heavens, no. I got married at the courthouse, in a regular suit. Just me and your uncle Rudy, and Reece. That's all."

"How come you didn't have a pretty wedding dress too?"

She started wrapping the pictures in newspaper, and she didn't look up when she said, "I was almost forty years old, Button. Why, I'd have looked pretty silly in a white dress made for a young girl, don't you think?"

"Well, how come there's no picture here of you in your suit, then?" I asked, and Aunt Verdella shrugged.

Aunt Verdella took all the pictures off of the walls and off of the tables. And as she did, she turned each one of them for me to see. "This here is your grandma Mae when she was still young, right before your daddy was born," she said. Grandma Mae wasn't smiling. Her face looked like a statue's face. She had a pointy chin and eyebrows that looked like fur cuffs. She was wearing an ugly dress that was buttoned up so tight around her neck that it looked like it might have been choking her. "She doesn't look young to me," I said.

Aunt Verdella laughed. "Well, your daddy was a change-of-life baby, so I guess she wasn't exactly a spring chicken. Still, it was taken while she still had some dark left in her hair." She rubbed the dusty glass with her hand. "That woman sure didn't have any time for kids. Not by the time I'd met her anyway. She just worked in her garden, or cleaned, or sewed, or canned, and she sighed every time your daddy had to ask her for anything. I don't think I saw her give that boy a hug once. Not once.

"When I married your uncle, Reece wasn't more than ten years old. Cute as a bug's ear too. One of them boys that never sits still." Aunt Verdella's eyes were full of laughs when she said this.

While Aunt Verdella yammered on about my daddy in the old days, I tried to shrink him down in my mind to a little boy as cute as a bug's ear. But no matter how hard I tried, the best I could see was a midget man, with arms like gunnysacks stuffed tight with rocks, and hair like fur crawling out of the top of his T-shirt.

"I remember Rudy helped him make Mae a bird feeder for her birthday, that first summer after your uncle and I were married. Making it was my idea. Mae liked birds in her yard, cardinals especially, so I thought she'd like a feeder. That poor boy worked for days on that thing, making it all square and nice. Paintin' it red so it would match the shutters on the house. It should have made her happy, but all she had to say was that it would be too much bother to traipse through the snow to keep it filled come winter, and that in the summertime, the birds could find their own food. She said the squirrels would just gobble up the seeds anyway. I was so mad!" Aunt Verdella's lips puckered up like the top of a drawstring purse tugged tight, then her mouth fell open and she clicked her teeth with her tongue.

"I didn't blame that boy for smashing it to bits. Even though I would have taken that bird feeder myself and propped it right in the front yard, proudly."

Aunt Verdella shook her head. "Then she dared resent me,

because that boy took to me. Your grandpa was dead by then, and your uncle Rudy had built our house across the road, because Grandma Mae said it never works, two women living under the same roof—even though Betty and Rudy lived with her the whole while they were married. So Reece just hung around Rudy when he wasn't in school. He helped Rudy with the farm chores, and they'd go fishing and hunting together. Things like that. And I made him peanut butter cookies, and pancakes, and rhubarb pie, because those were his favorites. And I listened to him when he talked. Not like her. Before you knew it, he was spendin' a night here and there with us, and little by little, his things got moved over to our place. I don't think Mae even realized he'd moved out. She'd work over there in her flower garden and not so much as glance over to our yard. Guess that's why your daddy is so special to me. It's like I raised him myself."

Aunt Verdella wrapped Grandma Mae's picture in newspaper and set it in the box next to her feet. "She was cold. That's all I can say about her. Cold, long before she went to her grave." I put my head down and rolled a little vase in newspaper, and I thought about those people who are cold before they get put in a grave. One night I woke from my sleep because I heard arguing, and I heard Daddy say to Ma that she was as cold as a corpse. So the next day I reached out and touched Ma's arm to see if it was cold, and it was, a little.

When Aunt Verdella came to Aunt Betty's picture—a little one that sat on the buffet—she showed that one to me too. Aunt Betty was pretty. Not the kind of pretty like Freeda Malone, but pretty in that churchy sort of way. "How come she died?" I asked, wondering that for the first time.

"Well, Button. She was gonna have a baby, but things didn't get that far. The poor thing, she wasn't far along when she lost it. Bled to death right on her bed while your uncle Rudy was taking your grandma into town to see the doctor because she had a bad chest cold. Oh, that must have been so awful for Rudy," she said, and tears squeezed out of her pale gray eyes.

"Losing his pretty, young wife and his one chance to become a daddy at the same time. He don't talk about it, but I know it still pains him to this day."

"Maybe you could have a baby for him," I said, and Aunt Verdella smiled a sad smile, then said, "Well, that's it for this box." She leaned over to fold the four flaps of cardboard so that the box would stay shut.

"Aunt Verdella?" I asked, still thinking about Aunt Betty bleeding to death in this house. "Is that bed she died in one of the beds upstairs, or the one down here?"

"Good Lord," she said then, slapping her skinny knees. "You're such a serious little thing that I forget sometimes that I'm talking to a little girl. I shouldn'ta said that about her bleedin' to death. You just put that thought right out of your head, Button."

All the talk about dead people made me think of Winnalee's dead ma. "Aunt Verdella," I asked, "is that really Winnalee's ma in that jar?"

Aunt Verdella was leaned over a box, her belly hanging low, bumping up against the top of her legs. She was still tipped over when she said, "Yes, it is, Button. And what a pity it is, a little one like that losing her ma, then carrying around her ashes because she can't bear to part with her."

"They burned her ma up?"

"Yes, Button. It's called cremation. It gives me the shivers to think of a body being burned up like a trash heap, but I guess some people don't mind such a thought. It about breaks my heart, though, seeing that little girl carrying her ma around like that."

"She ain't gonna carry her around forever, though. She told me that when she grows up and gets money, she's gonna buy her a nice stone and a final resting place."

"Bless her heart," Aunt Verdella said, and she looked about ready to cry. So then I thought about dead mas, and mas that aren't dead, and I realized that maybe I had just found one of those clues about life. So I made a place in my mind to keep it till I could tell Winnalee Bright Idea #85: *If your ma liked you, then even if she's dead and burned up in a jar, you can still talk to her. But if she never liked you, then even if she's across the road, you can't.*

For three days, Aunt Verdella and I worked hard. We packed up all of Grandma's pictures and knickknacks and her good dishes and silver. Then we packed up her clothes and put them in a box to go to people so poor they have to wear dead people's clothes. We put the boxes of clothes by the front door, and we hauled the dishes and stuff up into the attic. There was an old guitar propped up in the corner. The varnish was worn off right under the hole in the front, and there was a spider's web tangled over the four strings it had left. I wanted to strum it, but I didn't want the spider's web to cling to my fingers.

Aunt Verdella smiled as she picked up the guitar. "This was your daddy's first guitar," she said, touching it as soft as if it was a baby. "Rudy and I gave it to him for his fifteenth birthday. My, but that boy could play, right from the start. I was so proud of him the first time I heard him play with Owen Palmer at Marty's. Before your ma and dad were married, your daddy played out all the time. Rudy wasn't much for dancin', but we'd go down there on Friday nights, have their fish fry, then stay till closing time. Your uncle Rudy would waltz, that's about it, but I'd always find some women there to jitterbug with. Course, your daddy didn't just play at Marty's either. Sometimes they drove a good hundred miles on a Saturday to play for some wedding dance or other kind of party. Folks still shake their heads over your daddy quittin'. They all say he could have made it big." She set the guitar back down and it made a hollow-sounding ring.

Aunt Verdella started singing a couple of lines from a song I didn't know, then she grabbed my arms and started swinging them, her feet moving this way and that way, and her big belly rocking. We laughed, then she dropped my hands. "I'm gonna teach you to jitterbug someday," she said. She laughed again, then sighed. "It's such a shame Reece doesn't play anymore, but your ma said that was no life for a married man. I understand, I suppose, but I just think that it's such a pity when people stop doin' the things that make them happy. And I still say, if your ma would have gone with him, learned to dance, and let herself have a little fun, he'd still be playing."

When we had all the boxes in the attic, we took down the yellowed curtains from all the windows and washed them in Aunt Verdella's wringer washer. Then we hung them on the line to dry. It was a warm and windy day, and we giggled as those curtains flapped and snapped and wrapped themselves around us. Then we got busy washing the wallpaper, so it don't look dingy.

Me and Aunt Verdella worked till she said her arms and legs were aching like they had a cold in them. The house sure did look spiffy though, and it smelled clean too, from all that scrubbing and the breeze blowing in to air the place out, like Aunt Verdella said.

When we were done, Aunt Verdella drove to the Daverson's Motel to tell the Malones that the house was ready. Then, soon as supper was done that night, she made Daddy and Uncle Rudy and Tommy help unload the junk from the Malones' pickup and wagon. While they started unloading, I brought Winnalee upstairs, like Aunt Verdella told me to do, and I told her to pick out which of the four bedrooms she wanted for her very own.

Winnalee didn't pick the one I thought she'd pick—the one with curtains the color of Freeda's cheeks, and with flowers on the wallpaper in the same color—instead, she picked the room with wallpaper covered in pointy, dark green leaves creeping up the walls on brown ropes. The one with the ceiling that dipped where the room drooped down on the edges. "Why you want this ugly one?" I asked her, while she was setting her ma down on the bench that sat in front of two tall windows that overlooked the fields.

"Because," she said. "My ma always wanted a window seat. Now she has one."

"I bet your sister is gonna pick the pretty room across the hall, then," I said.

"No, she won't," Winnalee said. "She won't sleep in an upstairs. She'll use the one downstairs."

Winnalee and I put her play clothes under the lid of the window seat and her for-real clothes in the dresser and in the closet. We put her shoe box with her "special junk" in it on the shelf above where we hung her clothes. Then, as she was looking for a place to keep her book, I told her that I thought I might have found our next Bright Idea. I told her about how Grandma Mae didn't like my daddy much, and then I told her what that made me think. When I was done, Winnalee's eyes looked up for a time, then she smiled and opened her book and wrote down my bright idea, and titled it *Number Eighty-Five*. And this made me smile.

4

It wasn't but one day since Winnalee moved into Grandma Mae's house, and already it felt like she'd been my best friend forever. I jumped out of bed before Ma even had the chance to wake me, and I peed and washed and dressed so fast that she didn't even have to yell at me to get to the breakfast table, because I was already there. I couldn't wait, because Winnalee promised me she was going to show me a secret from her shoe box this morning.

Aunt Verdella said that what we get is *heritated*. Like the way I got eyes the color of mud with some green speckles in them from Ma, and the way Aunt Verdella got her happy-go-lucky ways from her daddy. I thought about this heritatary stuff when Daddy came to the table and didn't look at me. Not even once.

Daddy stabbed at his scrambled eggs with his fork and brought a wad to his mouth, then stopped. He turned his fork over and saw that the bottoms were brown, then dropped the fork. Ma was watching him. "I could make some more," she said. "I was busy buttering the toast, and answering the phone, and...well..." Ma was a good cook most of the time, but sometimes she wasn't.

"I'm gonna just have juice this morning," I said to Ma, quietly, when she tried to give me some burned eggs too. "Aunt Verdella is making pancakes this morning."

"Reece?"

"Never mind, Jewel," Daddy said. "I'll have something at Verdella's, like the kid." Daddy never called me Evelyn, or even Button. If "The Kid" was supposed to be another nickname, it didn't feel like one to me.

Ma took away our plates, with fingers that had nails chewed down so far that they looked like thin little half-moons. Her nibbled-up fingers shook a bit as she set our plates on the counter with a little clank.

"Is your coffee strong enough?" Ma asked, and Daddy told her it wasn't. She reached for the can of Folgers, saying she'd brew a fresh pot, but Daddy told her not to bother. That he'd fill it at Verdella's, along with his stomach.

"Why do you have to go there this morning?" Ma asked.

"I brought Rudy a tool from the mill yesterday," he said. "I'd best get it back there today." Daddy worked fixing machines at the Dauber Paper Mill. They made boxes, and toilet paper, writing paper, and whatnot. Daddy brought home free toilet paper that scratched your butt when you wiped, and he brought home notebook paper that they were going to throw out because it wasn't perfect. I used it to draw on, but I couldn't use it for school, even if it was free, because the lines were crooked, or the ink almost invisible.

Daddy grabbed his lunch bucket and his empty thermos from the counter. Then he grabbed a hunk of ham with his fingers as he passed the table. He headed out the door without saying good-bye.

"Did you put your pajamas in the hamper?" Ma asked me. I nodded, and she said, "I can't hear a nod, Button. You speak up when I ask you a question." She glanced out the window as Daddy's truck rumbled down the driveway. "He's going right over there, but do you think he could drop his daughter off and save me the trip? Like he's the only one here who has to get to work." She turned back to me, blinking like she just remembered I was there. Some sad was sitting in her eyes. "Get your sweater on, and get in the car, please."

When I got to Aunt Verdella's, Daddy was there, leaning against the counter holding a coffee cup and a piece of coffee cake. Aunt Verdella was standing at the counter making pancake batter. They were all laughing, so I figured that either Uncle Rudy or Daddy had just told a funny story. "Get over here and give Auntie a hug," Aunt Verdella said. She moaned like she was eating chocolate when she hugged me. "You ready for some breakfast?"

"Good thing you feed her, or she'd starve to death. Crissakes, you should have seen the eggs we had this morning," Dad said. "Like rubber. And they stunk like a skunk!"

"Oh Reece," Aunt Verdella said. "Jewel isn't much of a cook, that's true, but she is good at so many things. Don't be mean, now."

Daddy looked at his watch and said he'd better get going. He set down his cup and picked a big tool off of the corner of the table. Aunt Verdella handed him his filled thermos. "You have a good day, Reece," she said. She moved me in front of her. "Give your daddy a hug good-bye," she said, as she pushed against my back. I leaned back against her, not budging. "Bye, kid," Daddy said.

Winnalee came over while we were sitting at the table. She pressed her face against the screen—which wasn't easy, since she had her ma in her arms and had to lean over the vase—and we told her to come in. She was wearing another mesh skirt. Pink, this time, but she had on a girl's shirt and a pair of shorts under the slip so her undies didn't show.

Aunt Verdella poured three ladlefuls of pancake batter onto the skillet, then stretched the two blobs on top into long bunny ears with the back of her spoon. When the batter bubbled up, she dropped two raisins on the face for eyes, then flipped him over. "You eat breakfast yet, sweetie?" she asked Winnalee. Winnalee told her no, because they hadn't shopped yet, so Aunt Verdella told her she'd make her a bunny pancake too. Winnalee giggled, because she'd never heard of bunny pancakes before.

"Hey, where's my bunny pancake?" Uncle Rudy said, and all three of us giggled. Uncle Rudy shoved the last strip of his bacon into his mouth, saving the fatty part for Knucklehead—his old chocolate Lab with a jagged scar by his lip—who waited by his chair. Knucklehead caught it with a snap, then came over by me to see if I had some for him too. I didn't, but I had a pat, so I gave him that instead.

Uncle Rudy got up and grabbed his hat from the post of his chair. "Verdie, send Tommy over to the east forty when he gets here, will ya?" He smiled down at me and Winnalee. "We're fixing that fence up so good that those cows will have to grow wings if they want to get loose now."

Aunt Verdella wrapped her arms around him and gave him a big squeeze. "Don't you go working too hard or your back will start acting up again. Let that boy do the heavier stuff, Rudy. That's what you hired him for. You be good, and tomorrow morning maybe I'll make you bunny pancakes too." She started giving him noisy smooches on his cheek. Uncle Rudy spread his elbows a bit to break out of her hold, but Aunt Verdella just leaned over his arms and kept right on smooching.

"Verdie, you keep mauling on me and those cows are gonna have the time to grow wings before I get that fence fixed too." Aunt Verdella let go of Uncle Rudy, and he said, "Come on, Knucklehead, before she starts slobbering on you too." Me and Winnalee and Aunt Verdella giggled.

"Well, girls," Aunt Verdella said after Uncle Rudy left. "I've got orders for two more pairs of booties, so I'm gonna have to crochet as soon as I get these dishes done. Afterward, I'm gonna hightail over and see how Freeda's coming along. You girls got anything planned for this morning?"

Winnalee's mouth was full of pancakes and the corners of her lips were sticky with syrup, but she answered anyway. She had one elbow on the table too, which you're not supposed to do. "We're gonna look for fairies," she said. I looked down at my earless bunny, wishing Winnalee hadn't said such a stupid thing. Everybody knew that there wasn't such a thing as fairies. Winnalee promised me she was going to prove it to me today, but I doubted it.

"Fairies! Oh, I loved fairies when I was a girl! In school, we had to learn a poem to recite in front of the class. I learned a poem by some Yeats fellow. I don't remember the whole thing anymore, but I do remember one part." She set Uncle Rudy's dirty dish and coffee cup on the counter, brushed her hands on her apron, then folded them against her fat belly.

> There lies a leafy island
> Where flapping herons wake
> The drowsy water-rats;
> There we've hid our faery vats,
> Full of berries
> And of reddest stolen cherries.
> *Come away, O human child!*
> *To the waters and the wild*
> *With a faery, hand in hand,*
> *For the world's more full of weeping than you can*
> *understand.*

Winnalee started clapping her hands, so I did too, even though I thought that poem sounded sad at the end. Aunt Verdella took her skirt and held it out at the sides, then did one of those curtsies that fancy ladies in old movies do before they let a man dance with them. She giggled then and said, "Oh, I can't believe I still remember that silly ol' thing."

"Button doesn't believe there's such a thing as fairies," Winnalee said. "But I told her anything's possible."

I wanted to say something, but instead I just made that noise in my throat.

Aunt Verdella smiled with her lips closed, her head tipped to the side. "Oh, that's so true, Winnalee. Think of that Shepard man who went right up into space earlier this month. Who would have ever thought that we could send a man up there? But we did! I've always said that we've got to go on thinking anything's possible. Or else what's the point?"

Once me and Winnalee were outside, I told her—same as I did the day before—that there wasn't any such thing as fairies. "Fairies are just folklore. I learned about folklore in third grade."

Winnalee hoisted her ma up in her arms and gave a big sigh. "Course there's such a thing as fairies! I read about them in a book that was left in the attic of this one house we lived in last summer. It was an old book. Stinky old, the pages all crunchy. It was written by that very same man who wrote those Sherlock Holmes stories my ma used to read. It was called *The Coming of the Fairies*."

Winnalee headed across the lawn and I followed her. She stopped a second to peer at the Virgin lady in the bathtub, then kept walking. "It was a real story that happened by this place they called Cottingley Beck."

"Where's that?" I asked, and Winnalee shrugged. "Anyway, this girl and her cousin, they used to play by this water where there were fairies. The little girl, her name was Frances, and her cousin—well, I don't remember her name—anyway, one day they took a couple of pictures of the fairies. The pictures were in the book too, right there to see with your very own eyes."

"You have the book?"

"No, course I don't! That one was a *real* book, so if I'd taken it, that would have been stealing." She stopped till I stopped, then cupped her hand beside her mouth and leaned over to my ear. "But I did rip a page out, with one of the pictures on it."

"You still got it?"

"Yeah. In my shoe box. That's the surprise I'm gonna show you today."

So we headed over to Grandma Mae's house—which I decided right then I'd start calling "Winnalee's house" from now on.

We were just starting to cross the road when Tommy's black truck came rumbling down it in a cloud of dust. We ran as fast as we could—because it didn't look like he was going to stop—but it wasn't easy to go fast, because Winnalee was barefoot and the rocks on the road were hurting her feet. I got scared when Tommy's truck swerved like it was an arrow and we were the bull's-eye. I grabbed Winnalee's arm and yanked her along till we got to the grass, her ouching all the way. Tommy's truck braked fast, so that the back part bucked sideways some.

"Don't you kiddies know to get out of the way when somethin's coming? That's a good way to get your guts splattered." He was grinning so that his vampire teeth were showing.

"Come on, Winnalee," I said, but she ignored me.

Tommy spit out the window, then licked his skinny lip where some of the spit was sitting. He looked at the urn, then over at the house. "Where's that sister of yours?"

"Freeda? How do you know my sister?"

Tommy leaned his arm on the window and took a peek at himself in that little mirror sticking out of the driver's door. "Well, in this town, word of a newcomer spreads faster than the stink of a fart. Especially when one of 'em is good-looking and stacked. Heard about you too and how you carry your dead ma around with you." He squinted his eyes at Winnalee's urn. "That her?"

Winnalee was swaying from side to side, like there was

music playing in her head and she was wanting to dance. "Yeah. You wanna see her?"

Tommy's piggy nose scrinched up. "Don't think so."

He bent his arm and scratched at the dirty, dry patch of skin over his elbow. "You're a creepy kid, you know that?" He glanced at the house again, then back at us. "She's creepy too," he said, lifting one finger to point at me. "The way she's always watching people so close; never saying what she's thinkin'."

"We're going to look for fairies," Winnalee said, ignoring his comments. I put my hands behind my back and squeezed them tight. I knew Tommy was gonna make fun of us for playing such a baby game.

"Is that right?"

"We have to find a beck first, though. You know where there's one around here?"

I could tell by the way his snaky eyebrows scrinched in the shape of an *S* that he didn't have a clue what a beck was. Winnalee must have known this too, because she added, "That's a brook, I think. A little stream. I ain't sure, though."

Tommy gave one of those laughs that comes out half like a grunt. "I know that. What, you think I'm stupid?" He cocked his head, then pointed out past Winnalee's new house. "See that field there? If you cross it, duck right into that patch of white pine, straight west about three-quarters of a mile or so, you'll come right to a little stream that sits between Peters land and the Fossard property."

Tommy grinned at me after he said this, and I started biting the inside of my cheek.

"There's fairies at that creek too. Little fairy ladies with pearly wings. Pretty little dresses on 'em too. Lots of folks have seen 'em there. Course, you have to catch them right before dark, I hear."

Winnalee lit up, her eyes getting all round and sparkly. She hoisted her ma up higher in her arms.

One of Tommy's eyebrows scooted up, and the other one crouched down. "Course, you'll be takin' a chance on running into Fossard's ghost."

"Ghost?"

"Yep. Ask Button here about Hiram Fossard's ghost. She'll tell ya. He was the grave digger over at the commie cemetery, where the old atheists got buried. He was a skinny old guy, with a big ol' hump on his back. Couldn't even straighten up if he wanted to after spending so many years bent over, digging graves. He was crazy as a loon too. So scared of those Soviets nuking us that he dug himself a bomb shelter. Cut it right into that hill by his house with the very shovel that he dug the commies' graves with. Put a cot in there, a water barrel, guns, food, you name it."

"Lots of people have bomb shelters," Winnalee said. "That don't make them crazy."

Tommy nodded in quick little jerks. "Yep, that's right. But I ain't saying that's why he was nuts. It wasn't. He was nuts because he was so damn worried about those nuke bombs that he couldn't sleep nights. Stayed up around the clock in time, days on end, pacing and watching the sky, waiting for the big one to drop.

"Course, the nutty bastard was just as scared of being stuck underground too. So it weren't long before he couldn't get his mind off of being stuck under that hill of dirt if the Soviets did shit on us and he ended up trapped in that shelter. Worked himself into such a tizzy that one night he shot his dog and his wife, then he hanged himself from a tree."

Tommy cocked his head to one side and yanked on an imaginary rope around his neck. He made choking noises as his tongue flapped out of the side of his mouth. He laughed some, then dropped his voice down real quiet and leaned his ugly head farther out of the window. "His ghost still won't go into the ground. Walks all night long—and sometimes in the day too—pacing, still waitin' for the Soviets to come, that shovel he always carried scuffing behind him as he drags it across the ground. People who dare go there—looking for fairies, most likely—they all hear it."

Scared started swirling in my belly. I looked over at Winnalee, but she didn't look sick with fright at all. She just tugged her ma up again and lifted her head up a bit higher. "You're just trying to scare us. You think if you do, we'll be too afraid to go there to see the fairies. But you're not so smart after all. I ain't scared of dead people. If I was, you think I'd carry my dead ma with me wherever I go?"

I was real glad when Aunt Verdella leaned out the porch door just then, calling to Tommy, telling him where he could find Uncle Rudy. He waved to Aunt Verdella so she knew he'd heard her, then looked back at me and Winnalee. "I gotta get to work. I ain't got time to be sitting here talking to a couple of little kids." He put the truck in gear and it lurched forward, heading toward the driveway that led to the barn.

"Button, you going over to Winnalee's?"

I yelled back that I was.

"Okay, sweetie. But don't you go anywhere else. Auntie Verdella needs to know where you are."

As we walked across the lawn, Winnalee was all excited about going on an adventure to see those fairies. It was enough to make me start gnawing on the inside of my cheek.

"Aunt Verdella'd never let me go that far, Winnalee," I said. "She's always worried that I'm gonna get lost. I can't even leave the yard. And anyway, Tommy's nothing but a big liar. How do we know we could really find Fossard's property by going straight through the woods? And I'll bet if we did find it, there wouldn't be any fairies there anyway, because fairies aren't real."

As we walked up the porch steps, Winnalee shook her head. "Button, I told you. Anything's possible. You never know. Now come on, so I can show you that picture and prove to you that fairies exist."

. . .

I followed Winnalee through the house, and when we passed Freeda's bedroom to get to the stairs, I could see Freeda stretched across her bed in her underwear, the morning sun resting over her naked back. She was asleep, one pale arm dangling over the edge of the bed, her penny hair dripped over the side. "She was out last night, then came home with some guy," Winnalee said. "He left the toilet seat up, and I didn't see it when I got up in the night to pee. I got my butt wet too. Freeda said she'll pick up a night-light. I told her why don't she just make her stupid boyfriends put the damn seat down instead. Anyway, she ain't gonna get outta bed at least till noon—I can tell you that much. And you don't have to worry about making noise either, because she don't hear nothing when she's sleeping."

I followed Winnalee into her room, where she put her ma on the window seat, then opened the closet and disappeared inside. She came out with her shoe box. She dug out the folded page of the book, then brought it over to the bed that wasn't made, and we sat down.

She unfolded the page and laid it on the lap of her mesh skirt, which was scratching my bare leg and practically hogging up the whole bed. "See?"

"Holy moly!" I said, as I took the picture from her lap. I probably looked stupid with my mouth hanging wide open and my eyes all bugged out, but I couldn't help it. I ran my fingers over the glossy page where an old-fashioned girl was propped on a bank. Right in front of her were beautiful little fairies, their bare legs and arms dancing, their wings pointing up to heaven. "Wow!"

"See, I told you! Wish we had a camera to take pictures with when we find them."

I was thinking hard now. Thinking about how when Winnalee first told me that she had her ma in that jar, I didn't believe her then either, but it was true. Now here I was looking at pictures of fairies. I was having a hard time believing my own eyes, but maybe, just maybe, Winnalee was telling the truth this time too.

The thought of maybe seeing real live fairies made my belly start dancing. But then I thought of seeing Fossard's ghost, and suddenly it felt like my belly danced too close to a cliff and fell right off in one whoosh. "I won't be able to go all that ways, Winnalee. I told you. You heard Aunt Verdella tell me not to go anywhere else. She'd spy us before we even reached the edge of the field, so we can just forget about running off to find fairies today."

Winnalee took the picture and folded it back up. "I don't mean today, Button. You can't go out on a big adventure without thinking everything out first. We have to make plans. We need a map, food, things like that. Then we'll have to wait for just the right chance to sneak away."

My arms stopped itching when she said we didn't have to go yet.

5

One thing I thought about while I sat in the Malones' kitchen with Freeda and Aunt Verdella, while Winnalee splashed and sang in the tub (her first bath since she moved in, even though we'd gotten plenty dirty in the nine days since she got here), was how families are all different. At my house, it was quiet. So quiet that if Ma let a mouse slip inside (which she wouldn't), I was sure you could hear him breathing. Even when the TV set was on (which wasn't often), you had to scoot so close to it to hear anything that you had to worry about ruining your eyes.

Our house was clean too, with everything having a place and everyone having rules they had to follow. The towels all had to match, and after you used one, you had to fold it neat so that the hems hung straight like pictures. And nobody talked much, and nobody laughed, and nobody cried, and nobody touched anybody.

At Aunt Verdella and Uncle Rudy's, it was noisy all the time. The TV was going from the time they woke up till the time they went to bed—even if nobody was watching it, and even if that was wasting electricity. It was always turned up loud too. So loud that I was sure that if I ran to the end of the field, I'd still be able to hear the soap-opera people talking, and Aunt Verdella talking at them, or at Uncle Rudy. And the towels in the bathroom were folded over the rack, but if the hems hung crooked like bangs cut wrong, then that was okay. And if one of those towels was plain pink, and one green striped, and another one was busy with flowers, then that was okay too, because that was pretty like a rainbow. And there wasn't no special place to put anything either, so we spent a lot of time digging under mounds of yarn, old mail, or clothes that were folded but not put away yet for whatever it was we needed.

At the Malones', though, it was different still. Sometimes it was real noisy, with music playing so loud you could feel it thumping in your chest. But other times, like when Freeda was sleeping and Winnalee was drawing, it was as quiet in their house as it was in ours. The towels were usually left on the floor, or bunched up with just a wadded corner tucked over the towel rack. And sometimes they matched, and sometimes they didn't. And there was lots of yelling and cussing, and even slapping now and then, but there was lots of laughing and hugging too.

"That sure is a cute top," I heard Aunt Verdella say, so I stopped thinking and looked at the skinny, sleeveless blouse hanging over the back of a chair she was pointing to. "I wish I could wear things like that."

"Why can't you?" Freeda asked, as she ripped open a bag of Windmill cookies and ate a blade off of one. "I say, if you've got it, flaunt it." Freeda stretched out her arms and shimmied as she whooped.

"Oh good heavens," Aunt Verdella said with a laugh. "I'm fifty-eight years old and fat, that's why. Imagine how silly I'd look in something like that!" She giggled some more.

"Ah, piss," Freeda said, as she leaned back on her chair. She propped her feet up and hooked her long toes on the edge of the table. "If people don't like it, they can lump it. People should wear what they want, and do what they want. That's what I say. When I'm your age, I'm gonna wear whatever I damn please. And I'm gonna grow my hair all the way down to my ass too, and let it hang wild, just to piss off people who think that older women should have short hair. Just watch me."

Aunt Verdella giggled, then said, "I've no doubt you'll do exactly those things!"

"You want one, kid?" Freeda asked, tapping the cookie bag with the edge of her foot.

I kind of wanted one. Not because I liked the way they tasted, but because I liked the way they looked, but I couldn't make myself say yes.

Freeda popped the rest of her cookie in her mouth. She leaned forward and took another one out of the package, then flicked it across the table. It spun, then stopped when it bumped against my hand. I picked it up and chewed it with little bites.

Freeda set down her cup and, without excusing herself, shuffled into the bathroom on bare feet. She didn't even close the door behind her, even though we could see her drop her drawers and hear her piddling. I watched but tried to make it look like I wasn't. I saw drops of bathwater shoot sideways at her. She put her hands in front of her face, and her top part darted from side to side, like one of those fat-faced, poisonous snakes that dance when you play them music on a flute. "Goddammit, Winnalee. You stop that right now!"

Winnalee giggled, and Aunt Verdella turned to look. She giggled too.

"I mean it, you little shit, or I'll drown you when I'm off of here!" Winnalee kept flicking water till Freeda wiped, pulled up her pants, and ran out of the room.

"What a kid!" Freeda said, as she rolled her eyes.

Aunt Verdella turned and caught her reflection in the chrome toaster. She started picking at her hair. "You could get by with having your hair long when you're older, but not me. Oh, look at this frizzy mess. I've colored it so many times, I don't even remember what color it was before I started!"

While Aunt Verdella talked, I could feel Freeda staring at me. I set my half-eaten cookie down on the table and slipped my hands up over my ears—wishing my hands were as big as Uncle Rudy's so I could cover my knotty curls too.

"You like your hair like that, Button?" Freeda asked. I could tell by the way she asked it that she wouldn't like her hair to look like mine. Her eyes peered at me from over her coffee cup while she waited for my answer. I could feel my cheeks heat up.

"I didn't think so," she said. She set her cup down. "I've seen the way you look at Winnalee's hair. Hey, next time your ma gets out her scissors and that stupid perm kit, you just tell her, 'Fuck it, I'm not getting my hair whacked and fried. I'm letting it grow long like Winnalee's.' Then run like hell."

Aunt Verdella gasped. "Freeda!"

Freeda laughed and got up. She went to the stove and grabbed the percolator off it, put her finger on the glass knob on top, then tipped it sideways to refill her cup. "Ah, don't get your butt in a bundle, Verdella. That kid ain't gonna repeat what I just said. Look at her. She's so uptight she can't even say she wants a frickin' cookie without biting half of her face off, much less how she wants to wear her hair."

"But still…" Aunt Verdella said.

Freeda stood up. She stared out the window that over-looked the empty field and rubbed her belly. She yawned. "Shit, I've gotta find a job before we die of starvation and I die of boredom."

"Oh, that reminds me," Aunt Verdella said. "Marty's Place is almost remodeled now, honey, so you can go in and see him about that job. Reece said he's still looking for another girl." Aunt Verdella sighed. "You poor thing, having so much responsibility resting on your young shoulders. And with no one to count on but yourself. Maybe you'll find a nice guy to marry right here in Dauber who'll help lighten your load."

Freeda looked at Aunt Verdella and laughed. "Who says a man would lessen my load? What planet you living on, anyway? Damn, that's the last thing I need." She looked down at me, her green eyes lemony-colored with the sunlight shining through the sides of them. "Here's a tip for you, kiddo. Men are good for one thing, and one thing only. And hell, you don't even really need them for that either. Remember that."

Aunt Verdella glanced over at me, like I'd just heard something I shouldn't have, but I wasn't sure what that something was. Then she looked back at Freeda, her eyes still filled with worry. "Still, it's gotta be rough, having so much responsibility at your age. How old are you, anyway? Twenty-one? Twenty-two?"

"Twenty-five."

"Well, still, you must have been pretty young when you started carrying this load all by yourself. How long have your folks been gone now, honey?"

"Daddy, about fifteen years, I guess. Ma, four."

"Oh my, to lose your folks that young, and to have to raise your little sister alone."

"I'm used to being on my own," Freeda says. "I've been on my own since I was sixteen years old. I don't need nobody taking care of me."

"Since you were sixteen?"

Freeda picked up her cup and took another sip, but she didn't sit down. "Yep, that's how old I was when I took off. Sixteen."

"Took off, as in ran away?"

"That's right. I didn't step one foot back in that dump for five years. I just pulled into town the night before Ma died. Came home one day, went out that night, came back in around noon the next day, and found her deader than a doornail on the kitchen floor."

Aunt Verdella's freckly hand clamped over her chest, and she looked ready to cry. "Oh dear, how awful!"

Freeda's shoulders made a quick shrug. "Yeah, well...I called Ma's sister—she lived just down the road—and told her to call that piece of slime they call a brother from the bar, because Ma was dead and I'd called the funeral home to come get her and I was taking off. I grabbed my bags, a few things for Winnalee, told them where to send the ashes, and I got the hell outta there."

While Aunt Verdella was staring at her, her mouth hanging wide open, Freeda turned and shouted toward the bathroom, where Winnalee was still singing and splashing. "Crissakes, Winnalee! You've gotta be shriveled up like a prune by now. Get the hell out of there. I've gotta job-hunt today, and I sure as hell can't go like this. Now move it!" Winnalee kept on singing and splashing. Freeda cussed under her breath, then said, "Damn kid. You can't hardly ever get her into the goddamn tub. Then once you do, you can't get her out."

Aunt Verdella was watching Freeda, her face still looking upset. "But there were arrangements to be made, of course. And, oh my, you needed some support at a time like that, honey. I don't mean to pry, it's just that I'm trying to understand why you'd just take Winnalee and leave at a time like that."

"I don't mind you prying. Ask me anything, I don't care. I ain't got nothing to hide." She pulled a bobby pin out of her penny hair and opened it with her teeth, then retucked a loose strand back to the top of her head. "I wasn't about to hang around there and listen to my aunt and Ma's old biddy friends give me bullcrap about how I killed my ma by running off, then coming back out of the blue. And I sure as hell wasn't gonna leave Winnalee behind to be raised by her sister, that religious freak, or worse yet, their loser brother, the son of a bitch."

Freeda sat down, lifted her bare legs, and curled her long

toes over the edge of the table again, like they were fingers. "As if *I* had anything to do with her dropping dead. My ma didn't give a shit about me leaving, and she didn't give a shit about me coming home either. The only thing that woman ever cared about was eating. She goddamn ate herself to death, that's what she did. Just like Daddy drank himself to death. She had these big-ass stools parked all over that damn kitchen and pulled herself from one to the next, baking and eating till she looked like a bloated wood tick that fell off some mangy dog. I wasn't about to be blamed for any of that."

"Oh my. Poor little Winnalee," Aunt Verdella said, making her voice as small as she could. "She'd never even met you, right? How on earth did you get her to go with you, being a perfect stranger?"

Freeda got up and went to the refrigerator, opening it and peering in. "No, she hadn't met me, but my pictures were hanging around the walls—probably because Ma was too goddamn lazy to take them down—so Winnalee knew about me, of course. God knows what stories Ma told her, but I guess Winnalee decided I was her best bet. Not like I gave her a choice, anyway."

Freeda slammed the fridge door shut without taking anything from it. "Okay, enough, Winnalee! Now get the hell out of that tub!"

Freeda turned back to Aunt Verdella, her hands on her hips. "Hell, if you're gonna overindulge in something, it might as well be sex. At least sex won't rot your liver or clog your goddamn arteries. That's my theory, anyway."

Then her laugh stopped. She marched into the bathroom, where Winnalee was singing a made-up song about fairies.

"What are you doing? Don't let my water out!" Winnalee screamed. We heard a couple wet slaps and then some more yelling.

Aunt Verdella hurried to the bathroom door. "Come on now, honey," she said. "Button here is waiting to play with you."

I heard the bathwater gurgle as the last of it chugged down the drain, then Winnalee came into the kitchen, butt-naked, her long curls dripping. She didn't have any red slap marks on her crinkly skin, so I figured maybe she was the one who'd been doing the slapping.

"Come on," she called to me, as she ran through the kitchen, her feet padding wet prints across the floor.

"Get your ass back here and wipe up these goddamn puddles! You hear me?"

Winnalee ignored Freeda and kept running.

I followed her up the stairs, where she dug in her closet for something to wear. She grabbed a pair of red shorts with sailboats on them and a pink shirt with yellow flowers and put them on. She didn't bother to put on underpants first.

I watched the door, waiting for Freeda to race up the stairs and give it to Winnalee good for not minding, but she didn't come.

"Hey, I thought of something else we need for our adventure," Winnalee said.

"What's that?"

"A compass. Tommy said the beck is straight west. If we have a compass, we can find it."

Out of the two windows above the window seat, I could see the patch of white pine Tommy had pointed to. The one that led to the beck, he said. And to Fossard's ghost. Just looking out at that clump of trees made me scared.

Winnalee kicked at the dirty clothes on her floor. She watched me as she did this. When she heard a clunk, Winnalee rooted around with her foot. When she brought her foot up, the handle of a hairbrush was stuck between her toes. She took it from her foot, flicking aside the pair of underwear that was snagged on the bristles. "You're scared to go look for fairies, aren't you?" I bit the inside of my cheek and shook my head. "You are too," she said. She tilted her head and her hair dripped down her side, all the way past her hip.

"All because of that ghost Tommy talked about."

I shrugged. "I don't know if I'm so scared of that ghost," I lied. "It's just that I'm going to get in a heap of trouble for running off."

Winnalee brought me her hairbrush, then plunked down on her bed beside me and twisted herself so I could reach the back of her head. "Ouch! Start from the bottom first, then brush the topper parts," she said.

As I pulled the brush down, her hair straightened, then sprung back into loops once the brush left it. I watched it, thinking of how if I had her hair, I'd brush it all day long.

"You are too scared. Because you're afraid of dead people." She paused a minute, like she was thinking hard, then she said, "You're scared of live people too. But you don't have to be a-scared of either."

Winnalee got up. She turned and yanked the brush out of my hand and tossed it on the unmade bed. She grabbed me by the shirt and tugged me over to the window seat, where her ma was sitting in that jar. She leaned over, her still-damp fingers fumbling for my wrist. "Ma?" she said right to the jar. "Button's scared of dead people, so I'm gonna have her talk to you a bit so she can see that dead people aren't going to hurt her. Oh, and I washed behind my ears too." I grabbed at my cheek skin with my teeth. "Go on, Button," she said. "Just say anything to her. If you do, you won't be so scared of dead people anymore."

I'd been Winnalee's best friend for nine days now. Long enough to know that if Winnalee had something on her mind for me to do, she wasn't about to let up till I did it. I didn't lean down, but my head did, and I said, "Hi."

Winnalee waited, like maybe I was going to say more. I waited for her to stop waiting, but it didn't look like she was going to, so I leaned over again and added, "And I washed behind my ears today too."

When I backed away, she said to me, "You should practice talking to live people too."

Then she crossed the room and fetched her Book of

Bright Ideas out from under her pillow (where she said she was gonna keep it from now on, in case she got a good idea right before she fell asleep), and she opened it up and wrote: *Bright Idea #86: If you're scared of dead people, then you're probably scared of live people too. But you don't got to be scared of either.*

6

It was a Saturday, so I couldn't go see Winnalee. Ma made me clean my room, stripping down the bedding, and dusting, and then I had to dust the rest of the rooms. She checked on me over and over again and corrected me when I didn't make neat enough corners with my sheets and when I left streaks of Pledge on my nightstand. We were cleaning good because Aunt Stella was stopping by that night, while on her way to Minneapolis to see a friend. Aunt Stella lived about three hours away from Dauber. She looked just like Ma, but older, and not so tall, and not so skinny. She sniffed a lot, even when she didn't have a cold.

Since I couldn't have any fun, I busied myself while I worked by thinking about me and Winnalee's plans to go find the fairies. We already had a plan sheet that we kept in Winnalee's shoe box. So far, we just had a list of some of the things we needed to bring along. Things like peanut butter sandwiches and cookies, Kool-Aid, if we could find something that shut tight to pour it in, shoes for Winnalee, and a compass and a map to help us find that beck. While I stood on a stool and waited for Ma to take down her bell collection so she could wash them and I could dust the shelf, I wondered where we'd come up with a map to show us the way to the beck. Winnalee and me had been working on the plans for three weeks now, which told me that big adventures sure did take big planning.

"Evelyn?" Ma said. "Are you going to answer me or not?"

I started making those noises (that Aunt Verdella once called a "nerve tic," or something like that) in my throat, because I didn't know what the question was, so I didn't know what the answer should be.

"You weren't listening, were you?"

When I cleared my throat, it sounded like the sputtering of a car that just didn't want to start.

"I asked what you and that little girl do while you're at Aunt Verdella's," she said. Her voice was slow, and lower than it usually sounded.

The truth was, when we weren't making plans to go find the fairies, we played games Winnalee made up. Like riding out west on sticks to lasso wild horses, then sitting in the saloons while the cowboys hit each other over the heads with beer bottles, because they all wanted to be our only boyfriends. Or we'd play TV. We'd put on Winnalee's dress-up clothes, and then I'd sit cross-legged on the floor while Winnalee stood on the bed. I was the audience lady, and she was the actress. And, boy, did she have good stories! One day, when I thought up a story of my own, it would be my turn to be the actress. Till then, though, I was just gonna be the audience lady. I didn't tell Ma these things though. Instead, I just said, "We play."

"Play what?" she asked, and her voice sounded strange again. I stopped clearing my throat when a car sounded in the driveway. Ma peeked out the window. "Oh God, don't tell me..." she said.

I looked out the window, just as Aunt Verdella was getting out of her car. I watched her walk up the little stones leading to the house, Winnalee hopping alongside of her, her ma in her arms.

Aunt Verdella waved to me, then yelled, "Yoo-hoo!" as

she was coming through the door without knocking, like she always did.

Aunt Verdella gave me a hug first, then she told Ma she had to use the phone.

"What'cha doin'?" Winnalee asked. I was glad she was wearing real clothes today but wished she had on shoes. She started circling the living room, gawking at everything, her fingers smearing over the tables I'd just polished.

"I just got done cleaning," I said, remembering to say my *g* at the end, because Ma didn't like it when I sounded like a "country hick," like Aunt Verdella.

Aunt Verdella picked up the phone, then said, "Oh, sorry, Louise," and set the receiver down. She came into the living room and flopped down on the chair we weren't supposed to sit down hard in, because we'd break the springs, then said, "Oh, Jewel, Reece asked me to grab some electrical tape while I'm here. I know Rudy's got some layin' around somewhere, but you think I can find it? I couldn't believe it when I saw Reece at Mae's place so early this morning, workin' away. He fixed the front door so it doesn't scrape anymore too."

"What does he need electrical tape for?" Ma asked, and Aunt Verdella told her she didn't know.

"Button, honey, will you pick up the phone and see if Mrs. Slaga is still on the line?" I hated checking, because folks would get real crabby when you picked up the phone while they were talking. But I did as I was told. I held the receiver to my big ear, and sure enough, Mrs. Slaga was still talking. I put it down carefully.

"If Louise is on there much longer, I'll ask her if she'll get off for just a bit. I've gotta call Henry and reserve a place for the first sale. I can't believe that the community sale starts in two weeks already. Where does time go, anyway? I'm gonna tell him that he'd better not put me on a lot in the far back either. The old codgers like my baked goods, and that's too far for some of them to walk."

I took my dust rag and brought it to Ma, telling her I was

done. Ma gawked at the bell shelf, then at the floor where Aunt Verdella's cruddy shoes were resting. She looked over at Winnalee, who was touching the little glass doll who was riding a wire bike over the end table. I knew she wanted Aunt Verdella and Winnalee to go away so she could stay busy, making everything perfect for Aunt Stella.

Aunt Verdella went back into the kitchen and picked up the phone again. This time she asked Mrs. Slaga if she could use the line for a little bit. She told her why she wanted it and why she didn't want that back lot.

"Can we play while Aunt Verdella talks, since you're done cleaning?" Winnalee asked.

"Why don't you girls color," Ma said, so I told Winnalee, "Come on," and she followed me into my room. "I got a brand-new coloring book. It's all ballerinas."

As I got out my box of crayons, sixty-four count, Winnalee looked around my room. She grabbed my Barbie, who was propped in her doll stand on my dresser, and examined her. "It's a lady doll!" she said. "Ohhhh, she's pretty!" She looped her fingers around Barbie's blond ponytail, then poked at her bumps. "Hey, she's got boobies! I never saw a doll with boobies before!" She giggled, then she tugged down the top of Barbie's zebra swimming suit to look at them. I glanced at the door and wished I'd thought to close it. "She doesn't have any nipples," she said.

I hurried to fetch my coloring book.

"We have to color on the kitchen floor," I told Winnalee.

"Why?" she asked, and I told her I didn't know, but that was the rule.

Me and Winnalee picked out pages with two good pictures on both sides, then we stretched out on the floor, the linoleum cool against our bellies. "Hey, can I have that one instead?" Winnalee asked. "I like the way her arms are stretched above her head. Look, they make a heart shape!" I told Winnalee we could trade, and she rolled over the top of me, her hair tickling my bare arm as she went.

Winnalee didn't know about outlining the picture first so your crayon stops you from coloring outside of the lines. She didn't care when I told her either. She just started coloring the curtain on the stage, her fist going up and down for a few swipes, then back and forth; not all in one direction, like you're supposed to. She colored one side of the curtain green and the other side purple. She made her lady's skirt black, not a pretty color, then said, "I like black dresses. They're sexy." Then she leapt to her feet, lifted her arms, and shook her butt back and forth real fast, and said, "Sexyyyyyyyy!"

I didn't know what "sexy" meant for sure, but Ma obviously did. She must not have liked sexy at all either, because her face got so tight that it looked like her cheekbones were going to pop right through her skin. She set down the bowl she'd just pulled from the cupboard and came over to Winnalee, snatching the black crayon out of her hand. "In this house, we use pretty colors—girl colors—for ladies' dresses." I slid my fist off of my page so Ma could see that I was using pretty girl colors for my ballerina's dress. Pink, with yellow trim.

Aunt Verdella didn't hear this because she was busy on the phone with Harry. "Yeah, I'll have at least two tables. Long ones. And don't be tricky and try to put me way on that back lot, like you did once last year. So far back that the old people can't get to me."

I got more and more itchy as we colored and Aunt Verdella yammered, because Ma kept glancing at the clock, the gouge between her eyebrows sinking deeper and deeper with each glance.

When Aunt Verdella got off the phone, she plunked down at the kitchen table. "Well, I've got four afghans crocheted, twenty pairs of baby booties, and the squares cut out for two more quilts. I'm gonna sell some old junk too. A few lanterns we haven't used in years, some extra canning jars. Things like that, you know. I've got four crates of things ready. Then all I have to do right beforehand is bake. Those old codgers sure do like my sweets. I'm gonna get that color television set yet!"

When me and Winnalee finished our pictures, she took the sky-blue crayon and drew big, pointy wings on both of our dancing ladies. Then she tore out her page in one rip. "What are you doing?" I ask, scared.

"I'm taking my picture home."

I looked up at Ma, who was watching me out of the corner of her eye, and I didn't know what to do. I was glad when Aunt Verdella stood up then and said she had better get back home and get some work done.

"Can Button come to my house and play?" Winnalee asked.

Ma didn't look at her when she answered. "No, Button is staying home. Her aunt is coming by early this evening, and we've things to do before then."

"Stella's coming?" Aunt Verdella asked. Ma looked sorry that she let that slip.

"Well, just for a quick visit, and I'm not sure what time. She's coming through on her way to Minneapolis to visit a friend."

"Please, can she come over?" Winnalee asked. "Pretty please?" And then she did something that made my mouth drop open like I'd gone dumb. She grabbed Ma's arm and gave it a couple tugs, then she started swinging them like they were jump ropes. "Please, pretty please with a cherry on top? She got her cleaning done, didn't she?" She tipped her head back and bumped herself right against Ma. "Let her come. Please?"

Ma yanked her arms back to her sides and said, "Evelyn will be staying home today."

Winnalee's bottom lip poked out and she crossed her arms across her chest. "Whyyyyyy?" she asked.

"Button will be over on Monday, honey," Aunt Verdella said. "You can help me make bread when we get back, okay?" I looked down at my hands, which were busy twisting each other. Aunt Verdella baked bread on Saturdays, but sometimes (when Uncle Rudy gobbled it up before the next Saturday) she'd bake during the week, and I'd help her. I liked helping her bake bread. I liked the way the dough was soft against my hands and the way it smelled when it came out of the oven. Only today I couldn't help.

"Oh, if she'll be here for supper, I could drop off a loaf of fresh bread to go with your meal," Aunt Verdella said. Ma told her that that wouldn't be necessary.

"For all I know," Ma added, "she won't even stop."

Aunt Verdella rolled her eyes. "I don't know about that sister of yours, Jewel. You're her little sister by only three years. The only sister she's got that lives within five hundred miles of her. And you get over to see her twice a year, like clockwork, even though you rarely leave Dauber. She tramps all over the country, it seems, yet it's almost a cold day in hell before she'll stop here. Even when she does drop in, she only stays a few minutes. I just don't understand that. If I had a sister, you can bet we'd be as close as peas in a pod."

"She comes when she can," Ma said.

"Well, I hope she comes this time. By the looks of things, you've been getting ready for her visit all day long." Aunt Verdella patted Winnalee's back. "Well, sweetie. Let's get goin' and let these two get back to work."

"No fair!" Winnalee said, as they were heading out the door without me.

After they left, Ma called me to her and told me to bring my coloring book. "It's obvious that that child doesn't know how to behave like a little lady. You start acting like that, Evelyn Mae, and you won't play with her anymore. You understand me?" I said I did. She snatched my coloring book out of my hands and said it was too bad that I let Winnalee ruin my new book. Then she tossed it in the trash can under the sink. Even though only two pages got ruined, and even if it was my most favorite coloring book I ever got.

• • •

I didn't think I was gonna see Winnalee again until Monday, but I ended up seeing her that very afternoon, because a phone call came in with a message for Freeda Malone. Ma got all huffy as she took the message. "Well, yes, Marty, I'll give her your message, but I don't see why she gave you *our* number. She's just renting Mae's place. I don't even know the woman." Marty was the fat guy who owned Marty's Place. It was a real barn once, but after most of his cows died of something god-awful that made them diarrhea to death, he sold the cows he had left and ripped the whole insides of the barn out and built a dance hall inside instead. He served up food too. Fish and hamburgers, and things like that. Ma said she wouldn't even eat a soda cracker that was served in a barn, even if it was wrapped tight in cellophane, but Daddy and Uncle Rudy and Aunt Verdella ate there some Friday nights, because they said Marty fried the best fish in town.

"As if I don't have anything better to do with my time than running over there," Ma said after she hung up the phone. She looked around the house, which was so clean you could eat off of the floor without using a plate and not pick up even one germ, and at the mixing bowl and strawberries thawing on the counter, and sighed.

Even though I was nine years old, Ma thought I was too young to stay home alone when she was gone, so she told me to get in the car.

When we got to the Malones', nobody answered the door even though their rusty truck was sitting in the driveway. Ma hollered through the screen, while I looked across the yard for Winnalee. A yell finally came. "It's open!"

I gulped hard and my legs got stiff when Freeda Malone walked out of the kitchen, her hair up in a towel, and naked but for her panties and a man's old work shirt. Her shirt was hanging wide open on one side, so that one of her bumps was showing all the way. The pinker part was puckered like the skin of a plucked chicken, and seeing that made me glad my Barbie didn't have nipple parts.

Ma stared like she'd never seen a boobie on a grown lady before either, and her cheeks got blotchy.

Freeda pulled her blouse back over her bump and closed it with one button and a laugh. "I was pulling weeds in the flower bed out front. Crissakes, it's early June and already it's hotter than the blazes. I had to take a bath to cool down. Good thing we're all girls here."

Ma looked down and held her hands together, like she was trying to still them. "I'd be more careful if I were you, Freeda. Reece and Rudy, and that young farmhand, are always coming and going here."

I listened closely for sounds of Winnalee upstairs, but I didn't hear any.

Ma looked above Freeda's head. "Marty Wilson called our place with a message for you. He said you have the job and that you should come in tonight around six-thirty, ready to work."

Freeda laughed. "No rest for the wicked, I guess."

Ma turned to go, and I followed, but we didn't get to the door before it opened. "Jewel!" Aunt Verdella said, like she couldn't believe she was seeing Ma standing in the Malones' living room. Aunt Verdella had a jar of strawberry jam in one hand and a loaf of still-warm bread in the other. The bread was wrapped in a white dish towel so I couldn't see it, but I could smell it.

Winnalee said hi to me, then lifted Aunt Verdella's elbow and slipped herself under it, cuddling her face to Aunt Verdella's fattest ball. I looked down, feeling a little sad, because it was Winnalee hugging Aunt Verdella's fat part, not me.

"Jewel came by to tell me Marty called," Freeda explained. "I start work tonight."

"Oh, honey," Aunt Verdella said. "That's terrific! Why, let's celebrate with some warm jelly bread. You still have any of that yummy iced tea left you made yesterday?" Freeda told her she did.

Ma gave me a look, then scooted closer to the door. Aunt Verdella stopped her. "Oh, you can't go now, Jewel! Sit down with us and relax a minute." Aunt Verdella handed Winnalee the jam jar, then grabbed Ma's arm and tugged her toward the kitchen.

"Verdella, I have work to do before Stella gets here."

"Nonsense, Jewel. I saw your place, and it couldn't be more ready. And anyway, it's early. You don't have to stay long. Just long enough for a bite to eat and a little girl-talk."

Once we were in the kitchen, Aunt Verdella grabbed the breadboard hanging on the wall and set it on the counter. She put the bread on top of it and pulled the towel from it. She patted the bread a couple of times. "Maybe I should let this cool down just a bit more before I cut it," she said. "Sit down, Jewel. Sit down! And, Button, where's Auntie's hug?" I went to her and she wrapped her arms around me and kissed the top of my head with warm, breathy lips.

Freeda wore a grin as she watched Ma sip her iced tea, though I didn't know what was supposed to be funny.

While Aunt Verdella jabbered and Freeda grinned, Winnalee examined the bread that was cooling on the breadboard. "Why can't we have it now?" she whined.

"In a bit, honey," Aunt Verdella said. "If we cut it while it's too hot, it will flatten like a pancake." Aunt Verdella ha-ha-ed a bit, then turned to Freeda. "Stella is Jewel's sister. I've met her a few times over the years, and I don't want to say nothing bad about her, but she sure is critical of Jewel here. I just don't understand it. Jewel is just a peach. She keeps the cleanest house you'll ever see, and she can sew like a dream. Well, I know Stella is good at all those things too, but Jewel has nothin' to be ashamed of in the house department. Course, you'd never know that, listenin' to Stella." Aunt Verdella stopped, then made one of those faces that people make when they just told a secret.

"That's why I don't give a damn for relatives," Freeda said. "They're always ragging on you for something or other.

Always quick to tell you you're not doing things the right way—which is their way, of course."

Ma drank her tea fast, then stood up right while Aunt Verdella was talking. "Thank you for the iced tea," she said politely to Freeda, "but we do have to be going. Evelyn?"

"Oh, Jewel, you can't go yet. You're always in such a hurry. Sit down with us girls and relax a little."

Everybody was so busy fussing about us staying longer that nobody but me noticed that Winnalee had grabbed a giant knife from the block of wood the knives were poked in and that she was sawing on the bread. They noticed, though, when Winnalee let out a big scream.

Winnalee held up her chubby hand. Blood was running down from a gash sliced across the inside of her hand. Blood was splattering on the half-flattened bread and dripping to the floor.

"Owie! Owie! Owie!" she screamed, as she grabbed her cut hand at the wrist with her good hand and hopped around the kitchen.

"Stand still so I can see it!" Freeda yelled, as she hopped in circles to get in front of Winnalee. "Stand still, for crissakes, so I can look at it!" she yelled again.

"Bring her over here!" Aunt Verdella yelled from the sink, where she already had cold water running. They were all yelling so loud that I had to put my hands over my ears.

"Oh dear, I think she's going to need stitches," Aunt Verdella said as she held Winnalee's hand under the faucet, while Freeda held Winnalee still. "It looks pretty deep. Jewel, come look at this!"

Ma went over to take a peek, while I scooted back to stand against the wall.

"I'm not going to no doctor!" Winnalee screamed. "I'm not!"

"Yes, I'd say she'll need stitches," Ma said.

"I want my ma!" Winnalee cried, as Aunt Verdella tried to

wrap her hand in a white dishcloth Freeda got from the drawer. "Mama! Mama!"

Aunt Verdella looked at me over the top of Winnalee's head. "Go get her ma," she said.

"Upstairs, in her room," Freeda yelled to me, then she yelled at Winnalee for not minding and not leaving the bread alone in the first place.

I ran up the stairs and there her ma was, sitting right on the window seat, where she always was when Winnalee wasn't lugging her around.

I had never touched Winnalee's ma before, and I didn't want to touch her now. But downstairs, Aunt Verdella was yelling at me to hurry because Winnalee was still screaming for her ma. I picked up the jar, and I hurried downstairs, holding it out so it wouldn't touch anything but my hands.

When I got back to the kitchen, I held out the jar and Aunt Verdella took it. There were tears in her eyes. "Here, honey. Here's your ma." Maybe Winnalee's eyes were too teary to see through them right, because she pushed the jar away and kept right on crying for her ma, even though her ma was right there.

"We'll take my car," Aunt Verdella shouted, as we all made our way across the living room.

"Oh Jesus!" Freeda said, stopping so quick that Aunt Verdella ran into her. "I ain't even dressed!" Freeda ran into her bedroom to change, while we waited and Winnalee screamed.

As we were all hurrying across the porch to leave— Winnalee, Freeda, and Aunt Verdella for the doctor's office, and Ma and me for home to clean some more—Uncle Rudy appeared at the bottom of the steps. "My, my," he said. "I heard the commotion all the way from the oat field." He looked at Winnalee, who was being dragged out the door by Freeda. "She cut herself with the bread knife!" Aunt Verdella explained. "It looks deep, Rudy. Jewel said it'll need stitches."

"I'm not going!" Winnalee yelled. Her face was all

blotched with fear, and tears were springing out of her eyes and dripping down her cheeks.

Uncle Rudy always had a quiet voice, but when he talked now it was even more quiet than usual. So quiet that everybody had to hush to hear what he was saying. "It's okay, little one. You just close your eyes, and let Uncle Rudy have a peek, okay?" Winnalee was gasping and hiccupping as Uncle Rudy crouched down and took her arm gently. I looked away as he pulled the bloody towel away from her hand.

"Why, no wonder you're scared, these women carrying on like you're dying. But it's just a little cut. The doctor will have you fixed up in no time."

"No, no!" Winnalee pleaded. "I don't want to go to no doctor. He'll sew on me!"

"Aw, that's nothing. Lookie here." Uncle Rudy stretched out the neckline of his work shirt and pointed to the wrinkly indent that circled his neck like a necklace. "You think your cut there is bad, then take a look at this one. A few years back, I cut my head clear off. I had to pick it up and carry it under my arm like a cabbage, all the way to Dr. Williams's office." Winnalee giggled some while she sniffled. "Doc Williams stitched my whole head back on in just a few minutes, so it won't take him any time at all to stitch up a tiny cut like yours." He cranked his head from side to side. "See? Good as new."

"I'll get my purse!" Aunt Verdella said, as she bounced across the lawn toward her house.

Winnalee grinned a little, then the worried look crept back into her face. "Is it gonna hurt?" Fresh tears squeezed out of her eyes, which were already flag—red, white, and blue.

"I'm not gonna lie and say it won't," Uncle Rudy said. "But it's not gonna hurt any worse than it's hurting right now," he told her. "And if I'm lying about that, you can kick me right in the shin when you get back. Now, how about if Uncle Rudy carries you to the car?"

"Your back, Rudy!" Aunt Verdella yelled as she hurried

across the lawn, her big purse banging against her belly, her white sweater flapping from her shoulders.

Uncle Rudy crouched down and scooped Winnalee up. "If she breaks my back in two, then the good doc will just have to sew me back together, ain't that right, Winnalee?" Winnalee giggled, her giggles sounding like little, quick chirps.

As Ma and I got into her car, I watched Uncle Rudy in their driveway, putting Winnalee into the Bel Air.

The driveways sat across from each other, and Ma pulled out first. Probably because she was in a hurry to get the food cooked before Aunt Stella came. I turned around in my seat and got on my knees. Aunt Verdella was pulling her car out slowly, while Uncle Rudy made waving signs with his hand. Once she got the car out, he waved good-bye. I waved bye to him too, but he was busy watching the Bel Air head in the opposite direction for the nearest dirt road that would take them to town, because Aunt Verdella wouldn't drive on the highway, so he didn't wave back at us.

"Turn around and sit down, Evelyn," Ma said then, so I did, and the whole time I sat there, I worried that driving to town on those back roads might take so long that Winnalee would bleed to death, just like Aunt Betty did. "Maybe this will teach that child a lesson about listening to what she's told," Ma said.

As we crossed the highway, then slipped into our driveway, I looked down at my hands. The skin on the backs of them were white, the skin on the inside, pinky. There wasn't a scratch or scrape on them. And for a little bit, I was sorry about that.

7

There were two reasons I hated having big ears. One, they looked ugly. And two, they sometimes heard things I didn't want to hear.

I opened my eyes in the night, not sure at first what had woken me, but then I heard Ma and Daddy arguing in their bedroom.

"Crissakes, Jewel, I told you! I worked on Ma's house for a couple of hours, then I went to Marty's for a few beers. I work my ass off all week long. I don't see what's so goddamn wrong about me having a few beers with the guys."

"A couple of hours? Don't give me that, Reece. I saw your truck head to town at nine o'clock. You were at Freeda's earlier in the day, when Verdella came by to use the phone, but you weren't there when I ran over to tell Freeda about Marty's phone call. God knows where you were then, but you must have gone back before you went back to town."

"What to hell's your point? And since when do I have to hand in a time card at the end of each day?"

I switched on the little lamp on my nightstand and tipped my head backward. Above me were the two white-framed pictures that hung on my pink wall. In one picture, Little Bo Peep looked for her sheep, her mouth a pink circle of worry. In the other frame were her sheep, all topsy-turvy too, as they ran away from her. I wondered if they were running away because she couldn't cook eggs without burning them and because she was always harping at them about where they were.

"I went to help Rudy with the tractor. For crissakes, Jewel. I wasn't at Ma's house the whole day, if that's what you're getting at."

When Ma and Daddy argued, Ma's words were sharp like a crack of lightning, only not as loud. Daddy's were more like thunder, low and rumbly. I pulled the edges of my pillow up and folded them over my ears. It only helped a little, though, because Daddy got louder, and then Ma got louder.

"You weren't there this afternoon. But that's not even the point, Reece. The point is, you didn't come home, when I specifically asked you to. You knew Stella was coming. How do you think that looked to my sister, when you didn't bother to come home to say hello to her? I said you'd be here."

"To tell you the truth, I really don't give a shit what it looks like to Stella, snooty bitch that she is."

"I put up with your relatives, Reece. You could do me the same favor, instead of running off to chase anything in skirts."

"Jesus," Daddy said. "Here we go again! I've never had a thing to do with another woman since the day we got married, but you accuse me of it practically every goddamn day."

"Lower your voice," Ma snapped. "You'll wake Evelyn." Then Ma went on and on about him not being home when Stella came, her voice quieter, so that I couldn't hear the words, just the rise and fall of them.

Daddy didn't say no more. Ma called his name when she was done harping, but he didn't answer her with words, only snores.

I heard their door open and close, so I took the pillow away from my ears and listened. The bathroom door opened and closed. I thought I heard Ma crying, but I told myself I was imagining that, because Ma never cried.

Before I'd gone to bed, I knew Ma was upset with Daddy. She kept looking at the clock as we ate the supper Aunt Stella hadn't eaten, and she hardly touched her plate. She was standing by the window when I went to bed, her long arms wrapped so tight around her middle that they could have gone around her twice.

After I heard Ma leave the bathroom, I waited for the sound of their bedroom door opening and closing, but it never came. I tried to get right back to sleep, but I couldn't. I couldn't seem to do nothing but think about the day.

Ma had left the clothes I was supposed to wear for Aunt Stella's visit on my bed. She'd told me to come show her once I was dressed.

She'd laid out my best dress. The pink one that was made of those kinds of material that make you feel sweaty and hot if you wear them in the summertime and sweaty and cold if you wear them in the winter. The one with a slippery, stuck-on pink slip underneath and that see-through stuff over it, the skirt pressed into wide pleats. Next to the dress was a pink bow with a bobby pin stuck through it, to slide into my knots. A pair of new white anklets with lace trim was laid next to the bow, and my black patent-leather shoes were on the floor next to my bed. I had dressed quickly, trying my best not to think of Winnalee in Dr. Williams's office, him sewing on her as if she was made of taffeta instead of skin.

When I was dressed, I went to show Ma, like she told me to. She was at the table, moving the centerpiece—a basket of wax fruit—a bit more in the middle. "Just a minute," she said. Ma was wearing her best dress too. One she sewed herself. It looked pretty much like all the other dresses she wore, but it was made of softer, nicer material. Ma put two stubby candles on each side of the fruit bowl, then cocked her head all over again. "There!" she said, when she got it just right.

Ma looked at me and cocked her head some more. Then

she swirled her finger, so I'd turn in circles. When I got all the way around, she came to me and retucked the bow into my knots. She smiled—as if she thought I looked pretty—then she told me to go sit down and wait.

The whole house had too many smells: Pine-Sol, Pledge, shortcake, garlic, and a bunch more I couldn't name. The smells were so strong they made my nose sting inside.

By the time Aunt Stella pulled into the driveway, my belly was hungry, and I was sweaty and itchy. Ma tugged her apron off and dashed into the kitchen to put it away. She was back by the time the doorbell rang. Ma blew out air, patted her hair in place, and put a smile on her face. "Stella!" she said as she swung the door open. They kissed each other on the cheek.

Ma talked fast as she led Aunt Stella into the living room. She looked at me, and I knew it was time to stand up. "Hello, Aunt Stella."

"Hello, Evelyn." Aunt Stella's eyes raked over me, from the top of my ugly head to the tip of my glossy shoes. "My, look at how dressed up you two are. Do you have a program of some kind today, Evelyn?" I bit at the inside of my mouth and shook my head.

She turned back to Ma. "My Cindy never went through an awkward age. Isn't that amazing?"

"How are Cindy and Judy, anyway?" Ma asked in a voice that sounded more like a little girl's voice than my ma's voice. "Here, have a seat," Ma said, motioning to our best chair.

Aunt Stella sat down and set her purse down next to her feet. "Oh, marvelous! They're both still in dance class. Still both straight-A students. Judy just finished the tenth grade, and Cindy will be a freshman next fall. Oh, I think I brought pictures along. Let me see." Aunt Stella always wondered if she'd brought pictures along, even though she hadn't ever forgotten them. Aunt Stella scooped up her purse and rummaged through it.

"I'll go check on our dinner while you look," Ma said. "I found a wonderful recipe in *Good Housekeeping*. I hope it tastes as good as it looks! Reece should be home any minute. Coffee?"

"Oh, don't set a place for me, Jewel," Aunt Stella called out. "Martha is expecting me, and knowing her, she spent the whole day cooking. She'd be hurt if I didn't eat. I'll have coffee, though."

Aunt Stella handed me the pictures since Ma was still in the kitchen.

Even though the pictures were black and white, I could tell that their dancing dresses were as pretty as their faces. Judy's long hair had a cloth headband in it, and it curled up at her shoulders. Cindy's hair was braided on the sides, and two long curls hung from a bow behind each ear. They were fake curls, I knew, because I'd seen Aunt Stella make them when they spent the night at our house once, a long, long time ago. She had pressed long strips of torn bedsheets along her finger, then wound the hair around it and tied the rag to keep the hair in a loop. The hair looked real pretty when she first took out the rag curlers, but by afternoon the curls were drooping down their backs. I remembered too, that Cindy and Judy spent most of the day sitting on the steps, whispering into each other's ears.

When Ma looked at their pictures, Aunt Stella said, "These were taken at their dance recital in May. Can you imagine how proud Ma would have been of them both? Remember how she always said that I should have been a dancer? Of course, there weren't dance classes in town then, which was probably good for you. Remember how klutzy you were as a girl, Jewel? All legs and arms. Twenty feet of them!" She stopped to laugh. "Good heavens, you were at your adult height by what? Eleven years old? Of course, not that you would have taken a dance class had there been one in town anyway, being the tomboy you were. Even into your teens." Aunt Stella looked over at me. "Poor Ma used to worry about you so! I always said I'd marry a Baptist minister, just like

Daddy, and Ma was sure happy as could be when I did. But you, she didn't care who you married, as long as you found someone! I think she was afraid you'd be an old maid all your life. Remember when she told you that you'd better learn to be nice if you ever hoped to find a husband, since you didn't have much in the looks department?"

Aunt Stella took some more pictures out of her purse. "Oh, and here's pictures of the house. It has a greenhouse! Oh, and here's one of me at the ladies' social where I spoke in December. I got that dress in Chicago. I got more compliments on that thing!"

I felt sorry for Ma, looking at that stack of pictures. It seemed that no matter how much Ma scrubbed or fixed up our place, Aunt Stella never noticed. Like the sunburst clock hanging right above her head, or the new white trellis Ma had put up right next to the front door so flowers could creep up it.

"Did you make that dress, Jewel?" I smiled inside, because Aunt Stella noticed something. I held my breath, hoping she'd say it was nice. Instead, she said, "I suppose, you being so tall and long-armed, you pretty much have to make your own clothes." She looked over at me and added, "At least your Evelyn isn't too tall. She doesn't look like a tomboy either... or is she?"

Ma's face had funny blotches on it. She set her coffee cup back on its saucer hard enough for it to make a rattly sound. I tried to imagine Ma as a girl. A tomboy girl. But I couldn't see that in my head any more than I could see Daddy as a cute-as-a-bug's-ear boy. All I could see when I tried to picture Ma as a girl was a girl as tall as a man, with shoulders pinched forward and a head with nothing pretty on it.

"Evelyn is a perfect little lady," Ma said. "And she's a straight-A student too. Her fourth-grade teacher told me that if all her students were as well behaved as Evelyn, she'd pay *them* to let her teach. She earned the most patches in Girl Scouts this year too. Evelyn, go get your sash, and show Aunt

Stella." I hated Girl Scouts, where none of the girls saved me a seat at the table. And I didn't want to show Aunt Stella my sash—even if it did have lots of patches on it. Still, I got up to go fetch it.

I didn't have to show it to Aunt Stella, though, because she stopped me before I could reach my doorway, saying maybe we could save that for next time because she had to get going. "You haven't even finished your coffee," Ma said, and Aunt Stella told her that that was for the best, since she still had another two hours to drive and there weren't any clean restrooms along the way. "I'm sorry this visit is so short, Jewel, but I got a late start. Maybe I'll stop on my way back."

After Aunt Stella used our bathroom, Ma and I walked her to her car. "Well, tell Reece I'm sorry I missed him again. Is that man ever home?" Aunt Stella opened her car door and slipped her purse inside. Ma leaned over to give her a kiss good-bye, then told me to give her a kiss good-bye too. Aunt Stella leaned over and turned her rouged cheek to me. I kissed it quick, because her perfume was so strong that my eyes were stinging.

And that was it. That was my whole day. Cleaning, then running over to Winnalee's to watch her bleed, then getting gussied up for Aunt Stella's little bitty visit. Then falling asleep so I could get closer to morning and go by Winnalee and Aunt Verdella, only to get woken up by Ma and Daddy's fight.

I lay awake and thought about Aunt Stella's visit, and I thought about how I hated my ears that heard too much. I wondered if it was true, what Aunt Verdella said once—that if you put gum behind big ears and press them flat against your head, they'd learn to stay down like they're supposed to. And I thought about how I'd never know if it worked because Ma wouldn't let me chew gum, because Dr. Wagner said it wasn't good for a kid's teeth, but if I could, I'd stuff some in my ears too, just so I'd stop hearing bad things.

After I thought those things, then I thought about how, if I had my own Book of Bright Ideas, I'd write *Bright Idea #1: If you take an ugly girl and you dress her up in a pretty pink dress, lacy anklets, and plunk a homemade bow on her head, you're not going to get a pretty girl. All you're going to get is an ugly girl in a pretty dress, lacy anklets, with a bow plunked on her head.*

8

It was Aunt Verdella's idea to have a cookout. She said having one would help Freeda and Winnalee get to know their neighbors, and Ma get to know the Malones.

That Sunday, Aunt Verdella made some potato salad and baked beans and thawed frozen steaks and hamburgers for the grill, while I helped Uncle Rudy clean off the dusty lawn chairs that were kept in the shed and waited for Winnalee to take her bath and come over. I knew Ma was mad she even had to go to the cookout, much less go early so she could help Aunt Verdella put the food together, but Daddy didn't give her much choice.

"This is gonna be so much fun!" Aunt Verdella chirped, as she unscrewed a jar of pickles and popped the canning lid so I could stab them out with a fork and put them on a plate. "I've asked the Thompson twins—they're so good-looking, aren't they, and around Freeda's age? And of course, Melvin will bring his wife, June, and their kids. I'd imagine that the other one, Mike, is lookin' for a wife too, so who knows, Freeda just might meet her Prince Charming here in Dauber yet."

"It doesn't seem to me that Freeda Malone has much trouble meeting men," Ma said under her breath, as she stirred mayonnaise into a bowl of tuna, noodles, peas, and onions.

"Oh, and I told Tommy to tell his ma and dad to come too. Ada doesn't get out much, except to work at The Corner Store, and Elroy likes visiting with Rudy. And, let's see...oh, Fanny and John Tilman. I guess I sorta felt I had to invite them, since I ended up inviting Ada when I stopped for gas, and it turned out that Fanny happened to be back by the milk cooler. Not that I mind Fanny, of course, but, well, let's just hope that meeting Freeda at a social gathering will soften Fanny toward her a little."

Aunt Verdella rapped on the window above the sink, then yelled out, "Reece, did you guys bring out the tub for the beer? The ice blocks are in the freezer in the shed." She turned back to the table. "Oh, that's nice how you laid those pickles out, Button. Like a sunbeam."

"Aren't cookouts fun?" Aunt Verdella said, as she came to the picnic table carrying a pitcher of lemonade clanking with ice cubes and a stack of yellow plastic cups. Freeda, who was probably tired from staying up most of the night or was still trying to coax Winnalee out of the tub, still hadn't come out of their house. "I couldn't think of a better way to bring us all together." Aunt Verdella looked at Ma. "Why, you and Freeda hardly know each other, and you're neighbors."

Before I knew it, the Smithys pulled in, and the Tilmans right behind them. Fanny Tilman wore a button-up sweater, even though it was about ten hundred degrees, and both ladies were carrying bowls covered with Reynolds Wrap. "You're lookin' good, Ada. Doesn't she look good, Jewel?" I guess that meant that Ada had had a good recuperation from her operation. Ada, who was short and chubby, said she'd lost ten pounds since her surgery. Elroy, tall and skinny, and as ugly as Tommy, rolled his eyes. "She'll have it all put back on, plus another twenty, by the next time you see her, anyway."

Uncle Rudy and Daddy were at the grill, turning the steaks over with big metal pinchers, beers in their hands, so that's where the men headed. Aunt Verdella told me to bring them each a beer, so I grabbed some bottles out of the icy tub and brought them over to the grill. While the men yammered about farming over by the smoking grill, the ladies hovered around the picnic table, yammering about everything and anything. Mostly the Malones.

"So where are our guests of honor, anyway?" Ada said.

"Yeah, that's what I was wondering," said one of the Thompson twins, who'd come over to the table to set down some still-sizzling steaks. I didn't know if it was Mike or Melvin, since they looked exactly alike—both with blond hair on their heads and white hair on their sun-darkened arms. The other twin chuckled, then called over the exact the same thing. June, the lady with a baby on her hip and a scrappy little boy wiggling in her free hand, shook her head and rolled her eyes at the one who repeated the words like a parrot, so I guessed that one was Melvin, her husband.

"Oh, look, here comes Winnalee, Button!" Aunt Verdella waved hard at Winnalee, who was coming across their yard, her ma in her arms.

"What's she got on?" June Thompson asked, talking about Winnalee's pink mesh skirt that was dragging across the grass.

"Oh, and she's got that urn I heard about. Poor little thing," Ada Smithy said.

Fanny Tilman, who was sitting on the very edge of the picnic table clutching her purse, added, "I think it's disrespectful, carrying the dead around like a toy."

I raced across the yard to meet Winnalee. She was wearing three strings of pearly blue beads, and her eyes were red, like either she'd been crying or gotten shampoo in them. Her loops were still damp and her eyebrows were bunched, which meant she was grouchy.

When she got to the picnic table, Aunt Verdella grabbed her by the shoulders and stood Winnalee in front of her. "This here is Winnalee Malone," Aunt Verdella said proudly. "She's nine years old, and smart as a whip, just like our Button." Ada and June, especially, started clucking about how adorable Winnalee was. "I'm not smart like Button," Winnalee said. "But only because I never get to stay in one school long enough to learn much of anything."

A bit of worry passed over Aunt Verdella's face. "Well, you'll learn lots in school here, honey, won't ya?" she said.

Ada smiled. "Well, sweetie, I don't know what brought you to Dauber, but we're sure glad you're here."

"Harley Hoffesteader was going to blow our heads off. That's what brought us here," Winnalee said. Fanny Tilman's eyes stretched behind her glasses, and she clutched her purse to her middle all the harder.

"Where's your—?" Aunt Verdella stopped talking when everybody suddenly looked past her and Winnalee and out toward Grandma Mae's yard. "Oh, here she comes now!" Aunt Verdella said.

I looked up to see Freeda coming across their lawn. She was dressed in a pretty pink sundress, her coppery hair stuck on top of her head in a stack of curls the size of juice cans. It looked like her feet were naked. "What's she got?" Aunt Verdella said.

"A cake," Winnalee said.

A cake wasn't all Freeda was carrying though. She had a guitar too. Not the one from the attic, but a new one. A yellow-wood one.

"Where'd you get that thing?" Aunt Verdella asked, nodding toward the guitar as she took the cake from Freeda and waited for Ma to clear a spot on the table so she could set the cake plate down.

"Oh, some loser left it at my place last night. I guess he thought he was gonna serenade me." June Thompson giggled behind her hand as she glanced quickly at Mrs. Tilman. "Anyway, I thought Reece could play us a song." Ma held a clump of her oatmeal hair flat against her head, so the wind wouldn't pick it up again. Her eyes were squinched into little lines as she looked at the guitar, or maybe the sun behind it.

"My, what a beautiful cake! Jewel, look how she swirled the frosting. Isn't that pretty? I didn't know you baked, Freeda," Aunt Verdella said.

Winnalee stuck her finger into the chocolate swirls and Freeda swatted at her hand. "I don't do it often, trust me, so don't get used to it."

Aunt Verdella got busy introducing Freeda to everyone, and as soon as the "nice to meet you"s were said, Freeda went to Daddy. "Here," she said. She handed the guitar to him.

"What the hell you want me to do with this?" Daddy asked. Freeda grinned and shrugged, then, with her eyes still on Daddy, she backed up till she reached the picnic table and sat down, crossing her bare legs. Stupid Tommy rushed to sit next to her.

"I haven't played one of these in years," Daddy said. He had his hand wrapped around the neck part of the guitar and was staring at it, while everyone else stared at Freeda. One of the Thompson twins slapped Daddy on the back and said, "You son of a bitch, if I could play a guitar like you, I'd never set it down." Everyone nodded and added their two cents.

"Let's eat, shall we?" Ma said, standing up quickly and reaching for the stack of paper plates still in their plastic wrapper.

"Sit by me, Uncle Reece," Winnalee said, her name for Daddy making Ma's eyebrows leap halfway up her forehead. Winnalee plunked down on the bench beside me and set her plate down before her. "Scoot over, Button!"

I slid over to the very edge of the bench, slipped my hands up over my ears, and Winnalee scooted against me to make room for Daddy. Well, until Ma told me and Winnalee we had to sit on the grass, so there would be enough room at the table and on the lawn chairs for the grown-ups. She picked up a big spoon and jabbed it into the potato salad.

There was lots of food. Some that went together, and some that didn't. Just like the crowd filling their plates.

While we ate, Aunt Verdella kept coaxing Freeda to tell everybody about herself. "You know, so they can all get to know you better, dear."

"What do you want to know?" Freeda asked.

"Well, I don't know. Where you're from. Where you've been. Anything."

"Well, let's see." Freeda bit the tip off of a pickle and chewed it. "I went down to Chicago after I left home. Lived there awhile, then to Cleveland, then down to Orlando. I lived in the Dakotas for a time too. Hell." Freeda laughed. "Where haven't I lived?"

"Detroit!" Winnalee said, from the grass near the picnic table, where we sat cross-legged. "That's where we were gonna go." She leaned over then and wrapped her arm around my neck. "But I'm glad we ended up here instead, because Button lives here." She gave me a squeeze. Aunt Verdella and Ada and June's "aw"s sounded like a church choir.

"I've never been out to the East Coast, but one day I'll get there too," Freeda said.

"Seems to me, a child needs some roots," Fanny Tilman said, as she scooped some sauerkraut stuff that she'd brought onto her plate. Even when filling her plate, she didn't set her purse down but had it slung over her arm.

Aunt Verdella leaned forward. "Where'd you start from, honey? Where'd you grow up?"

Freeda sat up straight and tried peering over the top of the metal tub that was parked under a shade tree. "That beer over there?" she asked.

"Sure is. You want one?" Uncle Rudy asked.

"I sure do," she answered. Uncle Rudy was gonna get up to grab her a beer, but one of the Thompson twins hurried to grab her one instead, smiling at her with teeth white as the sagging plate he held.

"Where'd you say you were born and raised?" Aunt

Verdella asked again. Her eyebrows were stitched together, like she'd crocheted them that way.

"Hopested, Minnesota," Winnalee said, while she crunched a potato chip. "It was a hole. That's what Freeda said." Fanny turned around and glared at Winnalee. I think because Winnalee didn't know (or didn't care) that children should be seen and not heard.

"Where's that, exactly?" Aunt Verdella asked.

Freeda didn't look like she wanted to talk any more about where she used to live. It looked to me like she just wanted to drink her beer.

"It's in the east central part of the state," Uncle Rudy said. "Over by St. Cloud." Then all the guys tried figuring out how many miles St. Cloud and Hopested were from Dauber. Not because they wanted to go there, I don't suppose, but just because men always seemed to have to know how far away other places were.

I stopped listening to their boring talk and looked over at Winnalee's ma, sitting a ways over from the picnic table, and I worried that the Thompson baby, who was crawling in the grass, would knock it over. I felt Tommy staring at me. When he saw me looking at him, he showed me his vampire teeth and slipped his pointy fingers behind his ears till they were sticking out sideways. I turned my head away, slipping my hands up over my ears.

After we ate, Uncle Rudy got up to go get the ice cream, but Aunt Verdella told him she thought everybody was full, so maybe we'd better wait for dessert. All the men—and Freeda too—were talking as loud as Aunt Verdella, probably because they were drinking beers. "How about some music, Reece?" Freeda said. Daddy glanced over at the guitar a few times before he grabbed it. There was a pick weaved in the strings at the top, and he plucked it loose and gave the guitar a strum. It sounded bad, so he twisted the little knobs at the top while he plucked at the strings, one string after another, until it sounded just right. Then he started strumming. "Play something,

Uncle Reece!" Winnalee said. "I wanna dance!" Aunt Verdella grinned, and I knew why. She loved it that Winnalee was calling them all "aunt" and "uncle" now.

Daddy stood up then and propped one leg on the corner of the picnic-table bench. He hooked the curved part of the guitar on his leg and started to play.

"Oh goodie! 'The Twist'!" Winnalee shouted.

Aunt Verdella let out a whoop and jumped up fast. She grabbed Freeda's hand and led her to the grass. The two of them sang along, loud, as they danced that funny dance where you move your top part one way and your bottom part the other way. They looked silly with their butts poked out, the heels of their feet swishing from side to side as they twisted their middles side to side. June, who didn't seem to do much more than laugh, got up then too, dancing with her baby, whose head was bobbling all over the place. Her little boy, whose striped shirt was wet with spilled lemonade and watermelon juice, ran in circles around the dancers.

"Come on, Button! Twist!" Winnalee shouted, as she headed to join the ladies. I looked over at Ma, wondering if she'd dance, but one look at her face told me that the only thing Ma was going to twist was the wire tie around the hamburger-bun bag.

"Look at Freeda!" Winnalee yelled. I glanced up and saw everybody watching Freeda, who was twisting herself down so low that her butt was swishing across her heels. Mike Thompson joined her then, twisting just like her, while everyone laughed and clapped.

I never heard Daddy play guitar before, though I'd heard him sing along with the radio in the garage a few times. As his pick banged against the strings, the muscles in his arm rose and fell, making that tattooed red heart look like it was pumping. He sang and played so good that I felt proud that he was my daddy.

" 'Jailhouse Rock'!" Freeda called out when "The Twist" was over. "Yeah!" Winnalee and Aunt Verdella yelled at the same time. Daddy paused to take a long swig from his beer, then he started playing the Elvis song they wanted.

I didn't know how to dance. Not like Aunt Verdella and Freeda, who had stopped doing the Twist and were doing some other kind of dance now where they held hands and moved their feet fancy while they moved apart, then came back together. Winnalee didn't know how to do that dance either, but she didn't care. She just hopped and kicked and waved her arms wherever they wanted to go, while Uncle Rudy grinned at her from his lawn chair, as Elroy Smithy leaned over to yack in his ear. I didn't think I could do what Winnalee was doing, so I just started stacking the forks together, one dirty fork on top of the other.

"Come on, Button!" Winnalee ran to me and started yanking my arm, just as the song ended. "Play it again, Uncle Reece! Again!" Daddy laughed. He took another gulp of beer, then lit a cigarette. He took two puffs from it, then wedged it between the guitar and strings, up at the top part where the tuning knobs were. He sat down on the edge of the picnic table and propped one leg on the bench part, then started the Elvis song all over again.

"Come on!" Winnalee's hands were gripped around my wrists, squeezing so hard that they were pinching my skin. I leaned back and dug my feet hard into the ground, but they just slid across the grass when Winnalee pulled. When she got me as far as where the women were, Aunt Verdella grabbed my arm and pulled me into their circle. "Come on, honey!" she shouted, while swinging my arm. " *'Everybody in the whole cell block was dancin' to the jailhouse rock!'* " Even her singing sounded like yelling.

I watched Aunt Verdella, who was doing her own sort of dance now, her feet going, her bent arms rocking from side to side. Freeda was dancing her own kind of dance too. Her butt going this way and that, her arms lifted above her head. A clump of her hair had come down, but she was too busy leaning forward to shake her bumps at Mike Thompson to notice.

She didn't stop moving her feet as she tipped herself back and lifted her beer bottle, and she only laughed when two yellow streams poured out both sides of her mouth and sloshed over the front of her dress. I looked for Ma, but she was gone, along with half the bowls that had been on the table and Mrs. Tilman. I glanced toward the house and saw a shadow in the window above the sink. That shadow was not only skinny but tall too, so I knew it was Ma. Ada Smithy danced over to me, her shoulders shrugging, her fingers snapping, like she was showing me how to dance.

I started moving a little, this way and that. "Like this!" Winnalee shouted, as she waved her arms above her head and hopped in circles. She grabbed my hand and started running in a circle around me, so that I had to run too. With her hurt hand held out to the side, and her other hand clutching mine, she stopped running, and spun in one place, twirling me and twirling me until my belly got the giggles, and the little Thompson kid begged her to twirl him too. After that, I was like a windup toy, and dancing was a bit easier.

"I'm gonna die of heatstroke, dancin' like that in this weather!" Aunt Verdella said when the song ended. She went over to a lawn chair and sat down with a plop. She told Tommy to hand her a clean paper plate and started fanning her neck, where frizzy strands were glued to her skin with sweat. "Reece, what's that slow Elvis song I told you I like? You know, that pretty one that came out last winter."

Freeda headed to the tub where the beer sat in melting ice. She grabbed one and Mike hurried to open it for her. Ma and Fanny Tilman came out of the house then, both of them quietly watching as Freeda giggled, with one hand on the Thompson man's chest.

Daddy's fingers fumbled around, then he sang just one line of a song and asked Aunt Verdella if that was it. Freeda pulled the cap off of her beer and said, "That's 'Are You Lonesome Tonight?' "

Aunt Verdella clapped her hands. "Yeah, that's it!"

"I've never played it before, but here goes," Daddy said.

The minute Daddy started singing that slow, sad song, Knucklehead, who was laying next to Uncle Rudy's chair, started howling, so Uncle Rudy had to rap him a bit on the top of his head so he'd shut up, and the Smithys and June Thompson and her husband got up to dance. Mike Thompson asked Freeda to dance. "You couldn't wedge the ace of spades between those two if you tried," I heard Fanny Tilman say to Ma, while Tommy gawked at the dancers with the same look on his face as Knucklehead wore when he watched Uncle Rudy eat his steak.

Daddy played a couple more songs, then set the guitar down. He grabbed another beer, then reached for another piece of the cake Freeda had brought. "Damn, this is good. Homemade, right?" Freeda nodded. "Hell, I never thought I'd taste homemade cake again."

"Oh, stop!" Aunt Verdella said. "I make one boxed cake mix in my entire life, because I was busy getting things ready for next week's sale, and this guy's never gonna let me live it down."

Ma stood with her hands behind her back, watching everybody laugh.

"I wasn't talking about you, Verdella," Daddy said. "I was talking about Jewel. If she hadn't made friends with Betty Crocker, me and the kid would never get a piece of cake, period."

Freeda looked up at Ma, whose face had turned blotchy, then Freeda wrinkled her forehead at Daddy. "Too bad you can't buy a carpenter in a box," she said.

"What's *that* supposed to mean?" Daddy asked, as he crammed half of his cake into this mouth, then wiped the chocolate from his lips with the back of his hand.

"Sit down, Jewel. Sit down!" Aunt Verdella said, patting the lawn chair between her and Ada. "Tommy, bring that chair over here, will you? Come on, Fanny, you come sit too. Lord, it's hot." Aunt Verdella grabbed a plastic cup and asked Freeda to pour a little beer from her bottle into it. "I never drink, but, oh, what the hell." She clamped her hand over her mouth, because she said a bad word, and then she ha-ha-ed.

"It means what it sounds like it means," Freeda said to Daddy. She poured the rest of her beer into Aunt Verdella's cup, then grabbed another bottle from the tub. She came back to the table, sat down, and reached for the opener. Daddy grabbed it first and held it above his head. Freeda pretended she didn't notice.

"You guys, get a load of this one..." she said, while she bumped her side against Daddy. "Reece was supposed to fix the toilet so it wouldn't keep running after it was flushed."

"I fixed it!" Daddy said.

"Yeah. So you said." Freeda laughed, then went back to telling her story. "Anyway, he must have been in there a good hour, then came out and said it was fixed. I flushed it after he left, and it started making these gurgling noises in the tank, so I took the lid off, and a goddamn geyser shot out of the tank! I'm not kidding. A goddamn geyser!"

Daddy started to say something, but Freeda clamped her hand over his mouth. "Soaked the ceiling, my nylons hanging over the shower pole. Everything! Even the curtains were soaked!" Everybody laughed, especially Aunt Verdella, whose cheeks were pink from the beer she drained from her Styrofoam cup.

Daddy pulled his head away from Freeda's hand. "She's bullshittin'," Daddy said with a laugh. "I went over there to check it out, and it flushes just fine."

"Yeah, now and then, but just this morning, it geysered again."

"It did!" Winnalee said. "That's why I had to take a stupid bath. Because it geysered me! I was dressed already too!" Freeda reached for the can opener Daddy was holding again, and again Daddy lifted it out of her reach.

"Sounds to me like maybe I'd better stop in and take a look at it," Mike Thompson added.

Freeda must have been looking out the corner of her eye, because the second Daddy's hand started coming down, Freeda reached for the can opener. Daddy was too quick, though, and he jerked his arm back, the can opener going out of Freeda's reach again. "You don't talk nice about me, then you can't drink my beer."

"I'll get it!" Winnalee said. She dived at Daddy, her knee coming right down on his lap. Daddy's arms came in, and his back curled, as he let out one of those noises that is a mix of a gasp and a groan. The men really laughed then.

Winnalee grabbed the can opener and handed it to Freeda. "That'll teach ya," Freeda said to Daddy with a giggle. Winnalee jumped off of Daddy's lap, distracted by a blue butterfly bouncing across the grass.

Ma didn't wait for the laughing to stop. She stood up and said, "Reece, I think we should get going. It's going on nine, and I have to work tomorrow."

"You can't go yet, Jewel!" Aunt Verdella said. "We haven't even had our dessert!" Aunt Verdella hurried to the picnic table and started cutting more slices of cake. "Tommy, could you run in the shed and get the ice cream out of the freezer, please?"

"You heard Verdella," Daddy said to Ma. "We haven't had our ice cream yet."

"I think we had enough sweets for today," Ma said, propping her hands on her hips.

Daddy got up and grabbed two more beers from the tub. "One for the road?" he asked Ma.

"Since when do I drink?" Ma said.

"Since now?" Daddy said, tilting his head to the side. The way he said it made me suddenly able to see him as that "cute-as-a-bug's-ear" little boy Aunt Verdella said he once was.

"I'll have one," Aunt Verdella said. "That went down pretty good." June giggled right along with Aunt Verdella.

Ma picked up her purse, ignoring Daddy. "Thanks for

everything, Verdella," she said. "Fanny, Ada, June, nice seeing you all again. Elroy, John, Melvin, Mike." Fanny stood up too and jabbed John in the knee, waking him from his nap, his head sagged down against his chest. "I'm ready to go too," she said.

"Oh, Jewel, don't leave yet. Reece wants to stay a bit longer, and Button is having so much fun. It's not even dark yet!" Ma acted like she didn't hear Aunt Verdella, even though Aunt Verdella was talking so loud that even the crows circling the top of the trees probably heard her.

Daddy didn't make a move to get up. He just sat there as Winnalee jumped on his knee, her arm going around his neck. He patted her on the head.

Ma walked to the car and slipped in the driver's side. "Come on, Button," she said, her hand on the door, making ready to close it.

"Hey!" Daddy shouted. "You expect me to walk home or what?"

"I'm sure somebody would be more than willing to give you a ride," Ma said. "Of course, you'll probably have to take the back roads home."

Aunt Verdella ha-ha-ed. "Oh, I couldn't drive him home if I tried, because I think I might be drunk!"

"I wasn't talking about you, Verdella," Ma said, her voice as sharp as broken glass. "Button?" Ma said again.

"I think we should go too, Mel," June Thompson said, as she bounced her fussy baby, who was digging at her eyes with her fists.

Winnalee opened her mouth to start begging for me to be able to stay, but Freeda leaned over and gave her a big kiss on her cheek. "You're a pain in the ass. You know that, kid? Now tell Button you'll see her tomorrow."

"Here, wait," Aunt Verdella said. "I'll cut you two each a piece of cake to bring home. You gotta wait for Fanny and John to pull out, anyway."

Aunt Verdella gave me a hug, then handed me the plate. Uncle Rudy came to pat me on the head and walk me to the car.

I watched Ma out of the corner of my eye as we drove home, the cake plate on my legs. She looked extra saggy inside her gray and green dress. There was a little flinch jumping at that bony part right below her ear. She didn't say a word until we pulled into our driveway, then she told me to go take my bath.

The bathroom wasn't far from the kitchen, and with my big ears, I could hear Ma on the phone with Bernice. "It was downright humiliating," she said. "The two of them carrying on without an ounce of shame. And right in front of half the neighborhood too! Yes, yes! She brought over a guitar that one of her one-night-stands left there, and he played it for her. She danced like a hussy too, of course, and giggled at everything Reece said. Even Fanny thought it was terrible the way that woman carried on!" There were tears in Ma's voice that I didn't want to hear, so I started singing, just like Winnalee did in the tub.

I don't know who brought Daddy home. It was after dark, and all I saw was two headlights bounce down the drive. Daddy's eyes were shining like glass, and he was walking a little topsy-turvy. He looked around for Ma, but she was in the bathroom soaking in the tub. He didn't ask me where she was, or why I was still up, even though it was so late.

Daddy was humming some of that slow Elvis song as he took off his shoes and left them at his feet. He lit a cigarette and dozed off, his elbow propped on the chair, the half-smoked-up cigarette still between his fingers. Ma was in the bathroom still, so I couldn't tell her that he had fallen asleep with a cigarette in his hand. I didn't know what to do. I stood at the far end of the room and bit the inside of my cheek as I watched his hand. When I saw his fingers loosening and the cigarette start to slip, I ran and caught it in my cupped hands. It burned my skin a bit before I could drop it in the ashtray, where it smoked all by itself. Daddy's arm slowly sank down to the armrest. I looked at his dangling hand and wondered what it would feel like against my head. I looked down the hall and listened. I could hear more water filling into the tub, so I knew Ma wouldn't come out for a while. I got down on my hands and knees then and tucked my chin in. I took two creeps forward before I felt his fingers brush the top of my head. I stopped and concentrated real hard. I'd hoped that his fingers on my head would give me the same warm, happy feeling inside that I got when Uncle Rudy patted my head, but it didn't.

9

I felt groggy when Ma woke me up in the morning. She looked groggy too. There was no sheet or blanket on the couch, but the melon-shaped indent on the couch pillow said that she'd slept there.

I walked into the kitchen as quietly as I could and squeezed between the table and the chair to sit down. Even if I was going to be eating at Aunt Verdella's, I had to have juice and milk at home first.

Daddy didn't come to the table. He came into the kitchen and reached for a coffee cup, then headed to the stove for the coffeepot. Ma was making his lunch at the counter, and when he passed, they were like two magnets facing the wrong way, so that probably not even tornado winds could push them close enough to touch.

Daddy left his breakfast on the table and his lunch box on the counter, then he headed out the door. Ma thought he'd forgotten them, so she ran to the door and called out to him. He didn't stop.

"Sure," she said to herself as she marched back into the kitchen and slammed them down on the table. "Now it can look like his wife doesn't make him any lunch.

"Finish your orange juice so we can go!" Ma snapped at

me. I took a sip and tried not to make faces when the juice
stung the inside of my cheek I'd chewed in the night.

Winnalee was waiting for me in the driveway when I got to
Aunt Verdella's, her ma in her arms. "Aunt Verdella has a surprise for us!" she said, bouncing up and down. "I don't know
what it is, because we had to wait for you."

Ma smacked her lips, and I knew that meant that she was
annoyed. She didn't like when Aunt Verdella spoiled me. She
looked away as she backed out the driveway.

When we got into the house, Aunt Verdella was standing
at the table, both of her hands shoved into a big Ben Franklin
bag. She looked ready to burst. "First, something little.
They're the same, but different colors, so you girls decide who
gets the one in my right hand and who gets the one in my left
hand."

"I want the one in your right hand!" Winnalee said. She
set her ma down on the table so that she could hop high without dropping her.

"I'll take the left one," I said.

Aunt Verdella took out two plastic headbands. Not just ordinary ones (though that would have been okay too) but fancy
ones. A blue one for me in her left hand, and a pink one in her
other hand, for Winnalee. They had a row of little fake flowers stuck to them. White cloth flowers, tipped with pink on
Winnalee's and tipped in blue on mine.

Winnalee snatched her headband and put it on her head.
Not how you're supposed to—by starting at the front of your
face and scraping it back across your scalp so the little sharp
teeth can catch your hair and hold it back behind your ears—
but sticking it straight down from the top of her head so that it
disappeared in her loops, like she wasn't even wearing one.
"Thank you, Aunt Verdella," I said, as Winnalee tried snatching the bag, asking, "What else? What else?"

If there hadn't been even one more thing in that bag for

me, I'd have been happy. I'd wanted a plastic headband forever, just like some of the girls at school had. But when I'd
asked Ma for one, she said that those were for girls with long
hair, who needed help keeping their hair out of their faces.

"Just a minute, just a minute. Here, let me help you with
that, honey." Aunt Verdella took Winnalee's headband off
and put it on the right way. "Button, you need help?" she
asked when she saw me holding mine above my head, not sure
what to do with it. I didn't have any hair to fall in my face, and
I knew my short knots weren't going to stretch from the front
all the way back to my ears. I told Aunt Verdella I didn't need
any help, then I slipped it on as Winnalee had slipped hers on.
Aunt Verdella reached to correct me, then changed her mind.
"Well, it looks cute as a decoration, anyway," she said.

Aunt Verdella went back to the bag. She pulled from it two
red metal squares with teeth like a comb, only bigger, and bags
of multicolored nylon loops. "Well, I was thinking of how
you girls could make a little money at the community sale,
then I saw these looms. They make pot holders! Everybody
needs pot holders. And I'll bet they wouldn't mind paying
twenty-five cents for a pair of them from two pretty little girls."

Winnalee and I were happy about our weaving looms.
Well, until Winnalee held up her bandaged hand. Then we all
groaned. "Oh, what was I thinking!" Aunt Verdella said, whacking her head. "Well, you'll be able to do it in a few days, honey."

"Hey, there's something else in the bag. What else you got
in there?" Winnalee snatched the bag from Aunt Verdella and
peeked inside. "Penny candy! Look, Button!" She pulled out a
roll of white paper, with candy buttons stuck to it in neat rows.
"And there's Tootsie Roll Pops and Pixy Stix, and all kinds of
goodies!" She pulled two tiny bottles made of wax out of the
bag and handed me one. She bit off the wax top of hers, tipped
her head back, and drained the red juice from inside.

It took a whole week before Winnalee could make pot
holders.

It was hard making them at first, because you had to stick

one side of the loop on one tooth-thing, then stretch it to a tooth on the other side, going under and over, under and over the other row of loops you connected first. Sometimes you'd get goofed up and go over or under two times instead of one, and then you'd have to pull the loop out and start over again. It sure was fun though, seeing what pretty color combinations you could come up with.

I could tell that everybody thought the colors I used in my pot holders were prettiest. I made them in colors that would match people's kitchens, with two colors that matched each other. But Winnalee didn't. She'd pull out one loop because she liked green, maybe, then she'd grab a black one, because that was the color of sexy. And as if that wasn't bad enough, sometimes she'd grab five of one color—orange maybe, just because that morning she had orange juice, or white, because clouds were white and she liked clouds—until she thought of which color she wanted to use next. Her pot holder would turn out ugly then, and I knew nobody would want a pair like that hanging in their kitchen, the color and pattern all which way. Well, if they could even get a pair, which they couldn't, be-cause Winnalee never made two exactly the same anyway.

One morning, right after bunny pancakes and bacon, me and Winnalee and her ma went to sit in Aunt Verdella's yard to make pot holders. We sat under a big shade tree in the front yard, because the day before, we sat in the sun and I sun-burned my scalp so bad that I couldn't even get my headband on that morning. Winnalee's ma was sitting on the picnic table, which was right next to the shade tree. We were busy talking about how we hadn't had a bright idea in a long time, and how if we didn't get busy thinking up one, we were never gonna get to one hundred by the end of summer, no way.

"Look at that!" Winnalee said, pointing out in the field, where a cow was giving another cow a piggyback ride.

"Yeah," I said. "The bulls like to get piggyback rides."

"They're not playing piggyback rides. They're making babies."

I blinked at her.

"They are. Same as people do."

"Uh-uh," I said.

"It's true! He's putting his pee-pee inside her pee-pee."

"You're lying!"

"He is too! That's what grown-ups do too. I saw it with my own eyes."

"You did not."

"I did too! I saw Freeda do that with that guy who left the toilet seat up. You know that closet I got? Up at the top, there's a part where the boards don't come all the way up. I was up there getting my shoe box, and I knocked it farther back on the shelf by accident. So I had to get a chair, and I got up there, and then I saw into the bedroom. And I saw them doing that. But he wasn't up on her back. He was on her belly."

"That's not true! Freeda don't even use that room. She sleeps downstairs."

"Yeah, she sleeps downstairs. But when she brings a guy home to piggyback ride, she brings him upstairs into that room."

Winnalee started giggling. She flicked the loops off of her lap and stood up. She held her hands above her head and made her hips go frontward and backward. "They were going like this," she said. "And they did this too." She tossed her head back and opened her mouth, her tongue googling out, and she started panting like a dog.

Winnalee sat back down and picked up her loom. I felt something scratch the top of my head, right where my skin was feeling tight and hurting. I reached up, but there was nothing there.

She went on, "It must have hurt or something, because Freeda yelled out. And then she shoved him off of her and told him to get his sorry ass dressed and out of there."

"You telling the truth?"

Winnalee took her finger and made an *X* over her chest. "Cross my heart! That's what they were doing. And that's what those cows are doing too. I'll tell you this much though. When I get big, no guy is gonna do that to me. They have big pee-pees and that's gotta hurt."

"I'm not gonna either," I said.

Winnalee was busy looping a yellow loop over and under, so she didn't see me tap at my head again. "Anyway, we gotta think up another bright idea," she said. "That's the one thing peculiar about bright ideas though. The way you can't get one just because you want one. Sometimes you get ten good ones in one day without even trying, and other times you can think till your head hurts and you're still not gonna come up with nothing."

"Seems that way to me too," I said.

Winnalee held up her ugly pot holder, which was orange and black and green, with only one loop of yellow. "How does this one look?"

I didn't want to hurt her feelings, so I told her, "It looks nice. Somebody will probably buy it." I pulled my newly made pot holder off of the loom and patted it flat. It was yellow and white, like a kitchen. Next I was going to make a pink and white one. "We have five pairs made now," I told her. "That's a dollar twenty-five if we sell them all."

"We'll sell them all. And while we're at the sale, we'll take what we make and buy a compass. I bet we'll find one there. And if we have any money left, we'll buy hula hoops, just like we said we'd do."

While she was talking, I felt something on my scalp a third time, but this time it downright hurt, like a bee sting. "Ouch!"

That's when Tommy jumped out from behind the tree, bellowing like a monster. Winnalee and me jumped up fast and started screaming, the loops on our laps jumping too.

Tommy started ha-ha-ing so hard that he doubled over, his hand slapping his knees. In his other hand, he was holding the chopped-off foot of a real chicken. He held it up and yanked at the stringy things dangling from the cut ankle, and the toes of

that dead chicken scrinched in and out like they were grabbing. "Here's a bright idea for you kiddies. If you feel a
chicken foot scratchin' at your head, turn around. Well, unless
you're so busy talking about screwin' that you don't notice."

Winnalee's face was red with mad. She balled her hands
into fists. "You asshole!" she screamed. She dove at him then,
her fists pounding him good.

Tommy was still laughing as he put his arms up to stop her
punches. "Oh, owie! Owie!" he cried, making his voice high
like mine. Getting punched or not, Tommy lifted his arms and
made his hips move in and out, as Winnalee had. "Look at me.
I'm getting a piggyback ride!" he said. He started panting.
This made Winnalee all the madder, and she started kicking at
his shins.

Tommy backed up then, saying "Ow!" for real. The back
of his legs hit the seat of the picnic table and he stopped.
That's when Winnalee shoved him. She shoved him so hard
that she grunted when she did it. His arm swung back and
whacked Winnalee's ma's jar, and it went flying, just like
he did. I clamped my hands over my mouth as I watched
Winnalee's ma roll across the table, bounce off the bench part
on the other side, and land upside down on the ground.

"My ma!" Winnalee screamed at the top of her lungs.
Winnalee didn't peek under the table, like I did. She ran
around to the other side, then cried out when she saw that
the lid of the jar had come off and that some of her ma was
spilled out on the grass. Then dumb Tommy—trying to help,
I suppose—grabbed the jar and yanked it up, spilling a trail of
ash behind the heap already lying there.

I couldn't move. I couldn't do anything but hold the sides
of my face and stare at Winnalee's spilled ma, streaked across
the grass in the shape of a falling star.

"Jesus!" Tommy shouted. "Why'd you shove me? I was
just horsing around. I—"

"My maaaaaaaaaa," Winnalee cried. "You spilled my ma!"

She snatched the jar from his hand, then plopped down on her knees and started scooping up the ashes. Her hands were shaking so bad as she tried pouring her ma back into the jar that most of what she was pouring slipped down the sides of the vase. "Maaaaaaaaa..."

I felt like I was gonna puke.

"What happened? What happened?" Aunt Verdella yelled as she burst out of the house and sprinted across the lawn, her bumps and belly thumping. I'd never seen Aunt Verdella run so fast.

Tommy and I backed up when Aunt Verdella reached us. "I didn't mean it, Mrs. Peters!" Tommy said. "She started beating up on me, and I bumped it."

Aunt Verdella gasped when she saw the spilled ma on the grass, that dead chicken's foot lying next to it, and Winnalee on her knees, her face wet with tears, her eyes pulled wide with scared.

"I tripped!" Tommy said. "It was an accident!"

"Here, here, honey. Let me," Aunt Verdella said, as she cupped her hands under Winnalee's and waited for Winnalee to pour what she was holding of her ma into her hands. The breeze was strong, and it caught flecks of the ashes that poured from Winnalee's hands into Aunt Verdella's and carried them in the air. I held my breath so none would get into my mouth or up my nose.

Aunt Verdella scooped up the big mound, then spread the powdered blades of grass and pinched the ash that was sunk down to the dirt. The same way she had picked through my knots to examine my sunburned scalp the day before. While she did this, I put my hand on top of my head so none of the ashes that were floating could seep down and settle on my scalp either.

While Aunt Verdella got all of Winnalee's ma scooped up that she could, she kept telling Winnalee that everything was going to be all right. That those bits she couldn't get were just gonna go right into the ground when the rain came, and how then at least a little part of her ma would have a resting place in the ground, like people are supposed to have.

After Aunt Verdella screwed the lid on tight, she pressed Winnalee right up to her fat ball. She rocked her side to side as she patted her head and cried right with her. The harder Winnalee sobbed, the harder Aunt Verdella patted her.

Tommy had to go home, because Aunt Verdella said he should have gone straight home in the first place when Uncle Rudy told him he didn't need his help till after he got back from the hardware store. "I know you didn't mean for it to happen, but you just stay away from these little girls from now on." Tommy's ugly head nodded with little jerks. "Yes, ma'am, yes, ma'am," he said. Then he hurried off to where his truck was parked, half on the grass, half on the driveway, over near the barn.

I stayed behind to scoop the scattered loops back into the plastic bags, while Aunt Verdella walked Winnalee to the house. Winnalee was tucked under one of Aunt Verdella's arms. Her other arm was holding the jar.

Try as hard as I could to keep my eyes on only the loops, I couldn't make my head stop cranking around so that I'd have to look at those patches of dusted grass and that dead chicken foot—both of which were giving me the willies.

Even from the yard, I could hear Winnalee's cries pouring through the screen door. I felt bad, knowing I should just be feeling sad for Winnalee, not thinking about what I was seeing and breathing.

When she was mostly done crying, Winnalee went home to tell Freeda what had happened. "And I don't want to make pot holders anymore today, because my head hurts now," she said before she went out the door.

After she left, Uncle Rudy came home, and before he could even get his hardware-store bag set down, Aunt Verdella told him the whole horrible story of what happened. "I'm just so upset, Rudy! It's not right. None of it's right.

That poor child. That poor little girl. If you could have seen her face, Rudy." Aunt Verdella cried till she was shaking. Uncle Rudy patted her shoulder, but he didn't say anything.

Aunt Verdella marched out of the room then and came back carrying her jewelry box and the milk jug where she kept her change. She opened the jewelry box and took out a wad of rolled bills tied with a rubber band. She emptied the change jug, coins clinking onto the table and some rolling over the edge. "Help me make piles, Button," she said. She flattened the pile, then used her pointy finger to slide dimes out of the heap.

"What are you doing, Verdie?"

Aunt Verdella looked up at Uncle Rudy. Her freckly face was even more blotched than it usually was. "I'm going to use my savings to buy a plot and a gravestone for that poor little girl's mama. That's what I'm gonna do. That child wants nothing more in this world than for her mama to have a final restin' place. And by George, I'm gonna see to it that that's exactly what she gets.

"I'll find out where her mama's family's buried, and I'll go there and buy her a plot and a stone, once I have enough. Then when it's all set up, I'll take Winnalee and Freeda there to see it, and we'll put their mama to rest."

Uncle Rudy's bottom lip sucked in a bit—at least as much as it could, with that wad of Copenhagen tucked inside it. "Verdie, you've been saving that money for a color TV set for almost four years now. You sure about this?"

Aunt Verdella looked up. "Rudy, all the color television programs in this world couldn't give me as much happiness as one glimpse of that little girl's face when she sees her ma's final resting place. It will be our little secret, Button. We won't say nothing to Winnalee or Freeda until it's all set up, okay?" I nodded.

Uncle Rudy stood there for a minute, his thumb tucked under one striped suspender. He opened his mouth to say something, then closed it again. He picked up his bag from the table and then patted Aunt Verdella's shoulder again. "You're a good person, Verdie," he said.

While Aunt Verdella and I made neat rows of stacked money, Aunt Verdella chattered and counted out loud, while I counted to make sure each row had ten dimes in it. And while I worked, I thought up Bright Idea #87: *On days when your head hurts on the outside because you didn't know when to get out of the sun, or on days when your head hurts so bad on the inside that you don't want to make pot holders because your ma got spilled, it can still turn out to be a good day if even one good person does one nice thing for you.*

"You girls moving out?" Uncle Rudy said as he came out of the house and saw me and Winnalee and Aunt Verdella lugging boxes of junk for the community sale into the Malones' truck.

Aunt Verdella giggled. "It looks like it, don't it?" Aunt Verdella hoisted a box of junk into the back of the truck, then straightened up, brushing her hands off. "A couple more boxes, and I'd've had to ask Freeda to borrow the wagon too!" she said.

It was so early in the morning that the grass was still dewy, because the sun wasn't yet high enough to reach over the tree-tops to warm it. "Here, let me give you girls a hand," Uncle Rudy said.

"This box, not that. You're dirty from the barn," Aunt Verdella said when he tried to take the box of baked goodies.

We packed up the truck, then Uncle Rudy helped wave us out of the driveway.

Me and Winnalee were excited as we held our plastic bags of pot holders on our laps. We'd made a whole eleven pairs, and if we sold them all, we'd practically be rich. "Just smile cute, and when people come by, you just ask them nicely if they want to buy a set. You girls are so darned cute that no one will be able to resist buyin' from you."

"Me and Button are gonna buy a camera today, if we make enough money, and if we find one. And a compass too." I nudged Winnalee's leg with mine so she'd shut up.

"A compass? Now, why would you girls want a compass?" When Aunt Verdella asked that, my throat got all gunky and tight, so that I had to clear it a couple of times. Luckily, we didn't have to answer, because Aunt Verdella got busy whacking the horn so two deer would get out of the road. After they did and we got moving again, she'd forgotten all about the compass question.

"Oh, look at this traffic!" Aunt Verdella said, all happy when we got to the community sale. There were two lines of cars and trucks. One was parked on the right edge of the dirt road, and those were the customers who were waiting to get in, even though the sale wasn't gonna start for another hour. Then there was our line, where the sellers drove slowly, waiting their turn to be let in to the mowed field where the sale would take place.

There was a chain strung across the grassy dirt road that led inside the sale part. A skinny little man in bib overalls was standing by it, checking for a seller's receipt that told him that whoever was trying to get in early was a seller and had paid for their spot. "Good morning, Pete," Aunt Verdella said, as she dug in her fat purse for the little slip of paper.

"Mornin', Verdella. It's gonna be a hot one today," he said. "Hope the rain holds off."

"It will!" Aunt Verdella said as she pulled her orange ticket out of her wallet and held it up so Pete could see it.

"You got the front lot," Pete told her, after he checked his clipboard. "How'd ya fandangle that one?"

Aunt Verdella giggled. "Oh, I got my ways!"

He unhooked the chain, then waved us through. As we drove over the wavy field, the truck rocked so that me and Winnalee and Aunt Verdella were bumping into each other.

Even though it was early, the field was already busy with sellers lining their stuff up on tables. Aunt Verdella had her window open, her freckly arm braced on the door as she waved good morning to the old man pushing a rusty bike across the road, which was nothing but a wide path worn down to the dirt from people walking on it year after year.

It took longer than it should have to lay our stuff out on the tables, because Winnalee kept putting things in dumb places. Then I'd have to switch things around so that the baby-sweater sets were over by the tiny crocheted blankets, and not over by the canning jars or the kitchen junk. I was glad when Winnalee got busy digging around in the bottom of her foot, looking for what was poking her, so that I could lay out our pot holders on the card table Aunt Verdella brought just for us.

"Oh, honey, didn't Auntie tell you to go home and put on some shoes?" Winnalee didn't answer Aunt Verdella because she was too busy digging and flinching.

I spread my seven pairs of pot holders out in two rainbow-shaped lines, on the side of the table closest to my folding chair. I didn't want people thinking that I'd made Winnalee's ugly pot holders. Winnalee didn't find what was poking her foot, so she just stepped on the toe part and got busy putting her pot holders out, matching them into pairs (even if they weren't pairs) and plunking them any which way.

She didn't even have all of hers spread before sellers who already had their stuff laid out started wandering by, gawking to see what we brought.

"Oh, pot holders," an old lady dressed like a man, and wearing a patterned scarf, said.

Winnalee smiled up at her. "You wanna buy some? They're a real deal. Just twenty cents each. Thirty cents for a pair. So you save a whole dime if you buy two of them."

I leaned over and whispered in Winnalee's ear. "They're supposed to be a quarter a pair." She practically shoved her finger up her nose, trying to signal for me to hush.

While she was showing the lady practically every pot

holder and telling her about them, I went to Aunt Verdella and tattled into her ear that Winnalee was saying our pot holders cost more. Aunt Verdella just giggled and said, "She's one smart cookie, isn't she?"

Soon as all the sellers were mostly set up, Pete took the chain down, and a fat guy carrying an orange stick waved the waiting cars over to the parking field. The people looked like a swarm of bees heading to a flower bed, as they hurried from the parking area to get to the sale tables.

I was too shy to say anything when two old ladies came to our table and asked about our pretty headbands and if we were sisters. Winnalee wasn't though. She told them we were twins. I kept my head down when she said that, so they wouldn't see that I was too ugly to be Winnalee's twin sister.

The people didn't think my pot holders were ugly though. They bought every one of them, for thirty cents a pair. And by the time Aunt Verdella unpacked our peanut butter and jelly sandwiches and poured us each a glass of Kool-Aid, even Winnalee only had three pot holders left.

We wanted to sell those three pot holders bad, so we could go do some shopping of our own. "Hi, mister." I looked up to see who Winnalee was talking to. It was a man with a face as round as a baby's and a bald, shiny head. He was carrying a lantern and a paper plate filled with oatmeal cookies that he'd bought at Aunt Verdella's table. "You wanna buy three pot holders? All three of them for only sixty cents. That's a real steal, mister."

The guy stopped and smiled. He had teeth like a jack-o'-lantern. "What you say you're selling there, little lady?"

"Pot holders. My twin and me made them ourselves." I cringed a bit when Winnalee said this, because I didn't want him thinking I'd made those ugly-colored things.

As he strolled over to our table, Winnalee slipped our homemade sign with our prices on it off of the card table and scooted it under her butt. Probably so he wouldn't see that he wasn't getting any bargain at all. "I don't really have no use for pot holders. I'm a bachelor and I don't cook much."

"You don't got a wife?" Winnalee asked.

"Nope," he said.

"Well, mister, if you bought our fine pot holders and gave them to a nice lady, she'd probably be so happy, she'd marry you. Then she'd move in and make you good things like pot roasts and hams. Probably even some cookies. You'd have someone to piggyback-ride with too." The man gave her a funny look, but he must have thought that Winnalee had a good plan, because he scarfed up all three pot holders and paid us our sixty cents.

"We're rich! We're rich!" Winnalee shouted after we counted our money. "Three fifty. We're rich!" Me and Winnalee hopped up and down while we hugged, and Aunt Verdella, who was stuffing the things some lady bought into a shopping bag she brought from home, giggled at us.

"Can we go shop now, Aunt Verdella?" Winnalee asked.

Aunt Verdella looked down the lane filled with shoppers. Her eyes looked worried. "Okay, but you two stay right on the path between the rows of tables. No wandering off, you hear? I want to be able to see you when I look."

Winnalee limped as we walked, because something was still in her foot. We hurried from table to table, as fast as she could go, looking for a compass and a camera. Most tables were filled with so much junk that after a few we got smart and asked the saleslady or -man if they had what we were looking for.

We finally found one who said he had a compass. A guy as big as a giant, with long hair and a beard.

"It's an antique," the giant said. "It was my grandpa's. Twenty-five cents."

I looked at the compass he was holding. It did look old, but it didn't look very special to me. Not special enough to be worth a whole twenty-five cents. Winnalee must have thought so too. She put a real sad look on her face and said, "Ohhhhh. Our daddy wants a compass for his birthday, but we only have fifteen cents." She said it so real-like that *I* almost believed her. "Did you know that we're twins?"

The giant guy scratched his dirty head, then said, "Twenty."

I nudged Winnalee. We had a whole wad of money stuffed into the change purse Aunt Verdella let us use. We could afford a whole dollar if that's what he wanted for it, much less a lousy twenty cents.

"We'll take it," I said.

It was Winnalee's turn to jab me. Hard, with an elbow poked right into my stomach. She gritted her teeth at me, then looked up at the man. "We'll take it for that twenty cents, *if* you give us a lesson on how to use it."

The big man talked slow as he explained what the parts of the compass were. "Suppose you wanted to go straight west. How would you find it using one of those things?" Winnalee said, interrupting him.

"Well . . ." He scratched his head again. He didn't look really smart, so I figured even with the compass and his instructions, we still might get ourselves good and lost. "See this *W* on here? That's west. You turn this housin' part—this part right here—till the *W* is over the top of the direction arrow. Now, you keep it flat, mind you, and ya turn the base of the compass till the red end, the pointer end right here, is over the top of this arrow. Then ya just start moving. Following the direction arrow. And if you ever get lost and get rattled, the arrow's gonna get rattled right with you. So stand still and quiet, then the arrow will settle down too and point you the right way."

I guess he was so busy talking that he didn't notice that Winnalee had wandered off to look at a ratty green purse-thing. "How much for this?" she asked, holding it up.

"The army bag?"

"If that's what it is, yeah." I knew what Winnalee wanted

that bag for. She wanted it to be our traveling bag, to put our stuff in when we went on our adventure.

"I'll give it to you for twenty cents," he said.

"Fifteen," she said.

"A deal. Thirty-five cents altogether."

Winnalee turned around, so that he wouldn't see that our change purse was stuffed full, and she dug out a dime and a quarter and handed it to him. Just in time too, because along came Aunt Verdella. I saw her walking fast, her head cranking this way and that as she called our names. When she saw us, she waved. "Where were you? Auntie couldn't see you!" Winnalee grabbed the compass out of the giant man's hand and tossed it in our new adventure bag.

"What do you want with that old army bag?" she asked.

"Um, it's gonna be our purse," Winnalee said.

Aunt Verdella giggled. "That sure is one ugly purse. Fanny Tilman's got some old purses in her booth. They'd be better than that old thing. Come on, Auntie will buy you each one."

Fanny Tilman was wearing a jacket again, even though it was hot. "I get chilled easily," she explained to Aunt Verdella when Aunt Verdella told her she was going to die of heatstroke. There was a mirror on Mrs. Tilman's table, and I thought maybe if she peeked at her red, sweaty face, she'd probably see that she wasn't as chilled as she thought. While me and Winnalee dug through the box of purses on the grass, Fanny Tilman and Aunt Verdella talked. "I hear that that Thompson boy has been hanging around Marty's ever since your cookout," Fanny said. "I hear he's quite smitten with her—and I've no doubt about that, the way she was carrying on with him that night. I was telling..."

I glanced up at Aunt Verdella, who was shaking her head and pointing down to Winnalee, who was busy trying to open the gold clasp of a white purse.

"It might do her good to hear some common sense for a change," Mrs. Tilman said with a huff.

"Hello, ladies!" Ada Smithy called. "Hi, girls." Winnalee and me looked up and said our hellos back.

After Ada showed them the nice pair of shoes she'd bought, she opened a bag and offered us all a piece of home-made horehound candy. She laughed when I wrinkled my nose and shook my head.

"That sure was a fun picnic, Verdella," Mrs. Smithy said as she held out her candy bag to Mrs. Tilman. "And that Freeda. What a bubbly, fun girl she is! My Tommy has such a crush on her, you know." Ada giggled. "You should see him primp before he heads over your way. I had to make him change the other day. He was gonna wear a nice Sunday shirt to go do barn chores!" Ada and Aunt Verdella ha-ha-ed over this. While they talked, I was watching Mrs. Tilman suck on her candy like it was lollipop-good, until Mrs. Smithy made that sweet remark about Freeda, then her mouth puckered. I decided right then that people's feelings about Freeda were going to be a lot like their feelings about horehound candy. Either they were going to love her, or they were going to hate her.

At four o'clock, we packed up the rest of Aunt Verdella's stuff (which wasn't much, because she sold real good), and we headed back to her house. Winnalee and me were happy because we were going to get to spend the night there, since Freeda was working, and Ma and Daddy were going to be at Marty's too, for an anniversary party for Bernice's mom and dad. Then Aunt Verdella was going to run me home first thing in the morning.

Aunt Verdella walked us over to Winnalee's house so we could get some dress-up clothes to go with our purses. We each picked out some clothes, then before we left her room, Winnalee dug out her Book of Bright Ideas, and we wrote, *Bright Idea #88: If a giant names his price, but it's a price you think is too much to pay, don't listen to him. Even if he is a giant.*

She closed our book and was gonna tuck it back under her pillow, but I stopped her. "Wait," I said. "I want to write something that the giant man told us about how to find where we're going. In case I forget, since I don't think you were listening to that part. If we write in here, we'll have it for later."

Winnalee handed me the book and I wrote on the same page, *Bright Idea #89: If you ever don't know which direction to go in, or you start moving in the right direction but then get lost along the way, don't get rattled and start moving fast, this way and that. Instead, stand still and be quiet. Then you'll be showed which way to go.*

Me and Winnalee were so tuckered out by suppertime that Aunt Verdella let us eat on the couch, then she took our plates into the kitchen for us. We were gonna play after supper, but instead all we did was sit propped against each other and watch *Gunsmoke*. We fell asleep before Marshal Dillon even got out of trouble.

I don't know who carried us up to the spare bedroom, but somebody did, because that's where we were when Aunt Verdella's singing woke us up. The whole house was filled with the good smells of bacon and coffee as we headed downstairs. After we ate some Malt-O-Meal and bacon and toast, and Uncle Rudy left to do some things in the barn, me and Winnalee went outside to play.

We got on our horses made of sticks and rode off across the backyard. "Hey, look at that tree!" Winnalee said, pulling her horse to a stop when we got to the edge, where the woods began. The tree was old and big. It came out of the ground with one trunk, then split into three halfways up. There was a big, dark spot at its feet.

Winnalee dropped her horse and ran to the tree, getting down on her hands and knees and parting the tall grass more, so she could peer into a hole that was rotted away at the bottom. "Hey, we could hide our adventure bag in here! Nobody would find it!" Winnalee ran around the tree, looking it up and down. "Look! Right here, where the three branches start, there's a flat spot! If we swing up from this branch here, we can get up there."

I looked at the branch and bit my lip. Winnalee grabbed the lowest branch poking sideways, then swung her legs up and wrapped them around the branch. She grunted some as she pulled herself upright, then scooted herself along the branch until she reached the trunk. "Look! It's like a little floor!" she yelled as she swung her feet down to the flat part. "Come on, Button! This is fun! Hey, this can be our magic tree. It can fly us to other places. Like California and to the moon. Come on! Do it like I did!" So after biting myself a little more, I climbed up, just like Winnalee had.

We played on our new magic tree for a couple of hours, flying to far-off places, then getting down and looking around until some mean people or space monsters started after us. Then we raced back to our magic tree and hoisted ourselves back up so it could carry us to safety. When we got tired of being chased by bad guys, we snuck to Winnalee's house and grabbed our adventure bag. We brought it back to the magic tree and stuffed it into the hole.

We had just gotten our adventure bag hidden when Aunt Verdella called out of the kitchen window that it was lunchtime.

"Get out the milk, will you, honey?" Aunt Verdella said to me. While I was getting it, and Winnalee was getting our favorite pink cups from the cupboard, Aunt Verdella leaned over and peered out the window. "Your ma's here, Button." Winnalee groaned. I would have too, except that my throat was busy making that other noise because Aunt Verdella said, "I hope she's not upset that I didn't bring you home earlier."

Aunt Verdella handed me a plate with a ham sandwich on it, and potato salad, and pickles. "You know, Button, I don't think I heard you make those noises in your throat even once since yesterday. Not until now." She kissed the top of my head. "Stay happy, okay? And sit down and eat your lunch. I'm sure your ma will wait till you eat, and if she can't, then Auntie will wrap it up for you to take home." She handed Winnalee her plate too.

"Hi, Jewel," Aunt Verdella said when Ma came through the door. "Sorry I was running so late. We're just having lunch. You hungry? How was the anniversary p—" She stopped talking when she looked up from pouring milk and saw that Ma's face was pinched with mad.

"Verdella, I thought you said you'd be running Evelyn home this morning. I've been waiting for her since eight o'clock." I'd never heard Ma talk so mad-sounding to Aunt Verdella before. (About her, yes, but never right to her face.) Me and Winnalee had our purses slung over the knob of our chairs, and Ma stared at them with crabby eyes. "And I'd appreciate it if you'd stop buying Button things. Old or new. On her birthday or Christmas, that's fine, but not in between. You spoil her rotten. It's no wonder that she'd rather be here than at home."

Winnalee picked up her red purse and folded her arms over it. "They were only a dime each," she said.

Aunt Verdella's mouth made a circle. "Well, Jewel, I'm sorry. I did say I'd run her home in the morning. I just lost track of time, though, and I figured you and Reece might like to sleep in this morning, being up late, and it being Sunday and all."

Ma looked like she hadn't slept. Her eyes were puffy and dark underneath—what Uncle Rudy called "boxer's eyes," which meant eyes that looked like they'd gotten punched, even if they hadn't. "Listen, Verdella. I've had it up to here with you acting like you own Evelyn. And I'm sick of shutting my mouth about it too. Evelyn is *my* daughter, not yours. I decide when she comes here and when she comes home. And I decide what she can have and what she can't."

"Well . . . Jewel, I . . . I'm sorry. I didn't know that . . ."

Ma was so angry that she was shaking. She put up her hand, like Uncle Rudy always did when he wanted Knucklehead to stop barking. "Geesh," I heard Winnalee mumble.

"You take a lot for granted, Verdella. Especially when it comes to Reece and Button. It's not my fault you never had a child of your own, but I'm not going to let you steal Button from me, like you stole Reece from Mae. You got that?"

Aunt Verdella gasped.

Without saying a word out loud, I begged Ma to stop. The way she was shaking, though, her cheeks stained red, I knew she wasn't going to. Not yet anyway.

"I don't know what your problem is, Verdella. But I know it has something to do with the fact that you couldn't have children of your own. And probably something to do with that little boy you ran over years before you came into this family. But I'll tell you this much, Verdella. No matter what the reason, you don't have any right trying to fill that empty place with other people's children."

Poor Aunt Verdella looked like she'd been punched. Her hand went over her heart, and tears bubbled out of her eyes.

It was like every word Ma spoke was a bullet. A bullet that hit Aunt Verdella first, then bounced off her and pinged right into my chest.

For a little bit, Aunt Verdella just stared at Ma, her face going bedsheet white. Then she started shaking—more so than Ma—and big sobs started choking her breath. She stumbled to the table and almost fell before she could pull out a kitchen chair to sit on. Winnalee, who was standing right next to me, took my hand and squeezed it. For the first time since I knew her, Winnalee didn't have a thing to say.

Ma blew out one more angry breath, then grabbed my free arm and jerked me out the door, my lunch left on the table where I'd put it.

I was crying as Ma drug me to the car, and so was she, even though she was still stiff with meanness.

As we pulled out of the driveway, fast, I saw Winnalee running barefoot across the yard toward her house, her loops trailing behind her. I hoped and hoped that she was going to the field to get Uncle Rudy, or to her house to get Freeda.

Anybody who could help Aunt Verdella stop shaking and crying.

11

"Stop scratching your arms, Evelyn!" Ma snapped as we drove home. I looked down at my skin, which was blotchy with red patches and streaked with fingernail scratches, and I tucked my hands under my legs to keep from scratching them more.

When we got out of the car, Ma headed to the house and I followed, staying as far behind her as I could. As soon as we got inside, Ma told me to get to my dusting, because I'd missed cleaning day. I hurried to get some cleaning rags and the Pledge from under the sink. My hands were as shaky as Aunt Verdella's as I reached for them, and there was a lump in my throat that felt as big as my head.

I hurried into the living room and started on the coffee table, where I always started. I had to blink to clear my eyes enough to see if I was leaving streaks.

A couple of hours later, while Ma was doing dishes and I was wiping down the heating register right by the bay window, Freeda Malone's red truck came rushing up the driveway. She slammed the truck's door hard when she got out and marched to the house, jerking open the screen door and coming inside without knocking. "Jewel? Jewel!" she yelled.

Ma came from the kitchen, her dishcloth in her hand. She didn't even have time to close her mouth before Freeda lit into her.

"What in the hell do you think you were pulling last night? Making a goddamn scene like you did, and siccing those biddies on me? I went to the goddamn can to take a piss on my break, and there that bitch was—Bertie, or Beatrice, or whatever the hell she said her name was—and she lit into me good. Accused me of having an affair with Reece. She said you were onto the whole thing and that I wasn't pulling the wool over anybody's eyes.

"Listen here, Jewel Peters. I may be a lot of goddamn things, but the one thing I ain't is a home-wrecker. I wouldn't have a fling with Reece if he asked me to—which he hasn't— because I don't sleep with married men. I don't have many principles, but I've got that one. I don't care how much sweet-talkin' a married man gives me, or how goddamn cute his ass is. If he's married, I tell him where to go." Freeda was so mad that her whole body looked as if it was gonna snap in half.

"I just couldn't believe you last night. The way you sat there fuming when the band asked Reece to get up and play a few numbers with them. Yep, I did suggest it to them, but big goddamn deal. So did about twenty other people. And, yeah, Reece got a little flirty into the mic when he asked me to bring them drinks, but, honey, it was all a part of the show. And like it or not, Reece is a flirty kind of guy, just as I'm a flirty kind of woman. And you'd probably be one too, if you weren't such a tight-ass. But instead you made a scene, slapping Reece's face as soon as he got off the stage and came over by you, and taking off, leaving Reece stranded. Crissakes! What in the hell is the matter with you, anyway? You trying to get my ass fired or to just have me run out of town? Goddammit, I don't need this shit! If I wanted gossip, I would have stayed back in my own stinkin' hometown!"

Freeda stopped to take a breath. She was rocking from one leg to the other, like people do when they get so mad they're ready to explode.

"Are you that goddamn jealous that you want to scratch the eyes out of any woman who dares look at your man? If that's the case, you'd better keep your nails sharpened, missy. Reece is one good-lookin' guy. But then, you know that. That's why you keep his sorry ass glued to home whenever you can, isn't it? Jesus, Jewel. The man loves playing his music. Any idiot can see that! And he's damn good at it. Why in the hell do you want to rob him of the one thing he really loves doing?"

Freeda paused only long enough to take a deep breath. "What the hell's the matter with you, anyway? Creating a scene like you did at Marty's last night, then marching over to Verdella's today to create an even worse one!

"Winnalee came to get me. Verdella was a mess when I got there. A goddamn mess. She told me what you said to her. And what she was crying too hard to say, Winnalee told. After she settled down some, Verdella told me how you brought up that painful incident from her past. How could you be so goddamn cruel, Jewel? How? Did you know that that poor woman thinks that God Almighty Himself punished her for that accident by making her sterile? Jesus, Jewel! She couldn't leave her house for ten years after she ran over that little boy, for fear that if she did, she'd accidentally kill somebody else. She stayed holed up, punishing herself until her folks died and she was forced to leave home. Then you go and reopen that wound, and for what? To get even with her because your husband and daughter adore her?

"You know what, Jewel? You're a bitch. Just a fuckin' bitch. That woman is nothing but sweet to you. Even after you ripped her a new asshole today, she defended you to me. You're not even good enough to eat that woman's shit. You know that, Jewel Peters? It's not her fault that Reece and Button slipped under her wing to keep from shriveling up and dying without any love from their own mothers, now, is it? What in the hell you doing, blaming Verdella for who she is? What kind of mission you on, anyway? You flip your goddamn lid, or what?"

I don't know what I expected Ma to do, but for sure not what she did. The rag fell from her hand and her shoulders dropped till I was sure they'd snag on her belt. She leaned against the wall and tipped her head against it, as though even that part of her didn't have the energy to keep itself up. Then her face screwed up, and she started crying. "I don't know what got into me. I just . . . I just snapped. Last night, this morning . . . I just snapped."

"Well, what needs to snap is that rod you have stuffed up your ass."

Ma's arm went up slowly, and her hand cupped her forehead. Her shoulders pumped with each sob. "The truth hurts, don't it?" Freeda said.

All of a sudden, it was like Ma's tears washed clean every drop of mad Freeda had in her. Freeda took a big breath and it whooshed out of her. She groaned a bit, then went over to Ma and took her elbow. She led her to the recliner. "Come on. Sit down before you fall on your bony ass."

I knew that within a second or two Ma was gonna realize I was there and tell me to go outside or into my room and close the door, so I backed up and slipped inside my room. I left the door open a couple of inches and stayed just to the side of it, so my big ears could hear everything and I could take peeks if I wanted to.

Ma was crying hard. "Aw, Jesus. You got some Kleenex around here?" Freeda asked.

Freeda's feet stomped across the floor and came right to the bathroom across from my room. I heard the toilet-paper roller spin and then Freeda's foot stomps thumping back into the living room.

"Here. I couldn't find any Kleenex. Come on now, blow."
Ma did, and for a time there was no sound but for Ma's sniffling. I peeked around the corner and saw that Freeda had sat
down on the couch, right across from where Ma was sitting on
the recliner.

"Look. You aren't gonna like me very much for sayin' what
I'm about to say, but, hell, you don't like me as it is anyway....

"Jewel, if you bite the hands that feed you, you're gonna
end up even more bitter and ugly inside than you already are.
I don't think I need to say any more about what you pulled on
Verdella a bit ago. I think you know already just how wrong
that was. And I hope to hell you have enough decency to right
it, the best you can. So instead of harping more on that, I'm
just gonna say the rest of what I came here to say.

"Jewel, you go accusing a man of sleeping around every
time he steps out of the house, then sure as shit, that's exactly
what he's gonna end up doin'. It's like ... well, it's like owning
a dog—if you keep a dog on a short leash and give him nothing but bitchin' and swattin', and you never play with him or
scratch his belly, you'll keep him in the yard, all right. At least
while the chain holds. But sooner or later, that dog is gonna
snap it, and then he's gonna make a beeline for the hills."

Ma was still crying. I couldn't see her, but I could hear her,
and just hearing her cry was making my own eyes water.

"Now, it might look to most people like you don't give a
shit about either your husband or your little girl, but I don't
buy that. I think you love them with all your heart, but you
just don't know how to show it. You've about snuffed every
bit of joy out of that man. And that kid of yours, you got her
so uptight that she's gonna bite and scratch herself to death.
Obedience isn't love, Jewel."

Just hearing Freeda's words, even if I didn't understand
them exactly, made the water in my eyes roll down my cheeks.

"I can't compete with Verdella for Reece and Evelyn's affection. How can I? Verdella is so openly affectionate with

Evelyn. As for Reece...oh, Freeda. Just look at me. Look at Reece. How on earth can someone like me keep someone like him?" Ma said.

Freeda slapped her leg. "Is that what this is about? Your looks? For crissakes, Jewel. Look around once! There's all kinds of good-looking men paired up with women so god-damn ugly you could puke just by looking at them. You're not that bad-looking, Jewel. Or you wouldn't be at all, if you'd loosen up and smile a little, and if you'd fix up a bit. But you feel ugly, and that's the part that's hurting you. You got Button feeling ugly too.

"Look at me, Jewel. Look at me good. My nose is too big, but I got nice eyes, so I play up on them. And look at my thighs. If they got any thicker, they'd catch fire from the rub-bin' together they do when I walk. But I got big boobs, so I bring the eye up there by showin' them a little. I sweat like a pig when I'm worked up too. See how I'm sweatin' now? Anyway, what I'm getting at is the fine art of distraction. That's the trick, honey. Distraction! You got a full-length mirror around here?"

Ma nodded and led Freeda to the guest room—which was really the sewing room—and I stepped out of my room and followed quietly, knowing that if I got caught, I could just say that I was going to use the bathroom. Freeda drug Ma to the mirror (which was propped up against the wall because Daddy hadn't gotten around to tacking it on the back of the door, even though Ma asked him to about a hundred years ago), and she said, "There, now look at this, Jewel. Let's start right on top. The best thing you got going for you here is your eyes. Big, deep-set—but not so deep-set that they sink into your head—and nice, thick, curly lashes. Well, if people could see the pale things, that is. You know what a good eyebrow pluck-ing and a little makeup could do for those eyes? Well, proba-bly not." Freeda reached up and ran her fingers through Ma's oatmeal hair. "And this. What in the hell kind of hairdo do you call this, anyway? You're thirty-three years old, and I'll bet you haven't changed your hair since you left high school. Oh well, hair's the easy part."

Freeda's head dipped down to face Ma's middle. She clamped her hands on the waist of Ma's dress and bunched the material tight. "Just look at this, will ya? Starlets once had ribs removed to get waists as tiny as this! Course, you keep this asset hidden under these damn sacks you wear." Freeda patted Ma's chest where her boobies should be. "You don't have much up here, so you gotta bring the eye to that pretty waist-line. You see what I'm getting at, Jewel? Distraction! The trick is to learn distraction, just like I have."

Freeda backed up and leaned on one leg again. "Granted, I'm a pretty good-lookin' woman in spite of my shortcomings, but I'll tell you one thing, Jewel. Even if I was as ugly as a mud fence, I'd still be struttin' my stuff. And that's no goddamn lie. I don't care who we are, or what we look like, we've still got something worth struttin', and we should be proud of whatever the hell that something is. No matter what anybody says to us to the contrary."

I wasn't sure why, but those words were the words that made Ma cry the hardest. I pulled away from the door and leaned against the wall.

"That's what this is about, isn't it, Jewel? Ya took a lot of shit growing up about how you weren't good enough. Well, honey, I got dished up a whole shitload of crap as a kid too, but I'll tell you this. It wasn't your fault you got knocked down as a kid, but it's your responsibility to get yourself back up now. You gotta reach inside and find what you're made of, and you gotta prove them wrong. You don't, and you're not only gonna grow more bitter and ugly, but you're gonna grow a daughter just like you."

"I never say mean things to Evelyn!"

"You don't have to say them. That kid looks just like you, Jewel. And if your looks aren't good enough for you, how in the hell is Button gonna think they're good enough for her?

And you have that kid so afraid of doing something wrong that she hardly breathes when you're around. She can't ask for anything she wants, and she couldn't give a spontaneous hug if she tried. That's sad, Jewel. Goddamn sad!"

It was quiet for a time, then Ma said, "I never was good enough for them. Not my mom. Not my dad. Not my sisters. Not even Reece and Evelyn. They can't get away from me fast enough. They take every opportunity to go by Verdella."

"Course they do. Verdella makes everybody feel good about themselves. You know why? Because she loves everyone for who they are, that's why. And she digs deep if she has to, to find that one good thing. And because she does, just being around that woman feels good. And if it's true that those two run away from you to get to Verdella, it's certainly not because she's better or more beautiful, for crying out loud. It's because she knows how to love. Simple as that."

After Ma cried some more, Freeda said, "Look. It's a fact of life. If a woman doesn't feel good about how she looks, she doesn't feel good about herself, period. So what do you say you let Freeda Malone give you a hand?"

I heard Ma sniffle. "What do you mean?"

"I mean just what I said. I may not know much about a lot of things, but the one thing I do know is how to take what someone's got and make it look better. I worked in a beauty shop for a time. Not cutting hair—I never did finish beauty school, though I cut a lot of hair anyway—but I got a job in one, cleaning. The owner figured out real fast that I knew lots about hair and makeup and all that stuff, so she hired me to do makeovers. She said my mascara tube was a goddamn magic wand. So she started advertising 'complete makeovers.' I'd look the women over, say what I thought they needed, and Lucy would give them the cut I suggested, roll it up, then I'd fix it for them. I'd do their makeup too. Shit, I'll bet I was single-handedly responsible for half the pregnancies in that town during the months I worked there—which might not have been a good thing, because not all of them were married—but goddammit, those women felt like a million bucks when they left that place.

"I'll bet when you look in this mirror, you don't see nothing but a homely, skinnier-than-shit woman who can't do nothing right. But you know what I see when I look at you, Jewel Peters? Potential! That's what I see!

"Course, we can rat your hair up to the roof and slap makeup on you an inch thick, but it ain't gonna help your cause if you feel ugly inside. I can help with that too. Look at ya, Jewel. Fingernails like stubs—either from chewing on them or from working them to the bone, I ain't sure which. Wearing those clothes that cover up the little ya do have. And lemme guess . . . when Reece lays his hands on you, I'll bet you freeze up like a Popsicle. You must've heard before how a man wants a lady in the kitchen and a whore in the bedroom? Well, shit, with me, they get a whore in the kitchen too, but that's besides the point. The point is that I could have any man I set my mind on—and you can damn bet that I could keep him too, *if* I wanted to. I got a lot I could teach you, if you want me to.

"Okay, I've got to get back and get ready for work. But tomorrow I want you to come over. You hear? Marty's is closed on Mondays, so I'll be home when you get back from work. Fix up something for supper if you have to, and tell that man of yours it's on the stove. Then you head over to Verdella's and you make your apologies to her. If you aren't willing to do that, then I don't want a damn thing to do with you. But if you make things right with her, then you come over by me afterward. I'm gonna teach you how to loosen up, pretty up, and lighten up. You got it?"

I hurried down the hall and slipped around the corner of my room, just as Freeda and Ma came down the hall. I peeked out once they passed. Freeda headed to the door and put her hand on the knob. "And don't bother thankin' me either. I ain't doin' this because I'm particularly fond of you. I'm doing it because . . . well, I don't know exactly why I'm doing it. I guess I just like challenges." And with that, Freeda Malone was gone.

I expected Ma to head back to the kitchen after Freeda left, but she didn't. She sat down in the living room for the longest time, then she got up and paced. She cried a little here and there, her arms folded, her one hand rubbing the opposite arm. Finally she called for me. I waited for just a little bit— about as long as I thought it would take to walk from my bed to my doorway—then I went into the living room and blinked, like I had no idea that anything at all had gone on. "Yes, Ma?"

"We have to run over to Aunt Verdella's. You go on and get in the car while I get my purse." I did as she told me to do.

"Stay out in the yard and play while I talk to Aunt Verdella," she told me when we pulled in the drive.

I knew why she told me to stay outside. She wanted to talk to Aunt Verdella about the mean things she'd said to her, and she didn't want my big ears hearing any of it. What I didn't know, though, was what she expected me to play.

After she went inside, I looked over at Winnalee's house. I didn't see her in the yard though. I looked around for Uncle Rudy, but I didn't see him either, even though his black truck was in the driveway.

I walked over by the house, right under the kitchen window, and I sat down on the edge of one of those little cement boxes that sit around basement windows. From there, I could hear my ma and Aunt Verdella talking.

"...No, it's not okay, Verdella. I had no business talking to you the way I did."

"And I shouldn't dote on Button the way I do, Jewel.. You're right. She's not *my* daughter."

"That's true, but you're her aunt. And you're the best aunt a child could have."

Their words sounded good, if you read them on paper,

maybe. But spoken in stiff-sounding voices, they only sounded polite.

Ma cleared her throat. "About what I said, regarding your accident years ago. I'm sorry for that the most, Verdella. Freeda was right. It was cruel and mean of me to open that old wound."

I waited for Aunt Verdella to say that that was okay too, but she didn't. Instead, she said, "Jewel, that's something that breaks my heart every single time I think of it. I still have nightmares of that morning. And when I'm drivin', and I see any movement out of the corner of my eye, my whole insides shake, even if I am on a county road, and I still can't back my car up without shivering." I heard Aunt Verdella's voice gasp a bit from tears. "I don't think I'll ever get over that. And why should I? That little boy's poor mama and daddy will never get over it. You know?"

"Oh, Verdella. I'm just so sorry..." The politeness went out of Ma's voice, and sadness mixed with tears took its place.

"Freeda thinks that I believe God has punished me by making me sterile, but the truth is, I prayed to Him not to give me a child, even though there's nothing in this world I wanted more. But I told Him to give any child who would have come to me to that poor woman and man who lost their little boy instead. I had the local paper sent to me for eight years, and I scoured it every week, till I found what I was looking for. News that they'd become parents again. I finally could cancel my subscription when their third little one was born. A boy the third time. Somehow, that made me feel better enough to at least let go of it on some days."

Ma and Aunt Verdella were both crying by this point in the story, their words too muffled with tears for me to hear what they were saying anymore.

I felt Knucklehead's wet nose against my leg and looked up to see Uncle Rudy coming through the yard. I stood up quick, so he wouldn't know I was being all ears.

"Hi there, Button," Uncle Rudy said. He looked up at the house, the crinkles at the corners of his eyes crinkling even more. "Is your ma inside?"

"Yeah," I said. "She came to tell Aunt Verdella she was sorry for the things she said, I think." I said the first part so he wouldn't worry, and the second part so he wouldn't think I was eavesdropping, even though I was. He nodded his head once.

There were two metal lawn chairs over by the picnic table—one turquoise, one red—and that's where Uncle Rudy headed, telling me to come keep him company. He sat in the red one and saved the turquoise one for me because he knew I liked that one best. He pulled his Copenhagen can from his pocket and tapped the lid before opening it. He took a pinch, then held the can out to me, like he always did. "Snuff?" he said. He chuckled a bit when I shrunk away from his hand and made a face. He tucked the wad inside his lip and put the can back into his pocket with a chuckle. "Ah, nuts," he said when he settled down, like he'd say sometimes, for no reason all at.

We didn't say nothing, but that was okay. I liked sitting with Uncle Rudy whether we were talking or not. While he looked out at the field, I looked at the back of his neck where the sunshine had settled as he sat bent forward, his elbows resting on his knees. I looked at the way the wrinkles there were crisscrossed over his skin, making diamond shapes.

"Where's your little friend?" he asked.

"I don't know. In her house, I suppose. I forgot to ask if I could go get her before Ma went in to talk to Aunt Verdella."

I could feel Uncle Rudy looking at my arms, which were still rashed and scratched red. He opened his mouth to say something, but then Winnalee came out of her house. She jumped off the steps, set her ma down on the grass, lifted her arms, and started spinning in circles, the hot breeze wrapping her hair around her as she twirled. I didn't need to hear her to know she was singing. I could tell by the way she had her head tilted to the side and by the bouncy way she spun. She stopped, put her arms down, and must have seen Ma's car in the drive. She squealed when she saw me and hurried to pick up her ma. Her white mesh slip looked like it was waving at me, just like her arm, as she came running across the grass. I waved back.

There were only two lawn chairs, but they were plenty big for all three of us, so I scootched over and made room for Winnalee and her ma.

"Is Aunt Verdella done crying yet?" Winnalee asked.

"She is," Uncle Rudy said. "Or she was before Jewel got here. But you know how women are." He spit a brown wad on the grass, then looked over at us. At my arms, especially. "I suppose you girls were there when Jewel said those things to Verdie, huh?"

"Yeah," Winnalee said. "She made Aunt Verdella cry really hard."

"Yes, she did."

"Uncle Rudy, is it true what Button's ma said? Did Aunt Verdella really run a kid over and kill him?" My whole insides felt puky when she asked him this.

"Yes, Winnalee, but it wasn't her fault. It was an accident. It happened a long, long time ago. Long before I met her. Aunt Verdie was driving to work in the middle of winter, and the highway was icy. She was going real slow, because she hadn't been drivin' long and she wasn't real good at it yet. She was going so slow she couldn't make it up a hill, so she put the car in reverse so she could get a running start. She didn't have any way of knowing that a little boy was sledding in his yard, because she couldn't see him. He came over the bank as she was backing up, and he slid right into her. She didn't even know what she hit until she got out of the car. And I know it's hard hearing such a bad story, but I didn't want you kids thinking that your auntie Verdie did something bad by choice."

"And he was dead, then?" Winnalee asked.

"Yes, he was."

"That's sad," Winnalee said. I didn't say that it was sad too, but I sure felt it.

I looked over at Winnalee. She was staring down at the urn propped between her legs. "Could Aunt Verdella have killed that boy just from being mad at him?" she asked. "Like, if he said she couldn't wear her favorite dress, and it made her so mad that when she left for . . . well, for the store or something . . . that she thought she wished he'd die?"

Uncle Rudy reached over and patted Winnalee's bare arm. "No, honey. No."

For a time, only the birds and the wind said anything. I reached out and took Winnalee's hand.

"Uncle Rudy?" Winnalee asked after a while. "Is Aunt Verdella really trying to steal Button?" Uncle Rudy smiled slowly. He shook his head and the diamonds on his neck stretched and scrunched with each turn. "Course not," he said. "She's just lovin' her. That's all."

After a while, Ma and Aunt Verdella came out of the house. They walked down the steps side by side, their two arms twined together. They both had red eyes, patchy faces, and shaky smiles on their faces. I could see from just one glance at Ma that something in her had changed. And when I saw her look over at Freeda's house with something in her eyes that looked like both a "thank you" and a "please," I had a guess that the changes were just beginning.

12

Late in the afternoon, the Monday after the big yelling-and-making-up day, Ma came outside where I was doing nothing but sitting on the tire swing, missing Winnalee. "Button?" she called. When I got to the steps, Ma was dangling a key from her fingers. "You want to run over to the Malones' with me for a minute? I finally found the key to Mae's back door and thought I'd drop it off before I start dinner. Your daddy has to work late tonight, so we'll have time."

"Sure!"

I knew that Freeda never locked their doors, so she probably wouldn't exactly do flips when she got that key, but I didn't tell Ma that, because I wanted to see Winnalee. Even if it was only for a minute or two.

"Daddy's over at Uncle Rudy and Aunt Verdella's," I said when I saw a splotch of Daddy's truck peeking through the trees along their driveway.

"Oh," Ma said, "I thought he was working late." Ma didn't even look at his truck when we got level with the driveway. She was too busy looking at Grandma Mae's house. She looked a bit scared, like maybe she thought Freeda might yell at her for coming over, even if Freeda told her to come when she got done yelling at her yesterday.

Winnalee burst out of the house the second Ma stopped the car. "I saw you coming!" she yelled in a voice that sounded more like singing than talking. Winnalee was wearing a lady's dress I'd never seen before. It had big flowers on it. I think she must have had a belt strapped around the middle so she wouldn't trip, because the material was bunched up over something around her middle. She was barefoot as usual.

As soon as we stepped inside the house, we heard two voices laughing. One was Freeda's, and the other one sounded like my daddy's. Ma must have thought so too, because she got a sour look on her face.

"Freeda, Button and her ma are here!"

Daddy's laugh stopped quick, but not Freeda's. She came out of her bedroom shaking her head. "I don't know how you put up with that guy, Jewel," she said, while still laughing. She tossed her head back and turned her face some, like she wanted her next words to float inside the room where Daddy was. "He puts in a new light fixture, and it actually works, and he's so damn proud of himself that he gets cocky!"

Freeda waited a second, like she thought maybe Daddy would yell something smart-alecky back, but he didn't. She shrugged, then headed toward the kitchen, leaving Ma and me still standing in the dining room. "How about a cup of coffee, Jewel? I was just about to make some."

"Oh, I wasn't staying," Ma said. "I just stopped by to drop off a key for the back door."

"A key?" she asked.

Ma reached over and quickly set the key down on the dining-room table. Her face was redder than it usually was.

"Wanna see the pictures I drew?" Winnalee asked.

"Sure," I said, my eyes still on Ma.

"Come on," Winnalee said. Ma and I started following Freeda and Winnalee to the kitchen. We hadn't yet cleared the living room when Daddy came out of Freeda's room, coming face-to-face with Ma and me. He had his hand bunched around a screwdriver and was carrying a box with a picture of a ceiling light on the side. The old light was stuffed in it, poking out of the top of the box. Daddy looked a little red-faced. "Her ceiling light was shot," he said. "A short. So I picked one up in town."

Freeda appeared in the kitchen doorway. She had one of those little scoopers from a coffee can in her hand. She looked at Daddy first, her eyebrow on that side raised, then she looked over at Ma, and her other eyebrow lifted. "Thanks, Reece. Now get lost so us gals can talk about you." Daddy almost ran to get to the door. "Oh," Freeda called after him. "And before you put that little toolbox away, why in the hell don't you hang that mirror up in your wife's sewing room, huh?"

"See ya, Uncle Reece," Winnalee called, but I doubt Daddy heard her, because I think he was already halfway down Peters Road.

"Come on, sit down, Jewel."

Ma sat down, her back as stiff as the chair she sat on.

"Winnalee, get those papers off the table."

"Wait! I wanna show them to Button!"

Winnalee might not have been good at coloring (her crayon marks going every which way, her colors all goofy), but she sure was a good drawer. Her paper—which must've come from Daddy, because it didn't have good lines—was filled up with pretty fairies with skirts shaped like bells, and pointy wings coming out of their backs, both wings the same size.

"They're real nice," I told Winnalee, and she said thanks. "You want to draw some too, Button?"

"Out on the coffee table," Freeda said.

"No!" Winnalee whined. "I want to color here! All my stuff is already out!"

I started picking up the crayons. "I'll help you," I said quietly.

"No! I'm going to color right here." This time she screamed.

"I said move it, kiddo. You take cream or sugar, Jewel?" I glanced up at Ma, who was watching Winnalee hard.

"Um, no. Just black, thank you."

One by one, I picked the crayons up and tucked them back into neat little rows. That is, until Winnalee grabbed the box from me and shook them out onto the table. I held out my hands to catch the red-orange crayon that was rolling to the edge.

"Damn it, Winnalee. Now scoot! We're going to have coffee here. Go on!" When Winnalee didn't budge, Freeda scooped her papers into a heap.

"You're crumpling them!" she bellowed.

"I'm gonna dump them in the garbage next. Just try me, Winnalee. You gonna move into the living room, or do I throw them out?" When Winnalee grabbed the crayon box from me and shook them out onto the table, Freeda ran to the trash can. "I mean business, Winnalee. You get your butt out of here now, or they're going in."

I didn't know what to do, and I guess Ma didn't either, because she was staring just like me, with her mouth open.

"Stop it!" Winnalee screamed. She ran to Freeda and started slapping at her hands to get her pictures back. She whacked Freeda right in the bump, and Freeda cussed and tossed Winnalee's pictures into the air. Winnalee was crying and screaming both, as she tried to catch the pages. "I hate you!" Winnalee screamed. "And I hate the way you tell me what to do. You're not my ma!" Freeda stopped, her arms going limp at her sides.

Winnalee sobbed as I helped her gather up her papers. Freeda had tears in her eyes too.

I spread out the pages and crayons and pencils on the coffee table, while Winnalee sat on the floor, her arms folded tight over her chest. "I hate her," she hissed. "She crinkled my best fairy."

"You should have listened to her the first time," I said quietly.

In the kitchen, I could hear Freeda telling Ma how she didn't know what to do with "that kid" and that she should count her lucky stars that I was not as headstrong as Winnalee.

"Well, Freeda," Ma said. "Any kid would act like Winnalee if they knew they could get away with it."

"Well, what in the hell am I gonna do with her? You saw how she doesn't mind!"

Ma laughed a little. "Maybe I have something to teach you, in exchange for my beauty lessons. When it comes to discipline, I've got plenty to spare." And Freeda said, "No shit!"

In no time at all, the whole fight between Freeda and Winnalee was over, and Winnalee was drawing and chattering, and Freeda was telling Ma how she should update her hairdo. "I should give you a short, cute bouffant do."

"You cut hair? I thought you only set it."

"I can cut hair. I've cut lots of hair—just not in a beauty shop."

"No, here, like this," Winnalee said, right in my ear that was busy trying to hear the story Freeda was telling Ma. "You're making angel wings, but fairy wings are different. Like this." Winnalee was yapping so much that I missed the whole story, even though it had to be a good one, because it made Ma laugh. And not one of those soft kind of laughs either, but the kind that jiggles your belly. I'd never heard my ma laugh like that before.

Winnalee decided we should have some cookies then, so I followed her into the kitchen, where Freeda and Ma were still dabbing at their laugh-damp eyes. Winnalee hoisted up her lady's dress and leaped up on the counter to fetch the fudge-striped cookies.

Freeda got up quick. "Get your ass down from there, before you fall and crack your head open."

"I'm gettin' the cookies!" Winnalee grabbed the bag, then reached an arm around Freeda's neck, and let Freeda swing her down. Freeda kissed the top of Winnalee's head. "You're a sassy little shit," she said, "but I love you anyway."

"Love you too, Freeda," Winnalee said, meaning it this time, even though ten minutes ago she hated her enough to want her dead.

"Yoo-hoo!" Me and Winnalee glanced at each other and grinned when we heard Aunt Verdella's voice. We raced out of the kitchen and into Aunt Verdella's arms for our hugs. "We're gonna have cookies. Want some?" Winnalee held up the bag so Aunt Verdella could see what kind.

"Just a couple," Aunt Verdella said. "I've gotta watch my girlish figure, you know." We headed into the kitchen, our arms wrapped around each other.

"Hi, Jewel!" Aunt Verdella sounded surprised to see Ma sitting at the table having coffee with Freeda.

"Grab a cup, Verdella," Freeda said. "The percolator's here on the table."

We let go of Aunt Verdella so she could get a cup down from the cupboard. "Want to see the fairies we're drawing?" Winnalee asked.

Aunt Verdella sat down while Freeda poured coffee into her cup. As Winnalee ran to gather up our pictures, Aunt Verdella caught her reflection in the chrome toaster. She tilted her head this way and that while she plucked at the tufts of hair poking out from the bobby pins holding back the sides. The stripe on the top of her head had gotten as wide as a belt. "Oh, Jesus, look at this mess!"

"Funny you should mention hair. I was just telling Jewel that she should change her hairdo. Update it a bit. A nice bouffant."

"Oh, that would be nice. I should do something with mine—probably shave it off," she said with a laugh. "I don't know what color to make it this time." Aunt Verdella took the fairy pictures Winnalee handed her. "Jewel, you remember when I colored it with that off-brand that time, then permed it myself?" She laughed, her belly shaking. "The box said Bright Auburn, or something like that. Good God, I don't know if it was the coloring, or if I left my perm on too long, or what, but remember that? I looked like a red squirrel who tried lighting a woodstove with gas. Clumps of red-orange hair fell right out in my hands. Poor Rudy, he didn't know what to do when he came home and saw me. I know he wanted to laugh, but he was afraid to. Once he'd laughed at my coloring concoction—that time I went jet-black, and ended up lookin' like a witch—and I started cryin'. Course, that was back in the days when I'd get all emotional from the curse. Anyway, there we were, needing to go to a wedding, and I had that red-squirrel thing going on. I had to get a hat from Mae. She didn't have anything the right color for my dress, except this old thing with a fake flower on the side. I'll tell ya, I looked like a circus clown in that ridiculous thing. Bozo, with a dead red squirrel sticking out from under his hat!"

We were all ha-ha-ing over her story. Even Ma. "Oh, such pretty pictures, girls," Aunt Verdella said after we all settled down. "How about giving Auntie a couple to hang on her fridge? You each pick out the one you want me to have. Okay?"

"Hey, I know!" Freeda suddenly yelped. "Let's go to the drugstore and get some Clairol. We'll play beauty shop!"

"Right now?" Ma asked.

"Sure! Why not?"

"Oh, I don't know. I haven't even made dinner yet."

"Oh, let's do it, Jewel! Reece was having stew with Rudy when I left. So you don't need to worry about him," Aunt Verdella said. "Button, run over to my place and grab Auntie's purse, will ya?"

So off we went to Aunt Verdella's, then to the Rexall drugstore. We laughed and chattered, right there in the drugstore aisle, when Freeda grabbed a box with pale, reddish-brown waves on it and held it up to Aunt Verdella. "Look at that, kids. Auntie Verdella's gonna look like a peach in this, ain't she? Hot dog!" She shoved the box of color at Aunt Verdella, then started scouring the shelves for something Ma would look like a piece of fruit in too, I suppose.

"Here we go! A nice golden blond. You wait and see how this brightens you up, Jewel."

Me and Winnalee didn't play that afternoon, and we didn't talk about fairies either. We stayed in the kitchen and watched Freeda goop up Ma and Aunt Verdella's heads with that stinky hair-coloring stuff, while we ate bologna sandwiches.

After both their heads were rinsed, Freeda gave them each a haircut. "Don't cut too much!" Ma said, as tufts of hair rolled down her shoulders, and Freeda told her to hush up. That she was giving her a cute bouffant hairdo, like it or not, and that she'd love it when it was done.

When the floor around Ma and Aunt Verdella looked like a matted rug, Freeda rolled their hair in pink, foamy curlers. Then we had to wait till they took turns sitting under the dryer cap, to see what they were going to look like. "Is this thing turned up too hot, or am I just having a hot flash?" Aunt Verdella said as she fanned herself with the fairy pictures Winnalee had given her for her fridge.

"Can you color my head red like yours, Freeda?" Winnalee begged. "Please?"

Freeda laughed. "You'll have to wait a bit longer before you start that shit, Winnalee."

Winnalee crossed her arms. "But I want to play beauty shop too!" So Aunt Verdella, whose hair was dried but still in curlers, told Winnalee to get a couple rubber bands and she'd give her some braids. Winnalee ran to get the rubber bands.

"Button could use another hair trim soon," Ma said, while Winnalee's footsteps thumped on the ceiling above our heads.

Freeda looked over at me, and I slipped my hands up over my ears.

"Jewel, why in the hell do you do that to her hair, anyway?"

"What?" Ma asked. Freeda pulled the pink cap up so Ma's ears would be sticking out.

"Cut her hair like that, and perm it. You ever ask her if

that's what she wants?" My arms started itching like crazy the minute Freeda said that, because I was afraid Freeda would say that bad F-word, so I started making those noises in my throat, even though I knew that those noises would only make Freeda stare at me longer.

Ma shrugged. "Well, I, uh..."

"She hates her hair like that, Jewel," Freeda says. "She *hates* it!"

"But it's easy to take care of. It stays neat," Ma said.

"Yeah, well, your hair would be easiest to take care of too, if you shaved it off to your scalp, but I don't see you doing that. Jesus H. Christ, Jewel. Let the kid have long hair if she wants it. It's no skin off of your ass. She's old enough to take care of it herself." Ma squirmed a bit, and Freeda told her to sit still.

Winnalee came in the room then, carrying a few rubber bands. "Winnalee, get your butt over here," Freeda said. "Come on. Stand behind Button. There. Now lean your head right over the top of hers." Freeda's hands started rearranging Winnalee's loops, tucking them around the sides of my face until they tickled my cheeks and my arms. "Look at this, Jewel," Freeda said, loud enough to be heard over the hum of the dryer. "Just look at how cute your daughter would look in long hair. She's got the face of an angel, and she should have hair like one. Just look at her heart-shaped face. She's got your eyes too."

My whole insides smiled when she said those things, then she leaned over and kissed my cheek. Then Freeda told Winnalee to move, and she started rubbing her fingertips in circles on my scalp. "Button, every day you massage your scalp good, just like I'm doing. It stimulates the hair follicles and will get your hair growing faster. Before you know it, you'll have hair as long as Winnalee's."

The whole rest of the time we were there, even though I didn't get to play beauty shop, just knowing that maybe I'd get to grow my hair long now made me smile. And when I went into the bathroom, after I peed, I stood at the mirror and I rubbed my head, just like Freeda had done, while I looked for the heart shape on my face.

Freeda was busy taking the curlers out of Ma's hair when Mike Thompson yelled hello through the screen door. "Come in," Winnalee shouted, and Freeda gave her a crabby look. We all hushed up when Mike came into the kitchen.

"I knew it was your day off, so I thought maybe you'd like to go for a drive, or a beer, or something," Mike said.

"Sorry, Verdella and Jewel are here. We're doing their hair. Another time, Mike."

"We're almost done, aren't we, Freeda?" Aunt Verdella called out.

"Another time, Mike," Freeda said. Freeda didn't walk him to the door but gave him a wave and started talking to Ma about her haircut, as though he'd already left the room. "I really like Mike," Verdella said.

"He's nice enough, I guess," Freeda said.

"At least he puts the toilet seat down after he pees, so I don't fall in in the morning," Winnalee said.

Me and Winnalee walked Aunt Verdella home before I had to leave, so we could help her show Uncle Rudy her new hairdo. He might not have noticed, but Aunt Verdella saw to it that he did. She marched right in front of his head, blocking his eyes from the TV, and she turned her head this way and that, so he could see her light red-brown hair, cut short and spicy-looking, like Freeda said. "Holy cow! Who's this standin' in my living room?" Uncle Rudy said. "She's a real looker. Boy, is Verdie gonna be mad when she sees the beauty queen Button and Winnalee brought home for me." We all giggled when he said that.

Ma didn't stand in front of Daddy to get him to see her

new hair. She stood quietly at the sink when he came through the door and headed straight for the junk drawer. "Jewel, you see my Phillips screwdriver?"

"No," Ma said.

"Well, damn it. I thought I left it on the table when I came in earlier. You sure you didn't move it?"

Ma patted her new blondie bubble-hair that Freeda had made stand high by taking a rat-tail comb and running it backward down strands of Ma's hair. Then she made it smooth by combing some hair over the top of it to hide the ratty parts. When Ma had stood in front of Freeda's bathroom mirror, she patted her hair as though it were a new baby puppy. But now her pats looked more like slaps.

"Jewel?" Daddy said. "You hear——" Daddy stopped the second he looked up and saw Ma. His eyebrows scrunched down, and his mouth fell open.

I held my breath, wanting—and hoping—that Daddy would say something funny and nice like Uncle Rudy had, but he didn't. Instead, he said, "What the hell did you do?"

"Freeda did it," Ma said. "She did Verdella's too."

Daddy shook his head, then went back to rummaging in the drawer. "I picked up a box of files last time I was in town, but I can't find those damn things either."

The next morning, when Ma drove me over to Aunt Verdella's, she was wearing her best office suit and a sheer scarf, even though it wasn't cold or rainy outside. As she tugged the knot a bit so it wasn't so tight under her chin, I thought of how maybe that scarf was supposed to be like a pair of hands. Yet the farther she got down the road, the more I saw her glance in the rearview mirror, and by the time we reached Aunt Verdella's, I thought I saw a bit of a smile tugging at the corner of her lips.

After breakfast, when we ran to Winnalee's to get some different dress-up shoes for Winnalee because the ones she had on kept slipping off, I asked her if I could add another bright idea. Winnalee handed me the book, and I wrote, *Bright Idea #90: After you play beauty shop, your husband might say you look like a beauty queen, or he might just ask you where the Phillips screwdriver is. Either way, it doesn't matter, as long as your new hair makes you think nice things about yourself.*

13

That week, Daddy took two days he had piled up from his vacation time so he could go with Uncle Rudy to a cattle auction somewhere or other. It was a hot day. One of those kind of days where your skin, your clothes, and everything you touch feels sticky. I could feel it in my guts that it was gonna storm. I didn't like bad storms any more than Ma did. Especially when Daddy wasn't home.

While we weeded the vegetable garden, every now and then Ma would stop chopping at the ground with her hoe and look up at the clouds that were piling up like giant marshmallows stacked on a white plate.

Ma was always quiet when she worked, but on this day there was something different about her quietness. There'd been something different about it ever since the day she said those bad things to Aunt Verdella and Freeda yelled at her. Now it was like her brain wasn't just empty when she worked, but like maybe she was thinking really hard about some things. Sometimes, I figured she was thinking about sad things, because her face would get all droopy. But other times they must have been happy thoughts, because her lips would tilt up just a bit, and her eyes would look softer.

We didn't get to finish the weeding before the thunder

started grumbling in the distance, not loud, more like the sky was trying to clear its throat. "It's the calm before the storm," Ma said, as she reached down and ran her hand through the leaves creeping across the dirt, to see what size the cucumbers were. She looked up at the sky, then said, "We'd better go inside." She wasn't gonna get no arguing from me, even if I dared to argue, because the air was all foggy with those little black bugs no bigger than specks that always come out in the evening on summer nights. The ones called *nats* but spelled with a *g* in front. The mosquitoes were biting too.

We picked up the gardening tools and carried them to the shed, and by the time we put them away and cleaned our hands off with the hose, the sky was blinking like Christmas, and my stomach was swirling with scared. I wanted to go into the house and hide right then, but Ma spotted the clothes on the line and said we had to take them off first.

"Don't yank," Ma called when I tried to hurry because the wind was kicking up. We barely got Daddy's work pants in the basket when the rain started coming down. As we ran to the house, the wind and rain pressed our clothes to our skin.

Ma stood by the dining-room window folding pillowcases as she watched the black clouds roll across the field toward us. I wanted to tell her not to stand there (because even Uncle Rudy thought that standing by a window when it was lightning wasn't a bright idea), but only noises, not words, came up from my throat.

When the storm came full blast, we could hear hail clunking on the roof. Ma and I ran to the front door and watched it come down, popping on the grass and pinging off the metal garage like bullets. "I think we'd better go down to the basement," Ma said. "This isn't looking good." She had to say it loud, because the storm was noisy with howling wind and lightning and thunder.

Ma pushed the front door closed, and we hurried to the basement. We sat on the bottom stair. Out the basement window, I could see the ground, and a tree was bent so far over that it was almost lying down. I crossed my fingers, hoping me and Winnalee's magic tree wouldn't get blown over or struck by lightning.

When the storm ended, Ma and I went upstairs. "A tree must have gone down over the electrical wires," Ma said when the lights inside the house wouldn't switch on. We went outside then. The ground was white with hail the size of peas, and there were broken branches strung across the yard.

After we got back inside, Ma paced around for a bit, then said maybe we should go check on Aunt Verdella.

Aunt Verdella was just coming out of her house when we pulled in. She had her fists propped on her fat part. "That sure was some storm," she said. "You're out of electricity too, I suppose. Freeda's not. Course, they're on a different line than us." She looked out over at the field where the oats—still a lemony green—stood about doll-high. "The oats look fine, but they're gonna grow mold in the low spots now with this much rain. Corn's okay. It could have been worse."

Aunt Verdella rubbed the top part of her arms, which were goose-pimpled because the air was chilly after the storm. "Let's take a hike over to Freeda and Winnalee's," she said.

It was Freeda's idea that we should have a sleepover. Ma laughed a bit at first, like she thought that was the silliest idea she ever heard. "Well, why not? What are you three gonna do, anyway? Stumble around in your dark houses all night by yourselves?"

"Oh, stay, Jewel!" Aunt Verdella said. "It'll be fun! I always wanted to go to a pajama party."

So that's what we did. We had a pajama party!

Me and Winnalee made ourselves bologna sandwiches. I made mine just like Freeda did, with bologna and mayonnaise, and lettuce, and pickles and gobs of potato chips crushed over the whole mess. I made it so big that my mouth could hardly fit over it. Ma looked at me like she wanted to tell me to eat like a lady, but then she closed her mouth.

When we got done with our sandwiches, Freeda made us

all a banana split. My tummy hurt by the time I scooped up the last bit of banana, floating in a white, pink, and brown swirl of mixed-up ice cream and Reddi Wip.

Aunt Verdella said she almost needed a nap after that, but Freeda said, "No such thing as sleeping tonight!" Then she got out a case as big as a tackle box and opened it. It was filled with makeup and nail polish. "I used to sell cosmetics," Freeda said.

"She lies," Winnalee said. "She bought those at a garage sale."

"Sit your butt down here, Jewel," Freeda said. "You've got the good-hair thing going on now, but we gotta do something about that pale face of yours."

Winnalee grabbed a bottle of nail polish and shook it. "Let's do our faces too, Button," Winnalee said. I looked up.

"I don't think that would be a good idea," Ma said.

Freeda, who was taking out compacts of this and that, and tubes of lipstick, and lining them on the table, looked over at Ma. "Why in the hell not? What, you think the kiddie police are gonna crash our party and arrest you for letting a nine-year-old wear makeup? Loosen up, Jewel. For cryin' out loud." She looked up at Ma for a second, then she sprung up from her chair. She went to the cupboard and took down a big bottle filled with something that looked like water, though I didn't think it was. Then she grabbed the pitcher of orange juice from the counter, where me and Winnalee had left it.

"What are you doing?" Ma asked, as Freeda pulled down three tall glasses.

"I'm fixing us a little drink. Something to help you loosen up enough to let that rod slip out of your ass." Freeda clinked ice into the glasses, half-filled the glasses with the water-colored stuff, then poured orange juice up to the rims. "Ah," she said, as she took a big gulp of hers. "It's hotter than hell in this house. It cool off outside any?" she asked, and Ma said it had.

Winnalee unscrewed the bottle of pinky-red nail polish she'd been shaking. "You paint mine, Button, and I'll paint yours." I looked over at Ma, but I couldn't see her eyes because she had them closed so Freeda could yank out her eyebrow hairs with tiny metal pinchers. "Ouch! Ouch!" Ma said, and Freeda told her to stop flinching.

"Go on, Button!" Freeda said. "A little nail polish ain't gonna hurt nothing."

Aunt Verdella giggled every time Ma cried ouch, and Freeda said, "You just wait, Verdella. You're next!"

Freeda took another gulp from her drink and made Ma do the same, then she smeared some stuff the color of skin on her face. When she had her face all covered, she started drawing lines along Ma's eyelids with a tiny paintbrush. "You keep still too, Button," Winnalee said, as she brushed pink color on my fingernails. I liked the way the polish looked, all pinky and pretty, and I liked the way it felt too, all cool and wet.

"Jesus, I'm hot," Freeda said. She stopped what she was doing and pulled the front of her shirt out to blow at her boobies. She opened the back door wider. "These old houses take forever to cool down after a storm. I need to get a goddamn fan," she said. She peered outside. "Looks like more rain's coming."

When Freeda had Ma's eye lines drawn, she moved over to Aunt Verdella's chair and started drawing lines on her eyes too. "Oops," she said when her hand slipped and she drew a zigzag almost to the soft spot on the side of Aunt Verdella's head—the spot you aren't supposed to whack, because it could kill you or make you mental. Freeda giggled as she dabbed at Aunt Verdella's eye with a wet cotton ball.

After Freeda outlined their eyes in black, she started painting the lids up with eye shadow—green for Ma, and blue for Aunt Verdella. She brushed those colors on until she bumped into their eyebrows, which she'd already plucked into tipped-over half-moons.

Freeda picked up this funny-looking metal thing with finger

holes like scissors and clamped it over Aunt Verdella's eye. "Ouch!" Aunt Verdella cried.

"Sit still, for crissakes, so I can get ahold of your lashes to curl them. And stop that blinking."

"What eyelashes? I haven't had eyelashes for fifteen years! You might not be able to see that, in your drunken state, but trust me, all you're curlin' there is my skin!"

"Oh, Verdella. Stop pissin' and moanin'," Freeda said. "You gotta suffer to be beautiful. Now sit still so I can get this mascara on without smudging it, or I'll have to start all over." Freeda dabbed at Aunt Verdella's bent eyelashes with a teeny black brush until they looked like stubby black spider legs.

After she was finished with their eyes, Freeda stood back to admire her work, and me and Winnalee joined her, me keeping my fingers spread and my hands in the air, like Winnalee told me to do so I wouldn't mess my nails. "Now we'll color up your lips and cheeks," Freeda said. She did that, then dusted their faces with powder. "There! Done! Now go take a look, girls, but don't blink hard until your mascara dries."

Ma and Aunt Verdella raced into the bathroom, and Winnalee and me followed. They crowded in front of the mirror, blinking at themselves and each other. "Good Lord, Freeda!" Aunt Verdella said. "Whose makeup did you think you were doing, anyway? Cleopatra's?" We giggled.

"What? You two never looked better in your whole lives! Don't they look gorgeous, girls?"

"They look like movie stars!" Winnalee said, and Aunt Verdella added, "Godzilla, maybe!" then she ha-ha-ed hard.

"All I have to say," Freeda said, "is too bad the Peters men are out of town. Look at the two hot tamales they're missing out on tonight! Owee!"

"Oh my God," Aunt Verdella said, as she braced herself against the bathroom counter. "I keep laughin' like this, and I'm gonna wet myself!" This made Ma laugh all the harder.

When things settled down, me and Winnalee played

checkers and hula-hooped in the big part of the living room, while the ladies talked about hair and clothes, and dropping-down boobies and fat bellies, and all that other stuff I guess ladies talk about when they have a pajama party. After we hula-hooped, Winnalee wanted to play movie stars.

"Let's have a TV show for them!" Winnalee said, as we were clunking down the stairs in high heels that flopped at our feet. I didn't want to, though, because that would mean that Ma would be sitting in the audience. "I'll be an audience lady tonight," I told Winnalee. She didn't argue, because she thought she had a good story.

Downstairs, Freeda had the lights out and candles lit, even though the electricity wasn't out. In the candlelight, Ma's eyes looked like two pieces of coal and her skin ghost-white (but for those two dark stains on her cheeks). "Look at me, Button. Not your ma," Winnalee said right after she started her show, about a dancing, singing saloon girl.

Winnalee kept flashing her painted fingernails and fiddling to keep the balled-up socks in the pointed part of her too-big blouse. When she yelled to the cowpokes to watch her dance, then did that butt-shaking thing I knew meant sexy, I cringed. I glanced over at Ma, expecting her to be all crabby-looking, but she wasn't. She was laughing in slow motion, just like Freeda and Aunt Verdella.

Ma put her glass—which was almost empty—to her mouth and some slopped down her blouse. "Good grief," she said, "I think I'm drunk!"

Aunt Verdella giggled. "I *know* I'm drunk!"

When there didn't seem to be much left to Winnalee's story, Freeda stood up and threw a pillow at Winnalee. "Go play like a normal kid," she said.

Freeda went to the front door and flicked on the porch light. There were sparkles in the trail of rain dropping off of the eaves. "Okay, that's it!" she said. "I'm gonna cool off one way or another." And out the door into the rain she went.

She wasn't outside more than a couple seconds when she

rapped on the living-room window. "Come on out where it's cool!" she yelled, her voice some muffled through the glass.

Winnalee ran to the window. "She ran that way," she said, pointing toward the back of the house. Winnalee ran to the back door, and I chased after her.

"Ha-ha-ha, come see Freeda!"

I scooted beside Winnalee and looked.

"What's she yelling about?" Aunt Verdella asked. Even her ha-ha was slurred as she came into the kitchen and peered over our heads. "Freeda! What on earth..."

And there was Freeda, dancing across the backyard in her birthday suit—as Aunt Verdella called naked—her skin glowing and glossy in the light shining from alongside the door. She stretched her arms wide and swirled in circles, her bumps bouncing. "Come on!" she yelled. "It feels wonderful!"

Winnalee ran down the back steps and started tugging off her clothes, tossing them on the ground to join Freeda's. The night air filled with giggles as she ran after Freeda, waving her arms and legs, just as Freeda was doing. "Come on, you guys, while it's still raining!"

"What on earth are they doing?" I turned and looked around Aunt Verdella in time to see Ma's Egypt-lady's eyes stretch wide. "Oh my God, are they naked?"

"Come on! Button, Jewel, Verdella, come on!"

Winnalee didn't wait for us to come out. She ran up the steps and grabbed my hand and Aunt Verdella's and tugged us outside. "Come on! It's fun!"

I put my head back to let the soft rain cool my face, just as Aunt Verdella was doing. "Oh my, this rain does feel good!" Aunt Verdella said.

"Get naked, and it will feel a whole lot better! Come on! There's no one here but us girls." Then Freeda added, "Unfortunately!" and she tossed her head back and whooped loudly.

"Oh, why not!" Aunt Verdella said with a giggle, as she unbuttoned her dress. She pulled it off and set it over the railing. I clamped my hand over my mouth when I saw Aunt Verdella prance across the grass in her white bra and big, white undies.

"Come on, Jewel!" Freeda coaxed. "You chicken?" Freeda flapped her bent arms, leaned forward, clucked, and strutted like a plucked chicken.

I never, ever thought I'd see the day when my very own ma would strip her clothes off and dance in the rain in her bra and undies, but that's exactly what she did.

Winnalee came to me and started tugging at my shirt, then trying to pull it over my head. I helped her, because my clothes were wet and sticking to me. I stripped right down to my undies, and that rain sure did feel good slipping down my skin.

"Ouch!" Ma cried out, stopping her dance to hop on one foot.

"What's the matter?" Aunt Verdella asked, rushing over to Ma.

"I stepped on a sharp stick or something!"

Freeda laughed as she danced. "No, honey, that was no stick. That was the rod that just fell out of your ass!" And Ma and Aunt Verdella laughed till they had to lean on each other to stay on their feet.

Our ha-has filled up the whole night sky, as we danced naked till our hair was soaking wet and we felt chilly.

"Look! Lightning bugs!" Winnalee shouted, as we were heading inside. Sure enough, there they were, one here, one there, bright yellow blinks in the night. "Let's get a jar!" Winnalee's bare butt disappeared into the house. She came out with a canning jar and a lid and skirted around the women, who were going inside.

"Look at us," Winnalee giggled, as we chased lightning bugs across the yard. "With the porch light on, we are lit almost like the lightning bugs. Wish we could blink too!" It took us a while, but we finally got five bugs.

It started getting cold, so we picked up our clothes and went back inside. Freeda was just coming from her bedroom.

She was wearing a short nightie and carrying a stack of blankets and pillows and two folded nightgowns, which she tossed to Ma and Aunt Verdella. She dumped the blankets onto the couch. "Winnalee, you find something dry for Button to wear. And get the sleeping bag from upstairs." Freeda went back into her room and came back dragging the mattress from her bed. "There," she said, as she dropped it on the floor. "Jewel and I can sleep on this, and Verdella, you take the couch."

Winnalee ignored her. "Hey," she said. "Our lightning bugs stopped blinking!" I peered down into the jar, where our bugs were walking up the glass, looking like nothing but ordinary, ugly bugs. "One of the bug's butts lit a couple times, but barely. Why?"

"Oh, they don't blink real good once you put them in a jar," Aunt Verdella said.

Winnalee looked sad. "Why? Because they're scared or not happy anymore?"

"I guess so," Aunt Verdella said.

Upstairs we found a couple shortie nightgowns, then we got out our book and wrote *Bright Idea #91: When the weather's bad and your lights go out, have a pajama party. Eat till you feel sick, hula-hoop, paint your faces, catch fireflies, and dance naked in the rain. If you do, then your bare butt will light up like a firefly's after it's been let out of a jar.*

14

When we went back downstairs, Winnalee was bouncing one minute, then sound asleep on the floor, flopped across the sleeping bag, the next. I lay down beside her, my back to Ma and Freeda, who were sitting on the mattress, their backs resting against the couch, where Aunt Verdella sat, her legs stretched out to her side. I closed my eyes and stayed real still, like I was already asleep, but I wasn't.

"Aw," Aunt Verdella said. "Look at those two. All tuckered out from their fun. Sleeping like a couple of angels."

I could hear the clink of glass against glass. "Oh, Freeda, I don't know if I should have any more vodka," Ma said. "My head's still spinning!"

"Oh well. You only live once," Freeda said. "Besides, this is a pajama party!"

"Booze at a pajama party?" Ma snorted, as the booze glug-glugged into her glass.

"It always was at the pajama parties I went to!" Freeda said.

"This sure is fun," Aunt Verdella said. "I always wanted to have friends to do a slumber party with. I never really had close girlfriends though. Well, I had friends who'd talk to me at school—when they were having troubles at home, or with their boyfriends, things like that—but I never had friends who were my friends back, if you know what I mean."

"That's because girls are bitches," Freeda said.

"Oh, Freeda!" Aunt Verdella said. "You say the darnedest things!"

"It's true! That's why all my friends at school were boys. Even before I started letting them feel me up." She giggled. "Seriously, though—well, I guess I was serious when I said that—but anyway, boys just made better friends. They were never jealous of your big boobs, and they didn't run and tell every goddamn person in the can whatever you just told them in private. Hell, from what I saw, I didn't even want any female friends."

Freeda gulped from her glass and burped. "What were you like back in school, Jewel? No, wait. Let me guess. I bet you were the type that I couldn't figure out for nothing. One of those girls with her nose in a book all the time. The secretary of the glee club, and shit like that. You were, weren't you?"

Ma laughed. "Hardly! I was a tomboy when I was Button's age. I just didn't care about those girlie things, you know? I'd grown out of being a tomboy by the time I was in high school, but ... well, I don't know. I just didn't fit in, I guess. I did my work and pretty much stuck to myself. Most girls just ignored me. Most boys too."

"I would have liked it that way," Freeda said. "Well, except for the being ignored by the boys part." She laughed a bit. "Instead, everybody knew my business. Usually before I knew it myself. Okay, I guess I deserved most of that gossip. I *was* pretty wild."

Ma giggled. "Gee, we wouldn't have guessed that, Freeda." Then they all laughed.

"But still, the bitches didn't have to keep flapping their gums about me."

"You surprise me, Freeda," Ma said. "On one hand, you say you don't care what people think about you, but on the other hand, it sure does seem to bother you when people gossip about you." Ma's words sounded all slurry and lazy.

I could hear Freeda smack her lips after she took another sip of her drink. "Hey, it's not the gossip. People can say any goddamn thing about me they want, *if* it's the truth. It's people accusing me of things that aren't true that pisses me off. Hell, like I don't give them enough true things to talk about as it is." Aunt Verdella giggled.

I listened and waited, wondering if they were gonna start talking about that piggyback-riding stuff so I'd know if Winnalee had told me the truth.

Freeda left the room, her foot stomps going past my head.

"God," Ma said after Freeda had left the room. "If Reece and Rudy could see us tonight, they'd die!" And they both giggled, but in a nervous sort of way.

"I knew I had another one around here somewhere," Freeda said when she got back to the living room.

"Good Lord, Freeda," Aunt Verdella said, as the glug-gluggy noises happened again. "You're gonna have me and Jewel downright sick if you give us any more."

Freeda just laughed and said, "So?"

"Oh, as much fun as I'm having, I miss my Rudy," Aunt Verdella said with a sigh. "Did you know, Freeda, that I was thirty-nine years old when Rudy asked me to marry him? Old enough that I was sure I'd never hear anybody pop that question. Course, come to think of it, I guess nobody ever did!" She laughed, and Freeda asked her what she meant.

"Well, it just dawned on me that I never even let him get the whole question out. The poor man, he was fumbling around so much, I felt sorry for him. Finally, I just said, 'Rudy Peters, are you asking me to marry you?' and he nodded. I about crushed him, I was so thrilled. Oh, I loved him from the minute I met him."

"Where did you meet him, anyway?" Ma asked. "I don't think I ever heard."

"At the hardware store here in town. I'd just moved here, after my ma passed away. I came through town, just like you did, Freeda, and thought here was as good of a place to live as any. He'd come into the store to buy this and that. Pretty soon, I was bringing him a piece of cake, or some cookies I'd baked. Finally one day, he said he had to pay me back for filling him up, and he asked me to go over to the diner with him on my lunch break. I think I loved him from the first time I met him. He was kind and gentle, just like my daddy."

Ma burped, and they all giggled.

"Course, I didn't fool myself into thinking he loved me. I knew he was just a lonely widower. But I figured that I could put enough love into the marriage for both of us. I don't think he's unhappy, though. I feed him well. Both his belly and ... well, you know, that other kind of hunger."

"I knew it!" Freeda shouted. "I knew the minute I saw you, Verdella Peters, that you were a floozy at heart!"

Verdella ha-ha-ed so loud that Winnalee stirred, but she didn't wake up. "Well, I guess you could say that about me, though, Lord knows, I'd never talk about it. I don't want to put disgusting pictures in folks' minds. Two old, fat folks doing all that bumping and grinding and jiggling. Good Lord!" I heard someone's drink spray out of their mouth, and all three of them laughed till I thought they'd never stop.

When they got done laughing, it was Ma's turn to talk, I guess. "I don't think Reece loved me when he married me," she said slowly. And the way she said it made my insides feel like an empty mailbox.

"Nonsense, Jewel. He did so! I remember how he'd spend a good hour in that bathroom before your dates, slicking his hair, trying on one shirt then another!"

"I don't know about that. I think he married me because I

was the first girl his mother approved of. Verdella, you know the kinds of girls Reece ran with. I think he married me just to make Mae proud of him."

"Well, honey," Freeda said. "You're on your way to becoming the kind of girl Reece used to run with!"

"Freeda!" Ma said.

"What the hell, Jewel. We're just three women talking here. We all know about heavy breathing and horny men and all that good stuff. Why can't we speak our minds?"

Aunt Verdella giggled. "Oh my," she said. "Freeda, you're gonna corrupt us yet!"

Freeda laughed. "Hey, you two could use a little corrupting. Well, maybe not 'Frisky Fran' here, but Jewel sure as hell could.

"Hey, that reminds me!" she said. "Know what I just heard? That Washington approved a pill that will keep you from gettin' pregnant. Holy shit, will I cut loose then! No more of those damn rubbers. Can you imagine? Shit, I'll be poppin' those pills like candy!"

"Oh my!" Aunt Verdella said.

"I poked a hole in our condoms to get Evelyn," Ma said all of a sudden. The room went quiet. "He didn't want kids right away. For all I know, maybe he didn't want them at all."

"Well, you're not the first one to resort to that trick," Freeda said. And Aunt Verdella added, "You must have wanted a baby bad, honey. I can understand that part."

Ma's voice was so thick with sad now that it was hard to understand her. "Or maybe I just wanted to keep my husband home."

"Ah shit, you guys," Freeda said. "Don't go gettin' all melancholy on me now. I hate it when drunks get gloomy."

"Jewel?" Aunt Verdella said. "Maybe that was a bit dishonest, but it just tells me how much you love that man. And, oh, just look at what came out of it. Our precious little Button." I heard a couple soft pats of skin against skin.

I waited for Ma to agree with Aunt Verdella. I waited and I hoped. But all she said when she talked again was, "It didn't work, anyway. I can't help but think that if I'd given him a son, though, things would be different. Instead, I gave him another of what he already didn't want. Another one of me."

My ears were working like a sponge, sopping up Ma's words and wringing them out behind my eyes.

"Jewel Peters!" Aunt Verdella said. "There's nothing wrong with you. And there's certainly nothing wrong with Button! Reece loves you both. I know that's true, down to my bones. I'd stake my life on it! He just doesn't know how to show it, honey. I think he feels awkward showin' affection. Just like you do. He never got any affection the first ten years of his life. I think it just don't feel natural for him to give it, you know? But if you give it to him, like I do, like Winnalee does, why, that man practically rolls over like a dog who's getting his belly scratched."

"Bet he shows affection in the bedroom, though!" Freeda laughed, like she'd just said something funny.

"Is it still love if when he's done he rolls over and doesn't touch me again till next Friday night? And is it called affection if it comes and goes in five minutes and doesn't start with a kiss or end with a hug?" Ma asked, and she sounded both mad and sad.

"Apparently so, if you're a man!" Freeda said, then laughed again.

"I just wish he'd put some effort into it, you know? It's kind of hard to get . . . well, you know, excited, when it all happens while I'm still wondering if I shut off the living-room lights and it's over before I can even answer my own question." Ma gasped then. "I can't believe I just said that. I must be stone-drunk!"

"Jesus, Jewel. Just tell him what you expect out of him. I'm not married to the guys I get it on with—hell, most times I don't even know their last names—but still, you can damn bet that I let them know exactly what they've got to do to please me. And if I don't get it, they don't get a second try either!"

"She's right," came Aunt Verdella's slurred words.

"Oh my God, Freeda. I couldn't say that stuff to Reece!"

Freeda laughed. "Why in the hell not? You bare your ass to him, but you can't bare your mind? Tell him what you want. Tell him what ya like and don't like, then you pick up the pace, shakin' and movin' what you got, and let me clue ya. He'll be so damn grateful that you'll have to shove him away from you to get any sleep at all."

"I...I couldn't."

"Yeah, well, I bet you didn't think you could run half-naked in the yard either, but you did!"

"Gee, thanks for reminding me that I have *two* things to be ashamed of in the morning. What did you pour in my glass, anyway, Freeda? Truth serum? Oh, am I going to hate myself tomorrow!"

"Yeah, well, it works like an amnesia pill on me, so you don't have to worry about one damn thing you said. And as for Verdella, well, I guess it works like a knockout pill on her. Look at her. She's sound asleep."

"I heard that," Aunt Verdella mumbled. Freeda and Ma laughed.

Aunt Verdella didn't stay awake though. Right after she said that, she started making those snoring-that-sounds-more-like-snorting noises. "Good God," Freeda said. "She's snoring like a goat. Reach up and give her a nudge so she'll roll over, will ya?"

They talked in whispers after Aunt Verdella fell asleep, and I couldn't hear a thing they were saying. I dozed off, I suppose, then woke up when Winnalee's leg kicked into mine. After that, their voices sounded far away, like they were coming from dreamland. "You know when I said that stuff about girlfriends?" Freeda said. "About how I didn't give a shit if I had any when I was in school? I lied. The truth is, I always wanted a best girlfriend, even if I wouldn't have admitted it, even to myself. You know, someone to talk to about the things that mattered. My guy friends were great, but it's not like I could talk to them about everything. I guess I just didn't trust women though. Not after my ma. Hell, come to think of it, I didn't trust men either, but then, I had no reason to. I guess it's been the same for you, huh, Jewel?"

"Yeah, that's about it. I suppose I expected every girl I met to be as critical of me as my mom and sisters were. They just didn't like me, so I guess that I assumed no one else would like me either. And I'm afraid that in trying to teach Evelyn how to be better than me, I'm only teaching her that she's not good enough either." I don't know if I dreamed it or not, but I thought I heard tears in Ma's voice.

"Maybe, Jewel. Just maybe your ma and your sisters were being critical of you for the same reasons. Because they didn't like who they were, and they didn't want you to be inadequate like them." Ma mumbled that she doubted it, but Freeda kept on talking. "I make a lot of mistakes with Winnalee, I know, but I don't know how to make her mind without making her think that I don't love her just the way she is. I always told myself that I was doing okay as long as she knew that I loved her. Now I'm not so sure that's enough. Hell, I look at her sometimes and I think of how undisciplined she is, how rebellious sometimes, and I think, Christ, I hope she don't end up a mess like me."

That's all I remember them saying, so I guess I must have fallen asleep. The next morning, while Ma was complaining about her stomach and Aunt Verdella was complaining about her head, me and Winnalee went up to her room and we wrote in our book, *Bright Idea #92: If you have a pajama party, don't drink too much booze or you won't feel good in the morning. And if you have a makeup party at your pajama party, wash your face before you go to bed, even if you danced naked*

*in the rain, or you're gonna look like sick raccoons when you
wake up.* After Winnalee wrote that, I took the book from her
and added, *And don't just go saying anything when a kid is
around, because even if their eyes are closed, their big ears might
not be.*

15

After that pajama party, I started watching Ma more, and wondering who she was besides just my ma.

The day after our party, she was all squirrelly, like she half-expected the police to come and arrest her for showing her understuff, or Daddy to find out and have a hissy fit. She cleaned all day like she couldn't clean fast enough, or good enough, like she was trying to be extra good to make up for being extra bad. After a few days, though, she was like Uncle Rudy's cows when they got let out of the barn in the spring after a long winter of having their heads stuck in those metal stanchion things; when they got all happy and hopped around the field, running and kicking and making moos that I think meant, "I'm free! I'm free!" in cow-talk.

Ma started doing things she wouldn't have done before too. And doing them like a newborn calf who was trying to find her legs. Like one evening when she called me into the sewing room (which was really supposed to be the guest bedroom, except that it never had guests) and asked me if I wanted to see her new dress.

I stood just inside the door, sniffing, because I liked the metally smell that hung in the air when the sewing machine was turned on. "I'm making this dress here, with a few modifications," she said, picking up the Spiegel catalog and pointing to a fancy blue and white dress. She read the description of the dress out loud to me: *"Sheer nylon ruffles 'n lace beneath a boned petal bodice and filmy nylon net stole. Taffeta cummerbund, rayon taffeta lining, nylon net crinoline."* She set the catalog down on the little table to the side of her. "It's last year's catalog, but when we were looking at styles Freeda said it was the perfect style for me, if I cinch the waist a bit more. She says it will give me an hourglass figure. Of course, I have no idea where I'll wear it."

Ma looked up. "You can come in, Evelyn," she said, so I stepped inside the room. "I've got the skirt done. It's on the bed."

I glanced over at the bed, where a wide skirt of ruffles and lace was spread out like a fancy fan. It was black! Ma flicked the little handle, and the part of her machine that looked like a tiny robot's foot let go of the top part of her dress. She pulled it out and swung her knees out from under the sewing machine so she could swivel and show me the half-made top held up against her. It was black too! "What do you think?" she asked.

"It's the color of sexy!" The minute those words came out, I clamped my hands over my mouth.

Ma looked at me, her eyes stretching wide, and she said, "Evelyn Mae Peters!" She looked down quickly then, the corner of her mouth lifting up a bit like it was smiling, but I told myself that that couldn't be right, because Ma didn't smile about "sexy."

Just then Daddy's truck sounded in the driveway, and Ma got up. "Your poor dad," she said. "They had a breakdown at the mill, and he's been there since eleven o'clock last night. Come help me get his dinner, Evelyn. He's probably starving."

Daddy looked all crumbled, and his eyes were red. His face was picky-looking with stubby black whiskers. "Grab the bread out of the bread box, will you, Evelyn?"

Daddy fell into his chair and sighed. He lit a cigarette but left it in the ashtray, as though he was too tired to pick it up. He stuck out his arm and turned it this way and that and rubbed the side of his neck. "Damn, I'm beat," he said.

Ma hurried to fix his plate while I grabbed the butter dish that was still sitting on the table, even though I wasn't told to. The dish was almost empty, so I grabbed a new stick from the refrigerator, while Ma flicked on the oven and spooned a mound of chicken, rice, and peas onto a glass pie plate, tucking it into the oven. Then she poured Daddy a glass of tomato juice and set it down before him. "Your dinner will be heated in no time," she said.

I suppose Daddy was just as curious about what Ma was doing as I was, because he turned his head stiffly and glanced at her when she circled his chair to stand right behind him, and said, "Maybe this will help."

Daddy's red eyes got round as rubber balls when Ma set her hands stiffly on his shoulders. It got so quiet suddenly that even the sound of the wrapper coming off the butter sounded loud.

Ma's mouth looked twitchy at first—just like it had looked after she showed me her dress and didn't know what else to say—then her hands started working good, like they were just kneading bread dough. Daddy's whole body seemed to melt then, like the old butter I'd just scraped out of the dish, and his head dropped down to the side. "Ahhh," he said. I thought he'd fall asleep right where he was sitting, but when Ma stopped rubbing him to grab the plate out of the oven, he woke up enough to eat.

Just a couple days later, while we were punching out paper dolls, Winnalee said, "Your ma ain't so gray anymore."

"Am I still so gray?" I asked. Winnalee tilted her head and looked at me. "No," she said, and I smiled. "You're my best friend forever," I said when the thought popped up from my heart at just that moment. Winnalee smiled then and said, "You're my best friend forever too."

· · · ·

So I had a best friend forever, and I figured my ma did too. And that best friend for my ma was Freeda Malone.

On Saturdays now, while me and Winnalee went with Aunt Verdella to the community sale to sell a few pot holders and the stuff Aunt Verdella made or scrounged up around the house, Ma and Freeda went shopping over in Porter, where they had better stores. And once they even went to see a matinee, *Splendor in the Grass.* They were usually still gone when we got back from the sale, and when they came back, they'd bring back the yarn and sewing stuff Aunt Verdella asked them to pick up. I could tell that sometimes when Ma and Freeda giggled about something that happened while they were out, Aunt Verdella felt left out, but like she said to me, making good money at the community sale so we'd have enough money for Winnalee and Freeda's surprise was more important than anything else in the world right now, so she didn't mind working while Ma and Freeda were off having fun.

Aunt Verdella wasn't upset about Ma and Freeda becoming best friends, but Daddy was. He didn't like it the day he came home from that auction and saw Ma wearing makeup. "What in the hell do you have on your face?" he asked. He looked so shocked that all I could think about was how he probably would have keeled over dead if he'd seen her face right after Freeda had painted it. As it was, though, all Ma had on was a bit of eye shadow and mascara, and some pinky-red lipstick.

Ma cringed a little when Dad asked her about her face, then she straightened up tall and turned back to the stove. "You like makeup just fine on Freeda," she said.

Daddy stared at her back for a bit, shook his head, then opened the fridge and took the orange juice out. "Freeda's not my wife," Daddy said. "And she's getting quite a reputation around here. I'm not sure I like you running around with her."

Ma gritted her teeth. She stopped stirring the pot of stew

she was cooking and banged the spoon against the rim. She turned. "Owen's got quite a reputation. Everybody knows he chases anything in skirts. I don't see you leery of being seen with him."

"That's different!" Daddy said.

The screen door opened just then, and Freeda flashed into the room. "Speak of the devil..." Daddy said.

"Hi, Jewel. Reece, Button."

"Jesus, Freeda. Can't you knock?" Daddy said.

"Why? You afraid I'm gonna catch you butt-naked and find out that you're not quite as big of a man as you'd like me to believe?" Ma turned back to her pot, a grin on her face. I think she was trying hard not to laugh out loud. Freeda didn't stop herself though.

While she was still giggling, Freeda patted my head, then tugged gently at a few of my loosening knots. "I do believe your hair's growing, Button," she said. "You massaging it every day, like I showed you?" I nodded. "Good girl." She gave my head a final pat, then went over to Ma. "Your zipper got left in my bag, so I figured I'd drop it off here on my way out, in case you were planning to put it in tonight."

Freeda peered at the baking stuff on the counter and the recipe card next to it. "Homemade German chocolate cake?" she said, her eyebrows lifting. She turned to Daddy, while Ma turned on the faucet. "What do you think of your new wife? You got a pretty hot babe on your hands now, don't ya?" Ma glanced at Daddy as she poured flour-and-water paste into her stew.

Daddy looked crabby. "Jewel was fine just how she was. She didn't need new hair, or clothes, or goddamn clown makeup."

Freeda got up on her bare toes to reach Daddy's cheek with a quick kiss. "Oh, Reece. Don't go taking that rod Jewel just pulled out of her ass and shoving it up your own now." She shook her head. "You men are all alike, you know that? You like it on other women, but not your wife. Hmm, I wonder why that is? Could it be that you don't want other men looking at your women? Too much competition for ya? Well, you keep the little wifey satisfied and you don't need to worry about her wandering off." Daddy flinched when Freeda reached out and gave him one pat on the butt.

"I just don't know why Jewel would want other men looking at her," Daddy grumbled.

"Here's a news flash for ya, Reece Peters. Maybe she didn't exactly do it for other men, or even for you, for that matter. Maybe she did it so that when *she* looks at herself, she likes what she sees. You ever think of that?" Freeda looked at Ma and rolled her eyes. "Men can be such a pain in the ass, can't they?" This time Ma did giggle.

Freeda sure was right about that. Especially fourteen-year-old ones with ugly mold-colored hair and vampire teeth.

Me and Winnalee were in our magic tree the next morning when Tommy came out of the house carrying a jug, spotted us, and came across the yard. "What you kiddies doin'?" he asked.

"None of your beeswax," Winnalee said. She opened the grape Kool-Aid package she was holding a little wider, then dipped her purpled, pointy finger inside. She held the package out to me and I did the same. Our mouths puckered as we sucked the sour powder off our fingers, then dipped them again.

Tommy looked at the ground where Winnalee's ma was sitting, and he moved to stand in a different spot. "You go looking for fairies over on Fossard's property yet?"

"No! It takes a long time to plan an adventure like that, stupid."

Tommy laughed. "You're just making excuses, you scaredy-cats."

"Go away, Tommy," I said. "Aunt Verdella said you were supposed to leave us alone."

Tommy glanced over at the house, then shrugged. "What?

I'm not doing nothin'. Rudy and I are haying and he sent me back to refill the water jug. Haying's hard work, you know, and you have to drink a lot of water. Not that you two kiddies would know anythin' about working hard. All you gotta do all day is play stupid baby games and think about dumb fairies." Tommy reached down to pluck a weed. "What's this?" he asked as he stuck the root part of the weed between his ugly teeth. He took two quick steps with his skinny legs, then reached down, snatching up our bag.

"Hey! What do you think you're doing?" Winnalee yelled.

"What is it?"

"Put that down, you asshole!" Winnalee scrambled to get out of the tree.

"You kiddies joining the army?"

Winnalee dropped from the branch and landed on all fours, and I followed her down. She grabbed for the bag, but Tommy held it above his head. "Give it back, you son of a bitch!"

"You sure do cuss a lot for a little kid," Tommy said.

Winnalee screamed, "Give us our bag back, you creep!"

"Oh, must be something good in here, if you want it back so bad." Tommy opened the flap to dig inside, and turned his back to us. "Hmmm," he said. "A flashlight, papers, a watch—"

"It's not a watch, stupid! It's a compass." Winnalee rolled up her fist and slugged him in the back. "Now give it to me!" Winnalee punched him between the shoulder blades again, but Tommy didn't even seem to feel it.

Tommy turned back to face us and stepped back. He lifted the bag out of Winnalee's reach again. "A compass, you say. Dummies! You wouldn't need a compass if you took the road."

"What road?" Winnalee asked, her fists stopping. "You said the beck was due west, through the woods."

"It is. But you can get there by road too."

I knew by one glance at Winnalee's narrowed eyes that

she was plotting how to get Tommy to tell us the directions by road. "You lie! There aren't no roads to take to get there."

"What, you think that nut ball cut through the woods on foot every time he had to go to town? I just told you how to get there through the woods because, obviously, if you go by road you're gonna get caught runnin' off before you even get ten feet down the road."

"I don't believe you. Liar!" Winnalee said.

"I ain't lying. You just head down Peters Road here till you come to Marsh Road. Then ya hang a left. It's down the first road you come to on the left. The road with the dead-end sign."

"I'm gonna go tell Aunt Verdella if you don't give us our bag and get out of here," I said.

I didn't have to take more than one step before Tommy threw the bag at Winnalee's feet. "Here's your dumb bag," he said. "And don't think I don't know what it's for either. It's stuff you're takin' along when you sneak off to look for stupid fairies. Well, hope you got some holy water in that bag too to protect you from evil ghosts, because you kiddies are gonna need it." He grinned then, his ugly lips pulling back, the weed bobbing from between his pointy teeth. He turned while shaking his head. "You girls are so stupid," he said as he picked up the water jug and started walking away.

"Oh, yeah?" Winnalee yelled after him. "At least we knew what a beck is. And at least we aren't mean. We don't go around trying to scare people, and we don't go around spilling people's mas!" She stuck her purple tongue out at Tommy.

Winnalee put the Kool-Aid package between her teeth, then hoisted herself up onto the branch, our adventure bag swinging from her shoulder, and scooted herself back up onto the flat part. "Come on up, Button."

I climbed back up our tree and looked out at the hay field, where Tommy was heading. Uncle Rudy was riding the tractor, swiping long patches of hay down, making it keel over to lie flat against the ground. It would stay lying down until Uncle Rudy fluffed it up and made what I used to call "windows" until Uncle Rudy told me they were called "windrows."

I liked the different shades of green that the hay made and the way it was sprinkled with other colors here and there. Especially at the edges, where the clover and a few daisies dotted the green waves with pink and purple and white flowers. When I was real little, Uncle Rudy had taken me out there and showed me what some of those grasses were. I thought it was fun grabbing the thread-skinny stalks of timothy and racing my hand to the top where the clump of seeds were, then tugging quick so that the little hard seeds pulled off in my hand.

"You listening to me, Button?"

I looked at Winnalee. "Yeah," I said, even though I wasn't.

"I don't like the fact that Tommy saw our adventure bag," Winnalee said. "He could rat on us." She dipped her finger back in the Kool-Aid package and sucked on it, while she looked off at nothing, with skinnied eyes. "I think we'd better go see the fairies just as soon as we can, because if Tommy opens his big yap, then Aunt Verdella'll keep her eyes on us even more than she already does. Besides, if we don't do it, the next thing we know, summer will be over, and the fairies with it. I think they fly to find a warmer place when fall comes, just like the birds do, don't you? They aren't dressed very warm."

Sometimes, when Winnalee talked like that, it was like the notion that fairies really *do* exist seemed stupid, and for a little bit I'd have to struggle to get back to believing in them all over again.

Winnalee held out the Kool-Aid package and I took another dip. "I think we need to just pick a date and sneak off then, no matter what is happening. We'll just say we're going outside to play, then we'll take off," Winnalee said. "Today's Friday, so let's just plan on going Monday, or Tuesday."

"Winnalee, we can't go then!"

"Why?" she asked.

"Because Tuesday is the Fourth of July. *Marty Graw!*"

"It's the Fourth of July on Tuesday? And what's a Marty Graw?"

"It's what Aunt Verdella calls our Fourth of July celebration, even though Ma says it's not a Marty Graw at all."

"You got fireworks?"

"Yeah, and that's not all we got! We got a carnival too, and two parades!"

"Do we get to go to Marty Graw?" she asked.

"Course we do! Ma and Aunt Verdella were talking about it just this morning. We always spend the day in town on Marty Graw, and we have a picnic at the park. That's what they were talking about. What food to bring. After the fireworks, there's a dance at the park too, but we never get to stay for that."

"Okay," she said. "Then we'll go see the fairies on Monday! Then we'll have two magical days in a row!"

"We can't go on Monday, Winnalee. Because if we get caught, I'm gonna be in a heap of trouble, and Ma probably wouldn't let me go to Marty Graw then."

"Okay, the day after Marty Graw, then," she said doggedly.

"Button?" Aunt Verdella's voice boomed out of the window. "Your ma should be here to pick you up any minute. You girls come in and clean up now, okay?"

"Okay," I yelled back. We leapt down from the tree, and Winnalee got on her knees to put our bag back into the hollow of the tree.

"I don't know if it's a good idea, leaving our bag in the tree. Tommy might come back and steal it."

"Nah," Winnalee said. "I don't think he even saw the hole. And even if he did, it's not like he'd have a reason to go digging in there. You can't see the bag when we shove it far back. Anyway, Tommy's too dumb to figure out that we'd leave it here."

As we headed toward the house, Winnalee told me what she was going to write, soon as she got home: *Bright Idea #93: If you and your best friend have an adventure bag, and some dumb boy tries to steal it, or dig in it, or make fun of you for having it, just punch him in the back.*

16

It seemed that every day since Freeda and Ma became friends, Ma became a little bit more happy. Every work morning she'd wake up and put on the makeup Freeda helped her pick out, then she'd take out the rollers that she'd slept on, and she'd make the top of her head all poufy by holding up a clump of hair and running her comb backward in it to make snarls. Then she'd comb the top layer over that knot so you couldn't see the snarls, just like Freeda showed her how to do. Ma made herself prettier dresses now too. Dresses that weren't all saggy, and she'd make them out of material the colors of summer, instead of what Freeda called drab colors. Ma laughed more now too, and she didn't get such a worried look on her face when Daddy asked her where something was. A couple times, I even heard her tell him he'd just have to wait till she got done doing what she was doing before she helped him look. And she didn't spend time on the phone with Bernice like she used to either, griping about Aunt Verdella or complaining about this or that. In fact, I don't think her and Bernice were even friends anymore, because one day I heard Ma tell Freeda, "Carol, the hygienist, said that Bernice told her that I'm fixing up like a floozy because Reece is having a fling with the tramp who moved into his mother's place. She used those words too! She also said that I must be nuts, thinking that what's good for the goose is good for the gander and that I can get even, fixing up like a tramp myself." They laughed something silly over that. "Carol was upset, because she thinks I look gorgeous. She said Bernice is probably just jealous of you and me because we look so good." Then Ma had told Freeda how Daddy stopped alongside the road on his way home from work and picked her some tiger lilies, because he knew how much she liked them and we didn't have any growing in our yard.

"Wow!" Freeda had said. "Didn't I tell you things would perk up once you got brave enough to tell Reece to slow his ass down? Literally." Then they roared some more, though Ma's laugh was more like those embarrassed giggles.

When they were done laughing though, Ma got serious and said, "Sometimes I'm gloriously happy because I feel freer, but other times I can still hear those old voices in my head, telling me that I'm not good enough or that I'm not *being* good enough. It's hard, you know? Going against all those things you heard growing up."

And Freeda told her, "Tell me about it. Some of my old messages I got licked. But others, they're still running my life. I say, though, that when those voices come, just tell them to shut the hell up and carry on."

The morning of my second favorite holiday, I woke up early. Ma didn't have to work during Marty Graw, because nobody wanted to get their mouth hurt on that day.

"Good morning, Button," Ma called from the kitchen, her words sounding more like she was singing them than saying them.

After I brushed my teeth, I leaned over toward the mirror and turned my head to one side, then the other. My ears definitely looked smaller, so I tried to figure out if I was growing into them, as Aunt Verdella said I was, or if it was just the

fluffy hair behind my ears, filling in the gap between them
and my head, that made my ears not look so pokey-outy. I
tugged at the frizz right above my ear, to see if my hair had
grown while I slept. The tip reached down to the bottom of
my ear when I pulled on it, so I thought maybe it had. A little
anyways.

"Button? What's taking you so long? I need your help in
here," Ma called.

"Coming!" I yelled back.

When I got to the kitchen, Ma was slicing peeled eggs over
the top of a bowl of potato salad and sprinkling it with that
orange spice I hated. She was wearing a new red top and white
pedal pushers. Her hair and face were fixed up real nice.
"You'll have to have cold cereal this morning, Evelyn. Then,
after you eat, I want you to pack the plastic forks and paper
cups, napkins, and, oh, get out the checkered tablecloth we use
for picnics."

I was so excited, I didn't even want to eat my Trix cereal, because I loved the Marty Graw the same as I loved
Christmas. I loved the parade down Main Street, with the
Dauber marching band banging drums and tooting horns, and
the floats made out of Kleenex flowers, where girls in long
dresses were propped, waving and smiling, and trying to be
the prettiest so they could be the Marty Graw queen. Some
of the men driving the floats, and the clowns walking beside
them, threw candy. Afterward, there was a carnival down
by the river, where you could go on rides and eat cotton candy
or ice cream cones till your stomach hurt. And best of all was
the fireworks. We'd sit on blankets down by the river—the
carnival rides blinking with lights and pumping music behind
us—and we'd watch the decorated floats drift down the water,
the fireworks booming above them, the sparks whistling as
they fell, dying out just before they landed on the floats. After
fireworks, a band always played in the gazebo, but we never
stayed for that.

"Oh, look at the time," Ma said. "And you're still not

dressed yet. Never mind the packing, I'll do that. You just finish eating, then get dressed. I'll do the rest."

I scooped the last of the soggy cereal into my mouth, rinsed my bowl in the sink, then ran to my room. Even getting dressed that day was fun, because Aunt Verdella had made me and Winnalee matching outfits. Little blouses striped with red and white, and short navy blue skirts, with what she called "bloomers" underneath. After I put mine on, I ran to look in the mirror that hung behind the door in Ma's sewing room. My skirt looked just like an ice skater's skirt, so I leaned over and lifted my arms out like an airplane, then stretched one leg out behind me.

"Look at how cute you look," Ma said when I got back to the kitchen. I grinned, because I think she really meant it. She came to me and lifted the hem of the skirt to yank off a dangling thread. She examined the stitches along the hem part, which were a bit zigzagged, and she grinned at Aunt Verdella's sewing, but her grin wasn't mean. Then she went to the skinny closet where she kept the ironing board and broom and other tall stuff, and she pulled a bag off of the shelf on top. She handed it to me. "Verdella showed me your outfits, so ... well, here." The bag didn't weigh more than a feather. I peeked inside. "I know the ones you girls have are falling apart. Besides, they wouldn't match your festive colors."

I took out one of the navy blue headbands, dabbing at the one red flower off to the side, hoping it wouldn't fall off right away, like the flowers on our other headbands had, leaving a row of dried glue dots that looked like the swollen spots on a baby's gums. I don't know why I got a lump in my throat when I saw those headbands, but I did. I swallowed hard so I wouldn't start making those noises in my throat. "Thank you, Ma. They're real pretty. And they match our outfits real good too."

Ma tapped her fingertips together a few times and smiled. "Okay. I'd better get finished packing here. Your dad's taking a bath, and everyone will be here any minute."

I went outside and sat on the steps to wait, my big ears listening for the rumble of Aunt Verdella's car down Peters Road. My hands kept reaching up to my headband, and my eyes kept looking down at my little pleated skirt.

When I heard a car, I leapt off of the steps, sure that it was the Bel Air. But it wasn't. It was a white car coming from the direction of town. I expected it to drive right by our house, but instead it pulled into our driveway.

I stood up and cupped my hand over the top of my eyes to block the sun so I could see who it was. The car had to stop before I figured it out, though. And then, before they could even get out of the car, I raced into the house and straight to the kitchen. "Ma! Ma! Aunt Stella and her girls are here!"

"What?" Ma was at the table, putting a Tupperware bowl into one of the orange coolers. "Stella? She never said she was stopping by."

"Hello!" came Aunt Stella's voice. I could see Daddy stepping out of the bathroom, a towel wrapped around him like a white skirt. He looked at Ma, cussed, then hurried off to their bedroom.

"In the kitchen," Ma called.

I folded my hands behind me and backed up against the fridge when Aunt Stella and her tall girls filled the room. "Stella, what are you doing here?" Ma asked. Stella didn't answer right away. She was too busy gawking at Ma. So were Judy and Cindy.

"Jewel!" Aunt Stella said. "What on earth have you done to yourself?"

For a second, Ma turned back into her old self. Her shoulders drooped down, and her chin tucked down. She took a quick breath and blew it out before she looked up. She dabbed at her bubble hair, then her hand slid down over her round plastic earring and smoothed over the front of her new blouse. She smiled, her pearly lips a bit shaky.

"Your hair! And makeup? Good heavens, Jewel!"

In the worst way, I wanted Aunt Stella to stop right there and say to Ma, "I had no idea you were this pretty, Jewel. I'm sorry about every single, rotten thing I ever said to you." I wanted her to say those things so bad that I held my breath as I hoped.

"She looks terrific, doesn't she?" We all looked as Daddy came into the kitchen, his wet hair wearing little trails where his comb had been. I couldn't hardly believe my ears, because for as long as I could remember, I'd never heard my daddy say that my ma looked anything, much less terrific. "This cooler ready?" he asked, picking up the lid. Ma stood up taller and lifted her chin. "It's ready," she said. Her smile was as bright as the smile of a Marty Graw queen.

"Well, I, um..." Aunt Stella didn't seem to know quite what to say, so I guess she decided to say nothing and to just keep staring instead.

Ma repeated her question. "I didn't know you were stopping in, Stella. Where you headed?"

"Well, we're on our way back home. We were in Minneapolis for a few days at my dear friend's house. We were planning on staying there until tomorrow, but Ralph sprained his ankle bad yesterday while hiking with the church youth group. He's completely laid up, so I figured we should hurry home. The girls were getting hungry and had to use a restroom, so I told them we'd swing by this way." She turned to Judy and Cindy and smiled, then turned back to Ma. "The girls are funny about public restrooms, just as I am. I knew you'd want to see them anyway, since you haven't seen them in such a long time."

Ma looked at my cousins, same as I did. Judy wore a cloth headband holding back long hair that flipped up at her shoulders. Her chin was sprinkled with red pimples, and there were some gouges on her cheeks where other pimples had been. Those didn't show in her pictures.

The younger one, Cindy, wore her hair in a ponytail. Her front teeth stuck out some and stayed jabbed against her bottom lip when she wasn't smiling. Maybe Aunt Stella saw us staring at Cindy's teeth—I don't know for sure, but I'm guessing she did—because she gave Cindy a frown, and Cindy pulled her top lip over her teeth, tucking them inside her mouth the best she could.

Daddy closed the lid on the food cooler and said he'd take it to the car. Ice cubes clanked as he hoisted it off of the table. For a minute, nobody said anything.

Ma cleared her throat. "Well, Stella, I'm afraid you've come at an inopportune time. We're about to leave for town for the Fourth of July festivities."

Aunt Stella, who had her car keys in her hand and was working the clasp on her purse—to drop them inside, no doubt—stopped. "Oh," she said. "If you're not working, you're usually home, doing something or other, so I figured you'd be here on a holiday."

"We celebrate the Fourth every year, Stella."

"Yes, well…" Aunt Stella fidgeted a bit. "I suppose, then…"

While Ma put clear wrapping over a lemon cake, Aunt Stella yammered a bit, telling how they'd gone to a play in St. Paul, and how Judy thought she'd like to get into drama. Her words moved like birds walk, in quick, little jerky spurts. Ma glanced up at Aunt Stella now and then as she filled a grocery bag with napkins and plastic silverware, and said, "Oh," or, "That's nice," a few times, but she didn't sound like she was listening.

I didn't feel like there was anything more to see in my cousins, so I walked around them and went outside to wait for Aunt Verdella, Uncle Rudy, and the Malones.

I didn't even have time to sit down before I spotted a splotch of turquoise through the cloud of dust coming down Peters Road. Even before they crossed the highway, I could see Winnalee's hand waving out the window.

"Don't open that door before we stop all the way, honey. Good heavens!" I heard Aunt Verdella shout as Uncle Rudy slowed the car to a stop.

In seconds, the air was filled with the sound of slamming doors and ha-ha-ing. I liked the way everybody sounded so happy.

"Oh, look at Button!" Aunt Verdella squealed. She came at me with her arms stretched out, her purse rocking from one arm. "Doesn't she look cute?"

Aunt Verdella was wearing a nice cotton dress. She had her hair done too, and a bit of rouge and lipstick on. "Give Auntie her hug," Aunt Verdella said.

"Whose white car is that, Button?" Aunt Verdella asked as she let go of me.

"Aunt Stella's."

"Oh! I didn't know she was joinin' us today."

Daddy, who was busy carrying out the bag of paper and plastic stuff, balanced on another cooler, said, "She's not." And he grinned.

Freeda looked as pretty as the first day I'd met her, dressed up in a sleeveless yellow shift that fit her like a banana peel. Her hair was piled up on her head in big curls. She was wearing her rhinestone sunglasses, and she smelled like a bed of roses. "Hi there, princess," she said to me. "Your hair *is* growing, kiddo. Before you know it, it will be down to your cute little butt." I grinned when she said that.

"Look at me and Button!" Winnalee squealed, as she held her ma tight and ran to stand next to me, her shoulder and hip pressing tight against mine. "Now we really do look like twins, don't we? We got the same shirts and the same skirt, and we even both got on the same color sandals. Hey, where'd you get that cool headband?"

"From my ma. She got one for you too. Come on!"

Uncle Rudy held the door open for us and gave us each a pat as we passed him. He smelled like that good-stink stuff men put on after they shave, and he was dressed up in new work pants and a button-up shirt. He looked real nice but for the black speckles on his teeth and the snuff lump on his bottom lip.

Everybody was talking at once when we got inside. "You must be Jewel's sister Stella," Freeda said, pulling her sunglasses off and looking at Aunt Stella through narrowed eyes.

"Yes, I am," Aunt Stella said. She took her purse off of the table and slipped the strap up her arm. "Well, Jewel, I see you have plans, so we'll take off. Thanks for the use of the bathroom." She went to Ma and pecked her on the cheek. I smiled on the inside when I saw Aunt Stella standing next to my new ma, because my ma was the prettiest. I leaned over then and whispered into Winnalee's ear, "Is my aunt Stella a gray person?" and she nodded. "I thought so," I said.

Aunt Stella said to Ma, "We brought a bag of clothes for Button. Things the girls outgrew. I'll have Cindy bring them in." She gave me a peck on the cheek, then hurried out the door.

"I want to show you my dress quick before we leave. It's finished," Ma said to Freeda and Aunt Verdella, as soon as Aunt Stella and my cousins went outside. "Button, you go get those clothes," Ma said, as Freeda and Aunt Verdella tagged behind her down the hall.

I'd barely gotten to the door when Cindy stepped inside. She handed me the grocery bag, then hurried back out the door. "Let's see what's in there," Winnalee said, as she grabbed the bag out of my hand and set it on the floor. While Winnalee dug out one giant dress or shirt after another, I looked down the hall and wished Ma would hurry so we could go.

"Button, look!" Winnalee shouted. "Dancing costumes!" I turned to see two long, skinny costumes dangling from Winnalee's hands by straps as skinny as shoestrings. "Aren't they cool? One for each of us! I like the fur up at the top, do you?"

"They're too big," I said.

"Oh my! What do you have there?" Aunt Verdella asked.

Winnalee held up the costumes and ran to Aunt Verdella. "Can you fix them to fit us? Can you?"

"Of course I can, honey," Aunt Verdella said. Me and Winnalee cheered.

"I wish they had dancing skirts on them, like real ballerinas," I said. The stick-out little skirt is the best part. Winnalee gasped, "Hey! Hey! My pink slip! It's big. Real big! Aunt Verdella, could you make two little skirts from it, for our dancing costumes? Could you?"

Aunt Verdella ha-ha-ed. "Of course I could!" And we both cheered.

Winnalee was so excited about those costumes, Marty Graw, and her new headband that Aunt Verdella had to put her headband on her head because she was hopping so much I couldn't reach her head to do it. "Put the flower on the same side as mine," I told her.

Finally Daddy stubbed out his cigarette and said, "Are we gonna go, or are we gonna sit here all day and talk about dresses?" He looked at Uncle Rudy and shook his head. "At this rate, there won't be a beer left in all of Dauber by the time these women are ready to go."

On the way out the door, Ma stopped Daddy by putting her hand on his arm. "Reece, thank you for saying what you did to Stella. I know you don't like her, and that's the reason you said it, but thank you, anyway." I think Daddy was going to say something back, but Ma was already hurrying to the car.

We watched the parade first, and every time a clown or a man reached into his bag of candy, Winnalee ran out into the street, her mermaid hair flapping just like her jaw, and she waved both hands and screamed, "Throw some over here! Throw some over here!" And they did. Every time. We giggled as we ran to pick up the candy that pinged on the pavement, only half-hearing Aunt Verdella yell at us to back away from the floats.

The minute the parade was over, me and Winnalee wanted to hurry to the carnival, because just hearing the carnival music and seeing the top of the Ferris wheel out past the bridge was making our bellies excited, but we had to stop on our way to the car about a hundred times, because the grown-ups got stopped by this or that person to talk about dumb things like crops that needed rain and bad hearts and backs. At least three people told Ma right out that they didn't recognize her at first and then went on and on about how good she looked, and Aunt Verdella too. "We can thank Freeda for our new looks," Aunt Verdella said, and then whoever they were talking to had to yap to Freeda about their bad hair, or wide hips, or whatever. Freeda scooted right over to them then and started picking at their hair and touching their cheekbones and eyelids until their men got done talking about cows and the weather and hauled them away. Just before we got to the car, I heard Ma say, "Looks like Dauber's about to experience a population boom!" and the three of them laughed and laughed.

As soon as we got to the park, Winnalee and I jumped out of the car, and Winnalee started running. "Hey! Get back here, you kids! We have to find a picnic spot first and eat!" Me and Winnalee groaned as we headed back to the car.

"Why can't we go on the rides before we eat?" Winnalee begged.

"Jesus H. Christ, Winnalee," Freeda said. "That carnival isn't going anywhere. Everybody's hungry. We're gonna eat first." Winnalee started to argue, and Ma flashed Freeda that kind of look that says, "Remember what I told you?" and Freeda gave a little nod, sucked in a breath, then stared Winnalee right in the eye. Then, without even a bit of a smile on her face or a cussword on her lips, she said, "Winnalee. We're gonna eat first."

"I'm not even hungry! I'm going on the rides!"

Freeda made a pointy finger at Winnalee. "If you don't want to eat, fine, but you won't have any treats at the carnival either. Your choice. But whether you decide to eat or not, you'll sit quietly and wait until the rest of us are done. Then we'll go to the carnival."

Winnalee blinked and hoisted her ma up higher. She opened her mouth to argue, but Freeda put her hand up. "It's not up for discussion, Winnalee," Freeda said, then she hurried to help grab things out of the trunk.

Winnalee did decide to eat but said she was only going to eat the good stuff. When Winnalee and I were done eating, Winnalee watched Uncle Rudy stab another piece of Aunt Verdella's fried chicken, and her mouth got frowny. "Do we have to wait for *everybody* to get done eating?" she asked, crossing her arms.

"You better hope not, girls," Uncle Rudy said, "because with food this good, I might just keep eating till I pop." Winnalee groaned extra loud when he said that.

"Oh, he's teasin' you, girls," Aunt Verdella said. "You eat a few more bites, then we'll go on the rides."

Uncle Rudy said Winnalee's ma could sit with him under the shade tree while he took a nap and we went on the rides, so Winnalee set the urn down next to him. As we headed toward the rides, Daddy headed for the beer stand and Ma stepped on Aunt Verdella's heel because she had her head cocked as she watched him go. Freeda grabbed Ma's elbow. "Keep your eyes on where *you're* goin', Jewel Peters," she said.

My stomach was a bit scared because I'd never rode on the big-people's rides before, but scared or not, I was determined to ride them.

"Let's go on that one!" Winnalee shouted, pointing to the ride that said *Tilt-A-Whirl* on the sign above the steps leading to it.

"Auntie will buy you tickets, girls. You wait in line." Then Aunt Verdella ran off to the little wooden booth where the tickets were sold. She came back with two white rolls of them. She split one in half and handed them to Winnalee and me.

"I'll watch," Freeda said. "I puke on these things." And Winnalee added, "She does too!" She didn't have to wait by herself, though, because right then someone shouted, "Freeda!" and we looked to see Mike Thompson coming through the swarm of sweaty people, his little nephew propped on his shoulders, Mike's twin and his wife and baby tagging behind him. They stood next to Freeda while the rest of us climbed the metal steps to give our tickets to the carny guy.

Another carny guy, filled with tattoos, held the half-circle cage in place while we got in. After we sat down—Ma and Aunt Verdella on each end, and me and Winnalee in the middle—the carny guy flipped the metal-pole thing we were supposed to hang on to toward our bellies. "Here you go, ladies." He gave a wink, then rapped on the roof of the cage and went off to help some other ladies get into their seats.

"Did you see him wink at you, Jewel?" Aunt Verdella ha-ha-ed, and Ma rolled her eyes, but she was grinning.

When that ride started up, clanking and rumbling as it went over the wavy, wooden ramp, I felt scared. I held my breath as the ride started going faster and our seat started twirling. "Lean!" Aunt Verdella shouted. So that's what we did. We leaned to whatever side the ride headed in (usually Aunt Verdella's side) so that we'd twirl faster and faster. I screamed right out loud, just like everybody else, when it spun real fast, but not those real scared kind of screams, just the happy-scared kind. By the time the ride started slowing down to stop, I was yelling, "Again! Again!" just like Winnalee.

We rode on the rides until our tickets were gone and Winnalee was sick to her stomach. We packed the food cooler back in the truck, rounded up Daddy and Uncle Rudy and Winnalee's vase, and took our blankets and the cooler with drinks in it down to the riverbank. Mike Thompson came along with us, and I wasn't sure if Freeda liked that or not.

Sure, she smiled at him, and she laughed when he made a funny, but I noticed that when he tried to put his arm around her or take her hand, she moved away from him, though I wasn't sure why.

It seemed to take forever for the sky to get dark enough so the fireworks could start, but finally the first big boom came, telling us that it was time.

Me and Winnalee sat on our knees and watched the fireworks, screaming out when our favorites burst in the sky. Across the whole riverbank you could hear little kids squealing and big people saying "ooooh" and "ahhhhhh," till each firework hissed its way down, fizzling out just before it landed on the lit-up floats skimming along the water.

All too soon, though, it was over. From the park, we could hear the twang of guitars through amplifiers. Not playing songs, but tuning up. "Oh, a dance!" Freeda shouted.

Ma looked worried. "I don't know if we should stay. The girls—"

"But we wanna dance too!" Winnalee said. "How come we can't dance?" Winnalee whined, bouncing a little, like she always did when she begged.

"How about if they stay for a couple songs, Jewel? Then Rudy and I will take the girls home with us, if the rest of you want to stay."

I was real happy when Ma said, "Okay."

Freeda kicked off her shoes the minute the music started and headed out to the dance floor. She didn't seem to care if Mike followed her or not. Verdella hurried behind Freeda, dragging Ma right with her. And Winnalee grabbed my hand and drug me out there too.

I couldn't believe my eyes when Ma danced right along with Freeda and Aunt Verdella. And I suppose Ma couldn't believe her eyes when she saw me dancing right along with Winnalee. "Look at Button!" Winnalee shouted. "She's really dancing!" And I was too. And so was my ma. So for five whole songs, while the music thumped from black speakers and the rides whirled and blinked on the other side of the park, we danced, bunched up with other people on the cement floor, like no one was watching. All of us rocking our arms, and shaking our butts, and stomping our feet, and tossing our heads, and laughing and laughing.

I knew the second the singer announced that it was time for a little break that we'd have to leave. Ma gave Aunt Verdella a look, so Aunt Verdella put a hand on each of us to steer us toward the parking lot, when the guy who had been singing told everybody that while they took a break, their good friends Reece Peters and Owen Palmer were going to play a couple numbers. Nothing was gonna make Aunt Verdella leave just then!

I glanced at Ma quick, and my teeth went right to my cheek all by themselves. Ma was watching Daddy, and she seemed to be thinking hard, but she didn't say anything.

While Daddy and Owen put their heads together, talking about what song to do, I suppose, Freeda yelled out, " 'Jail-house Rock'!" Daddy nodded, and suddenly his voice came bursting out, till it was the loudest thing in that whole park. The crowd hooted and hollered when Daddy started singing the first words, and by the time the music started behind him, the drummer from the band forgot all about his break and leapt up on the stage and started pounding his drumsticks.

When that Elvis song got over, Daddy sang that song about a lady named Sue who liked to run around a lot. While he sang, I looked out at the people circled around the dance floor and saw how they thought Daddy sang better than anybody in that other band.

When the song ended, the people yelled, "More! More!" so Owen shouted into the microphone, "Here's a brand-new one by Roy Orbison, called 'Only the Lonely,' " and the crowd cheered some more, and so did we, as we danced and danced.

When that song finished, Daddy sang another Elvis song, the one Aunt Verdella said was her favorite, and he said right into the microphone that he was singing it for his two best girls, his wife, Jewel, and his sister-in-law, Verdella. Aunt Verdella led us to the side of the dance floor so we could see Daddy better, and me and Winnalee leaned our backs against her while he sang. Aunt Verdella had her arms wrapped around us, and I could feel her voice fluttering in her fat part as she sang along with Daddy. Ma stood beside us. She had her lips pressed together in that way people press their lips together when they feel soft tears in their stomachs.

Freeda was on the dance floor, her arms wrapped around Mike Thompson's neck, his arms holding her as gently as if she were a baby. I looked up at Ma then, and although she didn't turn her face down toward me, she smiled, and reached out, and pulled me softly from Aunt Verdella, and put her arms around my shoulders, and together we rocked side to side to the music.

After Daddy and Owen finished the song, the crowd hooted and hollered and begged for more, but Daddy pretended he didn't hear that part, as he told them to welcome the other band back.

Both him and Owen came over by us when they left the stage. Ma smiled up at him, and Daddy smiled back. Owen nodded and said thank you as everyone told Daddy and him how good they'd done, but he stopped when he saw Ma and told her how good she looked. Daddy put his arm around Ma and looked at her, then grinned. "She *does*, doesn't she?" And Ma smiled.

"Goddamn, I miss this, Reece," Owen said, while looking back at the stage and shaking his head. And Ma said, "So does he."

People came up to crowd Daddy and Owen, asking them when they were gonna get back together. I wanted to tell my daddy that I thought he sang real good. Maybe even wrap my arms around his waist like Winnalee was doing, but I felt shy even thinking about doing such a thing.

"Okay, girls," Uncle Rudy said. "This old coot's gotta find his bed."

"I'll keep the girls at my house, then you three can stay as long as you like," Aunt Verdella said. She added real fast, "Well, if that's all right with you, Jewel." And Ma said it was.

"Verdella, where's the can?" Freeda said, breaking into the little circle. June Thompson was with her. Aunt Verdella pointed to the brick building under another streetlamp, and Winnalee said she had to pee and couldn't make it till we got home, so all of us girls went. While we were standing against the cool, brick wall, waiting to get into one of the two stalls, I heard June Thompson whisper to Freeda, "I think Mike's fallin' for you, Freeda," and Freeda say back to her, "For his sake, I hope to hell not."

Winnalee and I didn't fall asleep as soon as we got in the car, like Aunt Verdella said we would. "Stop at my house first!" Winnalee said. "I wanna get my jammies, so I don't ruin my new outfit. And I want to get my pink skirt so you can fix it into two in the morning." I got excited when Winnalee said this, remembering that we'd soon have real dancing costumes.

Aunt Verdella waited in the car while me and Winnalee raced inside and up the stairs. Winnalee grabbed her pj's off the floor, then she pulled our book out from under her pillow. "Let's each write a bright idea before we go."

While Winnalee flipped pages to find where we'd left off, a bright idea came to me. "I got one!" I said, so she handed me the book first, and I wrote, *Bright Idea #94: If you always ride on the slow rides that don't lift far off of the ground, just because you're afraid of falling, you won't fall far, that's true, but you won't get many thrills either. And you won't be proud of yourself when the carnival's over.*

Winnalee took our book and read my idea. "Did you write

that about you? Were you scared of the big rides?" I nodded. "Wow, I didn't know that. You weren't even biting your face."

Winnalee took the pencil then and said, "I got one too." And she wrote *Bright Idea #95: When you sing, sing rowdy like Elvis. And when you dance, dance like you're at the Marty Graw.*

17

When Aunt Verdella threw her back out toward the end of July, trying to uproot the Virgin Mary's bathtub so she could move it to the back of the yard, for Lord knows what reason, Ma was worried about leaving me with her while she went to work. "Two girls to keep an eye on while she's flat on her back? I don't know about this, Reece," Ma said that morning.

"We'll be okay, Ma," I said. "Me and Winnalee are going to be her nurses and take care of her."

"They'll be fine, Jewel," Daddy said, so Ma ran me over to Aunt Verdella's like any other morning. Winnalee was waiting for me in the driveway. She was wearing an old lavender dress of Aunt Verdella's and an apron tied around her tight, to hold it up and in. She had bobby pins holding back the sides of her hair. "I got my dancing dress underneath," she told me. "You bring yours?"

"Yep, right here," I told her, holding out my arm so she could see the bag I carried. Me and Winnalee had worn our dancing costumes practically every day since Aunt Verdella had made them.

"Good. Then we'll put on a dance for Aunt Verdella later."

We all went inside, and Ma put the sandwiches and stuff she brought in the refrigerator, then we all went into the living room, where Aunt Verdella was stretched out on the couch, her curls matted, and her face all pinched up. "Oh Lord," she said. "Now I know what Rudy goes through when his back acts up."

"Where is Rudy?" Ma asked.

Aunt Verdella winced as she tried to prop herself on one elbow so she could see us better. "Oh, he's over at the Smithys'. Tommy came to get him. They had some pipe burst in their basement, and Elroy's gone. Tommy said the whole basement is flooded."

Ma looked nervous. "I don't feel right about leaving the girls here when you're laid up and alone, Verdella."

"Nonsense," Aunt Verdella said. "We'll be fine. And Freeda's right across the road if we need anything."

"She is now, but she ain't gonna be long," Winnalee said. "After they wake up—in about a hundred years—Mike and her are gonna go skinny-dippin' at Crystal Lake. That's what I heard her tell Mike yesterday, anyway."

"Skinny-dipping? Lord!" Aunt Verdella said, then she ha-ha-ed. "Ouch, that hurts," she said after she laughed. "Well, no matter. Don't you worry one iota about us, Jewel. The girls are gonna be my nurses, aren't you, girls? They'll take good care of me, and we'll all be just fine."

"Yeah," Winnalee said.

So Ma left, and Winnalee and I got busy being Aunt Verdella's nurses. "You go pick her a flower to put on her food tray, and I'll get her breakfast, okay?" Winnalee said. When I came in with a little clump of pink pansies, Winnalee was at the table, standing over a pile of crushed Shredded Wheat.

"What are you doing?" I asked.

Winnalee grabbed another raisin out of the Sun-Maid box. "I'm trying to make a bunny face on her Shredded Wheat, but they keep bustin'."

"You're crushing them because you're pushing too hard," I told her. "I'll do that, and you make her a piece of toast. She likes toast."

I used one point of a fork and jabbed carefully at the cereal that always reminded me of little hay bales, until there was two little holes in it, then I tucked a raisin in each one. "Put the broken ones in first, then the milk and sugar," Winnalee said. "And then we'll set the bunny one on top, careful, so his eyes don't fall out." We talked quietly as we worked, so Aunt Verdella wouldn't hear our surprise, which probably wasn't necessary anyway, since she was yelling out answers to the questions Allen Ludden was asking on *Password*.

When we got done, we brought Aunt Verdella her good breakfast on a sick-tray. Aunt Verdella laughed when she saw it. "Oh, you girls!" she said, her eyes tearing, either from our bunny cereal or from the pain of trying to sit up enough to eat.

After she ate, she fell back against her pillow and asked if I could get her a glass of water so she could take one of the pain pills the doctor gave her. "I wasn't gonna have one, because they knock me out for hours, but, oh boy, this back is hurtin' something fierce after I sat up like that."

It wasn't ten minutes after Aunt Verdella took that pill that her eyelids started getting droopy. "If I fall asleep, you girls be good and play inside, you hear?"

"We will," I told her as I took her water glass to the kitchen. I was emptying it in the sink when Winnalee came up behind me and whispered in my ear, "Today's the day!"

I turned to her. "What do you mean?"

"To go see the fairies! It's the perfect day! Your ma's working, Uncle Rudy's over at the Smithys', Freeda's gonna run off with Mike as soon as they wake up, and Aunt Verdella's out like a light."

I got scared the minute she said it. "Winnalee, we promised we'd stay inside and be good. And, anyway, we didn't even make a map yet."

"Nobody will even know," Winnalee said, as she stripped

off Aunt Verdella's old clothes and balled them up on the kitchen chair. "Look, I even have shoes on today. I wore them on purpose." She fluffed the fur at the top of her costume and told me to put mine on too, so that we'd look like fairies and maybe they wouldn't be so scared of us then.

My throat felt dry, so I cleared it a couple of times. "But Tommy said the fairies only come out right before dark. It's still morning!"

"If they're there, we'll be noisy and wake them up. As for the map, we don't need one. We'll take the road, like Tommy said. I remember the directions."

"We don't even know if he was telling the truth, Winnalee. I've never been down to the end of Peters Road before. How do we know there's another road on the other side?"

"We'll find out, I guess. Come on, Button, don't chicken out. We'll go fast and get back before anyone knows we were even gone." Winnalee picked up her ma. "Come on, Button. This might be our only chance."

"I bet Freeda will come over here to check on Aunt Verdella before she leaves for swimming," I said.

"Maybe she will, but she ain't gonna wake up till close to noon. Now, stop wasting our time talking, and let's get going."

There wasn't a sound anywhere but for the crunching of our shoes on gravel and one squawk of a crow flapping across the hazy sky, as Winnalee and I hurried down Peters Road, me carrying our adventure bag and Winnalee carrying her ma, even though I told her that urn would get heavy.

"What color dresses do you think fairies wear?" Winnalee asked. "I think some will have on blue dresses, icy blue. Or maybe a lavender color."

I didn't say anything, because once again, Winnalee was talking about fairies in a way that made them seem all the more make-believe.

"We have to start school next month," I said, just to change the subject. "There's three different classrooms for the fifth-graders. I hope we get in the same class."

"Me too," Winnalee said. "Then you can help me. I don't know how to do long division yet. Will we have to do long division?"

"Yeah, probably. How come you don't know how to do long division?"

She ignored my question and added, "I don't know how to multiply either. Well, except for my twos and fives, but I have to count up still."

I blinked at her. "You're kidding me!"

"No, I'm not. The school I was at hadn't started learning that stuff yet, then we moved. At my new school, they were already doing long division when I got there. The teacher made me stay in at recess to learn my tables, and the kids laughed at me 'cause I didn't know them. I hated that."

"Oh," I said. I felt sorry for her. "I can help you learn your math."

"I don't want to learn it," Winnalee said. "I'll just copy off your papers."

Just her mentioning cheating made another dose of scared thump down into my belly, to join the scared I was already feeling about sneaking off. I looked behind us to see how far we'd gotten. I couldn't see the houses or yards anymore. I looked ahead of us, and I couldn't see the road Tommy told us about either. I bit at the inside of my cheek, just thinking about how we might be lost already.

We didn't have to walk long before we were thirsty and Winnalee's ma got heavy. "Wanna trade?" Winnalee asked. The last thing in this world I wanted to do was to carry Hannah Malone. Even Winnalee asking made me hope hard that Aunt Verdella soon had enough money for that final restin' place for her. I looked at the urn, and for a second I thought about trading our loads, but only for a second. "Well,

I told you not to bring her, but you did anyway, so I guess you can just carry her."

Winnalee's sigh sounded half like a groan. "Fine. Then we're gonna waste more time resting, because my arms are gonna fall off." We sat down alongside the road, the long blades of grass tickling our bare legs, the sun hot on our backs. "Sorry about that, Ma. Button ain't insulting you. She's just a scaredy-cat."

I didn't want to talk about me being scared, so I talked about Mike instead. "You think him and Freeda will get married?" I asked, thinking about what Aunt Verdella said, how she thinks that they're falling in love and, if they do, she bets me and Winnalee could be flower girls and throw rose petals on the aisle for them.

"I don't know," Winnalee said.

"Do you want them to?"

Winnalee screamed, waving her hands. "A wood tick. Get it off me!" I grabbed the little round tick crawling up her leg and tossed it in the grass.

Winnalee stood up and picked up her ma. "Let's get going. My arms aren't rested, but I don't want those damn ticks crawling on me."

"Do you want them to?" I asked again, as I slung our adventure bag over my shoulder.

"No, I don't want ticks crawling on me. I told you that!"

Winnalee was crabby, which probably meant that she didn't get enough sleep, because Ma said that makes kids crabby. "No, I meant do you want Freeda and Mike to get married."

"I like Mike," she said. "He's funny, and he likes the shows I put on for them. He makes good hamburgers too. But I heard Aunt Verdella say something to Freeda about them maybe getting married, and Freeda said, 'Like hell!' so I think that means no."

Winnalee stopped and pointed. "Button, look! A stop sign! That's gotta be Marsh Road. Come on!"

We were panting by the time we got to the stop sign. "Look, there it is!" Winnalee said, pointing to the white sign. "Now we go left. We're almost there, Button!"

But we weren't almost there. We walked and walked and still didn't come to a road on the left, only on the right. "I have to pee," I told Winnalee. "Bad too," and she told me to go in the ditch. I never peed outside before, but Winnalee said it was easy if you kept your legs spread enough when you squatted. "Otherwise you're gonna pee on your leg or your shoes."

"You watch for cars!" I told Winnalee, even though we hadn't seen even one car yet. I set down our bag and hurried into the ditch. "Why you going so far? No one's gonna see you," Winnalee said.

"They might!" I yelled back, as I slipped just far enough into the woods that the brush and tree trunks could hide me.

"You're gonna get wood ticks on your butt!" Winnalee called, sounding a bit scared herself. I looked down at the ground, checking for snakes, or bugs, or anything else that might bite my bare butt, then, seeing none, I pulled the elastic of my pink skirt up high around my arms and pulled the snaps on my costume, which were tucked between my legs.

I'd just started peeing—tiny sprinkles of pee wetting my ankles, no matter how far I spread them apart—when I heard the rumble of a motor. "Oh shit!" I said out loud, then gasped. Not just because somebody was coming, but because I swore. "Winnalee?"

The rumble turned into a roar. "Somebody's coming!" Winnalee yelled. I saw the orange and pink of her dancing dress coming through the woods. I hurried to pull up my underwear, wincing as I felt a couple drops of warm pee between me and my undies. I didn't bother with the snaps, but just pulled my pink skirt down where it was supposed to be.

We moved away from the leaves I'd wet and crouched down so whoever it was wouldn't see us.

We heard brakes squeal and rocks spit into the ditch, as

whoever it was stopped. Winnalee's eyes got wide, and it was her turn to say, "Shit."

"Come out, come out, wherever you are!" a mocking voice sang out.

"It's Tommy!" Winnalee said. She got up and marched right out to the road, me following her.

"What are you doing here, Tommy Smithy!"

"Lookin' for you kiddies."

I gasped. "They know we're gone?" Scared buzzed in my ears.

Tommy leaned over the dusty black door of his beat-up truck. "Nah. Rudy sent me to check on Verdella and you kiddies, since he's still busy with the pipes. She's snoring on the couch. Never even opened her eyes when I came in. So I looked around the place and didn't see you kiddies anywhere. Didn't take no genius to figure out where you'd gone."

"He's gonna tell, Winnalee," I whispered. My legs felt like they were made of Jell-O, and the smell of the exhaust chugging out of Tommy's truck was making me sick to my stomach.

Winnalee shot me a look that said, "Shut up," then she turned back to Tommy. "We're just taking a walk. So what?"

Tommy scratched his greasy forehead. "So what? Not sure that's what Button's ma or aunt would say."

Winnalee tipped her head back a bit. "Button's ma is at work, and her aunt is snoring on the couch."

"I could stop and tattle to your sister," Tommy said. "Wouldn't mind an excuse to stop by and see her."

"Freeda isn't even home, dummy. Her and Mike went skinny-dippin'."

The minute Winnalee said that, Tommy's ugly eyebrows shot up. "You don't say."

"Come on, Winnalee," I said, not bothering to whisper this time. "Let's go home."

Winnalee tugged her arm out of my grip. "No way! I got this far, I'm gonna keep goin'." She hoisted her ma up higher, then started walking. Fast. I didn't have any choice but to tag after her.

"Go away, Tommy!" Winnalee shouted, as Tommy clanked his truck in gear and started coasting alongside of us.

"You stupids," he said. "You know how long it's gonna take to get to Fossard's and back? It's almost four miles, both ways. That is, if you *do* get back." Tommy made a creepy sound like a Halloween ghost.

Winnalee's steps slowed, but they didn't stop.

Tommy stopped his truck. I wanted to turn around and see what he was up to, but Winnalee told me to just keep walking and ignore him. We didn't walk more than ten steps before his truck was rolling again. "Okay," he called out his window. "I'll make you a deal."

I could tell that Winnalee wanted to stop and ask him what the deal was, but she didn't. She just kept walking and ignoring him.

"I could be coaxed to drive you there," he said.

Winnalee stopped. "Why would somebody who isn't even nice offer to do that?" she asked suspiciously.

"Well," he said. "You kiddies have given me a bit of a problem here. Rudy sent me to check up on things, I came lookin' for ya, and found ya runnin' off. I don't bring you home, and my ass is gonna get chewed out."

"Don't say you saw us, then," Winnalee said.

"Ain't gonna work," Tommy said. "He asks about you girls, and I say I didn't see ya at the house, then he'll ask why I didn't look for ya. And if I say I did see ya, then I'd be lying. Course, there's a solution to our little problem, you know."

"What's that?" Winnalee asked.

"Well, I could drive you two kiddies over to Fossard's, then drop you off back home, tell Rudy everything's fine, and no one would be wiser."

I got happy over his solution, because I was mighty thirsty.

"So what's in it for you, Tommy Smithy?" Winnalee asked.

"What?" he asked. "Who said there's anything in it for me?"

"Stop acting like you don't know what I mean. I can tell by the naughty look in your eye that you got something up your sleeve."

Tommy spit on the gravel, so close to Winnalee's feet that she backed up. "You ain't as dumb as you look, kid."

"So what's the deal?"

"Well, seems to me that if I help you get a glimpse of some pretty little ladies, you should help me get a glimpse of a pretty little lady too."

"You want to see the fairies with us?" Winnalee asked.

Tommy shook his head and rolled his eyes. "I guess you *are* as stupid as you look."

"What's the bargain?" I asked. "We ain't got all day."

"Well, neither do I, so I'll tell it to ya straight. You tell me where Freeda and Mike are skinny-dippin', and I'll take you to Fossard's."

"Don't tell him!" I said. "He wants to see Freeda naked!"

It was Winnalee's turn to roll her eyes. "Freeda don't care who sees her naked, Button. Come on."

I didn't have any choice but to follow Winnalee around Tommy's truck. He wouldn't let us in, though, until Winnalee told him that Freeda and Mike were going to Crystal Lake.

Tommy drove fast. So fast that Winnalee had to grip her arms around the urn so her ma wouldn't go flying off the seat. And when he turned down the dead-end road, Winnalee crashed into me, and the door handle jabbed into my side.

At the end of the drive, a tall, square house stood on a hill. The door was boarded shut, and the windows were broken, jagged triangles of glass glinting in the sun, like shark's teeth.

"Where's the bomb shelter?" I asked.

"It's here, but you can't see it till you get to it. It's cut on the other side of that hill, right there. Underneath those red pines."

"Who cares where the bomb shelter is," Winnalee said. "Where's the beck?"

Tommy brought the car to a stop, and Winnalee and I had to push our backs against the seat to keep from cracking our heads on the dash.

"The beck is straight that a-ways about fifty yards. Right through those trees," he said, pointing at an angle off to the left of the house. "I'm giving you ten minutes, then I'm honking the horn. You ain't back here in that time, and I'm leavin' without ya. And take that creepy urn with ya when ya go too."

As much as I hated Tommy Smithy, I was glad he was here, as I looked over at the hill where he said the bomb shelter was.

Winnalee opened the car door. "Come on, Button!"

We ran fast across the grown-over yard. Winnalee, because she wanted to hurry to the beck, and me, because I wanted to get past the bomb shelter.

"Keep going!" Tommy yelled to us. "Farther!"

When we got to the woods, Winnalee stopped. "Hear that, Button?"

"What?" I yelled, sure she'd say she'd heard the scraping of a shovel.

"It's running water! The beck!" Winnalee sounded like she was gonna cry.

It didn't take us long before we saw the silver sparkle of water showing through the trees. We hurried as quickly as we could, me in the front so I could hold the branches away, since Winnalee's arms were wrapped around the urn.

"Let's make a lot of noise, Button, so the fairies wake up!"

I called for the fairies too, but I didn't shout like Winnalee, for fear that what we would wake up was Fossard's ghost.

The beck sat low, trees close to the edge leaning over the sparkly water, like they were bowing. Winnalee stopped, her eyes looking up and down the bank of the stream. "Hello?" she called out. "Come out, please. We won't hurt you. We just want to see you."

The breeze, or a little animal, ruffled the leaves to the side of us, and Winnalee turned fast, sure that it was a fairy who'd made the rustle. "Did you hear that? Over there!" Winnalee rushed toward the noise, and I followed.

"Come on, fairies! We only have a couple minutes. Just one peek?"

Winnalee and I spun in slow circles, straining our eyes as we searched the underbrush for them. Then, all too soon for Winnalee (but not too soon for me), Tommy's horn sounded.

"Shit!" Winnalee said. Her pretty face crumpled, like she might cry.

"We'd better go, Winnalee." I felt sad for her, so I added, "Next time we'll come right before dark, then we'll see them for sure."

"But I want—" Just like that, Winnalee stopped, her pink mouth opening into a wide-open smile. "Look!" I looked where she was pointing, right above water that was so bright it hurt my eyes, and I caught the flicker of two tiny, rainbowy wings. There one second, then gone the next.

"Did you see that? Did you?"

Her voice was as soft as a sleepy baby's sigh when she spoke again. "They're here, Button. We've found them."

I didn't have the heart to tell her that all she'd seen was the wings of a dragonfly.

Aunt Verdella was still sleeping when Tommy dropped us off. We snuck in the house as quietly as we could, drank three cups of water each, then got out the egg-salad sandwiches Ma had put in the fridge for our lunch and the box of Lay's from on top of the fridge. We'd barely sunk our teeth into our sandwiches when we heard Aunt Verdella groan.

"Girls?" she called. We hurried into the living room as she was trying to get up. "Oh, there you are." She rubbed her head. "Good Lord, those pills make me goofy. Help Auntie get up, will you, so I can use the bathroom?" When we went through the kitchen—me and Winnalee propped under her arms like crutches—and Aunt Verdella saw our plates on the table, she said, "That's my girls. I knew I could count on you to be good while Aunt Verdella slept." I was glad she could only see the top of my head, since Aunt Verdella once said that you can always see guilt written on someone's face.

18

I knew right away why Aunt Verdella was smiling when we packed up the few baby sweaters and old junk that didn't sell at the community sale that second Saturday in August. She'd had her tables almost full, and she had sold almost every single thing, but for what was in the little box she carried. That meant that she probably had enough money now to buy Hannah Malone's plot and gravestone.

"I wish *I'd* have made money today," Winnalee said. She looked like a sad clown with her droopy lips and the skin around them stained red from cherry Kool-Aid.

I sighed one of those quick little sighs that people sigh when they get irritated. I'd told Winnalee that we should get busy making pot holders, since Aunt Verdella got us more loops, but she said, "Maybe tomorrow," she was sick of making them for now. Every day for two weeks she said the very same thing, until it was too late, so I just made some without her when I was at home.

Aunt Verdella stopped at my house first, and Freeda's truck pulled in right behind us. Aunt Verdella looked in her rearview mirror. "Oh, I thought Freeda was going off with Mike to Porter today."

"She was, but then she wasn't. He came," Winnalee said,

"but then they got into a fight. I heard Freeda tell him that she doesn't need his clingy shit."

"Oh dear," Aunt Verdella said.

Aunt Verdella got out of the car, and while the ladies talked, me and Winnalee danced in the grass in our dancing costumes. Finally, Aunt Verdella asked Freeda to take Winnalee home with her. "I'll stop by in a bit. I want to talk to Jewel about something first."

"No fair!" Winnalee said.

"Evelyn, maybe you should play outside for a while," Ma said, as she opened the front door.

"Oh no, she can come in, Jewel," Aunt Verdella said.

Aunt Verdella and I followed Ma into the kitchen. Ma set her bags on the table.

Aunt Verdella grabbed me by the waist and pulled me to stand by her chair. She gave me the same happy-secret look she gave me over the past few weeks every time Winnalee was around and we couldn't talk about our plan out in the open.

"It looks to me like somebody's got a secret!" Ma said with a smile.

Aunt Verdella ha-ha-ed, but then she got serious. "I don't know if Button told you what happened a while back, with Tommy knocking over Winnalee's urn and spilling some of her ma's ashes, but . . . well, I decided right then and there that I'm gonna use my TV money to buy Winnalee and Freeda's ma a headstone and a plot. I've been saving up every dime I make at the sales, all month, and I think I have enough now!"

Ma was leaned over, putting milk away in the refrigerator. She popped up and blinked at Aunt Verdella. "Your TV money?"

"Oh, Jewel, if you'd have seen her face when her ma's ashes spilled, well, you'd understand why I've gotta do this. Wasn't that the saddest thing, Button? That's why I couldn't give up my Saturdays at the community sale when you and Freeda would invite me along on your outings. I'd talked to

Mr. Parkins at the funeral home in town, and he gave me a rough idea of what a stone and a plot would cost here, and he didn't figure it would be much different in Hopested, so I knew I had to earn a bit more money for the surprise and, of course, the cost of the trip itself."

"What does Rudy say about this?"

"He says it's my money, and I should do with it what I want. I believe I've got enough now. Mr. Parkins gave me the name of a funeral director over there. A Mr. Hamilton, who will order the stone for me and set me up with a plot. Rudy's gonna drive me over there." Aunt Verdella gave me a grin, then said to Ma, "And, Jewel, I'm hoping that you'll let Button go with. This little girl has worked hard making pot holders, and she's given just about every cent she's made to Hannah Malone's burial fund, so I think it would be nice if she could go along. Winnalee is Button's best friend, and I know how much she'd like to help pick out a stone and plot for her little friend's surprise. I'd watch over her good, Jewel. You know I would."

"I know that, Verdella," Ma said. She looked over at me, and I didn't say nothing out loud, but in my head I was begging her to say yes. Not because I wanted to pick out one of those plot places, or one of those creepy Halloween stones, but because I wanted to help make Winnalee and Freeda happy. I also wanted to go away with Aunt Verdella and Uncle Rudy on a long car trip and stay in a motel like fancy people do.

"I don't see what harm there would be in her going along," Ma said.

Aunt Verdella got so happy about Ma saying yes that she shot up and gave her a quick hug. I was so happy that I tagged right after Aunt Verdella and gave Ma a hug too. I also gave thanks in my head to Tommy for not being a rat fink and tattling on Winnalee and me running off, like I worried he might (that is, until I saw him around Freeda two days after we'd gone to the beck and saw the way he couldn't look her in the eye and the way his cheeks burned like fire had started under his skin), or there was no way Ma would have said yes.

I walked Aunt Verdella to the car, and she chattered the whole way about our trip to Hopested. "I'm gonna ask your uncle Rudy to drive us there first thing Monday morning," she said. She clapped her hands together and looked up. "Oh, Button, Winnalee is gonna be so happy!"

I bounced more than I walked back to the house. Ma was still putting away groceries. "There you are. Verdella gone?" I nodded. "I can't believe I was gone this long. Freeda and I were only going to grab coffee, then get some groceries, but we ended up in Witmeir's Shoe Store instead. Good heavens, we've not done a thorough job on our housecleaning in about a month. Give me a hand, Evelyn, and we'll get at least some things done before your dad gets home."

"Where's Daddy?" I asked, just because I wanted to know how long we had to clean.

"He's over helping your uncle Rudy put a new hitch on the cattle wagon. Rudy's going to deliver a bull over to a farmer in Tomahawk on Monday."

"He'll be gone all day, then?"

"Yeah. Why?"

"Well, Aunt Verdella was going to ask him to drive us on Monday."

"Oh well, she'll have to wait till later in the week then, I guess."

But we didn't have to wait. Aunt Verdella came Sunday morning right after breakfast. "Yoo-hoo!" she called. I expected her voice to sound all droopy, but it didn't.

"Well, Jewel," she said, clapping her hands together. "I've made a decision. Since Rudy can't drive me to Hopested tomorrow, I've decided to drive myself. I hope you'll still let Button go."

"Yourself? Why don't you just wait until later in the week, Verdella?"

"The Smithys are going on a fishing trip to Canada, so Tommy will be gone all this week and part of the next. Rudy couldn't leave then, because he'd have no one to do the milking, with Reece puttin' in so much overtime. I decided that I don't want to wait till next week, so I asked Fanny Tilman to fill in for Ada, and I told Rudy I'm driving myself."

"Verdella, you never drive long distances alone, and you never drive on the highway. You try making a trip like this one on only back roads and it will take you forever!"

"You're right. I've not driven anywhere but to town and back, or to the sale, since we got married. And I never take the highways. Some days it's hard enough to make myself even do that much, because I get so nervous behind the wheel that to drive for more than a half an hour just ties me in knots. But it's about time I stop being so timid and just take the bull by the horns and go."

"And Rudy's okay with this?" Ma asked.

"Well, I don't think he was keen on the idea at first, but all he said was, 'If that's what you think you should do, Verdie, then that's what you should do.' He outlined my route on the map for me. I think I can find my way, and, well, if I get lost, all I have to do is stop at a station and ask for directions. Freeda's right. I've lived long enough being scared of causing more harm if I'm behind the wheel, and the only way I'm gonna get over it is to prove to myself that I won't. I don't know why, but I feel like if I do this trip and get back here safely, maybe I'll be able to let go of that old fear. I'll admit to you, Jewel, that at first I thought maybe I should go alone, because I got to thinking, 'what if...' but then I stopped myself. Anyway, I sure would appreciate it if you'd still let Button go. I plan to stay the night in Hopested before heading back, since my night vision isn't good. And as you know, I'll take good care of Button."

I bit my cheek while I waited for Ma to answer, then grinned as big as my mouth would stretch when she said I could go.

Monday morning Ma took me to Aunt Verdella's before the sun had even peeked its sleepy head above the treetops. She said she had some extra work to do at Dr. Wagner's office, so she didn't mind dropping me off at that hour.

I didn't expect to see Winnalee, since it was so early, but the second Ma stopped the car, the screen door across the road slammed and Winnalee came across the yard. She was wearing her dancing costume again, the pink skirt sticking out straight at the sides, and she had a rope tied around her waist, holding our Book of Bright Ideas like a holster.

I was carrying my little red suitcase with one change of shorts and a shirt, my baby doll pajamas, and an extra pair of socks and underwear. I had my jacket slung over my arm, in case it got chilly at night. "What do you got in there?" Winnalee asked, her breath blowy from running to get to our car. Her morning hair had a big snarl in it—or a "snot," as Freeda called those chunks of bunched-up hair that were half snarls and half knots. "And why you so early?"

I didn't know what to say, on account of I didn't know what fib we were planning to tell Winnalee. Lucky for me, Aunt Verdella hurried out of the house just then. She had on her best everyday dress, sky blue with white eyelet trim, and her white shoes. Her purse, which was slung over the crook of her arm, bumped against her fat part as she jogged to the car. She rapped on Ma's window, so Ma rolled it down. "Well, everything's set, Jewel. We'll be back sometime tomorrow afternoon."

"Hey, where you going?" Winnalee asked.

Aunt Verdella's voice was high and squeaky like Minnie Mouse's when she answered. "Well, I have to do a favor for a friend in another town. It's a long drive, so we'll be gone overnight. I have to take Button with me, because Jewel's gotta work today." I could tell by the way Aunt Verdella said it that she'd practiced those words just about as hard as she must have practiced that poem by the Yeats guy.

"She could stay at my house," Winnalee said. I felt sorry for Winnalee then. Standing there with her ma in her arms, looking lonely at the thought of her best friend being gone so long and her not being able to go with.

"Well, uh, my friend wants to see Button, because she remembers her as a baby."

Winnalee looked at her out of the corner of her eye. "If Button has to go, then can I go too, even if your friend didn't know me when I was a baby?"

"Well...you see, honey...um, I've got to cart her kids over to her sister's place. And there's a lot of them. So many that there'll hardly even be room in the car for me and Button."

"There'd be more room if Button stayed by me. It's Monday, so Freeda don't work." Winnalee looked down until all you could see of her eyes were long eyelashes curling against her cheeks.

Aunt Verdella put her arm around Winnalee. I could see by her face that she'd run clear out of fibs. "Button, would you and Winnalee please go into Auntie's house and see if I left my car keys on the table?"

"They're right in your hand, Aunt Verdella," Winnalee said.

"Oh, I meant Auntie's sweater. It should be right on the back of the kitchen chair. It's white."

I knew Aunt Verdella wanted us to get lost so she could ask Ma what she thought of her taking Winnalee along. As we were walking up the porch steps, I saw Ma shake her head.

When we got back to the car with Aunt Verdella's sweater, Ma was about ready to leave. I expected her to just say bye to me and tell me to be good and stay clean, but she didn't. Instead, she opened the car door and stepped out, then gave me a hug. It wasn't the warm, squishy kind of hug that almost hurts because it's so big, like Aunt Verdella always gave, but more like one of those whispery hugs like cousins who don't really know each other well give when their mas tell them to hug good-bye. But still, it made me happy inside. "Have fun, you two," she said.

After Ma pulled out, Aunt Verdella put her hand on Winnalee's shoulder and bent over so she could look her right in the eyes. "Honey, I know you don't understand why Auntie isn't taking you along or leaving Button here. I'm sorry, sweetie, but I can't explain any more right now. But when we get back, Auntie will bring you a big surprise, okay? A really, really special surprise."

Winnalee's eyes were already leaking, but when she realized that Aunt Verdella wasn't going to change her mind, big tears started rolling down her apple cheeks. One fell right on her ma's jar and slipped down the side. I felt like crying too. I knew why Aunt Verdella didn't change her mind, but at that minute I wanted her to.

Uncle Rudy came out of the house then, the screen door slamming behind him. He had a toothpick sticking out of the side of his mouth. He watched Winnalee walking toward home.

"Oh, Rudy. She feels so bad not being able to go with us. But how can I take her? It would ruin the surprise. And like Jewel said, it would be better with just one, since Winnalee is bound to get restless on such a long trip."

"She'll be fine, Verdie."

Uncle Rudy opened the car door and yanked the lever to open the hood. "I'm gonna check the oil before you go," he said.

"Rudy, you checked it yesterday!" Aunt Verdella shook her head.

"I wish you were waiting until I could drive you over there, Verdie. You sure you can't wait just three, four more days?"

"Oh, Rudy. We've waited long enough! And we'll be fine."

"You got the map I marked for you?" he asked, as he wiped the long dipper stick clean with an old rag he took from his back pocket.

"I got the map. Button's gonna help me navigate. And if I get lost, I'll just stop and ask somebody."

"I remember what you said, Uncle Rudy," I told him. "We take Highway 8 west for about four hours. Then we're gonna come to Minnesota and cross the St. Croix River at St. Croix Falls. And once we cross the river, we're gonna run into Highway 85—no, Highway 95, and then go on Highway 23, which comes like a split in the road. Then we're gonna drive about fifty miles."

"Well, what on earth was I worrying about, with this little smarty going along," he said.

"Wait," I said. "And I remember this part too. We're supposed to stop at that Barren town, and at St. Croix Falls to get gas on the way there and the way back. I remember how it looks on the map too."

Uncle Rudy was so proud of me for remembering everything he said that he gave me a teeth-speckled-with-snuff smile. And after he slipped the dipper stick back in the car and slammed the hood down, he patted my head at least ten extra times.

"You drive carefully now, Verdie. And you call Jewel at work, or at home, if there's any problems."

"There's not gonna be any problems," Aunt Verdella said. "Now, give me a hug good-bye and stop that fussin'. And your food is in the roaster in the fridge. You have sandwiches for lunch today and tomorrow and the pot roast and vegetables in the roaster for supper tonight, and for tomorrow night if you're hungry before I get home. I put heating instructions on the fridge door. And there's ice cream in the freezer for your pie too."

"Hear that, Knucklehead?" he said. "We're gonna eat like kings."

"Rudy Peters, don't you dare let that dog eat out of my dishes. You hear?"

Aunt Verdella grabbed him and gave him about a million kisses and then a big squeeze. Uncle Rudy opened her door and patted my shoulder as I climbed in. Then he picked up Aunt Verdella's suitcase and put it into the backseat. "You have the phone number of the funeral home that's going to make the arrangements, Verdie?" he asked.

"It's right here," Aunt Verdella said, patting her purse. "I swear, Rudy, you're soundin' just like me now!" She ha-ha-ed.

I scooted over to make room for Aunt Verdella. Uncle Rudy shut her door, then patted the hood of the car. He stepped back and started waving us on, like he always did when Aunt Verdella backed out.

"Stop! Wait!" came Winnalee's voice, then Uncle Rudy's, saying the same thing.

Aunt Verdella started shaking when she saw Winnalee's face right outside her side window.

"Honey, never, ever run up to a moving car like that. Oh good Lord, you scared Auntie about half to death!" Aunt Verdella dabbed at the little dots of scared that suddenly wet the skin above her lip.

"Sorry," Winnalee said. "But I wanted to give Button this." She slipped our book out from her rope belt and poked it through the car window.

"Why you want me to take it along?" I asked.

"Because when you go places, you find lots of bright ideas. If we don't get busy, we'll never reach one hundred by the time summer's over."

"You sure?"

"Yeah."

"Okay."

Once Aunt Verdella got the car twisted onto Peters Road, we waved to Uncle Rudy and Winnalee, who stood in the yard waving back at us, Uncle Rudy's arm on Winnalee's shoulder.

"Oh, I'm so glad she got done cryin'. I couldn't bear the thought of keeping that sad face in my mind all the way there and back. But you just wait, Button. When we come back and tell that little girl what we've done, she's gonna be so happy that she'll forget all about how sad she was when we left."

I tucked the book on the seat between us and unwrapped the map and laid it across my legs. I traced the route with my finger, paying special attention to the numbers alongside of the lines that drawed the roads. Uncle Rudy told me that while we were driving, I'd see those same numbers on the road signs, and I was to help Aunt Verdella look for them.

It was a hot, sunny day, so we drove with our windows rolled down and let the wind swirl inside. I folded the map, which flapped from the wind, and tucked it under my leg. Once we left Dauber, Aunt Verdella said that we'd be driving on that same highway a long time, so I didn't need to keep watching the map. Then Aunt Verdella and I munched cookies and sang "You Are My Sunshine," about twenty times, because that was her favorite song. After we stopped singing it, Aunt Verdella reached over and patted my bare knee. "You're my little sunshine," she said. And I told her, "You're my big sunshine. And Winnalee is my little sunshine."

While we drove down long stretches of county roads to get to the highway, there was nothing to see but more of what we had at home, trees and brush and high-line wires, so I waited for us to get close to a new town, because I liked that the best. I liked looking at the houses that started near towns. Some old and crumpled, some medium, with bikes out front and gardens off to the side, and some brand-new. I liked looking at them all, but I liked the old houses best. I liked wondering what they must have looked like when they were new, and I liked thinking about all the old-fashioned people who once lived in them. I liked wondering if they were happy people, or sad people, or somewhere in between. And I liked thinking about what kinds of things happened to them. So while Aunt

Verdella chattered about this and that, I listened to her with my big ears and I watched for the old houses, with eyes that Freeda said were pretty.

When I thought of a bright idea, Aunt Verdella said I could dig in her purse for a pen, and I did. Then I wrote, *Bright Idea #96: When you go on a trip to buy a special surprise for your best friend, sing "You Are My Sunshine" and think of all the big people and the little people who are your sunshines. Then look at the old houses you pass, and think about the people who lived in them, and hope that they were somebody's sunshine too.*

19

Aunt Verdella did fine until we got to the highway, then she sat at the stop sign at the end of the county road, staring out at the highway for so long that the car got oven-hot. I watched her from the corner of my eye. Her face was wet, the curls over her forehead clinging to her extra-pale skin. I could see a little shake in her hands, which were wrapped tight around the steering wheel. When her breaths started coming fast and hard, she fumbled for the door handle and got out of the car, leaving it running.

I got up on my knees and watched her go around to the back of the car. She was taking quick steps from side to side, one hand on her chest and the other on her forehead. She looked downright sick. I waited until she got still, then I got out of the car. Another car zoomed past on the highway, blowing a wind on me. I hurried to Aunt Verdella and asked her if she was okay. She had tears streaming down her face as she lifted her head and looked at me. "I'll be fine in a minute," she said, then she told me to get back in the car and that she'd join me in a little while.

Once in the car, Aunt Verdella slammed the door shut and dabbed at her wet eyes. She glanced in her rearview mirror. "I'm sorry about this, Button." She blew out hard, then took a jagged breath. "It's hard to explain, honey, but today is a very big day for Auntie. Like Freeda said, this drive will bring me my redemption." I wanted to ask her what *redemption* meant, but I didn't want to bother her, because I could tell by the way she was staring hard at nothing that her mind was busy.

She looked down the highway in the direction we needed to turn and took another breath, this one not sounding nearly as ragged. "All these years, since that horrible accident, I've been wrapped up in trying to find forgiveness. From God, from the family I hurt... Then, when Freeda came over to wish me well on my trip to my friend's house—because that's where she believes we're going too, of course—she told me that the only one who needs to forgive me at this point is me. And she said something else too. She said that when we can't find forgiveness for ourselves, or for somebody else, then we should just settle for acceptance. She said what happened, happened, and if I could just accept it and stop dwellin' on the 'if only's, forgiveness for myself would come in time." Aunt Verdella laughed a tiny bit. "That girl. Only in her midtwenties, but already wiser than most."

Aunt Verdella took her hands off of the steering wheel and wiggled her fingers. She took another big breath, this one softer and steadier. "There, now let's get movin'. I think I'm ready now." I didn't know what to say to her, so all I said was, "I love you, Aunt Verdella." This made fresh tears come to her eyes, but happy tears this time.

We stopped at a town called Barren to buy gas, just like we were supposed to, and we bought potato chips and Hershey bars with almonds and a couple of root beers. "We'd best not drink our soda pop right now, Button. Lord knows if there's another restroom between here and St. Croix Falls." Aunt Verdella sure was proud when she told the gas station guy how her and her niece were traveling all the way to Hopested to buy a plot and a gravestone for our little friend and how it was her first long car trip in years. "We're doing good too. Aren't we, Button?" I nodded, but the man didn't watch me nod. I don't think he cared if we were doing good on our trip or not.

When we got to St. Croix Falls, we stopped again, just like Uncle Rudy told us to, and we got gas and more potato chips and candy bars. Aunt Verdella looked a bit tired, and when she got out of the car, she walked as stiff as the Tin Man. She was happy though. She smiled the whole time she told the lady behind the counter at that gas station all about our trip too. The lady smiled back and told her that it sure was nice, what we were doing for our little friend.

It was about noon when we came to the sign on Highway 23 that said *Hopested*. Aunt Verdella laughed and shouted real loud, "Hopested, Minnesota. Population two thousand six hundred. We made it, Button! We did it!"

Hopested looked a lot like Dauber, with just one street for the stores and the few other streets for houses. Aunt Verdella drove us down Main Street till we saw a diner, then she parked the car. It took her four tries to line the Bel Air up with the curb, and when we got out of the car, she walked to the sidewalk and looked at the space between the curb and the Bel Air and said, "Well, a horse could probably fit into that space, but the street's wide, so I think it will be okay."

It was a real nice little diner, all decorated in red and white checkers, with a nice waitress who was almost as pretty as Freeda. She brought us each a hamburger and french fries, and two root beers that Aunt Verdella said we could drink now because the restroom was right there if we needed it.

"Miss," Aunt Verdella said when she paid our bill, "can you tell me where to find Hamilton's Funeral Home? We came to order a plot and gravestone for a little friend of ours. Well, not for her, but for her mama. Mr. Hamilton told me on the phone that I could order them right through his establishment, but, silly me, I forgot to ask exactly where he's located."

The pretty waitress stopped chewing her gum and said, "Sure. You just keep going here on Lincoln to the second stop sign, and then turn right. It's two blocks down on your left. It looks like a big white house. Three stories high. You'll see the sign propped on the lawn."

"Thank you, honey," Aunt Verdella said.

"Sure." The lady slid coins out from the register and counted them out in Aunt Verdella's hand. "And I'm sorry about you having to buy such things for your little friend's mother."

"Oh, no need to be sorry, honey. It's a good thing that we're buyin' them. Now she won't have to carry her ma around in a jar anymore." The lady gave Aunt Verdella one of those funny looks that means, "Wow, did you just say something kooky." Aunt Verdella put her change back into her purse and said, "You have a nice day, now, honey. And thank you for the real good service."

There was only one car in front of the big white house, so it didn't take Aunt Verdella long to park. As she reached for her purse, I looked up at the place, which was almost as pretty as the house Scarlett O'Hara lived in. I bit the inside of my cheek though, thinking about dead people being in there. Tommy told me once about funeral places. How they slap dead people on a concrete slab, point them upside down, and cut their armpits to drain out their blood. Then he told me how they put marbles where their eyeballs should be and stitch them shut so nobody could see that their eyes are gone. The whole idea of people laying in there with marbles for eyes and cut armpits made my stomach feel sick.

"What's the matter, honey?" Aunt Verdella said. "You're making those noises in your throat again. You scared?"

I couldn't lie. Not with my throat going nuts like it was. I nodded, then I told her that I didn't want to see dead people.

She reached over and petted my hair. "You don't have to be afraid, honey. We aren't going into the funeral part. Look. See that back door there? See the sign above it? Mr. Hamilton's wife sells the plots and gravestones out of that office right there. That's where we're going." I sure was happy to hear that.

I walked real fast down the sidewalk to get past the other part of the building, and I held my breath, in case Mr. Hamilton just carried a dead person inside and there were dead people's germs still floating in the air.

The lady inside was little and had a bump on her back. Her hair was sprayed stiff to her head, and it was a bluish color, like her dress. "Can I help you?" she said. She wore big, thick glasses that made her eyes look like marbles too, under a magnifying glass.

Aunt Verdella started telling her the whole story then. How this beautiful young woman and her little sister came into Dauber, the little girl carrying an urn with her ma inside. "It was the saddest thing I'd ever seen," Aunt Verdella said. "That child carries her ma with her everywhere she goes. She talks to her too. And she told Button here that when she grows up she's gonna buy her ma a final restin' place. Well, Tommy— that's my husband's farmhand—he accidentally knocked over the urn. That poor child was hysterical! That's when I decided to skip buying the color television set I was saving for and buy her mother a plot and a stone instead.

"Anyway, the woman lived right here in Hopested, ma'am, so I thought it would be a good idea to have her final restin' place be here. I know the dead woman has a sister and a brother living here, so it would be nice for them too. I ain't got much, mind you, but Mr. Parkins—the funeral director back in Dauber—he gave me a price quote on what both would cost in Dauber, and he figured it'll run about the same here."

While Aunt Verdella was talking, the lady's stiff hand kept spreading out toward the two fancy chairs facing the front of her desk, which meant we should sit down. Aunt Verdella didn't seem to notice though, so the lady waited for Aunt Verdella to take a breath, then she told us to have a seat.

Once we sat down, the lady with the marble eyes—who

said her name was Mrs. Hamilton—brought a couple big books to the desk and opened them. "Here we have our stones," she said.

"We want a white one. A pretty one. Not too expensive, like I said. And do you think we could have an etchin' of a little fairy cut into it?"

"A fairy?"

"Yeah. A fairy."

"Well, I suppose so. I imagine you'd need a picture for them to go by, but we'll see what we can do."

Aunt Verdella scooted the book over a bit so I could see, then she turned page after plastic-coated page, while she asked the cost on this gravestone and that one. I swore we were gonna be there for a hundred years till Aunt Verdella found a nice one we could afford. I about sighed out loud when she finally said, "This one. Yep, that's the one we want, ain't it, Button?"

Then the lady started talking about plots. "Golden Gate Cemetery is just at the edge of town," she said. "It's a lovely place. The plots all run about the same price, of course, but—"

"Oh. We have to have a plot next to a tree. I don't suppose you have apple trees there, but, boy, wouldn't that be nice, Button? If not, then of course any tree will do."

"There's a few trees, ma'am. And also some pretty lilac bushes. Perhaps we could find a plot next to one of those?"

"Oh, that would be wonderful!"

We were there a long, long time before it looked like we were gonna get any closer to being done with our business. And the longer it took, the more I thought about the dead people laying in the rooms just past the double doors behind Mrs. Hamilton. Tommy had said that some dead people turn into zombies. Out the window, I saw a man in a suit go down the steps and cross the street. He sorta looked like a zombie to me.

Aunt Verdella stopped talking right in the middle of a sentence and looked down at me. "Button, what's the matter? You have to tinkle?"

"There's a restroom just through these doors, down the hall and to your left," the blue-haired lady said. I shook my head fast. "No, I don't have to go."

The lady got out some forms. She asked Aunt Verdella for her name and her address first. Aunt Verdella recited them, spelling out Verdella, since the lady didn't know how to write it. Before Mrs. Hamilton could even ask another question, Aunt Verdella was talking about something else. Telling the lady how we were gonna need a minister to come say a few final words on the day the ashes got buried.

"I'm sure that can be arranged. Now, I need the deceased woman's name, the year of her birth and death, and any verse you'd like on the stone."

"Oh dear. I didn't think of what we might like written on it." Aunt Verdella dug in her purse until she found an envelope, then put it down on the lady's desk, scribbled side up. She turned to me. "What do you think, Button? Course, a verse will probably cost extra."

The woman picked up the envelope. She stared at it, her eyes stretching wide, then shrinking small, making it look like the lenses of her glasses were made from fun-house mirrors.

"Oh, can't you make out the name? I'm sorry. I don't have much for penmanship. It's Hannah Malone. Hannah, H-a-n-n-a-h, Malone, M-a-l-o-n-e. And I know that's the correct spelling too, because Winnalee—that's the woman's daughter—she's a real smart little girl, just like Button here, and she spelled the first name out for me. And I'm sure on the last name. Anyway, the dates are—"

Aunt Verdella didn't have time to finish giving the lady the dates, because Mrs. Hamilton looked up and said, "Excuse me. Did you say the child's name is Winnalee?"

"Yes, Winnalee Malone. She's the deceased woman's daughter. Her and her big sister, Freeda, moved into Dauber—that's where Button and I live. Anyway—"

"Excuse me a minute, please. Excuse me." Mrs. Hamilton hurried out of the double doors, closing them behind her (which I was glad about, because I didn't want to see no dead people with bloody armpits, or any zombies).

"Hmm," Aunt Verdella said. "Maybe she suddenly wasn't feeling well. She did look a little peaked there all of a sudden, didn't she?" Aunt Verdella stood up. "All this sittin' today. I'm not used to sittin' so long." She circled around the little room, looking at a vase of plastic flowers, then reading a poem about resting in peace that was hanging on the wall in a gold frame.

After what seemed like forever, the doors opened and a man came into the room, Mrs. Hamilton behind him. He held out his hand to Aunt Verdella, and it looked a bit damp, like he'd just washed it. I cringed, thinking that maybe he'd had to wash his hands because he'd been cutting armpits, so I was glad that he didn't expect to take my hand too. "Ma'am? I'm Charles Hamilton, and of course you've met my wife. Sit down, please." He had one of those slow, kind voices that sounded like it was saying, "I'm sorry," even when it wasn't. Both Mr. Hamilton and his blue-headed wife looked like they felt sorry, and a little scared, about what they were about to say. Aunt Verdella must have figured this too, because she groaned.

"Oh dear, don't tell me I need a death certificate to order these things, or something like that. Why, me and Button drove six hours to get here. Oh dear. The minute I saw your faces when you came through the door, I thought of the death certificate we had to bring in when we buried Mae, my mother-in-law."

"Sit down. Sit down," the man said, and that too, sounded like, "I'm sorry."

"Ma'am, a death certificate would certainly help in this case." He cleared his throat. "Please, Mrs. Peters, can you tell me some more about what you're doing here, and why?"

Aunt Verdella plucked at the eyelet trim around her collar as she quickly told him about Freeda and Winnalee and how they came into Dauber, Winnalee carrying that urn. She told him about the color television set she was going to buy too, and why she'd changed her mind. "Oh dear. I never thought of a death certificate till now," she said again. "And we drove such a distance. Oh dear."

The man and the lady exchanged looks, then the man cleared his throat again. "Can you tell me the name of the sisters again, please?"

"Freeda and Winnalee Malone." Poor Aunt Verdella looked ready to cry, because something was telling her—just like it was telling me—that Freeda and Winnalee's ma was not gonna get her final restin' place.

The man leaned back in his chair and then came forward again. He folded his hands, the tips of his pointy fingers and thumbs touching, kind of like he was going to start playing "Here Is the Church, Here Is the Steeple."

"Ma'am," he said, "I don't know quite how to say this, but..." He stopped and scratched behind his ear. "Well, Hopested is a small town, ma'am, and in my business especially, I've come to know every family, going back a good three generations."

I looked at him, and at Aunt Verdella, and my throat got so full of gunk that I couldn't stop clearing it. I knew what he was gonna say next was not gonna be good.

"Ma'am, I've known the Malones for years. I knew Freeda's granddaddy, and I knew her father. I buried them both, in fact. But, well, I never buried Hannah Malone. Do you understand what I'm trying to say here?"

"Well, of course you didn't," Aunt Verdella said. "She was cremated. Her poor little daughter carries her everywhere she goes. That's why we're here."

"Ma'am, I don't know how to put this delicately, so I guess I'm going to have to just come right out and say it. Hannah Malone isn't dead, Mrs. Peters. She's a member of our church, and we see her there regularly, when her health allows it."

"She was there yesterday, in fact," Mrs. Hamilton said. "In pain or not, from a ruptured disk, she was there."

Aunt Verdella gasped, and maybe I did too.

Mr. Hamilton cleared his raspy throat, but just once. "Ma'am, I don't care for gossip, but I don't see any other way to explain this to you but to come right out and tell you what everybody in this town knows anyway. Freeda Malone, Hannah's daughter . . . well, let's just say, she was on the wilder side. She ran away when she was young and then came back into town about four years ago. Anyway, the best any of us know, Freeda left her mother's house after they argued and went straight to the school. The little girl's teacher, Miss Miles, had taught Freeda herself, so she was able to tell Hannah for sure who took Winnalee."

Mrs. Hamilton continued the story, but not before she too, apologized for repeating gossip. "Poor Miss Miles believed Freeda when Freeda told her that her mother had just passed away an hour ago and that she needed to take Winnalee out of school immediately. After all, Miss Miles knew of Hannah's poor health, as we all did. Why, word spread of Hannah's death quickly. Within an hour, folks were calling Charles to ask when the funeral would take place, but we still hadn't gotten a call to pick up her body."

"I finally drove out to the Malones' to find out what was going on," Mr. Hamilton said.

"Hannah was heartsick when Charles got there, of course, because by that time, folks had called out to the Malone place, expecting to talk to Hannah's younger brother, Dewey, only to find themselves talking to Hannah herself!" Mrs. Hamilton stopped to take a breath, then continued. "Poor Hannah has been sick with worry since, as you can imagine. It's taken a toll on her already-precarious health. After all, once her husband passed away, and then after Freeda left, what did she have but that little one, for those few years? Granted, Dewey moved back in with Hannah just before Freeda took Winnalee, and although I'm sure he's fine company for Hannah, that doesn't help lessen her worry over the child."

Aunt Verdella got out of her chair and paced. "I . . . I just don't know what to say."

"We're sorry," Mr. Hamilton said. "It looks like you're another in a long line of good people that Freeda has duped."

Aunt Verdella was so upset that she dropped her purse. There were tears in her eyes and in her voice as she thanked the Hamiltons for their time.

Mr. Hamilton walked us to the door. "Ma'am, we are so sorry that you made such a long trip for nothing."

Aunt Verdella thanked him again, then asked him where we could find a room for the night. "I don't see well enough to drive in the dark, and as shook up as I am now, I couldn't drive back tonight if I wanted to."

The man told us where to find a motel, and out the door we went, walking like zombies.

20

Aunt Verdella didn't yack at the man who checked us into the motel, like she'd done to everyone else we'd met so far. She just quietly handed him the money he asked for, and then we carried our bags to room number 26.

The room was totally beige except for the nubby, dark green bedspread and curtains. Aunt Verdella sat on the bed, her hands limp on her lap. "I just can't believe this," she said. "Why would Freeda lie to that poor child and tell her that her ma was dead and in that jar? Oh my. Oh my. What on earth do we do with this, Button?"

We went back to the diner for supper, even though neither of us was hungry, but like Aunt Verdella said, it was better than staring at the walls. Aunt Verdella ordered us each a meatloaf platter, and some banana cream pie for dessert. While I ate the best I could, Aunt Verdella took a bite here and there but mostly sat without talking, staring out the big window to the side of us, her eyes not budging even when somebody walked by on the street. I watched her as much as I could without looking rude for staring, and I thought about how she looked old without a smile on her face.

We got back to our room and Aunt Verdella turned the television set on, but she didn't really watch it. "We'd best get ready for bed, Button. We'll head back first thing in the morning."

That night, the room was dark with the curtains drawn (except for the sliver of light coming from the bathroom door, which Aunt Verdella said she'd leave on in case I had to pee in the night) and we just laid there for a time, each thinking our own worries. Aunt Verdella sighed now and then, her folded hands rising up and down with each rise of her belly.

"I just can't believe this, can you, Button? That poor child thinks Hannah is dead. Oh my. It's almost more than I can bear to know."

"Aunt Verdella?" I asked. "Whose body is burned up in Winnalee's jar, then?"

Aunt Verdella sniffled. "I don't know. Probably nobody's. Maybe they're just ashes from a woodstove or something. I don't know." She asked me to go to the bathroom and get her some Kleenex. She dabbed her wet eyes, blew her nose, then said, "You know, when I told Rudy about the urn tipping over, he said that he hoped that Winnalee didn't see any bones or teeth bits, because that would be so traumatic for a child to see. I didn't question it then, but now that I am, I'm thinking about how I didn't see any bits of bones or teeth in those ashes either. What did I know, though. I've never seen anybody's ashes before."

"They looked like cigarette ashes to me when I saw them," I said. "I even told Winnalee that it looked like someone dumped their ashtray in that jar."

Aunt Verdella sighed. "I guess what we've got to think about, Button, is what we're gonna tell Rudy and your ma and daddy. And do I say something to Freeda or not? I just don't know the answers to those questions. Maybe the good Lord will give me some ideas by morning." She reached over and put her arm around me. She gave me a hug and a hard kiss on the back of my head. "Good night, Button. Auntie sure loves you."

Aunt Verdella fell asleep after a time, but she turned and

fidgeted so much that I felt like I was sleeping on a boat instead of a bed. Each time her moving woke me up, I ended up thinking about Winnalee again and about the lie Freeda told her.

I felt thirsty, so I got out of bed. I opened the bathroom door slowly and the light creeped up Aunt Verdella's stick legs. I didn't want the light to crawl all the way up to her face and wake her, so I opened the door just enough to slip inside, then drank water from a Dixie cup. On my way back to bed, I saw my opened suitcase on the floor and me and Winnalee's Book of Bright Ideas peeking out from behind my folded shirt. I picked the book up and ran my hand over the gold, dented-in letters on the cover. Winnalee said that an expectation was something you hoped for. What I hoped for was that even if Winnalee found out the truth about her ma, she'd decide that she wanted to live with Freeda instead. And that she'd stay my neighbor and my best friend forever.

I looked over at Aunt Verdella. Her face was tinged red from the letters that lit the top of the pole on the corner of the parking lot. I could see her eyeballs jiggling under her lids, which were still colored blue from the eye shadow she'd put on that morning. I didn't want to wake her to ask if I could use her pen, yet I wanted to write something in our book. After thinking about it for a time, I slipped my hand into her purse, which was sitting on the nightstand, and felt for a pen. Then I opened our book and wrote, *Bright Idea #97: A person doesn't have to be ugly and mean to tell a big lie. They don't have to be a stranger either. Sometimes the biggest lies come from pretty people who are in your own family.*

The next morning, we woke early and went back to the diner. It was filled with the smells of coffee and bacon and cigarette smoke. We ordered pancakes, but they weren't shaped like bunnies.

Aunt Verdella was quiet while we ate. She gave her half-eaten eggs back to the waitress and sipped her coffee some more. After a time, she said, "I was just remembering some-thing." She took a sip of her coffee, leaving red lip prints on the mug, then, while I swirled the rest of my pancakes into the syrup and ate, Aunt Verdella told me a story.

"One spring—a messy, messy spring where the weather turned so fast that the poor ground couldn't soak up the melt-ing snow fast enough—your uncle Rudy and I were taking a little drive over to Lincoln County so he could look at a heifer somebody had for sale. Your uncle Rudy's back was bad, and I didn't like the idea of him drivin' that far alone, so I thought I should ride along in case he ended up needing me to help drive. Anyway, on the way home, along the highway, we came across a man. Oh, he was a raggy-lookin' thing. Young, hair all askew, clothes all filthy and torn. He was downright scary looking!

"When he saw our car comin', he started runnin' right at us. Waving his arms and yellin', his face in those headlights, tortured like a madman's. Rudy started slowin' the car down and I got upset. 'Don't stop!' I yelled. 'He's crazy! Look at him! Lord knows what he'll do to us!' I was sure that he was some murderin' lunatic who would rob us, defile me, who knows what else. And with your uncle Rudy's back so bad, I knew he'd be no match for that young lunatic.

"But your uncle Rudy stopped, anyway, of course. And it was a good thing he did. What we couldn't see from the high-way was that this man's car was stuck something fierce in the mud, down this long driveway hidden from the road by trees. His wife was in the car, about ready to give birth to their first baby. Why, that poor man looked like a lunatic because he was crazy with fear. And who could blame him, him being still wet behind his ears and her in such pain and screaming for him to hurry and get her to the hospital?

"He was trying to get his car out of the mud when he heard our car. He ran out onto the highway then, hoping it would be a neighbor or someone who'd lend a hand. He was a filthy mess from rooting around in the mud. We got that poor little thing to the hospital, and all was well. Afterward, your uncle said to me, 'It just goes to show, Verdie. You can't judge a person by what they're doing, till you know why they're doing it.'

"Anyway, that whole night just came to my mind a bit ago, as I was trying to figure out why Freeda took that little girl out of Hopested like she did and told her such a horrible lie. It looks crazy to us, yes, mean even. But we don't know the whole story, Button. For all we know, she had a good reason for doing what she did, even if she did go about it in the wrong way. You understand what I'm trying to say?"

"I think so."

"And I was thinking of this too," she said. "Button, if I go telling your ma what we learned, and she judges it without knowin' the whole story, I'm afraid it's gonna change how she feels about Freeda. And worse yet, I'm afraid it's going to change how she feels about herself. Freeda has made your ma go from a little caterpillar into a beautiful butterfly. Your ma learns that Freeda lied about all those big things, and she'll believe that Freeda lied about the good things she said to her too. I don't want that to happen. So what we're gonna do is tell your ma and daddy that when we got to Hopested there was already a stone for Hannah Malone sittin' in the cemetery. And I'll leave it at that. I'll be telling Uncle Rudy the truth, though, 'cause I ain't gonna lie to him. But you know your uncle Rudy. It won't change nothing about how he sees Freeda. Your uncle Rudy is good like that, Button. He don't judge people, and he stays out of other people's business, like I shoulda done in the first place. Do you understand why I think it should be like this?"

"Yes," I said.

"As for Freeda, I'm not saying anything to her either. I'm gonna take a lesson from your uncle Rudy and just stay out of it and trust that Freeda is as good as I believe she is. It just ain't our place to say anything. To Freeda and Winnalee, we'll just pretend that we went to cart my friend's kids to their aunt's house, like we said we were gonna do. Do you think you can keep this secret, Button?" I nodded, and she reached over and patted my hand. "Okay, then let's head for home."

We stopped at St. Croix Falls for gas, and I reminded Aunt Verdella that we had told Winnalee we'd bring her home a special surprise. Aunt Verdella asked me what Winnalee would like the most, but I couldn't think of one thing past that final resting place for her ma.

We looked around in a Ben Franklin store. We didn't find nothing real special, so Aunt Verdella kept buying things that were only part special: new paper dolls, a new coloring book, a set of jacks—one for each of us—and barrettes just for me, because she said my hair was getting long enough now to need them. Then we went to a gift shop, and Aunt Verdella got busy looking at stuffed animals. Aunt Verdella picked up one teddy bear after another, hugging each of them to see which was softest. That's when I saw the glass jewelry counter, all lit up, pretty little necklaces laid out like sunbathers. "Aunt Verdella, look!"

She hurried to the counter and bent over, looking where my finger was tapping on the glass. "Oh my!" she said. Then she called a lady over to the counter to unlock it, so we could buy Winnalee the pretty silver chain with a silver fairy dangling from it.

When we got back into the car, I asked Aunt Verdella if I could borrow her pen again, and then I wrote, *Bright Idea #98: When what your best friend really wants is to have the one they love back again, but you can't give them that, or even help them put that person to rest, then give them a fairy instead. Because we all gotta believe in something good.*

21

We'd spent so much time looking for Winnalee's gift that Uncle Rudy was at my house having supper with Ma and Daddy by the time Aunt Verdella and I pulled in the drive.

"Well, if it isn't our angels of mercy," Uncle Rudy said when we came through the door. "How'd it go, Verdie?"

Uncle Rudy's smile faded when he saw Aunt Verdella up close.

Ma stood up. "I'll get a couple of plates. You two hungry?"

We said we were.

"Come on, Button. Sit down." Ma pulled out the chair I always sat on. She plunked a fried chicken leg on my plate and tapped a spoonful of mashed potatoes beside it. "Coffee, Verdella?" She put some corn on my plate too and buttered me a baking-powder biscuit.

"I'll get it. I've been sitting so long it will do me good to fluff my butt."

"How'd things go?" Daddy asked, his mouth full of chicken. "You get your mission accomplished?"

"No. Why, I guess I should have looked before I leapt. Turns out there's already a stone in the cemetery for Hannah Malone!" Aunt Verdella laughed, but it didn't sound like her usual ha-ha. "I imagine her sister or brother bought it for her.

Anyway, I've decided not to say a thing to Winnalee or even to Freeda about this. Freeda would probably feel bad, thinking about how I traveled so far for nothing. It was silly of me in the first place to run off without checking. Oh well, me and Button had a nice little vacation anyway, didn't we, Button? We made it, and we didn't get lost even once, and, best of all, nothing bad happened!" Verdella's eyes got sparkly when she said this, and I thought that maybe this meant she just figured out that she did earn her redemption.

Everybody went back to their eating and talking about what a nice drive it is to Minnesota. Then their minds went down other roads and other places. Now and then, though, I saw Uncle Rudy glance over at Aunt Verdella, like he was trying to figure out what she wasn't saying.

"Oh dear. Look at the time, Rudy! It's quarter after six already. Freeda's gotta get to work, and we've got to get back to look after Winnalee." She got up and grabbed her purse. "I'm sorry for not helping with the dishes, Jewel." Ma told her it was okay.

Aunt Verdella leaned over to give me a quick kiss and hug good-bye, then stopped and unpuckered her lips. "Jewel, I know Button just got home, but do you think I could bring her with me for just a minute so we can give Winnalee the gifts we brought back for her? The poor little thing was so sad about being left behind that I told her we'd bring her back something special. I don't want to give them to her without Button there, and, well, you know how Winnalee is about waiting." Aunt Verdella sounded like her old self when she laughed this time.

Ma looked a little disappointed. "Well, I suppose."

So off we went. Me and Aunt Verdella in her Bel Air, and Uncle Rudy in his pickup. And sure enough, Winnalee was waiting on their steps when we pulled in the drive, her fake ma sitting right alongside her. Her face was propped on her hands, her loopy hair spilled over her like a waterfall. When she saw Aunt Verdella's car, her whole body smiled, and she leapt off of the steps and ran toward us, bouncing until we got out of the car. She wrapped her arms around my neck and squeezed till it hurt. Then she wrapped her arms around Aunt Verdella's fat part and squeezed that tight too.

Of course, she begged for her special surprise right away. "Just wait, honey. Let Uncle Rudy bring my bag in so I can fetch it out of there."

Aunt Verdella gave her the little things first, and Winnalee liked them all, then Aunt Verdella made a drumroll sound with her tongue as she pulled the last, and best, surprise from the bag. I expected Winnalee to start squealing when she opened the box and saw that pretty fairy laying on a bed of cotton, but she didn't. Instead, she just stared and stared, then looked up at us, and her eyes filled with tears.

"Winnalee?" Aunt Verdella asked.

That's when Winnalee went nuts, laughing while she was crying and hugging us so hard I thought she might snap us in half. "I love it, I love it, I love it! I never in my whole life saw a fairy necklace! It's the bestest present I ever got!"

"Stand still, honey," Aunt Verdella told her, as Winnalee did little hops in a circle while I tried to hold up her hair so Aunt Verdella could slip the clasp through the little ring part.

After we got it on her, Winnalee went to the bathroom mirror so she could see how it looked on her. "Come see, Button!" she called, even though I didn't need a mirror to see how it looked.

When we came back to the kitchen, Aunt Verdella said that she had to bring me back home. Winnalee sighed and groaned at the same time. "She just got here!"

"I know, honey. But she's been gone two days and her ma and daddy miss her. She'll be back in the morning, bright and early."

"Okay. I'll ride with because I want to show Aunt Jewel my necklace." It was the first time Winnalee ever called my ma "Aunt Jewel," so it took me a bit by surprise and made me smile. I knew by the way Aunt Verdella smiled at me that it made her happy too.

"Did you get any bright ideas while you were gone?" Winnalee asked while Aunt Verdella dug around the junk on the counter for her car keys, which she'd practically just set down.

"A couple of them," I said.

"Well, sometimes it takes time before you can tell if they're any good or not. That's how bright ideas are."

"Oh, here they are!" Aunt Verdella shouted. She picked up her keys and jiggled them. "Let's go!

"Winnalee, honey, I can't see good when you stand up like that to see in the rearview mirror. Why don't you reach in my purse and grab my compact and look at your necklace with that. Okay?" Winnalee got out the compact and tilted it up and down until she got the right angle. Then all the way to my house she chattered, saying things like, "Ain't it pretty?" and "Doesn't she look real?" I made myself smile, but inside I was feeling some sad along with that happy. It was a nice necklace, for sure, but a necklace was just a thing. Not a person. I wanted so bad to just blurt out to her, "You know that lady, your ma? The one you still love a lot? She's not dead! She's in Hopested, still alive!" I could tell too, by the soft-sad look in Aunt Verdella's eyes when she had reached out to take the urn so Winnalee could climb into the car, that Aunt Verdella was wanting to say the same thing. But we couldn't, of course, because it wasn't our place.

When we got inside, Ma was wiping off the counter and the supper dishes were dripping in the dish rack. "Winnalee wanted to show Aunt Jewel her special gift," Aunt Verdella said to Ma.

"Is that right?" Ma smiled as Winnalee ran up to her and clasped her hands behind her back, moving like a washing-machine agitator. "Notice anything different, Aunt Jewel?"

Ma's eyeballs slipped down, then up, then down and up

again. Finally, they found the spot on Winnalee's neck where the little fairy shone. "Oh, isn't that lovely!"

Winnalee patted it. "It's a fairy, Aunt Jewel! A real fairy! Ain't she pretty? You ever see a fairy necklace before? I never did." Ma told her she hadn't either.

"Aunt Verdella said she was gonna bring me back something special, and she sure was telling the truth. I can't think of one thing they could have brought me back that would be more special than this necklace. Not one thing!" Me and Aunt Verdella looked at each other for two blinks, and then everywhere else but at Winnalee. "I can't wait to show it to Freeda, but she's gone to work, so I'll have to wait."

"Button, why don't you go unpack now," Ma said. "Be sure and put your dirty clothes in the hamper, please."

Winnalee followed me into my room. She reached for our book when I opened my suitcase. She opened it and read the bright ideas I'd put there, her head tilting, her eyes skinnying. "You have a pencil?" she asked. I handed her one, and she wrote: *Bright Idea #99: If your best friend goes away and you miss her, you don't need to cry and carry on forever, because she'll be back. And who knows? When she comes back, she might even bring you something so special that your heart almost bursts.*

22

It's funny how quickly we forget the things we don't want to remember. The day after we got back from Hopested, me and Winnalee took our lunch out to the picnic table and the urn was sitting right on the table across from Winnalee, where I wanted to put my plate. I didn't think nothing of grabbing that urn and moving it over under the tree. Winnalee looked at me cradling the urn in my arms as I moved it, and she smiled. I knew what she was thinking. She was thinking that I wasn't afraid of dead people anymore. But the truth of the matter was, I wasn't afraid of ashtrays.

A couple days later, though, after Aunt Verdella got her ha-has back, and after I'd seen Winnalee talking to the urn as if her ma was really buried in it, I found myself afraid to touch it all over again. And by the very next Saturday, I believed the big, fat lie Freeda had told Winnalee, as though I had never learned the truth at all.

It was Saturday—almost one week after we visited Hopested—breezy and muggy, and my guts told me it was probably going to storm. Ma and Aunt Verdella and I strolled over to Freeda's and were standing in the driveway, not sure if we should go in or not (even if we were invited to lunch), since there was a strange truck in the driveway. "I thought I heard two vehicles last night, about the time Freeda would have gotten home from work," Aunt Verdella said. "And it's been parked here since I woke up this morning."

Ma looked at Aunt Verdella and said, "Ah, Verdella. I know you were hoping that she'd get serious about Mike, but I didn't think that would happen."

Aunt Verdella looked down at the chocolate cream pie she was carrying for our dessert and sighed. "Mike's such a nice guy. And ready to settle down too."

"But Freeda's not, Verdella."

"Hey, you guys!" Winnalee called, her head appearing outside the screen door. "Freeda said, what the hell are you guys doing standing out there, and to come in." So in we went.

Winnalee hopped alongside of me and chattered all the way to the kitchen. "Oh, good. You wore your ballerina suit, just like I told you to!" she said.

"Hi, girls," Freeda said. She was standing at the table chopping onions into a bowl of tuna. Her penny hair was hanging loose and snarly, and she wasn't wearing anything that I could see but for a man's T-shirt that hung almost to her knees. The guy sitting at the table, smoking and drinking coffee, had a red scrape on one cheek and he wasn't wearing a shirt, so I figured it was his shirt Freeda wore.

"You know Jesse?" Freeda asked. "Probably not. He's on road construction, out on 47. No matter, he was just leaving anyway." The man cocked his eyes toward Freeda. "I was?" he asked.

"You got it, buddy."

With all of us staring at him, waiting for him to leave, I suppose he didn't have much choice but to lift his tired butt off the chair. He grabbed his cigarettes and matches from the table and stretched. "I'll get my shirt later," he said.

"Hold it," Freeda said. "You'd better take it now." She grabbed the hem and went to lift it up, but Ma cleared her throat and Freeda stopped, going into the bathroom instead and coming out in her robe. She tossed the shirt at him and he left.

"Oh, honey," Aunt Verdella said. "I thought you liked Mike."

"I like Mike just fine," Freeda said. "Or rather, I did, until he started spouting his mouth off about settling down."

"Yeah," Winnalee said. "Mike showed up here late last night too. And he punched that Jesse guy right in the face. Good thing that guy was too drunk to feel it, or it would have really hurt. I was scared that Mike had a shotgun in his truck, but Freeda said he didn't." Ma gave Winnalee a pat on the shoulder.

While we ate our lunch, Ma asked Aunt Verdella if I could spend the night with her, because Daddy and her were going out. Aunt Verdella said I could, and Winnalee clapped. Then Aunt Verdella went right back to worrying about Freeda not liking Mike Thompson anymore, and Freeda said, "I guess I'm just quicker to give away my body than to give away my heart." That's when Ma told me and Winnalee to go outside and play.

The skies were covered with ugly gray clouds heavy with rain by the time we reached our magic tree to play parade. We had to fiddle till we got our feet settled in the flat spot without stepping on each other, then started waving and smiling at the crowd, who thought we were stunning beauties too. We tossed candy, but only to the kids we thought looked nice. When Ma and Aunt Verdella came across the yard—Ma to leave, and Aunt Verdella to get busy in her house—Winnalee called to them, and they waved back at us like spectators at a real parade.

We played beauty queens until the breeze dried our teeth, then Winnalee decided we should play fairies instead. "We look like fairies in our costumes, don't we? I think we do." I wasn't sure how to play fairies, and I don't think Winnalee knew either, because all she did was flap her arms now and then, like they were wings, while she talked. "Guess what?" she said. "Uncle Rudy said that next weekend the corn and oats are gonna be ready to come in. He's gonna be busy all Saturday, then on Sunday Aunt Verdella is gonna have a big cookout to celebrate the end of the growing season, and the Smithys are gonna come, and the Thompson twins—well, maybe not them now—and a whole lot of other people. I figured that will be the best time in the world to go back to the beck. With so much going on, I don't think anyone would notice us slipping off. Only we'll go through the woods this time, because it's bound to be quicker, and we'll go right before dark."

Winnalee climbed down from the tree and dug our adventure bag out from the hole. She looked up at the tree. "Hey, I know what we could do now! Let's draw pictures of fairies and cut them out to hang from the branches! We could use Aunt Verdella's glue and glitter on their wings and fill up the whole tree!"

The first sprinkles of rain tapped the leaves above us. "But they'll get all wet and ruined. Daddy said this morning that it's supposed to rain heavy for a couple days."

"Uh-uh! Not if we iron waxed paper over them before we cut them out. The iron melts the crayon and the waxed paper sticks to it. We did it at school once. I think they'd hold up in the rain, don't you?"

I looked up at our magic tree, at the branches where leaves fluttered, and I could almost see those fairies hanging there. "Okay!" I said.

"I'll run home and get the crayons. And paper to draw on too. You go ask Aunt Verdella for waxed paper."

"Okay."

I'd barely reached the porch when the clouds opened up and started dumping so much rain that it moved like heavy curtains waving in the wind as it fell.

"Where's Winnalee?" Aunt Verdella asked when I got inside.

"She ran home to get something. She'll be right back."

Aunt Verdella glanced out the window. "It's rainin' cats and dogs out there. Button, go shut the front door for Auntie, will you? Rain always wants to come in and give my rug a bath."

I suppose it was the front door being closed that kept us from hearing Winnalee cry out when she jumped off her porch and rammed a nail up her bare foot. A stray nail left from Daddy's repairs on the front steps, we figured later.

Winnalee didn't yank it out. She hopped back to the house, screaming for Freeda the whole way. Freeda, whose stomach wasn't a bit braver than Winnalee's when it came to yucky things, tossed her in the car in a flutter of mesh and drove her into town to see the doctor. Me and Aunt Verdella didn't know where they'd gone. At first we just thought that Winnalee was waiting for the rain to let up a bit before she ran back, but then, when Aunt Verdella peered out the front door and saw that the red truck wasn't in their driveway, we both got a little worried. "Freeda's gotta go in to work at four o'clock, because there's a wedding reception at Marty's today, so you'd think she wouldn't have run off anyplace first," Aunt Verdella said, as she dried her hands and headed toward the bathroom.

I plucked a cookie off of a plate on the counter and sat down at the table. Even with the rain making noise as it dripped down off of the eaves above the window, I could hear the sound of someone pulling into the drive. "Somebody's in the driveway!" I shouted to Aunt Verdella.

"Is it your uncle Rudy?" Aunt Verdella called from the bathroom.

I spread my hands on the edge of the counter, then jumped up, bracing myself, my feet dangling. I looked out the window and into the driveway, hoping it was the Malones. It wasn't. "Nope. It's some lady in a white car." I strained, trying to see the face underneath the smudge of light brown hair, but with rain running down the car windows, I couldn't.

I lifted my knees up on the counter on account of my arms were getting shaky from holding me up. I watched the car door open and an umbrella poof open, hiding the lady's head. But that umbrella, though big, was nowhere near big enough to hide that enormous body.

I ran to the bathroom door, which was open just enough for me to see Aunt Verdella sitting on the toilet, her undies strapped around her white knees. "Aunt Verdella, there's a big, big fat lady here!"

"Oh dear, I hope it's not a Jehovah's Witness!" Aunt Verdella said.

"I don't think so. I didn't see her carrying any little magazines."

"Okay. Answer the door, Button. Auntie will be right out."

I opened the front door and waited as the fat lady struggled to get up the porch steps. She was huffing and puffing and had to pause at each step to catch her breath. Trails of rain were falling from points of the umbrella, wetting the parts of her that were too wide to fit under the umbrella—which was most of her.

I moved back a-ways from the screen door. I could hear the toilet flush and the bathroom sink running. "Hurry, Aunt Verdella," I yelled in my head, as I bit the inside of my cheek.

"Hello there, honey," the fat lady said, her voice all wheezy-sounding. "Is this the home of Verdella Peters?"

I was glad Aunt Verdella came then, so I didn't have to say anything.

Aunt Verdella scooted in front of me. "I'm Verdella Peters." Aunt Verdella looked at the lady's hands, and I knew why. Like Aunt Verdella said, she wasn't good with salespeople and always ended up buying something she didn't need and couldn't afford.

The fat lady stepped onto the porch and closed her umbrella, shaking it before closing it. She was still panting.

"Ma'am, my name is Hannah Malone."

Aunt Verdella's breath sucked in, and my ears started buzzing, like ears do when you get really scared.

"May I come in?" Hannah Malone asked.

Aunt Verdella opened the door. "Oh dear. Um, yes, please." There was no ha-ha in her voice now.

Aunt Verdella had to stand back to open the door wide enough for the fat lady to get in. I'd never in my whole life seen anybody walk like that lady: rocking to one side as she lifted one foot, then setting it down hard and rocking to the other side to lift the other, her whole body twisting with each step. Her eyes, nose, and mouth looked like little balls of Trix cereal dropped on a white pillow; two blue balls for eyes, and one red one for a mouth. She was wearing a cross on her neck, with Jesus nailed to it. You couldn't see His head with that crown of thorns on it, though, because it was buried in a crease of neck fat, but I knew it was Him because I could see His nailed feet sticking out.

"I understand you were in Hopested looking to buy a plot and gravestone for me, so of course I have questions," Mrs. Malone said.

"Oh dear." I heard Aunt Verdella mutter under her breath as she led Hannah to the kitchen table. Being polite, as she always was, she asked Hannah Malone if she'd like coffee. Then she set a plate with two pieces of coffee cake and a few cookies onto the table.

"A couple days ago, Mrs. Hamilton came to see me. She went back and forth, of course, wondering whether to say anything to me or not about your visit. But then she thought about how I've suffered with worry ever since Freeda took Winnalee, and she came to me and told me everything. My brother's going to be fit to be tied that I didn't wait for him to get home—he's a trucker and gone for the next two weeks—but I just couldn't wait another day to find out how my baby is."

Aunt Verdella's hand had the jitters as she patted the side of the percolator to see if it was still warm. It must not have been, because she lit the burner. She got two cups down from the cupboard shelf and brought them to the table. "Grab the creamer for Auntie, will you, Button?" Her voice sounded like it was stretched so tight that it could snap.

I got the creamer from the refrigerator—the cute little creamer in the shape of a cow that we bought for Aunt Verdella's birthday one year—and set it on the table. Aunt Verdella scooted a short stack of little plates across the table. She moved even quicker than she usually did when she was upset. The forks rattled in her hand as she brought them to the table.

"Mrs. Peters, this is very awkward for me..." Hannah Malone said, as she helped herself to a piece of coffee cake.

"Well," Aunt Verdella said. "This is awkward for me too. My, I didn't want to start up any trouble or get involved. I was just tryin' to do something nice. You see, I had money saved for a color television set, but then—"

"Mrs. Peters," Hannah Malone said. "I need you to tell me how to find my Winnalee. I know from Mrs. Hamilton that she and Freeda are here in Dauber, and I know about the horrible lie Freeda told about me being dead. Why, this has all taken a horrible toll on my health the last few years, worrying about if they were alive or dead. So uncomfortable or not, I hope you'll tell me what I need to know."

In fourth grade, a boy made a volcano out of flour and water stuff for his science project. When he blew in the tube at the bottom, some gunk that was supposed to be lava came spewing out. That's what I thought of when Hannah Malone's tears erupted into big sobs after she mentioned the part about her worrying about if Freeda and Winnalee were alive or dead: a big, white mountain rumbling and lurching, and then tears gushing out like hot lava.

Aunt Verdella always cried when she saw somebody else cry, so her eyes teared up the second Hannah Malone started in. "Button, would you go to the bathroom and get the Kleenex?"

I didn't know how much she wanted or how to get the crocheted lady off of the Kleenex box, so I just grabbed the doll and brought it into the kitchen. I set it on the table between Aunt Verdella and the fat lady. Aunt Verdella grabbed one for herself and some for Hannah. She patted Hannah's arm after she handed them to her.

"Please tell me what you know, Mrs. Peters," Mrs. Malone said. "I beg of you."

Aunt Verdella looked like a little kid sitting next to Hannah Malone. Not just because (in spite of her snowball middle) she looked tiny sitting next to that mountain of a woman, but because of the way she sat. With her hands folded on her lap and her head half dipped down. "Well, I'm finding myself in quite a pickle now, aren't I? I mean, I love Freeda and Winnalee like family. And now here I am, right in the middle of some family trouble I don't even understand. I feel awkward saying a thing. I hope you can understand that."

I tried not to stare at Hannah Malone's hand as she brought her fork down to her plate, but how could I not, with the strap of her silver watch almost buried in a crease of fat that hung over it like a puffy, too-long sleeve? "Mrs. Peters. Are you a mother?" Hannah Malone's voice was high like a girl's and jagged with tears.

I flinched inside when she asked that. Aunt Verdella shook her head. "No. Though Button here is my niece, and I couldn't love her more if I'd given birth to her myself."

"Well, then you know all about loving a child. If you understand, it might be easier for you to tell me what I need to know." I moved back from the table until I ran into the wall, then slid against it and out of the kitchen. I hovered just around the corner, standing in the dining room. I knew that if I stayed out of sight and kept quiet, no one was likely to notice me and ask me to go outside so I couldn't hear the grown-ups talk.

"You know Freeda, you say. Well, if you know her at all, then you know how headstrong she is. She was like that from the day she was born. Always contrary. Always opinionated and having to have her own way. A redhead in every sense.

"She was a handful from the start, but by the time she was thirteen, she was so wild I couldn't control her. I can't tell you the times I laid awake praying for that girl." I heard Hannah Malone sniffle, then I heard the scrape of a fork against a plate. I peeked around the corner just as Hannah was leaning back in her chair—well, the best she could, anyway.

"I can't tell you the gossip I suffered through." She burst into more tears. "I tried to raise her right, bringing her up in a good Christian home, but it didn't matter. It was like the devil himself burrowed into that girl early, and nothing I could do could drive him out of her."

"Ohhhh," Aunt Verdella said. "I wouldn't say that about Freeda. Why, she might be a little rough around the edges, but she is a sweetheart. An absolute dear."

Hannah Malone grunted, like people do when they don't agree.

"She got in the family way when she was only fifteen," Hannah Malone said, her words muffled from the mouthful of cake she chewed. "You can imagine how mortified and heartsick I was. Why, she couldn't even tell me who the boy was. Her daddy was gone by then, or I can assure you, he would have given her a thrashing."

Aunt Verdella put her hand up to her cheek and sat back in her chair. "Mrs. Malone, are you saying what I think you're saying?"

Mrs. Malone kept on talking, as if Aunt Verdella hadn't said a word. "I thought about sending her away to a school for, well, you know, unwed mothers, but I knew there wasn't a lock that could keep that girl inside an institution for the duration of her confinement. What choice did I have? My sister told me to force Freeda to put the baby up for adoption, because we knew that Freeda wasn't gonna take care of a baby. I did try to talk her into it, but she wouldn't hear of it. Not because she wanted that baby, I don't think, but because Freeda always turned her nose up at any suggestion I made."

Aunt Verdella's eyes were still big, and her hand was holding her chest. "Mrs. Malone. I'm ... I'm a bit rattled here, so help me out. Are you saying that Winnalee is *Freeda's* child?"

"Well, by birth, yes, but in no other way, I guarantee you! Freeda was gone within two weeks after Winnalee was born. Two weeks! My sister and brother and every one of my friends thought I was crazy, taking care of a newborn while I was in such poor health, but what could I do?"

I dipped my head out of the doorway again and stood with my back against the dining room wall until I could catch my breath, then I peeked back into the kitchen.

"Hard work or not, that baby was everything to me," Hannah said. "She was so beautiful, and smiley all the time. Just so full of love. My husband was dead and gone, and my daughter all but dead to me. Why, that sweet baby kept me from curling up and dying."

Aunt Verdella's eyes were still opened wide and blinking fast, but even so, she patted Hannah Malone's puffy hand, as tears curled over Mrs. Malone's cheeks.

"Can you imagine how upsetting it was for me to have Freeda show up out of the blue, after five whole years? *Five years?* She came into town every bit as unexpectedly as she left it and said that she was taking Winnalee with her. Imagine! She wouldn't tell me where she'd been or where she planned to go. She wouldn't even tell me if she had the means to take care of a little girl. Nothing! What reason did I have to believe that she'd grown up at all or repented her sins and settled into a decent life? Of course, I told her she couldn't take Winnalee. And what? See that little girl grow up every bit as bad as her mother?"

Hannah Malone sniffled, coughed a bit, then continued. "We argued, of course, because I was beside myself at the thought of losing my baby girl. I tried to reason with Freeda, and when that didn't work, I told her she was welcome to move back home or leave alone but that she couldn't take my Winnalee. I needed that child!"

"Oh my," Aunt Verdella said.

"She stormed out of the house. I was hoping she'd left for good at that point. But I knew better. She hadn't taken her suitcase, only her purse. She came home drunk and foul-mouthed in the middle of the night and started in on me all over again. How could I have in good conscience turned that precious little girl over to someone who it was clear hadn't mended her ways at all?

"I couldn't bear the thought of that little girl growing up thinking that her own mother had abandoned her, so when Winnalee started calling me Ma, I didn't correct her. And for good reason. Christmas would come, Winnalee's birthday, and not so much as a card in the mail," Mrs. Malone said. "I thought it was better if she thought I was her mama, so at least she'd feel she had one." Aunt Verdella put her arm around Hannah Malone—as far as it would reach anyway—and gave her a squeeze.

Hannah Malone was blubbering now, her whole body shaking. "Freeda thought I'd tried to turn Winnalee against her by having her call me Mama, but I never did such a thing. Freeda's pictures were up, and I told Winnalee that that was her big sister, who was working in the city, and that soon she'd come pay us a visit. Winnalee's an imaginative child, which I'm sure you know, and she concocted a story for herself, thinking that her pretty sister was a movie star. Even at four, she'd put on little shows for me, saying that when she grew up, she was gonna be a movie star just like Freeda."

Hannah sounded so wheezy that I'm sure Aunt Verdella thought she'd choke to death, so she told Hannah to take a breath. "And I think I'd better do the same," Aunt Verdella said. Hannah sucked in her breath and blew her nose some more.

"When Freeda ran away, leaving Winnalee behind, I had to bear up with the gossip before it settled down. After a time—well, because everybody in town respects me for the Christian woman I am, I suppose—they actually seemed to forget that Winnalee was really Freeda's child. I forgot sometimes too."

"Well," Aunt Verdella said, "I know even with my niece I can forget sometimes that she's not mine. So I can only imagine."

At the mention of my name, my breath sucked in and I backed away from the door opening again, sure Aunt Verdella would look up and see me and realize I was standing nearby being all ears.

"Well, and you can imagine how the gossip flew after Freeda came and took Winnalee away. Everyone in town, of course, heard about how Freeda went to the school, saying that I was dead and she needed to take Winnalee out immediately. What could Winnalee's teacher do but release Winnalee to her? She'd taught Freeda, and she knew Freeda was Winnalee's mother, so she knew Freeda had every right to take her.

"Mrs. Peters . . . may I call you Verdella?" Aunt Verdella told Hannah she could. "Verdella, you can imagine how shocked and hurt I was to learn that Freeda had told my little Winnalee that I was dead. Telling the teacher that was bad enough, but to tell Winnalee such a horrible lie too? Oh, it just pains me to think of it. And then to hear from Mrs. Hamilton that that poor little girl is still so devastated that she can't bear to part with me and carries around an urn that she believes contains my ashes? My God, is there no length of cruelty that my daughter will go to to hurt me? And doesn't she care that she hurts Winnalee in the process?" Hannah Malone paused then, as if she was waiting for Aunt Verdella to answer her.

"It broke my heart too, to see poor Winnalee carrying around those ashes," Aunt Verdella said. "You can see, then,

can't you, why I went to Hopested to buy that stone and plot?"
I peeked around the corner again.

"Verdella, I'm sure in view of what I've told you, you can
see that telling me how to find them is the only right thing
to do."

Aunt Verdella's hand came up to fidget with the neckline
of her housedress. "Oh dear. I've put myself in such a
quandary. My husband, Rudy, he tells me all the time to stay
out of other people's business. Oh dear, I feel so on the spot."
Aunt Verdella glanced at the back door. The heavy rain had
changed into a softer, steadier rain, and I knew that Aunt
Verdella was worried that Winnalee would show up at any
minute.

"And what do you plan to do, if I may ask, if I tell you
where Freeda and Winnalee are? Go to them out of the blue?
Oh my, it would be the shock of Winnalee's life! She believes
you're her mama, and she believes you're dead. She's carried
you everywhere for five years now. She's just a little girl,
Hannah, and if Freeda is her birth mother, then..."

Aunt Verdella spread her arms wide. "Do you think
Freeda would change her mind and turn Winnalee over to you
now? Is that what you're hoping for? She wouldn't, you know.
She loves that child something fierce!"

My mind was nothing but a mixed-up mess by now. I didn't
know what to do or what to think, only that I didn't want
Winnalee showing up to get the shock of her life, and I didn't
want Winnalee to go away. I turned around and leaned against
the wall, the taste of blood against my tongue.

"I don't think it's for you to decide, Mrs. Peters. Freeda is
my daughter and Winnalee is my granddaughter. I deserve the
peace of mind that only seeing Winnalee will give me."

I didn't need to see Aunt Verdella's face to know that she
was probably glancing at the door, wishing that Uncle Rudy
would walk through it and tell her what to do.

I leaned my face so close to the door frame that I could feel
my warm breath, and I slid to the side slowly so that only one

eye peeked into the kitchen. Aunt Verdella was still fussing with her neckline. "I don't mean to be disrespectful or difficult, Mrs. Malone, but this has all come as a shock to me. I'm afraid that the best I can do for now is to tell Freeda that you're in town and try to coax her to talk to you alone first. No matter how you feel, or how Freeda feels, Winnalee's the one we need to think about right now. You can't just go show up on their doorstep, Hannah, without that child being prepared somehow."

Mrs. Malone's arms flung up shoulder-high, then slammed down on the table. "You go telling Freeda I'm in town, and she'll be gone before you can even get all the words out!"

"Well, I'm sorry," Aunt Verdella said. "But that's the best I can do. I would imagine you're staying here in town tonight?"

"I plan to check in at the hotel at the end of Main Street," Hannah said. "This drive has been too much for me. Especially while I'm in this emotional state."

"Okay," Aunt Verdella said. "Then I'll bring Freeda over to Daverson's Motel in the morning, if she agrees to see you. I can't exactly say what time."

So it was decided.

And it was a good plan, I guess. Had it only gone right.

23

Mrs. Malone hadn't even hoisted herself off of her chair yet when the front door creaked open and Freeda's voice rang through the house. "Verdella? Hey, I came to see if you and Button can come over. Winnalee ran a nail up her foot and I had to bring her in to the doctor." I saw Freeda from the dining room where I was standing. Her sandal snagged on the rag rug, and she stopped to right it with her other foot. "She's carrying on like she's dying, of course. She says it hurts to walk, so she wants Button to come over to play paper dolls or something—and I've got to get to Marty's. I'm late for work already!"

Noises went crazy in my throat as Freeda slipped her foot back into her shoe, then clacked through the dining room. I glanced into the kitchen, where Aunt Verdella and Hannah Malone stood, still as icicles.

"Hey there, Button," Freeda said when she reached me. "Where's your—" And her voice stopped when she ran smack-dab into the same picture of those frozen ladies that I was looking at.

For a minute, Aunt Verdella and Mrs. Malone stood at the table staring at Freeda, their eyes big and round and scared.

Freeda was the first to speak. "What in the hell are you doing here?" I looked up at Freeda. Even from a side view, I could see that her eyes had changed into glowing slits. Like cats' eyes, when their ears go back and the fur on their back humps up.

"Freeda!" Hannah Malone's eyes, which were nothing but two red holes from crying, filled up like rain puddles.

"How in the hell did you find me?"

Aunt Verdella moved first. She rushed to Freeda and wrapped one arm around Freeda's waist, resting her free hand on Freeda's arm. "Honey. Just stay calm. I can explain everything."

Freeda looked at Aunt Verdella as though Aunt Verdella had suddenly turned into some kind of a scary monster. Freeda squirmed out of Aunt Verdella's hold and turned around until she was facing the dining room.

"Please, Freeda. Sit down. Let's talk. For Winnalee's sake," Aunt Verdella said.

Freeda shook her head like there were spiders crawling against her scalp. "There's nothing to talk about. I want *her* out of here right now." She turned back toward the kitchen and pointed toward the table, her finger wagging. "Don't you even think about coming near Winnalee. You hear? I'll blow your fuckin' brains out if you even try."

Aunt Verdella's gasp was the loudest. "Freeda! That's your mother you're talking to!"

"I don't give a damn who she is. I want her to leave me and Winnalee alone!" I could only see Freeda's back, but I knew from the way she was standing—all stiff, her hip banged over to one side—that she meant business.

"Young lady, don't you talk to me like that!" Hannah Malone said, and her voice didn't sound like a sad little girl's voice no more.

"Shit. My mother, my ass." I could hear something close to tears in Freeda's voice. She turned to Aunt Verdella. Her voice, when it came, was filled with anger. "Did you send for her? Did you?"

"No, honey. I didn't."

"Then how in the hell did she find me in this little rat hole of a town?"

"I can explain, Freeda," Aunt Verdella said. "I can explain if you'll only listen." Freeda crossed her arms, her fingers pressed hard against her skin.

"I didn't bring her here, but I am responsible for her coming. I'm sorry, Freeda. I didn't do it on purpose. I'd gone to Hopested to buy your ma a plot and a gravestone. For Winnalee's sake. So that poor child didn't have to carry that urn around anymore. That's when I found out that—"

"You had no right sticking your nose in my goddamn business!"

"I wasn't trying to stick my nose in anyone's business, dear. I was just trying to do something nice for Winnalee and you. That's all. The funeral home told your mother I'd been there. I'd given my name and address, of course, and I gave them the name I wanted on the gravestone. That's when they told me that your ma was still alive."

Hannah Malone, who was standing now, braced her hands on the table and glared at Freeda. "It doesn't matter how I found out, Freeda. What matters is that I am here now. And you, young lady, owe me an apology, as well as proof that my grandchild is well and happy. And if you had an ounce of sense in that head of yours, you'd hand Winnalee over to me right now, so that child could finish growing up in a good Christian home."

I could almost feel Freeda's rage then, so hot that it seemed it could burn us all in one swipe. I stepped backward and slid around the dining-room table, not wanting to be too close when Freeda went all the way berserk. "I don't owe you a goddamn thing. Not one fuckin' thing! And don't you talk to me about good Christian homes either!"

Hannah Malone slapped the kitchen table with one fat hand. "Stop that foul language right now. And whatever you do, do not take the Lord's name in vain in my presence. You hear me?"

I heard Aunt Verdella mutter, "Oh dear."

Freeda laughed, but there was no fun in her voice. "Yes, oh my, we could not have the family embarrassed by Freeda's foul mouth, now, could we?"

"You *should* be embarrassed!" Hannah said. "After the things you've done to our family. Dragging our good name through the mud, and breaking my heart as you've done!"

Freeda sprung at her then, her hands wrapped in tight fists. "Shut up, you self-righteous bitch! Shut the fuck up!"

Aunt Verdella grabbed Freeda's arm and held tight. "Freeda, please. Hannah. Let's all calm down, please! All this screaming isn't gonna solve anything. Don't go saying things you'll both regret later."

Freeda yanked her arm away and wrapped it back around herself. She was huffing and stepping from side to side, like she was waiting for one of those starting guns to tell her it was time to run. "I want her out of this goddamn town. Now. Or I'm gonna bolt. You understand, Verdella?"

"Freeda, please, say anything you want to me, but I can't bear to hear my Lord's name taken in vain," Hannah said.

Freeda laughed, but I don't think she thought what her ma said was really funny. "Isn't it a joke, Ma? That after all that happened, the issue to you is what cusswords come out of my mouth? Jesus H. Christ. Somebody slap me before I lose my fucking mind over the absurdity of it all."

"Will you sit down, Freeda? Please?" Aunt Verdella asked.

Freeda shook her head.

"Okay. Okay. Just calm down, then, dear, please. And maybe you and your ma can have a good talk and—"

"No, Verdella. This isn't my ma sitting here. My ma died to me, years ago."

More tears squeezed out of Hannah's puffy eyes. "Freeda, please. Don't be cruel now."

"Don't be cruel? Oh my God!" Freeda grabbed at the sides of her head and shook it. "I can't believe you'd dare call *me* cruel. My God!" She started crying then too, but those kind of angry tears that make people gasp and gulp, and growl.

"Calling your mother foul names isn't cruel?" Hannah asked. "Telling her own grandbaby that she's dead, and ripping away the child I raised by myself for five years, isn't cruel?"

"You want to talk about cruel, Ma? Is that what you want to talk about? Fine! Let's talk about cruel!

"Let's talk about a ten-year-old girl coming to you—your own baby girl—to tell you that her uncle Dewey has been slipping into her room at night and touchin' her pee-pee. And let's talk about you slappin' her face for saying a bad word like *pee-pee!*"

Hannah Malone gasped, as did Aunt Verdella. Aunt Verdella looked up then and saw me standing behind the table, watching and listening. "Button. You go over and sit with Winnalee. You hear me?"

I ducked away from the door and walked through the living room. My stomach felt sick, and I could taste blood inside my mouth. I knew I should keep walking. Right out the front door and across the lawn, just like Aunt Verdella told me to. But I couldn't get my feet to keep moving, and I couldn't get my big ears to stop listening either. And before I knew it, my feet were walking me around back to listen and peek at the kitchen door.

"Oh, I could spit on you, for that look of shock you just plastered on your face," Freeda said to her ma. "I could! I came to you after putting up with that son of a bitch's sick shit for months, and I was so scared to tell you what he was doing that I puked. Remember that? I puked before I could even get all the words out, just as I held puke in my mouth every time that sick bastard came and touched me like that, and made me touch him too. I was terrified, because he'd told me that if you ever found out what *I* was doing, you'd be so heartsick that it would kill you. I was terrified that you'd die on the spot when I told you, but I needed some comforting bad that day. Unfortunately, you didn't have any comfort to give me. You gave me a slap and a goddamn rag and told me to clean up my mess, because you couldn't bend. And after that, you said you couldn't make the stairs anymore because of your knees, and you let me sleep up there alone with that fucker every single night."

"Oh my," Aunt Verdella said, and there was pain in her voice. She went to Freeda and wrapped her arms around her. "Oh, honey," she said. Freeda let Aunt Verdella hug her a bit, but she pulled her head off of Aunt Verdella's shoulder.

"Is it any wonder, Ma, that I turned out the way I did? Hating men as I do? Yeah, I give them what they want, but goddammit, if I gotta play the role as somebody's whore, the way I had to play that role with my own uncle, you can bet I'll pick and choose the time, and place, and the guy. Because no matter what, I will never lay there helpless and scared while some sweaty, fat bastard paws me, telling me to lay still and be quiet. Not ever again in my life will I do that!"

"Stop this, Freeda. Stop it!" Hannah yelled. "You're making all of this up to justify taking Winnalee from me! What you said never happened. You're lying!"

"Lying? You dirty bitch!" Freeda pulled herself out of Aunt Verdella's arms. "You know damn well I'm not lying. You knew it was the truth then, and you know it's the truth now. Course, I believed I'd made it all up for a while, just like you'd said. It doesn't take much to fool a kid, now, does it? Especially when that kid *wants* to be fooled into believing something that horrible isn't happening. But that forgetting didn't last nearly long enough. All too soon, the truth came back to me. All of it."

"If that happened, Freeda, I'm sorry. I didn't know," Hannah Malone said. She didn't sound real sorry though.

"You didn't know? *You didn't know?* It happened right in front of your goddamn eyes! At the kitchen table, while you were cutting out doughnuts from a mound of dough. Dewey sitting right across from you. That fucker had me on his lap with you sitting right there, and his hairy hand went up my dress while he dunked a warm doughnut into his coffee cup. Don't you even try saying you didn't know! You sat there, your fat-ass cheeks red and bulging with a goddamn dough-nut, while tears rolled down my face. I was so ashamed, Ma. Ashamed of myself, as though *I* was to blame for what he was doing. And I knew by the look you gave me that you were ashamed of me too. To this goddamn, fucking day, I can't look at a doughnut, or sleep in an upstairs, without puke rising up in my throat.

"And later, when you found out that the neighborhood boys were having their way with me, you remember what you told me? Or did you conveniently forget that too? You told me that it was no wonder that Dewey did the things he did, with me throwing myself at him, the way I threw myself at the schoolboys. That's what you said to me!"

Freeda looked like she was shrinking as the mad seeped out of her, leaving nothing but the sad. "I was as loving as Winnalee, and, yep, I crawled up on his lap when he first came to stay with us, and I giggled when he tickled me, and even coaxed him to tickle me more. But goddammit, I wasn't ask-ing for *that*! I was asking to be loved, because I missed my daddy."

I batted at the tears that were falling down my face, tick-ling my chin.

"Stop this, Freeda! Kids remember things wrong some-times, don't they, Mrs. Peters?" Aunt Verdella didn't say nothing. "But I didn't come here to talk about the past. I have no interest in the past or anything except to see my grandbaby. I raised her for five years, Freeda. Five years! You had no right to take her from me as you did. Why didn't you just stay out of our lives. Why?"

Freeda turned more mad than sad again, her hands balling back into fists. "I came to get her because I ran into a trucker in Chicago who knew Dewey, and he told me that Dewey had left there to go back home to Hopested, where he planned to truck for his old company. I left that very same night, because I'd be damned if I was gonna let that motherfucker get his hands on my baby!"

Hannah Malone gasped. "You think I'd let anyone hurt that precious little girl?" Her fat hand came down to clutch the place where her heart should be.

"You let him hurt me!" Freeda screamed.

"That was different," Hannah said. "You were always throwing yourself at him. Don't think I didn't see that!"

"Hannah!" Aunt Verdella said.

"You're blaming *me* for what he did? I was a kid!"

"I don't want to talk about you anymore, Freeda. I want to talk about Winnalee. You can't do this, Freeda. I raised that child!"

"Yeah, you did. For five years. While I tried to get my head out of my goddamn ass. I was sixteen years old, and so fuckin' messed up from the shit that went on while I was growing up that I didn't know which way was up. But when I grew up, and I got myself together some, I wanted my kid with me. And I wanted her away from you, and safe from that sick freak!"

My head felt all buzzy, and my belly felt sick. I slipped out the front door, but I didn't go over to Winnalee's. I knew I couldn't look at her just then and pretend that it was just another day for playing. So instead I went around and sat on the porch steps.

I sat with my head down, my heels propped on the second step, a trail of raindrops falling from the eave onto the toes of my shoes. I wrapped my arms around my knees first, then I brought my hands up over my ears. Not to hide them from anyone this time, but to hide them from the yelling still going on inside the house.

"Button? You were supposed to come over!"

I looked up and saw Winnalee rounding the corner. She was hopping on one leg, her hand against the siding of the house to keep her steady. One foot was wrapped in white gauze, and she had that leg flipped up by her butt. Her loops were darkened from the rain, and she was dressed in real clothes.

"Freeda tell you what happened to my foot? I had to get a shot too, so I wouldn't get locked jaw. Whose car is here? You got company?"

I stood up fast. Not knowing what to do but knowing that, no matter what, I couldn't let Winnalee go inside that house.

"Let's go to your house and play paper dolls," I said quickly. "Or write something new in our book. We got a whole ninety-nine ideas now. We could write the one hundredth idea down, and then we'll know everything there is about living good. Let's do it, Winnalee." I grabbed her arm and tried slinging it over my shoulder, but she pulled it away.

"Who's Freeda yelling at?" Winnalee asked. She hopped to circle around me, her hand on my shoulder so she wouldn't tip over. "Okay, but first I want to show Freeda my arm. It's hot and it hurts where they gave me that shot." She reached for the railing and hopped up the first step, her head tilted toward the screen door.

"No. No. That's the TV. Let's go to your house, Winnalee. Come on. Now!" I tried my best to keep my voice little, so no one inside would hear me.

And then it came. Hannah Malone's voice. So loud that you could hear every word clearly when she said, "It doesn't matter, Freeda. You had no right stealing my baby girl from me and telling her I was dead!"

Winnalee turned around to face me. The color that normally pinked her cheeks was gone. She looked like she'd just seen a ghost.

She started shaking then. Worse than Freeda had when she set eyes on Hannah Malone. I reached out to touch her, but Winnalee hopped off the step, coming right down on her hurt foot. "Come on, Winnalee. Come on. It'll be okay."

I think Winnalee was too shocked to cry, or even to yell out. She backed away from my hand, as though she couldn't trust that it was really my hand, then she turned and started running as though she couldn't even feel her hurt foot.

Across the yard she raced. Not going toward home, but toward our magic tree.

I didn't know what to do. I hurried up the steps to tell Aunt Verdella that Winnalee had heard Hannah, and that she wasn't acting right either.

When I peeked into the kitchen, they were all standing. Freeda was rocking back and forth and making horrible noises as she cried those kind of tears that come when someone's so mad they can't hardly breathe, and Aunt Verdella was holding her up. "Leave now, please, Mrs. Malone," Aunt Verdella said. "Freeda's too upset to talk right now."

"Aunt Verdella?" I said. She turned and saw my face and hands pressed against the screen.

"Button, Auntie told you to go sit with Winnalee! Go on, now. Mind your auntie!" she snapped.

In my whole life, Aunt Verdella had never said a word in a mean voice to me. I backed out of the porch, then ran down the steps. The rain was falling heavy again, and a strong, colder wind was blowing raindrops against my wet eyes.

I could see Winnalee in the distance, crouched down beside our tree. I ran as fast as I could to reach her. Winnalee was sobbing, and her arms were buried inside the hollow part of the trunk.

"What are you doing, Winnalee? Come on. Let's go to your house and play, or write something in our book. Only one more to go, then we'll know all the secrets to life, remember?"

Winnalee was digging in that hole like a dog, kicking back bits of dirt and bark that clung to her wet legs. I looked at the house, then back at Winnalee. I didn't know what to do, because it was like Winnalee couldn't hear me.

Winnalee yanked our adventure bag out of the hole and got to her feet. She was bent over like she had a stomachache, holding the bag against her middle. Her bare knees were muddy, and her teeth were gritted, even though her lips were stretched wide so the screams could still get out. She turned then and started stumbling in the direction of her house.

"Winnalee?" I called. "Where you going?"

Her voice was thick with tears, and her loops were sagging under the weight of the rain. "I'm going to find the fairies!" she screamed.

"No. Let's not go right now. It's raining. See? We're going next weekend, remember? We made a deal!"

"No! I'm going now!" she screamed, her voice howling just like the wind. "Are you coming or not?"

"No. Not today. It's raining too hard, and your foot's hurt. We have to go to your house and wait. Aunt Verdella said."

"I knew you'd never go with me. I just knew it!" Winnalee screamed. "Even if it wasn't raining, you wouldn't go, because you're a scaredy-cat! You hear me? A scaredy-cat! Well, you might be a-scared of dead people, but I'm not! I like dead people! I love them even! I love dead people best!"

She turned then and started running, her sobs trailing behind her like her loops.

"Come back, Winnalee! Come back! Goin' now ain't a bright idea. You hear? It ain't!"

She didn't stop, but she turned her head to yell at me. "Leave me alone, scaredy-cat! You never believed in fairies, anyway. Well, I believe in them! I *know* they're real!"

I stood there, watching Winnalee get smaller and smaller as she raced past her house and across the oat field. I didn't know what to do. I swatted at my eyes and looked back at the house, then out at the field where I could only see Winnalee's head bouncing above the glossy, waving oats.

My throat was so thick with scared and tears that I couldn't run fast, but I tried my best to catch up with Winnalee. Even limping, she was going real fast. "Winnalee!" I screamed, but the wind against my face must have blown my voice behind me, because she didn't turn around.

I reached the oat field just as she was clearing it. I waved my arms, parting the oats as I ran. The scared I had in my belly ever since Hannah Malone had arrived wasn't nothing compared to the scared I felt when I saw Winnalee disappear into the patch of red pine. "Wait, Winnalee!" I called. "I'll go with you. Wait!"

But she didn't.

24

When I reached the edge of the field, I took a few baby steps into the woods, then stopped. "Winnalee? Winnalee!" I called out, then turned west and listened for her. All I heard, though, was the sound of the wind swirling the branches and the tapping of rain against the leaves.

I'd never been in the woods by myself before. I looked up at the sky. The clouds scooting across it were as fat as Uncle Rudy's belly, and their bottoms were the color of bruises. I knew that on a sunny day the sun could have been my compass, because west is where it goes to bed at night, but with the sun hidden behind dark rain clouds and the trees working like an umbrella, I knew I had to think of another way to find west.

I looked back at Winnalee's house and found her bedroom window. From there we could see due west, she'd said. I lined my back up with her window and stood facing the same direction. Everything would be okay, I told myself, as long as I kept walking in a straight line.

I tried to look for prints Winnalee's bare feet might have left on the ground, but walking in the woods, I could see, was nothing like walking through the fields. When you walked in the fields, you left a flattened trail wherever you stepped. But not in the woods, with the ground all bunched up with brush and dead tree limbs and last fall's rotted leaves. Uncle Rudy had told me once that in the old days, when the Indians would go out into the woods early in the morning to collect sap from the trees to make maple syrup, they used to bend willow branches so that the broken limbs would work like arrows, pointing the way to where they were strapping those weaved baskets to the trees. Then, when their kids woke up, they could go into the woods and find their mas without getting lost. As I listened for Winnalee, I wished that I'd thought to tell her that story. Then maybe she would have made tree arrows so I could find her if she left for the fairies before I did.

I knew Winnalee was way ahead of me. She was a fast runner, especially when she was riled up. And she had the compass too, so I knew she wasn't wasting time looking down at her feet to make sure they were walking in a straight line. Still—her being way ahead or not—I couldn't make myself run. It was like the scared in my throat had sunk down to my feet, making them so heavy that I couldn't move them fast enough to do more than walk.

I didn't let myself turn my whole body around when I looked to see if I could still see the empty field and Winnalee's house behind me. I was afraid that if I did, I'd forget which way I was heading and start going in one of those other three directions. I twisted my body and looked as hard as I could, but I couldn't see nothing but trees and brush behind me.

My chest was doing that fast, in-and-out breathing that people do when they're scared. I wanted to turn my whole body around and run as fast as I could for Aunt Verdella's house. I wanted to, but I couldn't. Not with Winnalee in the woods alone, all upset because the ma she thought was in a jar was right in Aunt Verdella's kitchen. Besides, me and Winnalee had a deal: We were gonna find the fairies together. So I walked on, stopping before a dead, tipped-over tree. It was a big one, its sticking-up roots black like giant, hairy spider legs. I thought of skirting around it, but that tree seemed to stretch on forever, so I swung my leg over it, the bark scraping against my bare skin.

I had one leg on each side when I heard something. I jerked my head up and saw leaves move, then stop. "Winnalee?" I called. "That you?" But it wasn't. It was only a deer. She peeked her black nose out at me. Her eyes were round and black and soft-looking. Around her skirted her baby, which wasn't real little, though it still had spots on its back. The mama snorted, and the baby stopped. Then they both turned and hopped away, their white tails pointing up like flags as they went. "Don't go," I whispered.

I suppose I was crying some. Not only because the woods were getting darker and I was scared of getting lost (or, worse yet, scared of getting found by Hiram Fossard's ghost), but because I was sad for Winnalee, and sad about all the things I'd heard. I thought of those things as I slid down the side of the broken tree and kept walking straight, my big ears sharp for any sound of Winnalee, or shovels.

Winnalee said once that a kid had to search for the secrets to life, because a grown-up wasn't gonna tell you shit. She knew what she was talking about there, because she sure wasn't told nothing. I thought of Winnalee talking to those ashes, thinking they were her ma, and how that wasn't nothing but a big fat lie. I thought of Hannah Malone too. I thought of how it must have been when she wrapped her fat arms around Winnalee. She seemed like a nice lady to me at first, yet she'd slapped Freeda when she was a little girl, just for calling that place between her legs where she got hurt a "pee-pee."

I didn't want to think about what Freeda said her uncle did to her when she was a girl like me and Winnalee, yet I couldn't help but think of that either. I didn't know there was bad uncles like that. I felt sad for Freeda, and I wished that she'd had a good uncle like me, who only patted her on the head and told her stories, instead of a bad uncle who touched her peepee and made her puke.

The farther I walked, the darker it got. I wasn't sure if that was because the sun was hiding behind rain clouds or if it was because it was turning into night. I came to a patch where the trees weren't so thick and tipped my head back to look up at the sky. Rain washed my face and I blinked my eyes. The sky had that dark, purple look to it that rainy skies get right before dark. "Winnalee? Winnalee, where are you?" I called, but all that answered was the wind. I paused a minute, then started walking again. My clothes were sticking to me, and the frizzy curls limping against my neck were dripping. I had smears of mud on my legs and cloud-shaped wet spots rimming my shoes. I didn't need anyone to tell me that I was in big trouble for running off and for getting all dirty.

Then it came. A moan so loud that I thought I'd jump right out of my wet skin. I froze, just like that mama deer did. I waited. I listened. My heart was rapping so hard against my chest that it seemed it should hurt. It was like I had two voices talking in my head then. One of them said the loud moan was nothing but the wind, but the other said that it was Fossard's ghost. Both voices were wrong.

I saw a glimpse of pale blue when I turned to run toward what I hoped was home, and then I heard the moan again. "Winnalee!"

I went to where she was sitting, her back against a tree, gulping for air as she cried. She flinched when she felt my hand on her and looked up quickly with eyes so scared that it made my tummy hurt. "It's me, Button," I said, even though there was still enough light that she could probably see that anyway.

For a second it looked like she was going to slap my arm away, but then she held hers up to me instead. I sat down beside her, and we hugged and cried.

"I heard my mama's ghost," she said. "Freeda stole me, so Mama's ghost came back to get me." Winnalee's teeth were chattering and snot was running out of one of her nostrils.

"No, Winnalee. That wasn't a ghost."

The way Winnalee felt in my arms when she cried made me so sad for her that I didn't even care that her snot was getting on my shirt.

She pulled her face off of my shoulder. "Then my mama was there? For real?"

"Hannah was really there," I told her.

Her wet loops were stuck to her cheeks, so I brushed them aside, even if it hurt more to see her face. "But my mama's dead," she said to me.

"No, Winnalee, she's not."

"Freeda said she was dead! She came to my school and said that. And then she gave me the jar and said Ma was in it, because I wanted my ma and I wouldn't stop crying. Why'd she take me if my ma wasn't dead?"

"Because Hannah wouldn't give you to her, that's why."

"But you can't take things that don't belong to you. Even Freeda said that! Why'd she steal me? I just wanted my ma."

"You got a ma, Winnalee. You always had a ma."

"No, I didn't!" Winnalee got up then, and her quiet tears turned noisy. "I had a ma in a jar. For all this time, I only had a ma in a jar. But I wanted a real ma. Why'd she steal me from my ma?"

I didn't know what to say, other than to say the truth. "Because she *is* your ma, Winnalee. Freeda's your ma. Hannah is your grandma."

Winnalee shook her head. "You're lying!" she screamed, as she backed away from me. I stood up too.

"No, I'm not. I heard the whole thing!"

"Liar! Freeda's my sister, and she's nothing but a liar too!"

"Uh-uh. I didn't hear it only from Freeda. I heard it from Hannah Malone herself! She said it just before you came. She said that you were Freeda's girl and that she let you believe she was your ma instead. She said it right in front of Aunt Verdella too."

The air had filled up with dark so quickly that Winnalee's

face didn't look like much more than a white smudge. "It's true," I told her.

"You're lying. You're all liars!" Winnalee turned then and started running, darting in between the trees so quickly that I could hardly keep up.

"Wait up, Winnalee!" I shouted, but she kept going, jig-zagging and zigzagging as she went. "You're gonna get lost!" I yelled. "We gotta stay due west, remember?"

"Leave me alone, Button! I hate all of you!"

I ran till I got tired, then I stopped. My breaths were coming fast, like Knucklehead's when he ran off to chase a deer, then back again. I looked this way and that, but I couldn't see Winnalee anywhere.

In the distance, the sky grumbled, and flashes of lightning lit the sky. I was crying hard by this time, because it was so black in the woods now that, if it weren't for the bit of muddy dark purple showing through the branches above me and the stabs of lightning, I wouldn't have known which way was up. I was cold and thirsty and my legs were tired, but, most of all, I was scared. I didn't know where west was anymore, so I didn't see much choice than to just keep walking, feeling my way. I flinched each time a sharp piece of brush or a heavy limb reached out to touch me, scared that it was Hiram Fossard's shovel poking me. I'd look up to the sky then, begging the clouds to move so that the moon could be my night-light.

I came to a hill and climbed it, because it was straight in front of me. I got halfway up the hill when the next crack of lightning showed me what was ahead of me.

I don't know what I was thinking, believing for even a second that house in the distance was Winnalee's and that I'd somehow turned myself around and made it back home. I knew that there wasn't a hill anywhere in the oat field that sat between the woods and her house, and besides, even in the moonlight, and from such a distance, I could see the jagged, broken windows. With the next flash of lightning, I saw the driveway off to the side of the house.

I backed down the hill until I bumped into a tree, then bent my arms back and wrapped them around the rough trunk. A tear slipped down my cheek and tickled my neck. I didn't know what to do, or where to go. I just knew that I didn't want to be standing alone in the field where a ghost might see me.

I thought of where the house was and where the driveway was, and then I realized where I was. I was standing close to where Hiram Fossard's bomb shelter had to be.

I didn't make a sound as I cried, because I figured Fossard's ghost could hear a kid crying. I took a big gulp, as if the air itself was made of bravery, and I headed toward the house. I wouldn't be able to get inside, I knew, but maybe just sitting with my back against the door would be enough to make me feel like I wasn't standing in the middle of nowhere, a sitting duck for Fossard's ghost. My head cocked this way and that with each step as I watched for a ghost, and for Winnalee.

Then, just like that, I could feel tall, wet grass up around my legs and wind on my face. I patted the dark, but I didn't feel any trees. I stood still until another bolt of lightning split the sky and lit the top of the house.

I hadn't taken more than a few steps when the sky lit with a web of lightning that brightened the ground and air, almost as if it were daytime. That's when I saw a smudge of pale blue across the field at the edge of the trees, right where Winnalee and I had slipped into the woods that led to the beck, when Tommy'd brought us here. I stopped to yell Winnalee's name in that direction, but in the time it takes to blink, the flash was gone, and I wasn't sure I'd seen that splotch of pale blue at all. Above me, dark clouds moved like ships on a black sea. I looked to my right, and that's when I saw a shape. A black shape of a person walking in the distance, right toward me.

I stood still as a fence post, not knowing where to turn next. My ear strained for the sound of a scraping shovel, but all I heard was the whimper of what was left of the wind and the steady stream of rain, which was coming down hard again.

I didn't know where I'd be the scaredest—pressed up against that old house where Fossard had shot his dog and his wife, or standing in the open, where his ghost roamed at night, walking straight toward me, scraping that shovel against the ground even if I couldn't hear it with the storm so noisy.

And then I remembered what Tommy said. He said that after Fossard built the shelter, the fear of being stuck in it if a bomb came down was so bad that he shot his dog and his wife and hanged himself. I didn't know if Tommy was telling the truth about why Fossard built the shelter, or why he killed them all, but when I started to hear scraping noises that could have come from a shovel, I decided real fast that I was gonna believe what he said about Hiram walking like a ghost because he was too afraid to go under the ground.

I turned to get out of the clearing and scooted down the hill, my shoes slippery on the wet grass, determined to find the shelter and hide in it till morning. The air was pitch-dark in the woods, even with the sky flashing, especially in the dippy part, so that my hands and my feet had to be my eyes again.

I cried out when my hands bumped into wood too flat to be a tree. My fingers fumbled to see what I was touching. I felt the wood strips on each side of the flat wood and a sliver that jabbed into my hand when I rubbed it. I pushed on the flat part, and the wood gave way, creaking as it opened. Tommy had said Fossard's shelter was cut into the side of a hill, underneath a thick patch of red pine. I looked up and saw the dark ridge of a hill above the door, and thick streaks that had to be trees, just like Tommy had said, and I knew that I'd just found Hiram Fossard's bomb shelter.

I lurched forward and shoved the door open. I stepped inside. The bomb shelter smelled like dirt and mold. I stood just inside the door. I was afraid of what was in front of me, and I was afraid of what was to the sides of me, but I was even more afraid of what was behind me. I moved deeper inside, spreading my arms wide as I felt for something, anything, but all I could feel was air.

I took a couple of steps to my right, my hand reaching till it bumped up against something and stopped. I'd learned to spell the word *mason* by running my fingers over the letters on the jars Aunt Verdella had out while she was canning green beans, so when my hand felt dusty, rounded glass with snaky lumps swirling in the same pattern, I knew I was touching jars of canned goods. I felt the whole row of mason jars, and the wooden shelf they were sitting on. I fumbled beneath the shelf and let my fingers trace the wooden rim of what I decided was a rain barrel.

I turned and took a couple more steps and figured I was in the middle of the room, because my toes or hands weren't bumping up against anything. I didn't like that feeling. I walked crooked, not on purpose but because it's hard to walk straight when you can't see, and I whacked my leg on something that was real hard. I reached out but felt nothing, so I bent over. It was a damp, thin mattress sitting on a low, metal frame that I'd bumped up against. And that's when I heard something I *knew* was Fossard's ghost!

I didn't think. I just moved. I slammed down on the floor and scooted myself under the cot. A spring grabbed at my hair and cobwebs clung to my wet face. The door started to creak and I slid myself over until I bumped against a wall. Every bit of me, from my feet up to the top of my ouching head, was shaking.

It's funny—but not in a funny sort of way—how lots of times when you get in a bad fix, you don't do what you thought you'd do at all. When Winnalee and me talked about going to see the fairies, sometimes I'd picture us lost in the woods or trapped in Fossard's bomb shelter. And every time I thought of this happening, I saw us both so terrified that all we could do was scream like Fay Wray in that King Kong movie Aunt Verdella once let me stay up late to watch, even though she was afraid it would give me nightmares. But when it happened for real, and I found myself huddled under a stinky bed in Fossard's shelter, ghosty voices coming from outside the doorway, I didn't scream at all. I just laid there all tucked up small, my hands clamped over my mouth, and I shook, and I stared hard into the darkness, and nothing came out of my mouth at all. Not even a breath. Not even when the door opened with a squeak and a clunk, and a stream of light jabbed inside.

I clamped my eyes shut, but I could still see some light flashing through my lids. "Shit, they're not in here." It was Freeda's voice! I pressed my toes against the floor to scoot myself out, then stopped when I heard my ma's voice. "I'm gonna give her the spanking of her life when I find her! I can't believe she'd run off like this! She knows better!" I'd never heard my ma so mad in her whole life.

"Shit, I'm wet!" Freeda said, as the murky beam from the flashlight zigzagged across the walls. "How far did we walk in that goddamn rain, anyway? Had to have been at least a good mile or more. Dammit."

"We should have taken my car, not Verdella's," Ma said. "Verdella said yesterday that it was making strange noises, and she hoped she could remember to have Rudy look at it."

Freeda cussed a few more times, then she said, "There's a candle. Look for matches, will you, Jewel? This flashlight's starting to fade."

There was a quiet sizzle noise, then the tiny room lit with soft flickering light. "Damn," Freeda said. "I don't know where else to look. The goddamn house is boarded shut... unless they found a way inside."

I could see the legs of a chair, now that the room had some light in it, and I could see Ma and Freeda's legs and their shoes and hear the squishy sounds their footsteps made. Ma's legs backed up to the chair and she sat down with a sigh. "I can't believe this," she said. "Evelyn's never done something like this before. I'm so worried about those kids, Freeda."

Freeda's legs scissored across the floor as she paced. "Do you suppose Button told Winnalee about Ma showing up? God, do you suppose? What if Winnalee talked Button into running away? They could be anywhere!"

"I don't think so," Ma said. "You heard Tommy. He said they'd been planning all summer to come here and look for fairies. No doubt they left after Button went to sit with Winnalee."

"But Button heard, Jewel. She was there when Ma showed up, and Verdella told her to go over to my place." Freeda's hands came down hard to her sides, and the slap her hands made against her wet clothes sounded sharp. "I can't believe Winnalee would run off, though, with her foot hurting. I had to carry her into the bathroom to pee before I left, for crissakes."

Freeda paced back and forth a few more times, her wet shoes leaving dark smudges on the floorboards. "I wish to hell we knew what was going on. Tommy's sure they headed here, but I just don't know."

"If they came here, they headed through the woods, like Tommy said. Let's just hope they got scared when the storm started and headed back to Verdella's, or that the men have found them by now and they're safe and sound. I guess we'll know as soon as they figure out that we should have been back by now and come looking for us. They know we headed here."

"Shit!" Freeda said again. "What a day this has been. Rushing Winnalee to the doctor; my ma showing up here; the girls running off and getting lost. Jesus H. Christ! And if Button told her about Ma..." The springs above me squealed as Freeda sat down, her butt sinking the cot so low that the springs touched my back. I laid as flat as I could so I wouldn't get squished.

"I shouldn't have lied to her. Ma might have been a bitch to me, but she was good to Winnalee. It was like she'd used up every bit of madness she had in her on me and so Winnalee was spared. That kid didn't know me, except for what Ma told her, and none of that was good, I'm sure, so I knew she wouldn't go with me unless she thought she had no choice."

They stopped talking for a bit, and all I heard was the sound of my own breathing. Quiet, short puffs that landed on the wood plank just an inch from my mouth and stirred dust that floated up my nose. Afraid I'd sneeze, I turned my head sideways and pressed my cheek to the floor.

There was nothing I wanted more in the world than to crawl out from under that cobwebby, smelly hiding place and have Ma wrap her arms around me. But I couldn't make myself do it. Not when there was still mad in her voice, and not after I'd waited so long that she'd be madder still to know that I stayed hidden, being all ears. I didn't know what to do, so

I decided to stay tucked underneath the cot until I figured that out.

"She's not going to understand why I lied, Jewel. When I told Ma that I wanted my daughter back, and she told me that I didn't deserve her because of the kind of mother I'd be, I just lost it. I suppose I conjured up that lie because at that time I was wishing she *was* dead. I didn't mean to hurt Winnalee though. I just wanted to get her out of there quick."

"Oh, Freeda," Ma said.

"I was barely sixteen when I had Winnalee. Just a kid. A scared, screwed-up kid. When I was in labor with her, they had to give me ether to knock me out because I wouldn't stop screaming. And I wasn't screaming just because of the pain either. I was screaming because I was scared shitless. They held her up to show her to me, and I started puking as much from fear as from the ether. There she was, her scalp still chalky, blood on her, looking so small and helpless, and all I could think was, 'What in the hell am I supposed to do with her?' I lost it, Jewel. I did! I didn't hardly know how to take care of myself, for crissakes! What in the hell was I gonna do with a little baby?"

"Wouldn't your ma have given you a hand, Freeda?" Ma asked.

Freeda grunted that kind of grunt that means, "What? Are you crazy?" Then she said, "I'd dropped out of school when I started showing and sat home for a good four months. I thought I'd lose my mind, sitting in that house with that woman preaching at me. The thought of spending the rest of my life sitting stuck out on that farm, taking care of a kid with that fat ass harping at me, about sent me up the wall.

"Course, when I left, I didn't plan to be gone for so long. I was just gonna catch a ride with this young guy who was making a run to Chicago. He said he'd be swinging back through Hopested in a few days, and I'd planned to come back with him. My last hurrah, you know? But, shit, before he could even turn his car around and point it north, I was gone."

"You were just a kid, Freeda. A scared kid."

"Ah, shit, that's no excuse, and you know it as well as I do." Freeda got up and started shuffling across the small floor again. "One week dragged into another. Then a whole year had passed. I told myself I'd go get her when I turned eighteen, but by then I was waitressing, living in some dump with a couple of losers, and barely making ends meet. I couldn't support a baby. Then one year turned into two, then three, then four. I felt guilty, of course, but at the same time, I felt some comfort in knowing that the kid was at least being fed and clothed.

"I was twenty-one when I learned that my uncle Dewey had moved back in with Ma. I didn't think about the money, the dump I was living in, or anything but getting my kid out of that house and away from him. I jumped into my old clunker, and I drove back to Hopested, hoping to God that I wasn't too late and that that worthless, sick son of a bitch hadn't touched her yet. If he had, I swear to God, I would have taken a gun and killed him."

"Oh, Freeda. I didn't know about your uncle," Ma said. She sounded teary.

"Yeah, well, water under the bridge at this point, I guess. The important part is that I got there before that bastard could do to her what he'd done to me."

Freeda was crying, softly, and maybe Ma too. "You know what's the goddamn truth, Jewel? That if it hadn't been for hearing that Dewey was back, I probably wouldn't have gone for her."

"Of course you would have," Ma said. "As soon as you grew up a bit more."

"No," Freeda said. "I wouldn't have. As much as I loved her and thought about her, I wouldn't have gone back, because I knew I was no good for her."

"Oh, Freeda, don't say that!" Ma sat down on the mattress next to Freeda, and I did my best to make myself bunny-pancake flat.

"It's true. I'm all fucked up, Jewel. You know it's true. I spread my legs for anyone who wants me to spread them, and I don't even know why. What I do know, though, is that it ain't good for Winnalee. Neither is all the moving around I've put her through, trying to stay ahead of Ma, or Dewey, or maybe the lie I told her itself. I don't know, but I just can't put down roots. I feel safer this way, somehow. Like a moving target, I guess."

"You want to hear something that might make you feel a little better, Freeda? When I first met Winnalee, I told myself that I didn't like her because she was so undisciplined. But you know what the truth was? I didn't like her because looking at her made me feel sorry for Evelyn."

My insides stiffened when Ma said this, sure that what she was gonna say next was that looking at Winnalee made her feel sorry for me because I was ugly.

"You shittin' me? Why?"

"Because I could tell that no matter how unstable—tragic even—her life had been, she still felt secure because she felt loved and accepted. And I knew Evelyn didn't feel the same. I guess in a way that's why you bothered me too. Because even though it was obvious to me that you had your demons, at least you didn't feel like you had to apologize or hide who you were and how you felt."

"Hell, you probably rubbed me the wrong way for the same reasons," Freeda said. "You had a grip on all the things I didn't. Like I needed more reminders of how many things I was failing at! Shit, though, at least your kid knows where home is."

Freeda got up. She sighed. "Crissakes, our kids are only nine years old, and already we've got regrets. How damn bad is it gonna be by the time they're grown?"

Ma and Freeda laughed together then, though their laughter had a lot of sad in it.

"It's all guesswork, isn't it, when you don't have a decent blueprint to follow?" Freeda said.

"Tell me about it," my ma said.

Freeda went to the door and peered out. "It seems to be letting up some now. Christ, where are they?" I didn't know if she meant me and Winnalee, or Daddy and Uncle Rudy.

For a minute I couldn't hear nothing but the patter of rain outside the shelter door, then Freeda spoke. "Having someone mess with you when you're little, it screws a person up, Jewel. Bad. It took me a long time to get past that. Hell, I suppose in reality, I ain't over it yet, because I still do things that I don't understand, but at least I can stomach looking at myself now. And at least I'm trying my damnedest with Winnalee now."

Ma walked to the door too and stood with Freeda. "If it's any comfort to you, Freeda, I was scared to be a mother too. A few minutes after they wheeled me back to my room, I locked myself in the bathroom and cried. I cried because that poor baby looked like me. I remember praying the whole time I carried her that, boy or girl, God would have enough mercy to let the baby look like Reece. Then there she was, all pale and skinny, just like me. Her ears so thin they folded over when her head rubbed against my arm. My heart broke just to look at her, and I felt guilty for passing my bad genes on to her."

"Christ, Jewel, you had no reason to pity her. There was never anything wrong with you, inside or out, and there certainly isn't anything wrong with Button."

"I'm learning that now, Freeda. Thanks to you. I looked at Evelyn in that outfit Verdella made the girls for the Fourth, and I could see, really see, how cute she is."

"You hear that?" Freeda said. Her foot lifted off the floor as she leaned out the doorway. "I hear a vehicle, Jewel!"

"Oh God, let them have found the kids," Ma said. She hurried to the little table and there came a quick puff, then the light from the candle went out. "Hey! Hey! We're over here!" Freeda yelled from outside the shelter.

"Hello?" Ma called, her voice already sounding far away, as I scooted out from under the cot.

I hurried out the door. The rain and wind had stopped, and the clouds had broken up enough to let the moon shine, but still it was black with the trees so tall and full of branches.

I scrambled up the bank and reached the field to see two poles of light stretched from our car to the old house, and two poles of light shining on our car, from Uncle Rudy's truck, which was parked behind it. I could see Uncle Rudy and Tommy standing in the light, Knucklehead dancing in circles around them, and I guessed that the big, dark shape coming toward us was Daddy. Ma and Freeda were running toward the driveway, their arms waving, their bodies only dark, bouncing shapes. "We didn't find them!" Ma yelled, and Daddy cursed.

The tall blades of grass flicked raindrops against my legs as I ran toward them, shouting, "I'm here! I'm right here!" I yelled louder than I ever yelled in my whole life.

The smaller shadow stopped and spun around. "Button?" Freeda's voice called. "Button? That you?"

"Yeah!"

"Reece, it's Evelyn!" Ma screamed. I squinted as a beam of light hit my face.

They all started rushing toward me, but Daddy was the first to reach me. "Jesus, Kid. We looked all over for you!" he said. Then, for the first time that I could remember, my daddy scooped me up and hugged me. "You okay?" he asked, and I told him I was.

"You sure had us worried, Kid," he said, and this time, "Kid" *did* sound like a nickname.

"Oh, Evelyn!" Ma half-screamed, half-cried, when she

reached us. "Are you okay? Reece, is she okay?" She hugged me, and not one of those whispery kind of hugs either, but a big, Aunt Verdella kind of hug that almost squeezed the breath out of me.

"Button, where's Winnalee?" Freeda asked, just as Uncle Rudy and Tommy reached us. Knucklehead licked my leg that dangled against Daddy's thigh.

"I saw her heading in there," I said, "to the beck."

"The beck?" Daddy asked.

"I know where she means!" Tommy said. "The creek!"

"How long ago?" Freeda shouted.

"I don't know. Right before you and Ma came."

Daddy set me down, and Ma pulled me to her. Daddy took a couple steps, then stopped and turned. "No, Freeda, you stay here." He grabbed her shoulders. "We know this area well, and we'll find her. We don't need to be searching for both of you." Then Daddy hurried off in the direction Tommy and Uncle Rudy and Knucklehead were heading.

I wrapped my arms around Ma's skinny waist and cried as she rubbed my back. "Come on, let's get you to the car," Ma said. She nudged me to her side, her arm still around me. She wrapped her other arm around Freeda's waist. "They'll find her, Freeda," she said. "They will."

"Button," Freeda asked when we got back in the car, "when you came to the door at Aunt Verdella's, while my ma was there and we were arguing...was Winnalee with you?"

"No," I said, because that was the truth.

Freeda sighed. "Thank God."

"She'd already started running off by then," I said.

"Why? What does Winnalee know, Button?"

My teeth started searching for some skin to bite.

Ma turned my face to hers. "Evelyn, don't be scared now. None of this is your fault, and I'm not angry with you. Just tell Freeda what she wants to know, okay?" I nodded, tears warming my eyes. Ma brushed my damp bangs out of the way and kissed my forehead.

I turned to Freeda. "Winnalee came over while Mrs. Malone was saying that you stole her." I rubbed my teary cheeks. "And Winnalee got all upset and took off for the tree where we keep our...well, our bag where we put the things we planned to take with us when we went to find the fairies." I turned to Ma. "But I wasn't really gonna go, Ma. I just pretended I was." She patted me and told me to finish telling what happened.

"Did she say anything?" Freeda asked. I turned to look at Freeda again, who was slouched down in the seat.

"Just that she was going to find the fairies and that she liked dead people best." Freeda started crying then, so Ma reached over my head and touched Freeda's hair, just like she was touching mine.

I felt scared to say the next part, but I'd already been bad and I didn't want to be double-bad by not telling the whole truth. I turned back to Ma. "Winnalee wanted to know why Freeda stole her from her live ma, so I told her the part I'd heard. How Freeda was really her ma."

Ma pulled me to her and she rubbed her hand down my head, softly. "It's okay, honey."

"I said it because I didn't want her thinking that she didn't have a ma this whole time."

"It's okay, Button," Freeda said, then sighed.

It seemed like we sat forever, shivering because the night had turned cool and straining to see the flicker of flashlight beams through the trees. "They'll find her. They will," Ma kept saying, but still we waited, sniffling, and holding our breaths each time we heard Knucklehead bark.

"They're coming!" Ma shouted. I scooted up so I could see over the dashboard and, sure enough, there were four beams of light bouncing through the dark.

"Do they have her? I can't tell!" Freeda cried. She opened the car door and started running toward them. Ma and I got out too.

"Winnalee?" Freeda cried out as she ran.

"We found her!" Tommy called back, and the whole night seemed to sigh with relief. That is, until Winnalee started slapping at Freeda's hands when she tried to take her from Daddy.

26

When we got back to Aunt Verdella's, she came flying out the back door, her arms outstretched. "Oh my God, you found them!" Aunt Verdella was crying and laughing at the same time as she gathered me in her arms and hugged me. "Oh, Button, Auntie was worried sick about you!" She rushed to Uncle Rudy, who was carrying Winnalee, and in one swoop of her arms, she hugged them both. "Winnalee, oh, honey," she said, and then, "Oh, you're all soakin' wet! Come on, let's get inside. I got fresh coffee, and these girls must be starving by now."

Once inside, Aunt Verdella led me and Winnalee into the bathroom. "I'll give them a quick bath," she said, and Ma said, "They're probably too hungry and tired for that, Verdella. Just dry them off, okay?"

Aunt Verdella stripped us down and rubbed a wet wash-cloth over our faces and our arms and legs, and put Band-Aids on our worst scratches. "You can wear Uncle Rudy's T-shirts for now," she said, slipping them over our heads. Ma came in the room and helped rub our hair with towels. "My, I was so scared," Aunt Verdella kept saying.

I watched Winnalee as Aunt Verdella dried her loops. She was scratched here and there from tree branches and dotted with pink mosquito bites, just like me, but unlike me, she didn't flinch when Aunt Verdella's washcloth dabbed at the scrapes, or even when she cleaned her hurt foot and wrapped it in a new bandage. Instead, she watched the door, and I watched her, searching for something that would let me know what was going on inside of her.

The door was open a little, and I could hear Daddy and Tommy and Uncle Rudy talking, exchanging stories about their search. "This old guy deserves a steak," Uncle Rudy said twice, talking about Knucklehead, who had found Winnalee at the beck, and Tommy said that *he* deserved a steak too, since he's the one who figured out where we'd gone.

When Aunt Verdella brought us out of the bathroom, everyone stopped talking. Uncle Rudy patted our damp heads and called us his little adventurers, and Daddy made jokes about how he'd thought for a minute that we'd run off to New York to join the ballet. Winnalee didn't smile at his joke.

"I'll fix you all something to eat," Aunt Verdella said. "I don't know what that'll be quick, but I'll come up with something. In all the excitement today, I didn't give a thought to supper."

"How about some breakfast food, then," Uncle Rudy said, and Aunt Verdella told him that was a good idea. "And bunny pancakes for my girls!" she said.

Ma led Winnalee and me into the living room, and Freeda followed, her fingertip in her mouth. Winnalee sat right up tight against me and fumbled for my hand without looking for it, because her eyes were busy glaring at Freeda.

"I'm thirsty, Ma," I said, and she hurried to get me a glass of water. She touched Freeda's arm as she passed her.

As soon as Ma was out of the room, Freeda came to the couch and squatted down beside it. She put her hand on Winnalee's knee, but Winnalee pulled it away, pressing her leg closer to mine.

"Honey?" she said. "I know you must have a million questions, and I know you must be confused and upset, but—"

"You lied!" Winnalee said, the words coming out in a burst. "You told me she was my ma! You told me she was dead!"

Freeda shook her head. "No, I never said she was your ma. She did. Not me. But, yes, I did tell you she was dead, and for that I can't apologize enough. It was wrong of me to tell you that. You should have always known the truth." I looked across the room at nothing, not knowing where else to look.

I could feel Winnalee's legs jumping, her skin cool against mine. "Don't touch me!" Winnalee screamed when Freeda reached out with both hands and tried to still them. "I don't even know who you are!" Winnalee bellowed, bringing Ma and Aunt Verdella rushing into the room.

Ma reached out and took my hand, pulling me off of the couch to stand by her, but Winnalee didn't let go of my other hand, so she came with me. Freeda reached for her. "I'm your ma, Winnalee. Your mama! You grew in my tummy, not Hannah's. She raised you those first five years, yes, but that didn't make her your mother. I was always your mama, even if I wasn't there in the beginning."

"No!" Winnalee said. "You're not my mama. You're my sister. My sister, Freeda! Mas don't go away to the city without their babies!"

Freeda was crying hard now too, just like Winnalee. "I'm sorry, baby. I'm sorry I told you she was dead, but I wanted you back. You understand? I was afraid you wouldn't go with me if you thought you had a choice, and I wanted my baby girl with me."

Winnalee shook her head. "I don't know who you are!" Then she looked at me, and Aunt Verdella, and at Ma, and she pointed at us one by one and asked, "Who are you? Who are you? I don't know who you are, any of you!" Then she pointed at herself, and she screamed out, "Who am *I*?"

"Oh dear," Aunt Verdella muttered.

I heard doors slamming outside and saw the headlights of Uncle Rudy's truck jiggle as he backed out of the driveway.

Daddy and Uncle Rudy, it seemed, were going to run Tommy home. I bit the inside of my cheek and wished that I were going with them.

Ma handed me my water glass, then she moved in front of Winnalee. She took her by the shoulders and bent over, putting her face close to Winnalee's. "Winnalee? Honey, look at me." Winnalee was crying so hard that her chin was quivering.

"Winnalee, you had a terrible shock. Come on, honey, let's sit down. Auntie Jewel will sit right by you, and so will Button, okay?" Ma motioned with her head that I should sit on the other side of Winnalee. "There, see? Now, you just hold on to my hand, and Button's, and we'll stay right here beside you, okay? You know Button. She's your best friend, and you know Auntie Jewel." Winnalee nodded, and Ma said, "Good. Auntie Verdella is going to get you a nice afghan to put over your legs, so they warm up and stop shaking, okay? Everything's going to be all right."

Ma looked up at Freeda, even though she was still talking to Winnalee. "Now I want you to listen to Freeda. She's going to talk to you real slow and soft, and she's gonna tell you all the things you need to know." Ma took the afghan Aunt Verdella handed to her and shook it over Winnalee's legs. I grabbed the other end and helped. "She's going to tell you how you started growing in her belly when she was not more than a girl. And how she ran off because she was scared—just like you ran off to see the fairies because you were scared. And maybe you won't understand all of what she's saying, but the part I think you will understand is that she loves you. Isn't that right, Button?"

I had tears in my eyes as I nodded.

We sat for a long time—Aunt Verdella in her favorite chair, her eyes teary, her hands held together as though she was praying, and me and Ma alongside of Winnalee, our hands holding hers—while Freeda talked, and Winnalee looked down at her lap and cried softly. Daddy and Uncle Rudy came back, and each time Freeda took a little pause, I could hear the soft clatter of a pan, or the sizzle of bacon, or the low hum of their voices coming from the kitchen.

Winnalee didn't say a word until Freeda got to the part about her going back to Hopested. "Why didn't you just leave me there, then?"

"Because," Freeda said, "I loved you and I wanted you with me. And because I didn't want Uncle Dewey to hurt you. He hurt me when I was a little girl, Winnalee. I didn't want him to hurt you in the same way, so I came back and took you, even though I didn't have a nice place to bring you to or enough money to get you all the things a little girl should have."

Winnalee's tears had quieted to little, soft gasps.

"I know it's hard for you to understand why I did the things I did. It's even hard for me to understand. But the part I do finally get is that no matter how hard I want to, I can't go back and undo anything that happened, so I have to just accept it and move on, and just try to do my best now. That's what I'm trying to do, Winnalee. Just do my best now. And I hope that'll be enough for both of us."

Ma got up from the couch then, so Freeda could take her place. Freeda gathered Winnalee in her arms and pulled her onto her lap and rocked her and rocked her, saying, "We're gonna be okay, Winnalee. We're gonna be okay." Freeda told Winnalee that she loved her, about a hundred times, and she kept kissing Winnalee's wet face.

Winnalee looked like she was sleeping for a time, then she opened her eyes, and without taking her head off of Freeda's shoulder, she said, "What about M—my...my grandma. I wanna see her."

Freeda's teary eyes looked up toward the ceiling. "I know, honey. But not right now. I just can't see her again right now, Winnalee, but we'll figure something out."

When they were done hugging and crying, both of them looked tired and crumpled. Freeda got up to go to the bathroom, and Ma followed Aunt Verdella into the kitchen to see what the men were burning.

I sat down by Winnalee and took her hand. We sat quiet as the grown-ups talked in the kitchen. Ma was teasing Uncle Rudy and Daddy about the mess they were making and the bacon that they'd burned, and the men were teasing back. All of their laughs sounded like sighs.

"She's gonna move us again, you know," Winnalee said after a while, talking in almost a whisper, probably because her voice was hoarse.

I shook my head. "No she won't. School's almost ready to start. I heard Freeda and Ma say that next week they're gonna take us school-shopping in Porter. We're gonna get in the same room, and keep right on being best friends, and—"

Winnalee shook her head. "No. She'll move us now," she said again.

"You can't move, Winnalee. We don't even have our Book of Bright Ideas finished. We gotta get to one hundred, so we know all the secrets to life and can live good, and not make the same mistakes over and over again, remember?"

Winnalee looked at me with eyes that—even though they were as red as blood, and dry-looking now that her tears had stopped—still had a light shining behind them, and she said, "Button, if she makes me move, we'll still go on being best friends forever. And one day we'll find each other again, and we'll write that last bright idea together, just like we said we would. Let's promise, okay?" So we squeezed our fingers tighter around each other's hand, and we whispered our promise.

27

The next morning when Ma and I went to check on Freeda and Winnalee, she slowed the car down and we both looked out at the empty spot where the red pickup and wagon always sat. Aunt Verdella stepped out of their house then, moving like the wind had just gotten knocked out of her. She shrugged and held up her hands, palms up to the sky, as if she expected some explanation from God Himself to drop onto them. Ma pulled in the driveway. "They're gone," Aunt Verdella said.

We got out of the car and followed Aunt Verdella inside. "Freeda's coffee cup's still on the table, and the milk was left out. It's room temperature, so I think maybe they left in the night. They didn't even bother taking their bigger pieces of furniture, just their personal things. And not all of those either." Aunt Verdella put her arm around me and patted my upper arm a couple of times, while she dabbed at her eyes.

"Maybe they just went somewhere," I said.

Aunt Verdella shook her head. "No, Button. All of Freeda's clothes are gone, and most of Winnalee's."

Once, on the local news, I saw a family whose house just burned down. The news guy showed them walking through the rubble, picking at this and that, trying to find anything that the fire had left behind. We reminded me of those people as we wandered through the house to see what was left, our faces pale and our eyes teary. Ma followed Aunt Verdella into the kitchen to see the half-filled coffee cup and milk that was left out, and I tagged after them.

Aunt Verdella looked at Ma. "It's my fault," she said. "If I hadn't stuck my nose where it didn't belong, they'd still be here. I was just trying to do something nice for them . . ."

Ma bent to pick up an empty box of Saran Wrap and the brown paper tube that had fallen out of it and rolled across the floor to rest against the bottom of the stove. "Of course you were," she said. "Verdella, don't blame yourself for any of this. You've spent almost a lifetime blaming yourself for something you couldn't help already. Don't do it again."

I left Ma and Aunt Verdella to rummage through the downstairs, while I ran up to Winnalee's room.

The lid to the window seat was propped open, but I didn't go look inside. Instead, I went to the bed and pulled up the pillow. Our Book of Bright Ideas was gone.

I crossed the room, which was littered with a pair of shorts, a dress-up blouse, and a stray sock. My foot stepped on something lumpy and poky under the forgotten blouse. I bent over and tossed the shirt aside, then picked up Winnalee's hairbrush. A few loopy strands were wound around the bristles. I kept the brush in my hand and went to the closet, which was mostly empty, except for a girl's dress Winnalee never wore. I hopped in place, my neck stretched as far as it would go. The shelf was empty: Winnalee's shoe box, gone.

"Button? You up there?" Aunt Verdella called.

"Yeah." My voice sounded like I had a sore throat, but I didn't.

I heard two pairs of footsteps trudging up the stairs, and then Aunt Verdella and Ma were in Winnalee's room too. Ma went over to the bed and tossed the blanket back in place. She didn't bother making neat corners.

"I can't believe they're gone," Aunt Verdella said. She

crossed the room and went to the window, looking out at nothing first, then looking down. "Ohhhhhh," she said. She bent over and reached inside the window seat. When she straightened up and turned around, she was holding the urn in one hand and the lid in the other. She tipped the urn upside down and a few specks of ash drifted out and floated to the floor. "She emptied it in the window seat," Aunt Verdella said, her eyes filling with brand-new tears.

We looked around the room some more, not talking. I think Ma and Aunt Verdella felt just like I did. Like a pumpkin after the insides have been scraped away. Ma and Aunt Verdella walked in front of me down the stairs, moving slow, just like me. I guess at that moment I learned that there's nothing heavier to carry than emptiness.

We were just about to walk out of the house when Aunt Verdella stopped. "Oh no! Look." She pointed to her driveway, where Hannah Malone's white car was parked, Uncle Rudy standing next to it.

"Let's wait a bit," Ma said. "Rudy will explain things to her." Aunt Verdella closed the door again, and we stood without talking, waiting until the whirr of Hannah Malone's engine sounded and the crunching of gravel told us she'd gone. Aunt Verdella didn't say a word, as she locked the door behind us.

For a long time after they'd gone, our world was like that parched land Uncle Rudy once talked about: bare and singed gray. We went about our business, Aunt Verdella knitting baby booties and afghans, and filling in again at The Corner Store for Ada Smithy when Ada went out east to visit family, and Ma going to work and coming back to make supper and cleaning on Saturdays. Ma dropped me off at Aunt Verdella's every weekday morning to catch the bus, and sometimes while we ate our pancakes, we'd hear a noise on the porch and we'd both look up, as though we were expecting Winnalee's face to be pressed up against the screen, that urn in her arms. But it was never her, of course. Just Knucklehead or the wind. Then Aunt Verdella would look at me and get teary-eyed, and she'd say, "They were like family, weren't they, Button?" And then I'd get teary-eyed too.

It rained for days after Winnalee and Freeda left, and on the first sunny Saturday, Uncle Rudy came from the barn and found me in the yard doing nothing. "Where's your ma and dad?" he asked, and I told him they went shopping. Uncle Rudy patted me on the head, then he told me it was time for lunch, so I followed him inside. As soon as we finished eating, he said, "Okay, girls. Go pretty up your hair, or whatever it is you girls do before you leave the house. I'm taking you two into town for ice cream at the A&W."

Aunt Verdella blinked at him. "You have to go to town for something? You were just there yesterday, Rudy."

"Yep," he said. "I've gotta go to town for ice cream."

Aunt Verdella tilted her head to the side and gave him a closed-mouth smile. She knew, same as I knew, that Uncle Rudy was just trying to help us feel better.

"The weather pattern's finally changed," Uncle Rudy said as we sat three-close in the front seat of Aunt Verdella's Bel Air. "It looks like we'll see some cooler days now."

When we got to the A&W, Uncle Rudy ordered a strawberry malt, Aunt Verdella got a hot fudge sundae, and I got a big vanilla cone dipped in that waxy cherry stuff. We each got a root beer too.

Uncle Rudy wanted to sit in the shade on the picnic table behind the A&W to eat our ice cream, so that's what we did. While we licked and made those moans people make when their tongues get happy, Uncle Rudy watched me. "You miss your little friend, don't you, Button?"

Aunt Verdella reached across the table with a sad smile. "She barely does anything since little Winnalee left."

I cracked off another bite of cherry coating and popped it in my mouth.

"I miss her too," Uncle Rudy said. "She was quite a little ray of sunshine, wasn't she?"

"I miss them both," Aunt Verdella said.

I was sitting beside Uncle Rudy because the bench had less bird poop on his side. And while I licked my cone, I watched Uncle Rudy suck on his straw as he looked at this and that before settling his stare on the sweating mug in front of him. While he stared at his root beer, I stared at him. I liked the way his wrinkles reached out like sunbeams from the corners of his eyes and curled around his cheeks like one of those oval frames that hold special old pictures. He must have felt me watching him, because he looked down at me and smiled. "Button? You ever see a stick caught in an eddy?"

"What's an eddy?" I asked.

"Well, take down at Dauber Falls, for instance. Remember when you and me and Verdie went there last summer to pick raspberries, and you said that the water looked like the foam on root beer when it crashed against the rocks?" I nodded. "Well, sometimes you'll see a stick float down the rapids, and now and then, when the water's movin' it around a boulder, that stick gets caught in the swirl just below the rock. And it stays there, just twirlin' and twirlin' in that same stuck place."

"And it twirls there forever?"

"Well, it seems likes it's gonna. After all, a poor little twig ain't got no arms and legs to swim his way out of that whirlpool, now, does he?"

Aunt Verdella and I giggled.

"So there that poor little stick is, caught up in a swirlin' eddy, spinnin' and spinnin' until it's sure it's gonna be stuck in that one spot forever. But then a most amazing thing happens. For no reason that anyone can really be sure of, the water spits that little stick right out of that stuck place and off it goes, floatin' on down the river to find new adventures."

I put my cone straight in my mouth and sucked on the ice cream, moving it in a quick circle to try and make the top get a curlicue again. I thought Uncle Rudy was done talking, because usually he didn't say any more once he told me how something worked, but instead he looked right at me and said, "Button? Right now you're swirlin' in a sad eddy, but you ain't gonna stay stuck in that place forever. Sooner or later, somethin's gonna happen to spit you out of it."

"You ever been stuck in a sad eddy before, Uncle Rudy?"

"Yep. Course I have. We all have."

"One you got stuck in because your best friend went away?" I asked.

Uncle Rudy used his thumb to swipe at the sweat drops that ran down his mug, though I don't think he knew he was doing it. "Yep."

"Then what happened?" I asked.

"Well, I guess in time, life just spit me out of that place and moved me on downriver, where I found a new best friend." He glanced at Aunt Verdella, his wrinkles sinking deeper as he smiled.

Aunt Verdella's mouth puckered up then, and her eyes teared up. She didn't look sad though. She looked happier than I think I'd ever seen her.

Once Aunt Verdella got her ha-has back good, me and Uncle Rudy went with her over to Porter to buy that color television set she wanted forever. She insisted that she drive herself, even though we were taking Uncle Rudy's truck so the new console could ride in the back. And when Uncle Rudy lingered out in the driveway to wave her out, she told him to get back into the truck. That she'd use her rearview mirror, same as everybody else.

Me and Ma and Daddy went over to watch TV that night after supper, and we sat till the stations went off the air, flicking around the knob so we could see every program on all three channels, to see which of them were in living color. Aunt

Verdella didn't seem to notice that everybody's face was blue, or if she did, she didn't care. She just grinned from ear to ear, then went to make us some Jiffy Pop popcorn and lemonade.

For a time after Freeda left, Ma stopped wearing eye shadow, and before long, she didn't put on lipstick unless she was going out at night, which wasn't often. And when her roots grew out, she colored her hair again, but this time a color more like oatmeal. She stopped making it puffy too. Soon she was cleaning like we were getting company, even though we weren't, and harping at me again to make neater corners with my sheets and to take more care with my cleaning. She started harping at Daddy again too, asking him where he was going, and when he would be back, and where he'd been.

Her mouth pulled so tight that her lips turned as white as her face when Daddy came home one day and told her that he'd gone to Adam's Music Store in Porter and ordered himself a new guitar: a red-colored Epiphone, with an amplifier to go with it, since they didn't have what he wanted in stock. Ma watched his back as he talked on the phone with Owen, telling him when it would be delivered and that he cleared out a spot in the garage so they could start practicing again. Just looking at Ma's mad face made me scoot my mouth over to the side so my teeth could grab some skin, but then I stopped myself. The insides of my cheeks had healed smooth and soft, and I thought maybe I'd like to keep them that way.

Ma stayed crabby until Owen came to practice, bringing with him a guy named Al who was going to be their drummer and a lady named Linda who was going to be Al's wife. Linda had bouffant hair and the kind of face that looked like it could only smile.

Ma liked Linda, I could tell, and while Daddy and Owen and Al played songs in the garage, Ma and her talked about wedding dresses. Ma got hers out of a big box in the attic and unwrapped it so Linda could see it. "I took a pattern and altered it how I wanted it," she said.

"Oh my, it's lovely!" Linda said, and then she asked Ma if she'd sew her a wedding dress, since she still hadn't found exactly what she was looking for. Ma said she would.

That night, after Owen and Al and his girlfriend left, and Ma was clearing away the coffee cups and dessert dishes, Daddy told Ma that he was taking some days off from work. "I have a couple of vacation days comin', so I thought we could head out Friday afternoon and go set up some bookings. We just have to call the places where we used to play, but I'd like to hit some new places too. I want to head over to Pine Lake, stop at Porter, and hit a few more bars south of that. Pine Lake has a new supper club and dance hall called The Rusty Nail. They're looking for bands, and a guy at work said they're already packing them in. We'll be ready for bookings in a month's time, easily."

Ma stopped up the sink and started running dishwater. "Linda didn't say anything about Al going away this weekend."

"Al?" Daddy reached for his cigarettes. He stopped, one cigarette half pulled out of the box. "Oh. You thought I was talking about going with the guys?"

"Weren't you?"

"No. I was talking about you and me. I thought we could have a nice dinner at The Rusty Nail, check out the band, dance a little. Maybe spend the night in that nice place across the lake. What do you say? Can you get Friday off?" Daddy made dancing steps and hummed as he waited for her to answer.

That Friday, Aunt Verdella and I stood in the driveway talking with Daddy, as he put their suitcase into the trunk. "I'm so glad you're doing this, Reece. Jewel seems so lost since Freeda left."

"I'm all set," Ma said, coming out of the house with her purse and a small carrying case. She'd gone to the beauty salon that morning and got her hair put back into a blond bouffant, and she had her face painted up. Not like an Egypt-lady, but just enough to make her look like the color of summer.

Daddy grinned at Ma, then patted his back pockets. "I must have left my wallet on the nightstand." He sprinted toward the house.

Aunt Verdella giggled at Ma. "You look like a new bride, going off on her honeymoon," she said.

When Daddy came out of the house, he was carrying Ma's dress, the color of sexy. "You forgot your dancin' dress," he said. He whistled as he opened the back door and hung it up.

Ma gave me a hug before she slipped into the car, and Aunt Verdella gave Ma and Daddy a hug. "You two have fun, now," Aunt Verdella said, then she stood back. "Reece? Aren't you forgettin' something?"

Daddy tapped his back pocket, then pulled the car keys from his front one. "Nope, I think I've got every—" And then he stopped, his eyes on Aunt Verdella. I tilted my head back and looked at her. She had her hands folded over her fat part, and her chin tucked down. Her head was tilted over to my side. "Ohhhh," Daddy said. He moved forward, his legs kind of stiff. "See you, Kid. You be good for your auntie, okay?" He reached out and patted me on the head, and his hand *did* make a warm feeling in my belly. I smiled and said, "Thanks, Daddy," and that made him smile.

28

It seems to me that after someone sweeps across your life like a red-hot flame, peeling back the shutters that sat over your heart and your mind and setting free your sweetest dreams or your worst nightmares, after things cool down you've got two choices. You can either slip back into your old self, your old life, tucking those things you were too scared to look at back into hiding, or you can keep those parts of yourself out until you get so used to them that they don't scare you anymore and they just become a part of who you are.

Right after the Malones left, Ma tried tucking those parts of herself back again, but they didn't stay tucked away for long. She came back from that little trip with Daddy with a shine that stayed with her. Not just for those months until my little brother, Robert Reece Peters, was born either.

Ma quit working for Dr. Wagner so she could stay home with Bobby while he was a baby. Those were her plans anyway. But right after Linda and Al's wedding, Ma got called to make dresses for two more brides and their brides-maids. And after those two weddings, she got more calls. With the sewing room turned into Bobby's room, soon half-made gowns were hanging all over the house, and Ma was running herself ragged trying to make sure there were no beads or stickpins left out for Bobby to swallow. What choice did she have, then, but to rent a little store two doors down from Dr. Wagner's office and set up her own bridal shop?

Women come from Porter and beyond to order their gowns now, and lots of times they take the cards left on the counter advertising Daddy's band and book them for their wedding dances. I doubt I'll ever see Ma dance half-naked in the rain again, but I see her grow brighter and warmer every day. She doesn't harp at Daddy about where he's going and when he's gonna be back anymore, but sometimes *he* harps at *her* for those things. When he does that, Ma usually just pats his cheek and says, "Keep your eye on where *you're* going, Reece Peters."

It was Ma's idea that Aunt Verdella take in a few more little kids, since she was so happy to have Bobby to look after when Ma opened her shop. "If you're going to watch Bobby, you might as well watch a couple more and make a few extra dollars while you're at it," Ma said. So that's what Aunt Verdella did, and she greets them with a morning hug, just like she still does with me, even though I'm not a little kid anymore.

As for me, about two weeks after the Malones left, I'd found myself missing Winnalee so much that I'd gone to our magic tree. And while I stood in the flat center, the wood cool against my bare soles, and thought about the fun we'd had and about how much I missed her, I realized that I wasn't standing in the magic tree anymore. I was standing in that place they call "bittersweet." That place that, if you could find it on a map, would be the mountain that sits between happy and sad. And I thought about how when you stand on that mountain, you can almost feel God's hand on your head and you just know, deep down inside, that even if you don't understand everything that happened to cause those mixed feelings, you still know there was a good reason for them happening.

When I was done crying, I grabbed the branch and swung down, landing on my butt, right in front of the hole at the bottom of the tree. The setting sun worked like a flashlight, lighting the inside of the tree with an orangey glow, giving me a glimpse of something inside. I reached in and felt the heavy canvas of our adventure bag.

I held it for a long time, just remembering, then I untied the flap and took out our compass and papers, and things, and lined them up on the grass. And then, at the bottom, I saw it. Our Book of Bright Ideas wrapped in thick layers of Saran Wrap.

I unwound the plastic wrap and ran my hand over the indented letters that spelled out the words *Great Expectations*.

I fanned the pages to get to the end of the book, hoping that on that last page would be Bright Idea #100, a bright idea Winnalee had just minutes before they left. If it was there, I told myself, then both me and Winnalee would know all the secrets there are to life. But when I got to Bright Idea #99 and turned the page, what I found instead was a note Winnalee had scribbled in pink crayon. *Button, It can be your turn to keep our book. Bring it when we meet, okay? Your best friend, Winnalee.*

I guess Uncle Rudy was right when he said that nobody stays stuck in a sad eddy forever. That school year, I made a new friend named Penny. She liked horses, not fairies. Penny came to my house for a sleepover and we played dress-up with some old clothes of Ma's. Penny wanted to fix her hair like a lady's, so she grabbed Winnalee's brush off of my vanity. "Don't use that one!" I yelled, and she stopped.

"Why?"

"Because it's not for using. It's just for remembering."

And Penny put the brush back down and picked up the one Grandma Mae gave me. "Can I use this one?" she asked, and I told her she could.

At quiet times, when I think of Winnalee most, I wonder what she looks like now, and if she's happy. Mostly, though, I wonder if she ever forgave Freeda for the lie she'd told, and I wonder who, in her heart, she calls "Ma."

Winnalee never did tell me why she wanted to find fairies so badly. Back then, I figured it was just so that she could see them (because what little girl wouldn't want to see magical, tiny ladies with pearly wings?), but now I'm starting to think that it might have been about more than just that. Maybe a part of Winnalee always sensed a lie hiding someplace in her life, and maybe... Well, I guess I really don't know, but somehow it seems like her hope for finding the fairies and the lie she carried in that urn were somehow tied together.

When Uncle Rudy told me what happens when a wildfire comes along, I asked him if the tiny seeds burned up in the flames, and I still remember his answer. "Nope," he'd said. "The sap around those tiny seeds keep 'em safe till the danger passes." I guess that's my biggest hope for Winnalee. That her innocence—or maybe childhood itself— was the sap she needed to keep her safe until the heat of that lie cooled.

As for Freeda, I think of her often too, just as I know Ma and Aunt Verdella do. I don't understand most of what happened to Freeda, but what I hope for her is that her fiery spirit keeps shining bright, in spite of how badly her childhood burned her.

Just last night, Aunt Verdella and I were talking about the Malones, and I brought up my plan to find Winnalee someday. Aunt Verdella's eyes dipped down at the edges, and her smile faded. "It's not gonna be easy to find her, Button. Not with all the movin' they'll have done by then."

I let Aunt Verdella go on for a while, then I smiled, and I reminded her of what she and Winnalee had both once told me. That you have to go on believing anything's possible, or else, what's the point?

ACKNOWLEDGMENTS

My love and appreciation to all of you who made my first year as a published novelist so endearing. To Lynn, Sylvia, Brenda, Sheilah, and Eric, who carted me to my readings, knowing I'd still be lost if they hadn't. To my wild and crazy friends at the Brantwood Literary Society—Deon, Frances, Nadine, Sylvia, Lynn, Susie, Brenda, and Sariah—who remind me often of the value of old friends. Also, to my newfound friends at *Curves*, who so generously share their laughter and lives with me, and who never fail to ask me how my writing is coming along. And, of course, to the readers who wrote to tell me how much they loved *Carry Me Home*, and those who invited me into their book clubs, their homes, and their hearts.

My thanks also to the talented writers in my life who continually root for my success, even as they strive for their own. To Jerry, Abe, Kelly, Darlene, Sachin, and most especially, to Vikas, my "bestest," who has cheered me on every step of the way and repeatedly gives me reminders of my resoluteness, as well as the pleasure of reading some of the most beautiful writing imaginable. My thanks to each of you. May your writing dreams come true soon.

My heartfelt gratitude, also, to those who helped make my work on this book so pleasurable. To my agent, Catherine

Fowler, whose trust in me as a writer helps me better trust myself. To my editor, Shannon Jamieson Vazquez, whose patience and attention to detail have been invaluable, and to my publisher, Nita Taublib, as well as those at Bantam Dell who so aptly captured the spirit of this story in its design. And to Kerry, who eagerly shared his knowledge of nature with me whenever I asked, and who helped me proofread for errors.

And of course, to dear Gerta; my MM; my littlest angel, Sophey; my children, Shannon, Natalie, and Neil; and to Vishal Kochhar, who didn't have a thing to do with the writing of this novel, but who wanted to be mentioned so badly that I couldn't refuse him!

Thank you all for loving what I do.

ABOUT THE AUTHOR

SANDRA KRING lives in the north woods of Wisconsin. She has run support groups and workshops for adult survivors of trauma. Her debut novel, *Carry Me Home*, was a Book Sense Notable pick and a 2005 Midwest Booksellers' Choice Award nominee. Visit her on the web at www.sandrakring.com.